The Dog Who Digs Heavy Metal

By June Carter Powell & G Alan Bettz

The Dog Who Digs Heavy Metal
By June Carter Powell & G. Alan Bettz © 2024
'Farewell my Friend' Words and music © G. Alan Bettz
2013
ISBN 978-1-989092-92-7

Cover illustration by Jolyon S. Joslin

Celticfrog Publishing
Clearwater, BC

ONE

Lance's comfortable farmhouse was dark and silent as he pulled the van into the driveway and shut off the motor. He quietly tiptoed into the music room to set his bass guitar on the rack. Lance was accustomed to arriving home in the wee hours of the morning. It had been a great concert, and he smiled to himself as he thought over the performance. He knew he had played well. He couldn't help smiling when he thought of the enthusiastic audience calling for more music.

He returned to the van and put his concert amp on a dolly and wheeled it into the house. While putting it against the wall, he knocked over a music stand, triggering a chain reaction of indescribable noises. He was picking up the cymbals, the noisiest piece of percussion equipment when his wife came through the doorway. Andrea was pulling her navy blue robe around herself. She tied the belt around her waist before she retrieved the drumsticks from the wastebasket where they had fallen. She picked up the scattered pieces of torn paper, gum wrappers, and apple cores and put them back in the basket before she hugged him.

"You're like the infamous bull in a china shop," she said, looking at him with an indulgent smile. "Are you okay?"

"Yes. I'm fine," he answered. "Just clumsy."

"What was that crash? That was more than just the drumsticks falling."

"The snare drum fell over, and the cymbals went flying. I hope the noise didn't wake the kids up?"

"It would take more than that to wake up Lanny. I can

see why the kids in your band love banging the cymbals together. They make a neat sound." Andrea giggled as she spoke. "I think you like them too."

"I do, but not at three in the morning," Lance said. "My eyes are still smarting from the bright lights in the auditorium tonight."

"How about a hot drink?"

"Yes, please. Do you have any hot chocolate?

"I do. I'm wide awake myself now, so I'll have one with you." She stood with her hand on the doorknob while they chatted. "You must be tired."

"I am tired. The band was very loud tonight, but it was a good concert. The Rusty Hinges used to be rock and roll, but they are borderline heavy metal now. Big audience and not just kids either. Funny how lots of older people come out to rock concerts. I guess Elvis made rock famous, but mostly kids and a few old *metal heads* come out to the Heavy Metal shows."

"Yes, but Elvis was king of them all and we'll never forget him. I can't imagine why an older person would go to the loud concerts," she said.

"Oh, they like to remember when they were into heavy metal, but most of them don't want to play it now." He laughed as he cupped his hand so it resembled a horn and held it up to his ear.

"Don't laugh!' Andrea warned. "You'll be deaf soon enough yourself if you keep playing that loud stuff. Now, sit down, and relax while I make our drinks. I won't be more than a minute. We can drink them in here instead of going to the table."

Lance watched her with admiration as she left the room. She was a beautiful woman, her tousled hair giving her a distinctive beauty all her own. The glow of robust health showed in her every move.

2

He took off his shoes and socks and put on his warm plush slippers. When she came back with the drinks, she asked, "Anything interesting happen tonight?" She handed him a steaming hot cup of his favourite hot chocolate with whipped cream and a marshmallow floating on the top.

"Mmm!" he uttered as he stirred it. "This smells good. Remember Igor, the theatre cat? Well, I was playing a little bass rhythm solo, and he suddenly appeared on the stage chasing a mouse. That cat has nerves of steel. He didn't pay much attention when the audience began to applaud. The mouse disappeared and Igor spent the rest of the evening looking for it."

"How comical!" Andrea said. "Did anyone get a picture?"

"Yes," Lance replied. "Nicolas Barren was covering the concert for the *Meldrum Tattler*. Nick tried to interview him, but Igor was too busy hunting for the one that got away. He said Igor's picture will be in the paper on Monday."

"How come he didn't try catnip?" she asked with a chuckle.

"Igor is so pampered already with band members and even those in the audience bringing him cat treats. Even if the mouse got away, Igor still came out ahead." Lance noisily scraped the dregs of chocolate off the bottom of the cup and licked the spoon.

"How long has he lived in the theatre? He probably thinks he owns it by now."

"I'm sure he does," Lance said. "About four or five years, I think. He just turned up one day, a tiny, scared kitten, lost and alone. He was so hungry he nibbled on a bit of cheese from one of the theatre staff's lunch. He doesn't mind people, but he doesn't like Heathcliffe. After the show was over, he joined them for snacks in the foyer."

"Who is Heathcliffe?"

"The security guy's dog-partner."

"I'm getting tired," she said, rubbing her eyes. "It's almost three o'clock, honey. Wipe the whipped cream moustache off your face and brush your teeth. Time to go to bed." She stood up and held out her hand to him.

"Me, too," he said. "Nobody realizes how hard we work when we're onstage. I guess they think it's all fun and games.

"Oh, wait! Something did happen tonight that I wasn't expecting. After the show, Freddy Bastable, an old student of mine, came backstage. He said he was in the audience, but I didn't see him there."

"Do I know him?" Andrea asked. She sat down on the couch opposite him and pulled her robe around her legs again.

"Probably not. Anyway, I sure got a surprise when he said he owns The Sinkholes, the band that's playing this weekend. His stage name is Freddy Gonzaèlas. He worked in the Bastable music store when he was a kid. He's Jem Bastable's younger brother. He asked me to play the concert this weekend."

"Really? I saw the posters for The Sinkholes, but none of the band members looked familiar. Are you sure it was him?"

"Yes. You couldn't mistake Freddy for someone else. He and Jem both have one blue eye and one brown eye. It never seemed to bother Jem, but Freddy had a hard time in school because of it. I bawled him out for not keeping in touch, but he said he wanted to make his name first before he contacted me."

"Will you do it?" Andrea asked. "I wonder sometimes how much heavy metal your ears can take."

"Sure, it doesn't bother me. My ears are still young. He said The Sinkholes, the band that's coming here this weekend. Would you like to come to the concert?"

"No way! The kids make enough racket for my tender ears. I know you like playing with these visiting bands, but I don't want to go to the concerts," Andrea said. "Let's go to bed. We can talk about it tomorrow." They both laughed as, hand in hand, they made their way upstairs to the bedroom for a few hours of shut-eye.

TWO

Lance had barely closed his eyes when he was startled by the persistent ringing of his land line bedroom phone. He sat up and made a grab for it.

"Yeah?" he said, checking out his bedside clock. "Who the hell makes phone calls at seven-thirty in the morning? You out of your mind?"

"Not yet," a cheery voice said. "Don't tell me you don't know who I am? It's Freddy. I wanted to make sure you took me seriously last night when we talked in your dressing room."

"Yes, I did," Lance said. "I told my wife when I came home. She was surprised."

"Was she okay with it?"

"She doesn't mind, but she probably won't come to the concert. Too loud for her. She sent her regards and asked why you changed your name. She had seen the posters downtown but didn't recognize you," Lance said.

"It's not easy to make an impression when your last name is Bastable. I guess I've lost a few pounds over the past six years," said Freddy, "First time I've been back here to play since I graduated."

"Don't change too much," Lance said. "I hope you're still the same old Freddy. Yes, you do look a bit gaunt. I noticed that right away. Are you eating properly? Maybe the hours are a bit much and eating on the run."

"You sound like my mother! She still lectures me as if I haven't been on my own for six years. I'm fine. Only the name is changed," Freddy assured him. "I told the guys last night I was getting the best bass player this side of the equator. I hope you'll still do it."

"The Rusty Hinges concert was the only time you've heard me play for years. Do I get an audition?"

"That's the only audition you need. My brother Jem says you play in bands all over B.C., so I want you for the concert Saturday night. Will you do it?" he asked once more.

Lance hesitated for a moment. "Sure, I told you last night that I would," he finally said.

"Thanks, Mr. Bishop. I knew I could count on you," Freddy said.

"Hey, drop the Mister-stuff, eh? You're grown up now. *Lance* is fine by me. It was great to see you last night. Surprised you came to our concert."

"I saw your name on the billboard, and I wanted to surprise you., so I came. Good concert. I enjoyed it."

Lance laughed. "You did that alright. I'm famous too," he said, "but just in Rocky Creek. Nobody knows me anywhere else. Maybe after this week, they'll know me in Meldrum City though." He laughed at his own joke.

"I'm sorry I woke you up," Freddy said. "I didn't realize it was this early."

"You should be sorry," Lance said jovially. "However, I really do want to see you."

He banged his fist on the bedside table to accentuate how happy he was and knocked the receiver onto the floor. He got down on his knees to pick it up and dragged the whole phone over by the cord.

"What the devil are you doing?" Freddy asked. "You trying to deafen me or something?"

"Sorry, I dropped you on the floor," Lance said ruefully, "I had a late night, so my co-ordination is a little off. Just dusting the cat hair off ya is all."

"Gee, thanks. I don't get a welcome like this very often." Freddy said.

"Consider yourself lucky," Lance said. "I don't greet everybody like this. When do we rehearse or are we just going to wing it like we did in the old days?" "

"Tonight, in the basement of Mom and Dad's house, about seven o'clock. Will you be awake by then?" Freddy asked, with a throaty chuckle.

"I hope so," Lance said. "In fact, I'd better get the lead out right now and turn on the hoses."

"Good to chat with you, Mr. Bishop."

"You forgot already that you can call me *Lance*."

"I'll try, but it won't be easy," Freddy said. "Sorry I haven't called or written to you for ages, but I've been all over the place. I do have some news I will just share with you, though. I'm tired of running back and forth trying to be in two places at once because the band members won't leave Meldrum City."

"What do you mean by that, Freddy?" asked Lance.

"I know it sounds ominous, but The Sinkholes are joining up with players in the States, without the B.C. group. This will be the last concert with the original bunch," Freddy said. "Steve can't afford to travel, and Morley has a hospital job now, and Brutus says he has responsibilities to his family."

"Are you sure that's what you want to do, Freddy," Lance asked. "Jem told me you just came back from a tour to Europe. I thought you had it made."

"I would if the guys played fair."

"Getting the information second-hand is not the same as receiving a letter or a phone call from you," Lance said. He opened a drawer and pushed it shut with a bang after he got out a pair of clean socks. "So, you haven't told the guys yet?"

"No, I'll tell them after the concert," Freddy said. "I'm sorry I haven't written. I guess I was just thoughtless."

8

"It's not too late to start all over again," Lance said.

"You're right. I'll keep in touch from now on. Now what are you doing, Mr. Bishop—oops, I mean Lance?" Freddy asked. "You're the noisiest person I've ever talked to on the phone."

"Getting dressed. Nothing exciting," Lance said. He smiled into the receiver as if Freddy could see him. "This drawer sticks sometimes so I pushed it in hard. Didn't mean to be so violent. I'm not much good until I've had my coffee."

"For heaven's sake, go and have a cup then," Freddy insisted. "I'm going into the shop this morning to see my brother. Jem can't wait to put me to work."

"He just wants to spend some time with you," Lance said. "You know how big brothers can be."

"Yeah, they are bossy and know everything, but he admitted he has missed me. Anyway, I better get off the phone and let you have your coffee. See you later," Freddy said. "Goodbye for now. I can't wait to see you."

Lance hastily finished dressing and came out into the kitchen where Andrea was busily rinsing the new-laid eggs she had just gathered.

"Andrea!" Lance called. "Where are you? Great news. Freddy's back in town."

"Tell me, who is this Freddy person?" she asked.

"Lead singer with the Sinkholes. I thought I told you already. He's that talented kid I gave guitar lessons to just before we were married?"

"Vaguely," she said. "Is he the boy you stood me up for on our second date?

"Yeah, Freddy Bastable. He's in town."

"Well, if you stand me up again for him, it's all over," Andrea said, giving him a playful poke. Lance leaped out of her reach. "Too late for that," he said. "You've already got priority in that department, but I can't think until I've had my coffee."

He walked to the cupboard and found an extra-large cup with a dark blue initial L on it. He noisily filled it from the coffee maker and sat down at the table with a grin on his face.

"Did I ever meet him?" his wife said.

"I think so. He was one of my music students in high school. His parents own the music store here. I don't know if having a stage name makes much difference, but he seems to think so. The concert is Saturday night at the Coral Reef Theatre. Can you believe that?" Lance replied.

"Yes, I can," she assured him. "You're popular, too, but aren't they just kids playing with the Sinkholes?" Andrea asked with a skeptical look on her face.

"Yes and no," he said. He paused and took a deep breath. "Freddy is twenty-five now. Years ago, I promised to play with his band if he made good. He's been out of school for about six years. I still think of him as a kid. I was his band teacher the year he graduated."

"If that's what you really want to do, then it's okay with me," she said.

"Thanks," Lance said. "I knew you'd understand. Soon as I finish my coffee, I'm having a shower. Bet I look awful."

"You do," she said, "but I love you just the same."

THREE

Lance emerged from the bathroom, his head loosely covered by a blue bath towel wound like a turban. Stray strands of his long hair had escaped and dripped water down his neck and onto the floor. Andrea handed him a wad of paper towels and headed toward the dining room. "I thought you wanted to sleep in this morning?"

"I planned to, but when Freddy called and asked me to play for his concert, I forgot everything else," Lance said as he hesitated by the door. He went to the bathroom to comb his hair and tie it back.

"What did Freddy want this time? Was that him who called you again?" his wife asked when he came back.

"He wanted to make sure I had taken him seriously last night," Lance said, getting down on his knees to clean up the water spots he'd left behind.

"If he's your friend," she said, "he must know you always keep your promises." She paused, and added, "Now you're up, will you drive the kids to catch the school bus? I was going to, but they'd enjoy it more if you would do it."

"Sure," he said. "I guess it's sort of quality time we have together. What on earth are they doing? Sounds like they're just having fun instead of getting ready for school." They could hear giggles coming from the hallway as the three teens chatted noisily over the important job of putting their homework assignments into their backpacks, along with their lunch bags.

"Come on, you guys. Stop fooling around. Your dad will drive you this morning, so you'd better behave, or you'll get me, and you know how I drive," she warned, her voice filled with laughter, as she opened the hallway door.

"Yikes," Lanny said. "Coming. How come we have to go to school during the holidays this year? We don't even get a holiday."

"Because of the fire in April. Did you forget that the deal was that in order to pass all your subjects you have to go two days a week during the holidays to catch up."

"Oh, yeah!" he said. "I did forget. We must be about finished now though. How many more do we have to do this?"

"Two weeks more."

"No-o-o-o!" whined Roy. "I want to quit school."

"You enjoy it once you get there. From the giggling you were doing to get ready, I think you are already enjoying it. Just make the best of it. It won't be forever."

Lance hurriedly pulled on his shoes and hollered, "Let's go! The train is leaving in two minutes. All aboard!" There was a race as they all rushed for the door at once and then jostled for the front seat next to their dad.

"Can we make fudge when we get home?" Jeannie asked as she crowded into the seat beside him.

"Ask your mother," Lance said, playing it safe. "She's in charge of nutrition." Lance grinned as he waved to Andrea who was standing at the kitchen window.

When he came back after seeing that they were on the school bus, he was deep in thought. "Were we that excited to go to school when we were kids?" he asked.

"Probably," she said. "I don't recall it being a party atmosphere, but I liked school." She took his sweater and hung it up for him.

"I did too, but I wasn't that thrilled to get up and get ready. I'm hungry after all that. What's for breakfast?"

"You'll find out in a minute," she said.

"I'm a lucky man," he said aloud. "Three healthy children, a beautiful wife, and a job I love."

He studied Andrea as she moved around the kitchen wearing a purple apron over her red, fluorescent green, and hot pink summer skirt. Her blonde hair curled around her ears. Colours that didn't quite go together still looked good on Andrea, a woman pretty enough to get away with wearing all sorts of odd combinations.

"I think so anyway," he muttered," but perhaps I'm biased." He thought Andrea looked even prettier than she had yesterday.

Lance washed his hands, took his place at the head of the table, and waited for her to sit down before he picked up his fork.

"Why did Freddy change his name?" Andrea asked.

"He's always had problems with the name Bastable," he explained. "Bullied in school about his eyes being two different colours, and some kids called him Freddy the Bastard."

Andrea passed him a plate piled high with sausages, eggs, and toast. "How awful. I wonder when they are going to put a stop to that kind of bullying?" she said.

"There has always been some bullying in school. I put up with it too, but my dad said it's all part of growing up."

"I guess it is," Andrea agreed, "but some children get it worse than others. I remember a shy girl at school who had awful things said and done to her. The boys who assaulted her got to stay in school, but she was asked to leave."

"I remember her too. Seems unfair, but that's the way it is," Lance said as he wiped the crumbs off his moustache. He studied his wife. She was frowning so he quickly changed the subject. Not going to go there. He knew it was wrong, but the law still blamed the girl for 'getting herself assaulted.' Nothing he could do about it. Nobody else was doing anything about it either, he mentally noted.

"Has changing his name made a difference?" she asked.

"Maybe," he said. "People are funny."

"I remember you taught a boy called Freddy," she said, her forehead furrowing. "I know his brother Jem because he works in the music shop."

"Yes, he's several years younger than Jem. We rehearse tonight at the Bastable house. Do you mind? Would you like to come to listen?" He touched her hand.

"Heavens no," she said. "They're too loud for me. You love playing with these bands, and I want you to be happy. More coffee?"

"I can get it," Lance said. "You want a refill while I'm up?" He continued talking while he walked to the counter and got the coffee pot. "It's sort of a tradition to have a stage name, but don't worry, I won't be changing mine."

"Good," Andrea said. "I like being called Mrs. Bishop so don't try it."

***

Lance opened the door and walked into Freddy's music room where the band was already setting up and waiting for him.

Freddy greeted him dressed in a tatty pair of green shorts that looked as though he had rescued them from the rag bag. Lance noted the other band members looked very little better. He felt over dressed in his white T-shirt and blue jeans.

"I'm here," Lance announced. "My amp's in the truck," he said. "I don't want to blow your parent's ears, but I'll bring it in unless you have a practice amp."

"Hi, Mr. Bishop, I mean —-Lance," Freddy said. "Use your practice amp tonight. I have an extra one, but it's better to use your own. The concert amp would blow the house down, and I don't want to be responsible for doing in my parent's home. They soundproofed this room for me, you know," Freddy said.

"Where do you want me to sit?" Lance asked.

"Over here." He pointed to a chair to the right of the keyboard. "We can sit down to rehearse tonight, but we stand at the concert," he said.

"Good," Lance said.

Lance liked the way Freddy was in command. He looked around at the other young people. He recognized Brutus and thought he may have seen the rhythm guitarist before.

"Morley Frontenac, drummer, and Steve plays keyboard and that wretch of a Brutus Faulgaar is on rhythm." Freddy continued. He grinned at Brutus.

"Morley, do you work at the Meldrum General Hospital? I think I've seen you before," Lance observed.

"Yep," Morley said. "I try to hide but people keep recognizing me. I can't imagine why."

"Could be that you're taller than everybody else in Meldrum," Brutus said. "How tall are you—my guess is about eight feet."

"Not quite. Try six feet seven," Morley said as he absentmindedly combed his fingers through his hair.

"That is still mighty tall."

Brutus waved at Lance in greeting, his open vest showing off the pot leaves tattooed on his torso. One bare forearm sported the words *I love Mama,* printed in dark red Roman letters to match his watch band. When Brutus stood up, Lance felt like one of those little elfin creatures reported to hide behind toadstools in the garden. Brutus' dark complexion and heavy-set physique combined with his innocent smile created an element of surprise.

His own forearm appeared skinny in comparison to the one Brutus displayed with such a flair. Lance mentally vowed to start working out in the gym. "Are those real tattoos or just painted on," Lance asked.

"My dad would disinherit me if I had real ones," Brutus said with a smirk.

"If you're talking about money, I can understand," commented Freddy. "This guy is my friend. When he was my teacher, Big Lance Bishop gave me my first guitar."

Lance wished Freddy hadn't described him as Big. He looked ruefully at the three younger guys. At six feet four, Lance hadn't met too many men who were taller. However, it wasn't their height, except for Morley, which caused his concern... It was the brawn.

"This is Steve, keyboard player. He goes to the barber every two weeks to get his head flattened so it looks like a tabletop."

"Yep," agreed Steve, patting the top of his blonde head. "He's worn out two levels already this year, trying to make it look even."

"I thought levels were just used for carpentry," Lance said. He grinned, thinking that even though the popular brush cut of the forties was out of style in the nineties, it still suited Steve.

Morley Frontenac's long legs were slim, but Lance couldn't keep his eyes off his enormous shoes. Size fifteen? Do they even make shoes that big? For the Sasquatch, maybe. It wasn't just Morley's shoes that were noticeable. His auburn hair stood out six inches all around his head in tight curls. Lance wasn't sure what held it in place or what cut it represented. Afro? It seemed to fan out around his face, reminding him of the famous MGM Lion of the movie world.

"Lance," Freddy said, "We are a noisy bunch, and you may have heard that we have a light show to introduce us, and there will be fake gunshots and exploding props that are loud but harmless. "

"Nobody gets hurt and it's all in fun," Brutus piped up.

"Our audiences get a real charge out of it. Be prepared for a noisy evening."

"Glad you warned me," Lance said.

Three hours later, one by one the group packed up their instruments and the equipment needed for the concert tomorrow evening. With a lot of back-slapping, last-minute suggestions with meaningless threats and promises, members of the Sinkholes floated out into the night.

When they were gone, Freddy engaged Lance in a discussion and held him there for what seemed forever.

"I should go home, Freddy," Lance finally said. He opened the door again and stepped out onto the narrow wraparound trellised deck. "It's late, and I won't feel like getting up in the morning if I don't hit the hay soon. We could meet for lunch tomorrow at the Gateway to talk some more."

Fred looked uneasily over his shoulder. "Wait, don't go yet. I have a favour to ask you."

"Okay, what would you like?" Lance asked, thinking that surely Freddy wouldn't be asking for money; or would he?

"Close the door again, then," Freddy said.

"Why the secrecy?"

"They still watch me like a hawk," he whispered. "Mom and Dad treat me like I'm twelve instead of twenty-five."

"Shoot!" Lance said. "I have to get home, or I'll fall asleep at the wheel."

"This," he said, stepping back inside the practise room. "I need you to hide this for me. It would fit in the back of your amp." He walked to a cupboard against the wall and pointed to a rectangular parcel, which looked surprisingly like a concrete brick.

"If that's what I think it is, the answer is 'no'," Lance said, emphatically. "Why me?"

"I trust you," Freddy said. "You smoked dope. You can hide it in the back of your amp real easy."

"My concert amp?" Lance asked in surprise. "I smoked pot a few times when I was younger, but I didn't know the dangers of it then. I don't do drugs."

"Sure. It would fit in there just right," he said.

"I told you already I want nothing to do with it. Do you have any idea how much that crap is worth on the street?"

"Yeah, a cool seventy-five thou. Crazy, eh?"

"More than my house. "

"We'll both come out on top."

"What are you talking about?"

"I'll give you a couple lines for free. Good deal, eh? You know the ropes."

"No deal. You must know what that stuff will do to you. Are you addicted to cocaine?" Lance said. He put his hand on Freddy's shoulder.

"Oh no, I can quit any time I like," Freddy insisted. He shook off Lance's hand and glared at him.

"No, Freddy, you can't. Cocaine is highly addictive. Do the other band members use that stuff too?"

"Brutus is scared of his daddy," Freddy said with a sneer. "Steve is a chicken shit, and Morley works at the hospital and knows it all. All he does is fold the towels." Freddy laughed rudely.

"Morley's an orderly," Lance said, folding his arms. "He's studying after work to get the courses he needs to go to medical school. I discovered last night at the concert that I know him already."

"Oh, come on! I can't see that idiot in a white coat with a stethoscope in his hand. He works there so he has easy access to drugs," Freddy said, with a rude snort.

"That's not true, Freddy. He's a good drummer, but he wants to do something permanent with his life," Lance said,

18

making an effort to be patient. "He doesn't do drugs, and he is not an idiot. It takes a lot of money and brains to become a doctor, and that's what he's working toward. I just told you that I know Morley. He does not use drugs."

"Much you know about it. That's what heavy metal's all about. Really vamps up the music. With that stuff, there ain't nuthin' you can't do. There could be a million people in the audience, and you don't give a darn who's there. You ought to try it."

"No, thank you," Lance said. "I do care who is in the audience."

"That's silly. The audience doesn't care about you. Anyway, you could get away with it, and it's just for tonight. By next week I'll be gone, and nobody will know the difference." Freddy looked at Lance and snickered rudely. "Learn to have fun. Take chances."

"Not interested. I hope you don't intend on taking it to the concert? You just told me yesterday I taught you how to size up your audiences."

"Oh, come on! You can't be that naïve or that stupid. Of course, I do," Freddy said with a rude laugh.

"My decision has nothing to do with my mental capacity." Lance felt his anger rising. "You need to think this over, and I want to go home. See you tomorrow at the Gateway at noon, eh?"

Freddy said. "I think you'll change your mind. Let me know tomorrow, eh?"

Lance shook his head. "No, that's my final answer. Do you want to meet me for lunch or not?" he asked, with an agitated edge to his voice.

"Of course." For a fleeting moment, Freddy looked almost sorry for his behaviour. "I haven't become completely complacent, you know. I still care about keeping our friendship. I thought you might do it just this once."

Lance shook his head again. "No, I can't and I won't. I'll see you tomorrow."

Fifteen minutes later, Lance arrived at his home and dragged his equipment into the house. He had enjoyed the rehearsal, but there was a sadness in his heart as he got ready for bed. Suddenly very weary, he skipped the shower and just washed his face and hands and crawled into his bed beside Andrea. She didn't stir as he quietly laid his head on the pillow next to her,

Did Freddy use cocaine and gimmicks like gun shots and exploding instruments to replace talent? Lance was shocked at Freddy's disrespectful opinion of his audiences too. Did he not know that without his faithful followers, he would be a failure? Stars are not born; they are made by careful planning and hard work. Hopefully, Freddy would find that out before it was too late.

FOUR

After the kids had gone to school, Lance set the sprinkler over the hay field. When he came into the house, he joined Andrea at the kitchen table.

"Thanks for cleaning the barbecue for me, honey," she said. "I sure appreciate you doing that job. We had such a nice visit with your parents over dinner last night. "

"I enjoyed it too, even though Dad gives me a bad time about my part-time farming. I tell him that, to a farmer, there is nothing so beautiful as a sun-drenched field of wheat," Lance said with a smile.

"And to the farmer's wife! I like the flowers and produce, but I can do without the weeding," Andrea said. She poured them each another cup of coffee.

"He admits that farming is a lot of work, but those who choose it say there is no other career like it." Lance nodded as he got himself another muffin and heated it in the microwave. "Mmm! These muffins are sure good!" He wiped his mouth with the corner of his napkin.

"They are good, aren't they? I like my own cooking. That's not boasting though. Mom always said if she didn't like her cooking, she wouldn't ask anyone else to eat it."

"Good philosophy," Lance agreed with a smile. "That's the reason I don't offer to cook." He pointed to the can opener by the sink and laughed.

"I'm glad of that," Andrea remarked. "Beans are nice sometimes, but a steady diet of them straight out of the can would be a bit much."

"I see you have my number!" he said. "I'm a can opener specialist."

"Good. I value my health. Will you see Freddy before

the concert tomorrow night? Or will he just use you now and go away for another few years again?"

"I don't believe he'd do that. He told the guys I gave him his first guitar. We plan to meet at noon at the Gateway for lunch. Do you mind?" Lance asked.

"Not at all." She sat down across from him and put a spoonful of sugar in her coffee. "It's nice to have a few minutes just to chat with you alone, though. Life sure gets hectic," she said wistfully.

"Yeah, it does. Should I invite him to come here instead?" he asked.

"I don't know him, but you two must have a lot to talk about. Your friendship goes back a lot of years," Andrea said. "Actually, I want to put the zipper in my new skirt."

"Okay," Lance said, with a chuckle. "Then you definitely don't want interruptions. Will a couple of hours work for you? Jem says Freddy doesn't communicate that well, but he does want to see him today."

"It won't take me that long." She paused, then remarked, "I suppose Freddy has been so busy making his fortune that there was no time for family or friends. Did you enjoy the rehearsal last night?"

"Yes, but too loud for me. He's a good leader and he sure knows his music," Lance said, focussing on the good points of the rehearsal.

"If you taught him, my dear," Andrea said, "he had no choice. You are a good teacher. I bet you worked him hard."

"He worked me hard too," Lance said. "I suspect I'll work even harder tonight to keep up with him."

"What were the other guys like? Has Freddy changed in the years he's been away?" she asked.

Lance deliberated before he answered. "I didn't think so at first," he said, "but he looks really gaunt. Maybe the pace, or eating out at odd hours, but either way, he doesn't look healthy.”

“I understand groups like The Sinkholes go from one concert to another without a break,” she said. “It would be exhausting to constantly be on the road and sleeping on buses or hotels every night.’”

“I’ve never done it,” Lance said. “I’m tired enough after a symphony weekend, as we call it. We have two rehearsals on Thursday and Friday night and often one Saturday afternoon, then the concert that night. I don’t know how professionals do it on a full-time basis.”

“It’s the lifestyle they chose,” Andrea said. “Some families travel with their musician parents. It wouldn’t be easy for the kids to adjust. I probably could, but I’m glad you are a teacher.”

“Me too,” Lance said. “Have you seen the posters advertising the concert? I hardly recognized him.”

“Yes, but I didn’t recognize the band members. I did notice there were no girls.”

“Brutus said they did have one for a while, but she got tired of Freddy’s snide jokes. Odd, because none of the groups I’ve been in would have tolerated that.”

“Were the jokes suggestive?” she asked, with a frown.

“He didn’t say, but I knew that’s what he meant.” Lance agreed.

“I don’t blame her. I take it, he’s not married.”

“No, but he told me he’s in a serious relationship,” Lance said. “She’s a singer with another group. He does have some strange ideas about marriage. He thought I would have to bargain with you to be able to see him today at noon.”

“Did you tell him we don’t have that kind of marriage?”

“I did,” Lance said with a chuckle, “but I don’t think he believed it.”

“If I had to check up on you for every little thing,

marriage wouldn't be worth it," Andrea said. "We have few secrets, but we don't suffocate one another. I like it the way it is."

"Thanks, honey, you've made my day."

At noon Lance slipped into a booth at the Gateway Coffee Shop and ordered a coffee while he waited for Freddy to arrive. Ten minutes later, Freddy walked through the door. His blonde hair looked damp, and he smelled of shampoo.

Lance looked at his watch "I was beginning to think you'd forgotten me," he said. "Almost seven minutes late!'

"Sorry about that," Freddy said. "No way I'd ever forget you—you're the reason I still play."

"I see you were half asleep when you put your shirt on," Lance said, determined to keep things light. "It's inside out."

Freddy looked down at his shirt and laughed. "I didn't notice that. I never sleep very well after a rehearsal. I really get involved in the music, and then I think about it for a long time before I doze off."

He snickered as he strolled into the washroom to put his shirt on right side out. When he returned, he had the buttons done up wrong.

"Maybe your mother should have come with you," Lance said. "Now it's lopsided."

"She was working in the store today, so she sent me out on my own." They both chuckled. "I had a bad night. The hours are catching up to me, I guess."

He dropped heavily into the seat across from Lance and fixed his buttons. He studied the list of menu choices tacked on the wall.

"I guess you've been keeping a busy schedule recently," Lance said.

"Yeah, but I'm used to it. Did you enjoy the rehearsal last night?" he asked.

"I wasn't sure I'd fit in with you young guys, but after the first two pieces I felt myself getting into it." Lance noticed that Freddy hastily pulled his sleeve down to cover his wrist. Needle marks? "How come heavy metal is your bag?"

"A phase, I guess. I'll get over it when it no longer makes money." Freddy ordered a cup of coffee and two maple cream-filled doughnuts when the waitress stopped at their table. He smiled at the flustered young woman.

She had probably just realized she was serving the star of tonight's concert. Lance couldn't help smiling when he overheard her telling the other waitress by the kitchen door that she had just served Freddy Gonzaèlas his lunch. He leaned forward hoping to hear more, but they disappeared into the kitchen area.

"You fit in well with the group," Freddy said, not appearing to notice the waitress's reaction, "but I knew you would." He hesitated a moment while he sucked the cream filling from both of his doughnuts, wiped his chin, and began chewing, unaware that Lance was watching him in fascination. He had never witnessed anyone sucking the filling out of a doughnut before. A bit messy but it must be enjoyable, to judge from the look on Freddy's face. He might try it himself if no one was home.

When he finished, Freddy said, "One thing you taught me when I was your student was to size up the people you are playing with as well as your audience and act accordingly. Last night I watched you interact with the guys at the rehearsal."

"Gosh," Lance said, "I hope I didn't lead you astray!" He laughed guiltily. He bit into his hamburger, after sizing it up carefully to make sure he was taking the first bite out of the appropriate spot. After Freddy's demonstration, the burger was almost a letdown. One could not even hope to put much drama into a hamburger unless the mustard dripped out on his pants.

"I do follow some of the wisdom you shared with me, and I always use it with my audiences. I like to improvise so I start with three or four straight lines and pretty soon my mind is off and running. The louder I get, the more I can make it up as I go along. And the more I improvise, the more excited everyone else gets."

"I see," Lance said. He downed his cup of coffee and signalled to the waitress he wanted a refill.

"I know heavy metal isn't really your bag," Freddy said. He twirled a lock of his hair around his finger. "The dog that comes in with the security guy seems to dig it though. He looks like a neat dog."

"Oh, you mean Heathcliffe?" Lance asked. "He probably recognizes some of the performers or people who work at the theatre, but I wouldn't want to get on the wrong side of him or his partner Brad."

"I wonder if he's trained to sniff narcotics," Freddy said, looking worried.

"I've never thought about it, but it would make sense that he uses his sniffer. He's a dog, so instinct would tell him to be attracted to a strong smell," Lance said, after a pause. "I couldn't tell you what his reaction would be."

Freddy threw back his head and laughed. "Do you have security at your concerts?" he asked.

"Yes, but they are low profile. It's nice to know we have them, but we seldom have anything happen that needs heavy security. We play, they applaud, we have a reception and go home."

"Why do people even come to your concerts?"

"The audience? To hear the music," Lance said. "They

like to see local people perform. It's a gift to be able to hear it in our own little city."

"They're missing all the fun," Freddy said.

"It depends on what you see as fun." Lance put his elbows on the table. "After a concert, I like to pack up my instrument and go home. I'm too old for that after-show partying."

"You are not!" Freddy exclaimed.

"Heavy metal has an important place in the music world, but don't give up other types of music," Lance said, leaning forward as he talked. "Remember that all music, even with the strong beat that occurs in heavy metal, hasn't really changed that much. A riff is still a riff, no matter who plays it."

"Really? I hope you won't try to convince me Mozart played power chords," Freddy said with a rude laugh.

"They weren't called power chords in his day, but he used a lot of fourths and fifths in his harmonies, the same as today," Lance said.

"Oh?" Freddy replied, "I still have that old guitar you gave me years ago. I won't do a concert unless I have it with me. I don't play it in concert, but I feel more secure if it is close by. It's my good luck guitar."

"When I gave it to you it was already battered up from being in the attic for ages," Lance said, glad to change the subject. "I asked you to try it and your eyes lit up; then we both forgot all about the piano lesson I was supposed to be giving you."

"Right, I even forgot to go home for dinner, and my mother phoned and gave us what for," Freddy said, his voice full of laughter. "We were both in the doghouse that night."

"Your mom wasn't pleased, and neither was my fiancé," Lance said with a chuckle. "We had a dinner date that night, and I wandered over to her place looking like a rebel. She actually married me a year later though."

"Lucky you! I'm still single," Freddy said, "but I have a girlfriend and we're pretty darn serious."

"Great to hear that, Freddy. A man should not live alone," Lance said.

"Jem says you have a beautiful wife. Can't wait to meet her. I remember you had a thing going with somebody from the symphony. Is it her?"

"Yes that *thing,* as you put it, turned into marriage," Lance said. He bellowed with laughter. "She keeps me on a short leash, but she'll have to let me out for this gig."

"Wow, that's awesome, Mr. Bishop--I mean Lance. A high society girl! The prettiest girl around these parts. I remember her. And who wouldn't remember a babe with a shape like that? What was her name?"

"Andrea St. Michaels. I was surprised when she said 'Yes'," Lance said.

"Remember the day I sat outside your house all afternoon because you forgot I had a lesson?"

"I think there were more than one or two days like that!" Lance said. "You sometimes waited for me when we hadn't even scheduled a lesson."

"I know," Freddy admitted. "You always treated me like an equal, so I wanted to be with you. I grew up thinking I was ugly because my brother and I have funny eyes." He looked down at the floor. "Jem didn't let it bother him, but I got teased in school."

"You are not ugly," Lance said. "You're imagining things. Who's the girl?"

"Shauna Worthington," Freddy said. "She sings with us sometimes. After this tour is over, I think I'll ask her to marry me. Most of the guys just shack up, but Shauna is special. She doesn't look down on me. Kinda like you." Freddy stared out the window.

28

"That's good news, Freddy. You have my blessings. Married life is good."

"Thanks," Freddy said. "When I get back, I'll tell her."

"We probably need to head home, Freddy, so we'll have time for some dinner before the concert," Lance said, glancing at his watch. "I'll give Andrea a call and ask her to get something quick for me."

"I guess you probably need time to bargain with her," Freddy remarked.

"No, of course not. I've never had to bargain. My wife doesn't try to change me from what I am."

Freddy shrugged his shoulders. "Well, don't forget about the stash I mentioned last night. I'll slip it into your amp before the concert, when the stagehands put all our stuff on the stage. They won't bother to look. Then before it's taken off stage, I can get it out. Okay?"

"I told you last night I won't have anything to do with it. If I thought you were really going to do that, I'd pack up my bass and go home," Lance said, his brow wrinkled angrily.

"Well, you don't need to get mad. It's just a little favour. I don't have respect for guys who don't follow through with a promise."

"And I don't have respect for guys who ask me to do something illegal," Lance retorted. "I only promised to play the concert. I'm insulted that you would try to put me in that position."

"What would they think if they knew *you* smoked pot when you went to school?" Freddy said, getting belligerent. He smiled as he spoke, but Lance felt that the smile was more sarcastic than genuine. Maybe even a veiled threat.

"I was honest when I applied for my job. Most kids in that era tried it. Even adults smoked the stuff. Now that we all know the danger of using any substance that alters the mind, it wouldn't be tolerated. Eventually, pot will be legal, but I won't use it."

"Skip the lecture. You're chickening out, eh? I thought we understood each other."

"Whoa!" Lance exclaimed. "That's a heavy-duty remark. Our long-time friendship is why I'm telling it like it is. Cocaine is not child's play, and if you insist on bringing it to the theatre, I won't play the concert. That's the bottom line."

"I have to get out of here. You make me sick with your goody-goody foolishness. You signed a contract. You'll play the concert, Mr. Perfect. See you there. Don't be late," he snapped. With that, Freddy walked out the door without a backward glance, leaving Lance to pay the bill.

Lance sat quietly for a few minutes before getting up from the table. He watched in stunned silence as Freddy leaped into his bright blue convertible and drove from the parking lot, paying no attention to the speed limit or to the car carrying a family of four that dodged to prevent a collision.

Lance went to the counter, paid for the two lunches, and left a sizeable tip for the waitress before he left the café, knowing that Freddy had him over a barrel.

FIVE

Lance and Brutus enjoyed a friendly chat when they met in the wings before the concert. "How come you're so early?" Brutus asked. "There's thirty minutes before we have to go onstage,"

Lance glanced at his watch. "I know I'm early. I brought my dinner so I could share some time with Charlie. I guess you will have your meal at the café with the guys?"

"Maybe. Is Charlie that fugitive who's hiding from the government? Why are ya feeding him?" Brutus asked.

"He's not a fugitive. He's a refugee," Lance explained. "He wants to become a Canadian."

"You mean he entered Canada without the proper papers?" Brutus wanted to know.

Lance shook his head. "No, he came here legally. You don't understand. Let's not talk about it now, eh? Too many people milling around." He put the take-out box in a grocery bag.

"Hey, that smells good. What's in there?" Brutus wanted to know, leaning over to breathe deeply.

"Hamburger and fries from Wendy's. It does smell good."

"How long you gonna keep bringing him food?" Brutus asked, refusing to drop the subject.

"I'll help until they get it sorted out. Eventually, he will need to have a more healthy diet, of course, but for now, it's been easier to pick up fast food for him."

"What did he do to make them want to deport him? Must have been something real bad."

"No, Brutus. He was doing research for a course he was doing at his university. Someone started a rumour that he was probably a spy so now his country wants him to return home and answer charges. Now let's not talk about it anymore. I have to get this up to him," Lance explained.

"If he came here legally then why is he worrying about being deported? Shouldn't he go home?" Brutus persisted.

"Now don't worry about it anymore. I have to get up there and back or I'll be late."

"That doesn't make sense."

"It's the way it is, Brutus," Lance said, beginning to feel annoyed. He walked away as he spoke.

Lance quickly climbed up to the catwalk where Charlie was putting away his flashlight and the book he'd been reading.

"Hi, Charlie, did I scare you?" Lance asked when he saw Charlie look startled.

"Ya, I see guys carrying big parcel from room down there," he said, pointing down toward the stage. "What they doing?"

"Many things go on in a theatre, Charlie," Lance said. "Costumes, equipment, instruments. Could be anything."

"I guess so," Charlie said. "I like look down, see guys work hard. Get muscles. I see them go to stage. Not come back."

Lance laughed at Charlie's words, thinking that although he couldn't express himself well in English, he had a unique way of making himself understood.

"I'm sure they'll come back before the concert begins. They could have taken the stairway on the other side so they didn't have to walk around. Anyway, I have time before we go onstage so I thought I'd share my dinner hour with you. I brought you some food and a gift too." He handed Charlie a guitar case. "Open it right now. It's for you."

"For us—I mean, for me?" Charlie asked, stumbling over the words in his haste.

"Yeah. I thought you might have fun with this old guitar I found at home. The kids all have their own instruments now," Lance said. "This is an extra one we had. An instrument needs playing."

"How you know I want to play?" Charlie asked, grabbing Lance's arm.

"It wasn't hard to guess," Lance said, with a chuckle.

"Tanks," Charlie said.

"I hope you enjoy playing it, Charlie."

"Oh yes, I leave my guitar and piano back home."

"I wondered about that," Lance said. "I knew you were a musician."

"How you know?"

"Oh, it's just one of those things. I could tell you really liked listening to music," Lance said.

"Tanks, but why you call me Charlie?" he asked.

"The theatre manager called you Charlie, so I thought it was your name," Lance said. "What is your name?" He handed Charlie a take-out box from Wendy's with a hamburger and fries in it, and some chilli. "I thought it would be fun to visit you and we can have a dinner party."

"Ya!" Charlie said. "I not go to dinner for long time. Nobody say my name."

"I could try. Tell me."

"You no say Stanislav Gladysuiski." Charlie said the words so quickly Lance could barely follow him.

"I can so. Stanley Slav Gladly Sue Ski," Lance said, purposely pronouncing it wrong. When Charlie laughed, he said, "That's okay. I know it's funny, but you can teach me next time I come to see you. Charlie is easy for me to say so I hope you don't mind if I use it instead."

Charlie laughed out loud and then quickly put his hand over his mouth. "I not allowed to make noise. Solly. I just tease. Charlie good name."

"Do you still have that little room by the stairs?" Lance asked.

"Not now. They move me close ticket booth and bathrooms, and I can have shower when no concert," he said. I have a table and two boxes for chairs."

"That's good," Lance said. "That's much better for you. You will have room to put the guitar away safely too."

"Fanks," Charlie said.

"No, say it this way," Lance said. "I could teach you to speak English, too," Lance said. He stuck his tongue out again and said "THH!"

Charlie tried to copy. "FFFFanks," he said.

"Stick your tongue out and hiss. This way." Lance demonstrated.

"THHHH!" Charlie said.

"Good!" Lance said. "Practice it. I'd like to just talk, but we'd better eat now because the time goes so fast. Wipe the spit off your chin."

"You said stick out tongue and hiss," Charlie said as he wiped his entire face with a piece of pink toilet paper.

"Practice makes perfect," he said.

"Oh?" asked Charlie. "What you mean?"

"Our language is very hard to learn," Lance said. "We use slang terms which might not make sense to you."

"Slang?"

"I'll help you," Lance said. "I'm a teacher in Meldrum Secondary School."

"You play in band," Charlie said. "How you teach?" He frowned as if trying to understand.

Lance chuckled. "I teach music, and grammar too, so I'll help you learn to speak English. I'll come back with more food in a few days, and we will talk," he promised.

"You teach Gramma? Where your gramma live? Like me, huh? Need help speak da English?" Charlie wrinkled his nose. "I not understand."

"Not my grandmother, Charlie. Grammar is the guide to speaking to each other and for writing. I will help you learn to read and speak English." Lance accented the 'rrrrr' at the end of the word *grammar*, hoping it would help Charlie to understand.

"Like this? 'rrrrr'?" he said, trying to mimic Lance.

"You got it. Let's finish eating. Have some coffee?" he asked, taking the lid off a plastic cup. He handed it to Charlie. "I even brought you some cream for it. Have you tried Wendy's chilli? It's really good." He gave the young man a clear plastic spoon. "There won't be any dishes to wash because I'll take away the dirty ones."

"THH," Charlie said, leaving out the rest of the word. Lance snickered and Charlie followed suit. "I forget," he explained.

"I should get back downstairs, Charlie. I have to tune my guitar yet. Are you coming to the concert tonight?"

"Yes, I see good from catwalk. Good view of guy's head tops."

Head tops? That was a new one. Lance was still laughing as he got up. "I hope you enjoy the guitar," he said. "I'll be back soon."

"Th-thanks," Charlie repeated with a big smile. "When you play my songs?"

"I'm really interested in your music, but tonight I'm just here to play bass guitar. Freddy's keeping his promise to me," Lance said.

"I wanted sing my song first," Charlie said.

"What's the name of it?" asked Lance, as he began to move away.

"Suzanna," Charlie said.

"Did you write that?" asked Lance, in surprise.

Charlie nodded his head. He looked down at the floor.

"Freddy stole my song, and he sing it first."

"You mean that you wrote the song that Freddy's singing tonight?"

"Yah, It my song. She afraid to come with me. We get killed maybe."

"I'll be back to talk to you about that, Charlie. How did he get the music?"

"I no give it to him. He take."

"I believe you. I'll be back to talk about it. If you write more songs, I'll help you copyright them so that won't happen again. Bye! I must go. Wish me luck."

"Break foot!" Charlie said.

"Thanks, Charlie." Lance walked away with a big smile on his face, after gathering up the empty food boxes and napkins to put in the trashcan in the dressing room. With such a good wish, it had to be a great concert. He'd often been wished the usual "*Break a Leg*" as he went onstage, but "*Break foot*" was even better.

After he had visited with Igor and delivered the fries to Charlie, he slowly manoeuvred his way across the narrow walkway to the stairs down to the men's dressing room to retrieve his guitar and get in the lineup to go onstage.

The catwalk, twenty feet above the stage wasn't Lance's favourite place to be. It was easy to get spooked. Like right now. Footsteps?

He heard rustling coming from somewhere behind him. Or was it further down the catwalk? He couldn't tell. Were the footsteps coming toward him? Or going away?

He could have sworn nobody else was on the catwalk but Charlie. The steps were barely audible and definitely not the gait of the man he had just spoken to. Maybe not a man at all? Lance was aware he was not alone.

He stood still and listened to the sounds that echoed in the passage, designed for the stagehands, and where the sound technician made his magic from a small office in the centre. There the lights and sounds were all manipulated using levers and switches and sound keys. There was a sound board covered with buttons, with complicated letters and numbers all meaning something to the guy who read them. He'd been in the room once, impressed with the huge amplifiers, woofers and sub-woofers, laser beams, and dozens of keys that meant something to the operator.

Lance heard the unmistakeable whisper of footsteps on the landing as he passed the closed door. He wasn't certain from which direction the sounds originated, but he did know they were creeping closer and closer, so he pressed his body up against the wall and made himself as flat as possible. Then he heard a voice so sad he thought it had to be a young person.

When he heard something scurrying close behind him, he shuddered. Who else but Charlie or a stagehand could be up there? Unless the theatre ghost was making a visit? Lance felt a crawling sensation in the roots of his hair.

"Granddad used to say his hair stood on end," Lance muttered, "and I believe it." In panic mode, he smoothed his hair uneasily and wiped the sweat off his forehead.

All theatres are reputed to have at least one ghost, but Coral Reef was said to have three. Were they seamen from long ago forced to walk the plank? Which one is out tonight?

He tried not to let it bother him. Things ethereal have a habit of upsetting people, and Lance was no exception.

He knew the reef on which the theatre stood had a historic past, from pirates to rum runners and American counterfeiters using Canada as a haven for their dirty deeds.

There were signs of its bloodthirsty history everywhere; the hanging tree, with what was reported to be the remnants of a buckskin noose still suspended high up in the branches, and numerous unnamed graves hidden in the rocky slopes.

Lance had trouble believing it was the original noose, but he did see the graves.

He'd always wondered why Meldrum City seemed to revel in its gory history, even using it as a tourist attraction. At the summer fair, a replica of a pirate ship from the seventeenth century was a featured display.

There was no time to worry now. It was show time, so he brushed the thoughts from his mind.

With a surge of renewed vigour, Lance made a run for it. The old cliché, 'Caution is the better part of valour,' fit perfectly. Who really wants to confront a ghost?

Just as he was about to sprint towards the spot he was certain the stairway must be, he was startled by something soft and furry rubbing against his hand.

"Argh!" he exclaimed. He hurriedly covered his mouth. Then he heard the cry again. It seemed much closer. Right by his head, in fact. This time it seemed more like an ear-splitting "Meow!'

Lance chuckled, although he felt like a fool when he realized the beloved theatre cat was resting on a ledge behind him.

"Igor! I'm glad to see you, but you scared the daylights out of me. Here, give me a peck."

He leaned over and put his cheek next to Igor's nose and received a swipe of his rough tongue in return. With difficulty, Lance tried to control his mirth.

A great way to start a show. He patted the old fellow on the head. "I might have a little treat for you," he whispered.

He dug around in his pocket and found three potato chips wrapped up in Saran Wrap left over from his dinner.

"Sorry, it's all I've got," he whispered. He offered them to the cat, and as he walked away, he could hear the vigorous purr of the Russian Blue. Igor was a good guy. He'd lived in the theatre since he was a kitten, but he stayed mostly on the catwalk with the stage crew. He'd been known to wander around during a concert if he thought the performers carried cat treats. Quite often they did because Igor was popular.

When Lance joined the Sinkholes. Brutus asked, "Did you get lost?"

"Yes," Lance said.

"How could you get lost in this theatre?" Brutus asked.

"Ask Igor."

After Lance had tuned up his instrument, he and Brutus waited for the opening band, The Shotglass Five, to finish playing so they could walk on the stage and take their places.

"They're a good band," Lance said. "Someday they'll give the rest of us the runaround. Almost ready to do a whole concert on their own."

"They've done well," Brutus said. "I wonder where the light tech is tonight? I haven't seen him around yet, and we are on in less than ten minutes "

"The opening band had plenty of light, so we'll be fine," Lance said. "We're playing by ear or memory anyway, so no big deal."

When the lights went out, Brutus said, "Okay, smartypants, now see how we'll do. Where is he?"

The door swung open, and a well-dressed man stomped into the hallway, slamming the stage entrance door behind him.

"The lights went out!" Brutus whined.

"Here, use this if you're scared of the dark," snarled the man, as he flung a black bag down on the floor with a clatter. He grabbed a flashlight from the bag and tossed it at Brutus, leaning threateningly toward him. The flashlight rolled across the floor. When Brutus picked it up, he shone it at the newcomer.

"Stop!" the man protested, running his fingers through

his short dark hair. "You trying to blind me? You're shining that thing in my face." His words were aggressive, but his voice had a smooth, theatrical quality. Lance studied him with interest, his active mind filled with questions. An actor, musician, or lawyer? His pants were well pressed, his white shirt probably just back from the laundry. The clean-shaven man was obviously a professional in his field, whatever he did for a living when not operating the light or the sound system. Tonight, the lights would be part of the show with exciting changes and background sparks and thunder claps co-ordinated with the music. Freddy had ordered the best to be had in Meldrum.

Brutus turned the beam toward the floor and uttered an oath under his breath.

"Hold on, Brutus," Lance said, taking charge. Turning to the man, he said, "I'm sure it wasn't intentional. There's no time to fight. We have a show to do. When the lights come on, we move to the back of the stage. You know the routine."

"I'm not that late anyway," the newcomer said belligerently. "Traffic jam on Maine Street. It was fine for the opening band, wasn't it?"

"Yes," Lance said calmly.

"Who are you?" Morley asked, standing up.

"Sound and light technician," the man said. "Who the hell do you think I am—the cleaning lady? So I'm five minutes late."

"No worries," Lance said, to cover for Morley and Brutus, both appearing to have foot-in-mouth disease. He held out his hand. "My name is Lance Bishop."

"Zeke," the tech said, ignoring Lance's outstretched hand. "Gotta go before Herr Freddy blows his top. Bad-tempered brat. One of these days somebody will put him in his place." With a cigarette hanging out of the corner of his

40

mouth, against fire regulations, he slammed the door and ran up the stairs to the control room. The backstage area vibrated and echoed with his footsteps.

A few minutes later the lights came on again in the theatre, and Zeke came down the stairs with a clatter and disappeared into a room across the hall, with a sign on the door that read *NO ENTRY STAFF ONLY.*

"He has a funny scar on his face," Brutus said, holding his ears.

"Yes," Steve said, coming forward again. "I've seen him before. Good sound man. Great reputation."

"He's an excellent worker," Lance agreed. "This is the first time I've spoken to him, but I've seen him many times at symphony concerts. Knows his stuff."

"Well, I don't like him," Brutus said. "Always snotty."

"Hey, Brutus," Lance said, abruptly changing the subject. "Did you go to school in Rocky Creek? I've seen you somewhere before. Maybe in another band?"

"Yeah," Brutus said, settling down after his encounter with the sound man. "Rhythm Band, Grade two. Played first tambourine."

"That's why you're playing rhythm guitar tonight. I knew I'd seen you before. Who was your teacher?"

"Mrs. Clow. My mother wouldn't allow me to dye my hair green for the Christmas concert, so Mrs. Clow gave me a shiny green star to pin on my shirt. You probably recognized my talent."

"I noticed last night at the rehearsal that you are very talented. Did the other kids dye their hair green?"

"No, but I wanted to dye mine green for Christmas."

"How come it was a green star?" Steve asked.

"She offered me a red one, but I blew a tantrum because I wanted a green star. I was in love with her after that. I asked her to marry me, and she said she'd have to ask her husband first." Brutus chuckled as he told the story, obviously enjoying it.

"How comical," Lance said. "That's why it is so rewarding to teach children. Mrs. Clow was a very good teacher. You were lucky to have her."

"I thought she was lucky to have me," Brutus said.

"Not conceited or anything?" said Steve with a snicker.

"No chance of that with three sisters," he said. "They put me in my place quickly."

"I remember Mrs. Clow too. She had a whole box of stars. I liked the red stars best, but I wasn't spoiled like Brutus," Steve said.

"The opening band's coming offstage now, so we're next," Lance said, taking his place in the lineup.

SIX

The opening band walked off stage, and The Sinkholes took their places in a seamless changeover. While Freddy waited in the wings to make a grand entrance, Lance and Brutus walked on carrying their guitars. Morley's drum set was already onstage and ready for him. He grinned at the audience and acknowledged the crowd before he took his place. Lance was more laid back until someone called out "Yay! Lance!" He turned his head in the direction of the voice and nodded.

Lance thought Brutus looked magnificent in his buckskin vest, open at the front to show off the well-known green pot leaves tattooed on the right side of his chest. and a wreath of red and green poison ivy on the left. He'd just stepped up to his microphone when his guitar exploded, sending a mass of coloured stars over the front rows of excited concert goers.

He threw up his hands and tossed down the remnants of his guitar and gave the pieces a mighty kick off the stage. He stomped across the platform to grab another instrument and continue playing, hardly missing a beat. The walls of the old building vibrated with the thundering applause that followed.

Lance was horrified until he realized the exploding guitar was only a replica timed to play for so many minutes before it self-destructed.

"Thank God it's not the instrument he will play," he murmured.

Morley covered his eyes in mock terror when a life-sized effigy of Freddy Gonzaèlas slowly floated across the stage before it continued out the second exit behind the baffles.

The squeals of the youthful concertgoers mingled with the drumbeats and the sudden bursts of applause, while various pops and bangs could be heard.

Melodrama was Freddy's trademark. Lance would have preferred to skip the gimmicks and rely on talent. As a paid performer, however, he had no choice but to follow suit.

Morley started with a quiet drum roll which got louder and louder. When his orange Afro fanned out, Lance again thought he resembled Leo the lion of MGM fame.

He'd thought his kids were loud, but they were nothing in comparison. Who was responsible for the maniacal laugher that filled the air, blocking out any semblance of music that had existed?

It might have been fun to just wing it on stage years ago when everyone did it, but Lance wasn't prepared for all this melodrama. He comforted himself with the knowledge it was only for tonight.

Just as he thought it was coming to an end, the theatre lights were dimmed, and an amp exploded, followed by a shower of sparks, a signal that Freddy would soon appear. It was spectacular for sure, but probably unsafe. What about fire regulations?

When Morley's drum blew up and an avalanche of drum skins and broken guitar parts covered the stage, the audience cheered. Throwing himself to the floor with both feet extended in the air, his arms flailing, Morley moaned in mock pain.

Another bang announced the singer's entrance. Wearing an all-white costume, the bell-bottomed pants embroidered with red chain-stitch, his blonde hair loose on his shoulders, Freddy appeared to literally float across the stage as if in a trance. Lance had fleeting thoughts that this

44

may have been influenced by the use of cocaine to get him through a concert. He tried not to dwell on it, but the thoughts were there.

After the hair-raising introduction, the silence that followed was almost a shock. As smooth as silk, Freddy took over. The girls screamed and the guys banged on the floor and hollered a mixture of compliments and insults at the performers.

The show began with Charlie's piece. Lance wondered why this was first on the programme. He slowly moved to the back of the stage to wait, having no bass part to play.

"Suzanna" was one of those songs that would stay in his mind well after the concert. Lance liked the way Freddy slid into it, gently at first and then a gradual crescendo. He wondered if Charlie was happy with Freddy's rendition. Helpless on the catwalk, listening to his song being sung by another man must have broken his heart. Lance felt the hurt in his own heart, knowing how passionate love can be.

Was Freddy heartless or did he simply not realize how this must hurt the composer? Even worse was the possibility that the cocaine Freddy used was responsible for the way he thought. He'd told Lance that he no longer cared for his audience, but perhaps he also no longer cared for the feelings of others, especially a helpless refugee seeking asylum.

Had Freddy realized he had skillfully changed the words to express his own sexuality just to please the crowd? He had also omitted the words that would have told of Charlie's love for her. Charlie had shown the words to Lance that very afternoon, so he knew the words sung by Freddy tonight were not all written by Charlie.

It wasn't fair. Surely Freddy didn't do it on purpose? It must have been an accident. Freddy couldn't have changed that much.

The sound effects got louder and louder until Lance wanted to cover his ears. Freddy certainly went for realism. Lance could hear explosions going off in the background. If they were done by the sound man, Lance had to give him credit for knowing his craft.

The band played on while Freddy went off the stage for a quick costume change. Everything appeared normal, but Lance still felt uneasy. He thought he heard some strange sounds coming from backstage, but it was obvious that neither Brutus nor Steve had heard them.

Freddy appeared again in a cobalt blue costume, the wide flared legs swinging seductively when he swaggered onstage. He reached for the microphone, and with his lips close to it, wooed the audience into near surrender with his voice.

The screams of the girls almost drowned out the music entirely. Lance could hear the boys mouthing off in the background as if they didn't really come to hear the music at all. His uneasiness mounting, Lance began to feel anxious.

Freddy had improved a great deal as a singer in the last few years—as much as Lance could hear it over the din. Even so, he felt very proud of the way Freddy won over the patrons, as if he was not just a hometown boy they had come to hear but because he had real talent and was among the known celebrities.

Freddy seemed to take his time with every song, heavily breathing into the microphone the last strains of each verse with the seductiveness of Elvis. The hidden meanings of each stanza were becoming a clear invitation to join him backstage with a promised tète è tète. Or more.

The band segued into their regular set-list. Lance began to thumb his bass from his position beside Morley on the drums. Freddy wooed the crowd into submission when he accompanied himself on the guitar.

Freddy returned briefly to acknowledge the applause, with flair but no humility. "I'll be back in five," he promised as he went off stage for yet another costume change.

Leaning forward, he thanked his fans for being there, but something was missing. Lance would have been more impressed if Freddy had shown less pride in his own performance and said a few words to acknowledge those who had supported him. Most solo performers were aware that they needed accompaniment, but Freddy gave the impression it was all about him, and no one else counted.

After the break, the crowd waited with bated breath for Freddy's return. Lance glanced at this watch and observed that Freddy had been 'changing his costume' for almost twenty minutes. Suspense was Freddy's trademark, but when it became too cumbersome. Brutus picked up Freddy's microphone. Five more minutes went by, seven minutes. The tension was building up.

Lance thought he heard some strange sounds backstage. The audience was getting restless. Lance asked both Steve and Morley if they had heard anything different. They both shook their heads. Perhaps it was his own finely tuned musical ears that picked up the unusual sounds?

"What the hell?" Brutus whispered. "What do I do now?"

"Cover for him, I suppose. Give him five minutes more."

Lance picked up his bass and improvised a few chords and Steve and Morley followed suit, while Brutus took over the microphone again. Tuning up his golden tonsils a second time, he crooned for a few minutes, looking back several times as if waiting for Freddy to appear.

When he heard strange sounds coming from the wings once more, Lance stopped playing and looked around in horror. This didn't fit into the script.

"What's that funny noise?" he mouthed to Brutus. "Sounds like someone gargling."

"You're hearing things. We told you at the rehearsal it would be noisy. Relax. Nothing unusual yet. Wait 'til things really get noisy."

Brutus took the microphone and tried to fill in with some idle chit-chat. "While we wait, I'll just sing "Gravel Pit Slide," one of my favourites. When he finally gets here again, he can take over and sing for ya." Brutus paused dramatically for that to sink in. "Freddy has a good show fer youse peoples," he announced, trying his hand at being a comedian. "I'm sure he won't be too long. "Pothole Rock" comin' up as soon as he comes back." Instead of applause, cries of, "Kill the creep!" shocked Brutus.

"Shush!" Lance said.

"You said to improvise," Brutus complained with an injured air.

"You're doing fine," Steve said. "The audience is disappointed, and they'll take it out on us, so be aware."

"Imposter!" someone screamed. "Who wants to listen to a fake? We paid to hear Freddy. And we *want* Freddy."

Drowned out by a chorus of, "We want Freddy, we want Freddy," Brutus finally gave up trying to sing at all.

"I don't understand," Brutus asked Lance. "Won't Freddy be back?"

"They want him now. I wish he'd hurry up and get out here."

The security guard walked past the stage with Heathcliffe beside him. The animal was dressed for work, his dark blue vest printed with the name of the Canine Unit and the words, *Working Dog* in red.

"Thank God!" murmured Lance. "Somebody else besides me knows it isn't right."

48

A book hurtled toward Brutus and knocked him off his feet. He stopped pretending that everything was alright and closed his mouth tightly, disengaging his talented tonsils.

"What was that?" he inquired as he looked up. The teen patrons screamed for more.

The light tech walked quickly onstage and removed the object.

"I thought he just did the lights —is he one of the roadies, too? Shhhhhhhh!"

"Nobody can hear us over the din. They think it's part of the show. I'm getting out of here!' Brutus mouthed to Morley.

"I s'pose they think this is normal. Is it?"

"Not this loud," Morley whispered,

When two more loud explosions startled them, Lance said. "Those sounded like real gunshots. Get off the stage before someone gets hurt. This is too dramatic for me. Come on, let's get off the stage. There's no time to try and figure it out. Somebody is trying to tell us something."

Steve shoved his keyboard aside and knocked over his microphone, then stopped to pick it up. While he fussed around as if nothing had happened, Lance glared at him in disgust. "Get off the bloody stage, you fool," he said.

"Yeah, yeah, I'm going. Don't get your stomach in a knot." Steve said, as his feet flew out from under him. "What was that?"

"Oh, damn. I don't know, but it just hit my bass," Lance croaked. "I'm not putting up with any more of this BS. Now GET OFF THE STAGE NOW!"

"Ouch!" Steve yelled... "I hurt my arm. It's bleeding. I got shot. I'm dying," he yelled, He examined his hand.

Lance finally grabbed him by his sleeve and dragged him bodily off the stage.

"Why did you do that?" Steve whined,

"Because you are going to get us killed is why. Whatever it was, it hit my bass. "

"Not my fault." Steve protested. He pulled himself onto his feet. "I didn't do it!"

"Let me take a look at your arm," Lance said. He pushed Steve's sleeve up and checked for an injury." You didn't get shot. You'll live. You don't need an ambulance. It was just a damn ice cube."

"Well, I don't like it!

"Grab your stuff and get out. You'd like it less if it was a bullet. A little blood won't kill you, but a riot might, and this looks like it could turn into one."

"Riot?" mumbled Steve.

"Get out of here NOW. You're gonna get killed."

In seconds, it was every man for himself. The scene was one of chaos as guys punched other guys they didn't even know. Girls ran for their lives, and the sound of broken glass filled the once-beautiful Coral Reef Theatre.

Lance clutched his guitar by the long-necked fingerboard and ran for safety, colliding with the effigy of Freddy still floating on a guy wire where it was pushed from the stage. It blocked his escape route.

"Sorry, "he muttered. "I forgot to duck."

He wanted to laugh when he realized he had just apologized to the stuffed figure of Freddy. Obviously, this was no time for humour. When the effigy swung toward him, socked him over the head, bounced back and got him a second time, he definitely wasn't a happy camper. A lump was beginning to rise on his noggin. How could a stuffed figure deliver such a wallop?

He opened his mouth to warn Brutus to look where he was going but didn't get the words out before Brutus attempted to dash through the stage door at the same time someone else made the same decision. Brutus stood up in time to take a blow to his head.

The intruder stumbled over his own feet, and they were both sprawled across the floor. He kicked Brutus several times with the toes of his black boots.

"Get off me, you idiot!" Brutus hollered, struggling to stand up. "You're not even a member of the band."

"Fire!" Lance roared, in an effort to take the guy's mind off fighting with Brutus.

"The place is on fire," yelled someone else. "I'm getting out of here."

The sound of seven hundred pairs of feet running aimlessly through a crowded theatre was like a herd of wild boars.

When Brutus leaped up and started to run, he knocked the piggy-back rider into the door jamb. The fellow shrieked like a banshee and took advantage of Brutus' clumsiness to jump him again.

Lance saw him pick up a microphone and swing it toward Brutus. He grabbed the little guy's arm in time to stop him, then he angrily aimed the microphone at Lance. Loud popping sounds caused by the short-circuiting microphone were amplified as it exploded in a shower of sparks. Lance was getting fed up with the silly little man trying to pick a fight with him. He certainly didn't want to fight with someone half his size, so he put a heavy hand on the man's head and held him firmly in one place. Finally, Lance spun him around several times and let him go suddenly while he moved out of the way. The last Lance saw of him was when he spied Brutus again.

Brutus closed his eyes and began flailing his arms aimlessly, not once connecting with the jaw of his assailant.

He didn't appear to be a vindictive guy, but Lance could imagine that he was probably slow and methodical.

"Stop! There is no fire!" yelled Lance, trying to diffuse

the situation again. Nobody heard him; they were all so busy pushing their way to the exits that Lance's voice was drowned out.

"Take that, you fool!" the little guy screeched. "I'll teach you to get in my way. And you too!" he hollered when he saw Lance, who was at least head and shoulders taller.

"Yikes!" Lance said, doing some fancy sidestepping to avoid the lethal black boots again. "I'm an innocent bystander," he mumbled, putting his hands up in a gesture of surrender.

The miniature guerrilla fighter finally jumped off the stage, cursing in a mixture of undecipherable words, and blended in with the confused crowd.

Lance breathed a sigh of relief. "I'm doggoned glad he's gone! Anybody know who he is?" he asked.

"No," Brutus said. He scratched his head. "Never seen him before."

"We have to get out of here—those sounded like real gunshots," Lance said one more time. "Are you sure they're only fireworks?"

He looked around in shocked realization that he was talking to himself.

Some people were picking fights with whoever happened to be there, but others were actually beginning to throw tables and chairs into the aisles and destroy the upholstery. One of the heavy curtains at the end of the stage had already been yanked off the rod and thrown on the floor. Lance flinched when he saw a young man kick the curtain off the stage where it got even more abuse from being stomped on and torn.

Brutus looked shocked, and Lance concluded that he was probably beginning to realize he'd just gotten the wind kicked out of him by somebody half his size. He saw Brutus put his hand to his head as if it ached.

"Come on, Brutus, move it!" Lance grabbed the rhythm guitarist by the arm and shoved him off the stage.

"What's going on?" Brutus asked.

"No idea," Lance said, "but I do know we need to get out of here as fast as we can. I don't exactly relish getting things thrown at me by people I don't even know."

"Would you feel better if you knew who was throwing things at you?" Brutus asked, stalling again.

"Come on, Brutus," Lance said, taking his arm. "Time to leave."

Within seconds, there was a rush to the main exit by the unhappy fans. The theatre was already a mess. There would be no concert and the band would not get paid. Someone could even get hurt before the night was out. Theatre rental and security costs weren't anything to sneeze at. They still had to be paid, concert or no concert.

Lance looked around for Heathcliffe and his handler. The dog was always business-like, but it was obvious by the doggie grin on his face, the well-trained Labrador-Shepherd cross enjoyed covering the heavy metal concert beat. He had never spoken to the dog handler although he'd often seen him at other concerts.

Lance felt sorry for the other band members who had nothing to fall back on should the evening turn out to be the end of The Sinkholes. He looked around hoping to see someone familiar, but it seemed no one was sticking around to help. Even Brutus and Steve had disappeared.

He grabbed his equipment and tried to push it out past the bleachers hoping to get out of the building before anything else happened.

"Please would you help me get this amp out," he said to a guy who looked familiar. "It's too heavy to carry, but I want to put it in my trailer before it gets broken."

"Sure. You're name's Lance, ain't it? I seen ya 'round.

How much?" When Lance didn't answer immediately, the man disappeared.

Lance nodded. He was trying to think clearly. So much to worry about, like what would happen to Igor if the theatre burned down? Charlie, or whatever his name was, could escape, but Igor would be helpless.

Maybe he should go back and get the cat. He knew he would if there really was a fire, but he couldn't see any flames or smell smoke. He suspected Igor would travel well enough in his duffel bag. He was a mellow cat.

"There ain't no smoke, so there ain't no fire," he muttered. "A good first line for a new song! When I write it, I'll dedicate it to Igor."

He tried to drag the big bass amp toward the exit, but the casters kept jamming up with all the garbage people had thrown on the floor. Along with the two bags he was carrying as well as his guitar, he didn't get very far.

"Ain't 'cha the bass player?" asked one of the guys Lance recognized from other shows. He'd been sitting in the front row. Maybe one of the roadies.

"I'm just a freelance musician," Lance said, making an effort to hide his identity from the man. "What was his name?

"Hell, I don't know. Jack? Something like that anyway," the heckler said.

"Oh yeah? Who are you?" someone else said. "Ain't that a bass amp?"

"Hey, let's get out of here," Lance replied. "I need help to carry this thing out. It's too heavy."

"Money—the green kind!" The stranger held out his hand.

"What are you talkin' about?" Lance asked.

"You got lotsa cash. How much are ya payin'?" The man loomed over him with a greedy smirk.

Lance didn't see it, but he must have signalled to his friends because in seconds he was surrounded by a group of men.

He saw someone in the distance who looked like the lighting tech. He was about to wave to him when the man caught his eye and came over.

The youth who asked for cash wandered away and the rest followed, looking back at Lance several times. None of it was lost on Lance, although his mind hadn't yet processed the meaning of it.

"Where did you come from?" Lance asked.

"Oh, I was just watching what was going on when I saw you. Were you being harassed by those guys hoping to make a buck?"

"Yeah, I was getting a little nervous," Lance admitted. "Too many of them for me to handle. They sure took off when you turned up. Wonder why?"

"Who knows?" Zeke said. "You're in good hands now. Our best bet is to go through the backstage exit to avoid the crowd. Come on, I'll give you a hand. Look what I found?" He pointed to a handcart. "Just pile your stuff on here and I'll get it out for you. Where's your trailer?"

"Parking lot. Left side. Man, am I glad to see you!" Lance said.

"You're in good hands now," Zeke repeated, with a smirk on his face.

When he and Zeke moved on, they overheard a girl saying, "Stop kicking."

"Maybe one of the groupies you see at most of these concerts," Zeke said. "You should see the teenaged girls who follow guys from place to place. He leered at a girl standing in his way.

"Good heavens, man," Lance exclaimed. "She can't be more than thirteen. What's wrong with you?"

"Nothing," Zeke answered, snickering. "It's not me who's at fault. It's her parents. They know right well there's drugs and things going on when they let her come!"

Lance knew all about that, although he never did have an interest in underage girls. Out of the corner of his eye, he saw a girl holding her hip, as if in pain.

He wished he hadn't yelled, "Fire!" in hopes of stopping the fight onstage. It was poor judgement on his part and Lance knew it. Before he walked away, he saw one of the girls crawl under the row of seats.

"What's she doing that for?" he asked Zeke

"Come on, we gotta get this amp and stuff outta here fast. I'll come back for the girls. She probably thinks she'll be trampled. I'll tell them I'm coming back."

Lance couldn't help admiring how the young man appeared to be everywhere at once without looking as if he was hurrying. He also noted that there was something about Zeke he didn't trust, but he couldn't put his finger on it.

Lance piled his equipment on the handcart and cinched the amp with a bungee cord that dangled from the handle.

"I knew you were out there somewhere trying to get your equipment out, so I headed toward the stage," Zeke said.

Lance noticed that Zeke's scar was not as pronounced as it was earlier. He suspected that Zeke had applied some stage makeup to hide the prominent scar.

They retraced their steps and went out through the rear stage exit, startled to see there had been a fire in the parking lot after all.

"I parked my van and trailer in this area," Lance said.

"Tell ya what," Zeke replied, "let's take the cart over there and put your stuff in my van before we decide on another move. If that's your trailer, it don't look very bad to me. Looks like somebody just set fire to some trash or somethin'. Maybe to scare ya. It's probably too smelly to put your stuff in it." He pointed to a smoking vehicle, "That yours?" he asked. "I wonder who set it?"

"I don't know," Lance said.

"People do a lot of silly things when they get excited. Sure odd that Freddy didn't come back onstage tonight. He probably doesn't even know he started a riot, or if he does, he's still hiding," Zeke said.

"Do you think something really happened to him?" queried Lance. "I had coffee with him today. He seemed fine then. He was my music student years ago, you know. I was hoping to talk with him again before he leaves Meldrum City because I haven't seen him for ages."

"He's a strange one," agreed Zeke. "His car was parked behind the theatre about six o'clock. Did you see that guy aiming at the stage with a pellet gun? Kind of funny, eh?"

"I didn't find it funny, "Lance said. "There's a small crack in the front of my bass. I'll have to have it repaired." He studied Zeke's sardonic smile.

"Let's go," Zeke said. "No sense sticking around here. I saw someone with a knife stabbing holes in the seats. When they get excited it doesn't take much to start stabbing people." He led the way until they were close enough to see that some papers were still smouldering near Lance's trailer and the car parked next to it.

"What the hell would I have done with the bass amp if I was stuck dragging it around? The thing weighs a ton," Lance said.

SEVEN

Zeke watched Lance struggling to pull the cart with one hand, the guitar held under his arm, without offering to help. Even with the wheels, Lance had to reconfigure the load every few steps. When the guitar fell to the concrete with a crash, Lance wanted to throw up his hands and just go home, but he said nothing. Why was the guy just standing there watching him? It was irritating.

His precious amp was on a dolly out in the middle of a parking lot while a riot was taking place inside. Now his guitar probably had a large crack in it. He had no phone so the only way to get home was with Zeke, and…well, everything was a mess, including his livelihood.

"Hold it, old man. You're doing fine. Funny the police aren't here," Zeke said, turning to look over his shoulder. He pulled his keys out of his pocket and jingled them while he talked to Lance. "I'll deal with those girls and call the cops while I'm there. My van is on the other side of the lot." He indicated with a wave of his arm. "We'll leave the amp there while you come back to your trailer. I'll open the van and give you the key so you can load as much as you can and wait for me." He finally put his hand on the dolly and steadied it while Lance pushed it.

"You'd actually give me your keys?" Lance asked, breathing a sigh of relief.

"I don't know what else to do," Zeke said. "Besides, I know where you live! Your trailer might not be badly damaged. and the fire is almost out. Let's get out of here." He led the way.

Lance said nothing, but he studied Zeke from the shadows, admitting to himself that his words, although used in jest, were too much like a veiled threat. He brushed the thought from his mind with difficulty, realizing that he'd made himself vulnerable by not having his phone handy.

After Zeke helped Lance unload his amp and put it in his van, he handed him the keyring.

"Now get to work," he ordered. "When I come back, we'll load the rest of your stuff, and I'll drive you home. See you in a bit!" With that, he started at a dead run back to the theatre.

"Wait!" called Lance. "Do you intend on bringing them here?"

Zeke stopped and turned around just long enough to say, "No, I'm gonna shove the one girl up onto the catwalk, and she can walk to the other end and find the exit, but the other one is tough, and I doubt if she'd listen anyway. Wouldn't put it past her to have already gone off with the guys she was talking to."

"Catwalk?" asked Lance, in alarm. "There's a guy living up there. He might be startled to see a girl there."

"I know about him. Harmless. Joanne can handle it. Betty is just a follower, but she knows her way around too. Not as young as she looks, either. Anyway, I have to let myself back into the theatre. Don't worry about me, I know what I'm doing."

Zeke took a pack of cigarettes from his pocket and selected one, lit up and offered Lance a cigarette. Lance shook his head.

"You don't smoke?" Zeke asked.

"Occasionally. Can't play and smoke at the same time."

"Oh, scared of gittin' your precious gee-tarr smelly?"

"Yes, if you put it that way," Lance replied. He watched Zeke disappear in a cloud of smoke, thinking that it was obvious there wasn't much Zeke hadn't experienced. He marvelled at the man's generosity. Almost too good to be true.

Another fleeting thought came to mind—his mother always said if it seemed too good to be true, it probably was.

While he waited, he took the hand cart back to his trailer, pulled some stuff out, discarded some that smelled too smoky or were too damaged, and some stuff he just abandoned, hoping that he'd be able to come back and get the rest tomorrow.

He held up a blanket that was still smouldering, threw it down, and stomped on it. So much for his grandmother's last gift.

He wished there was more police evidence. Were the police aware of the fights going on inside the theatre and the hooligans hanging around by the door?

No one else appeared very concerned about the gunshots, though. Probably Freddy's audiences had become immune to loud noises because of all the sound effects he used. It was a sobering thought.

Everything seemed to be going wrong tonight. Right from the moment Lance had come into the theatre, going up to see Charlie—or Stanislav, or whoever he really was. No lights, no stage crew on duty.

He walked back to his trailer pushing the cart, thinking that even if Zeke took a long time to come back, he had no choice but to wait for him. He worried about the girl going up on the catwalk. Charlie is probably just frustrated with his life right now, but then again, frustration can lead to foolish behaviour too.

What were Zeke's plans? He seemed really nice, but Lance felt somewhat uneasy when he realized that Zeke was his only hope at the moment. A man like himself who enjoyed being independent should never get himself into such a predicament. He wasn't the worrywart type, but when

60

his independence was compromised, Lance allowed his mind to play tricks on him.

Lance was going through the contents of his trailer when a heavy-set guy with an unkempt beard stuck his head in the door and asked, "Do ya need help?"

"No," Lance said, "I have help, but thanks anyway."

"You look worried," the man said.

"Well, I'm worried about the cat who lives there," Lance said, trying to move the focus from himself.

"Cat? Hey, I know you. You play in the Meldrum Symphony. I thought you looked familiar."

"Yes. Do you go to symphony concerts?" Lance asked with a smile.

"No, I wouldn't be seen dead at one of them concerts, but I drive my mother to the theatre. I seen yer 'physog' on her programme."

"My what?" asked Lance.

"Yer face, Stupid. Don't you know anything?"

"I see," Lance said, choosing not to answer. "I'm glad your mother doesn't feel the same way. My ride will be here any minute, so everything is okay."

"Why were ya worried about a cat? I don't see no cat," he said.

"The cat lives in the theatre. He's a good mouser. Likes music and sings a real good baritone," Lance said, making an effort to show he was not worried. "We use him now and again."

"Ha ha! You're a joker, ain't ya? Should have used him tonight. Hey, are ya gonna give us our money back? Never saw no show."

"Drop into the ticket office tomorrow and ask them," Lance advised.

"They're gonna hear about it if I don't get a full refund. And you are too. You bet," he said belligerently. He walked closer to Lance and loomed threateningly toward him. Lance felt uncomfortable with him although he was a smaller man. His aggressive manner was probably an indication he wasn't alone.

"Thanks. Oh, there's my ride now," Lance said, thankful that he had spied Zeke in the distance.

Zeke strode through the parking lot and without a word, systematically began getting Lance's stuff loaded in his vehicle.

"Did you see those guys trying to bash the door open so they could all escape?" Lance asked, as he and Zeke got into the van and moved it out of the parking lot.

"Yeah," said Zeke, "I was going to join them, but when the door finally gave way and everybody landed in a heap on the asphalt, I was glad I hadn't. It was rather funny, wasn't it? No cops around and I don't see why. Not even Brad with his dog."

"Is that his name? "Lance asked as he automatically locked the front passenger door.

"Yeah, Brad Thomas. He's almost sixty-five. Been on the force for a long time. Could have retired at sixty but the dog has a year or two left yet. He and the dog do all the band concerts. Dog's real smart. I think he digs heavy metal," Zeke said.

"Right, the dog looks happy. Did you say Brad Thomas? Sounds familiar. Who is he?" Lance said, taking his time to process the information.

"Started out as a cop, but a few years ago he trained as a dog handler. He's good, but the dog has a better nose," Zeke said with a sly grin. "He sure busted me his first year, and all I had on me was a pitiful little baggie of weed."

"You smoke that stuff?" Lance asked.

"Everybody does. Illegal, but that's what makes it fun."

"The motto used to be, 'Make love not war.' Lance

quoted. "I have kids, so it wouldn't do for me to get busted. What will happen to the dog when his teammate retires?"

"He'll retire too. He's worked with the same handler since he was a pup," Zeke answered.

"It didn't take long for the mob mentality to kick in but there's usually plenty of security around. They just look like guys going to a concert. Of course, we don't have to worry when we play in the symphony. Did you call the police to let them in on what was happening here?" Lance asked.

"Yeah, I called 911, and they said it was already covered, but I didn't see anybody who looked like they were in charge."

"They probably have plainclothes men on the job," Lance said. "I never bring my cell phone to concerts anymore. Too easy to forget where you put it."

"I had a hard time convincing that silly girl to go up on the catwalk. I had to shove her up there." Zeke said as he manoeuvred the van onto the street.

"Nervous of heights?"

"No, not that one. I hadn't expected her to even be there. I sent the other girl home with an off-duty copper I know. Originally, she was the one I was going to put on the catwalk. Don't think she really wanted to have a cop take her home, but her boyfriend took off and joined a bunch of toughies. Nice kid, but I'm not sure of the other one."

"She sounds like a winner."

"Not as tough as she pretends to be," Zeke said, rolling his eyes. "You should have heard her squawk when I pushed her up onto the catwalk."

"How did you finally get her up there?"

"She said she hated me, and I said I didn't like her either, but I ain't gonna be responsible if she gets beat up."

"Sounds like the beginning of a grade one romance, eh? When we were kids, if a guy pushed a girl, that meant he was interested in her," Lance said.

"Works for me," Zeke said with a rude sneer. "Keep them pregnant and barefoot, I always say. Give them a good beating early on, and you never have any more trouble with the silly bitches. You must know that. You're married to one."

"I beg your pardon." Lance frowned at Zeke. "My wife is not a silly bitch. I wish I had my cell phone so I could call her."

"Cell phone? Oh, shoot!" Zeke said, abruptly changing the subject. "I forgot to pick up my phone after I called the police. I'll just break in and get it.

"Why not enter legitimately," suggested Lance. "I have a passkey."

"More fun to break in," muttered Zeke.

Lance was impressed with the easy way Zeke handled the cumbersome van, but he disliked the rude innuendos he made in reference to people.

The van was of a much earlier vintage than most vehicles on the road, but it was big, and he appeared to keep it in good mechanical shape. Zeke was different, and Lance puzzled over his crass remarks and odd mannerisms.

"Where are we going? I thought you were going back to look for your phone."

"I am. Not about to park close to the theatre again. We'll drive just out of town and walk back. I do that all the time. Nice area." Zeke swung onto the highway and put on some speed as he left the city.

Lance watched the scenery change from city to suburbs. Homes became smaller, and further apart as the city lights dimmed. After forty minutes or so, he said, "Where are we going? I've never been this far out of town before."

"We'll soon be there," Zeke said. "It's not as far as you think. Relax, you'll enjoy the walk." He swung onto Billy

64

Goat Lane and parked the van. "The truck stays here until tomorrow, so take what you need and get out."

"Is this village called Predator Hills," Lance asked. "I saw a sign with that name on it, but I've never been there. Is it even on the map?"

"Sure," Zeke said. "Lots of big birds out here like ospreys and eagles. Owls too. There's a path that leads to downtown Meldrum. Just follow me; I know the way. Take anything you'll need because we aren't coming back here. The van stays here for the night."

Lance reached into the back seat and picked up his sweater. "It gets quite cool once the sun goes down," he commented.

After Zeke had parked, he got out and slammed his door shut before he flung open the back door and reached in for a sweater.

Lance looked around curiously and concluded this was an older part of Meldrum. It's lack of streetlights proved it was a rural part of the city. Most homes were lit dimly, and there were few porch lights.

"We'll cut through here," Zeke said. He leaped over a low picket fence and stomped through a garden. He started off at a dead run, leading the way.

"Hang on! You are going so fast, and in the dark, I can't follow you because I can't even see the path," Lance begged.

"The moon will soon be up over the mountain, and you'll be fine," Zeke said. "I want my phone tonight. I don't want anyone getting into it."

Lance didn't answer. He got a glimpse of a pile of broken shingles on the pathway as he picked his way carefully around them where the path cut through someone's back yard.

When Zeke shoved a rickety fence to the ground and

stomped through the middle of a flower bed, Lance felt he'd had enough. Broken plants littered the ground.

"Zeke, come back here this minute and pick this stuff up. I'm not putting up with any more of your selfish behaviour," Lance said, in his most persuasive teacher's voice.

When Zeke turned and walked toward him, Lance felt a moment of concern, but all Zeke did was stare for a moment and, without arguing, obediently came back and said, "Yes?"

"You don't need to destroy what little these people have," Lance admonished, amazed that Zeke was actually doing as he was told. "Hold that fence up while I put it back together."

Zeke didn't speak as he worked. However, as soon as Lance had braced the fence upright with a broken broomstick he'd picked up beside the shed door, Zeke was off and running again.

It seemed out of character for someone as angry as Zeke to take orders without arguing. Lance allowed himself a smile as the light tech raced ahead. He noted that he didn't break any more garden plants along the path, but he didn't bother to see that Lance was following him either. What a strange man!

Lance breathed a sigh of relief when he saw the west tower of the theatre in the distance. He was watching the tower looming up ahead when he heard a splash and an angry string of expletives coming from Zeke.

The full moon had just begun to climb over the mountain. He rushed ahead and when he came around the corner of an old shed, in the first beams of the rising moon, he was startled to find Zeke had fallen headfirst into a child's inflatable swimming pool.

Lance was half inclined to leave him there, for the man

really didn't deserve his attention, but it wasn't in the teacher's character to do that. Besides, he still wasn't sure just where he was, so he gave the fallen man his hand and helped him up.

"These damn idiots, and their blasted kids…" Zeke said.

"Stop it right now!" Lance snapped, feeling his anger rising again. "It's not their fault you fell into a pool, while you were trespassing in someone else's back yard. You weren't looking where you were going. Now, stand up and I'll help you. Don't destroy anything else or I'll go back to the theatre without you."

"You sound like my mother!" Zeke complained. "She never did anything for me. Didn't even bother to get my dinner. Threw me a can of beans as she left for what she called 'work. Silly bitch!" he said. "All she did was count the money. Never did know who my father was. She said I was hatched." He laughed bitterly.

"You must have some good memories, Zeke," Lance said, trying to overlook the obvious references to his mother's character and possibly her employment. He felt his blood run cold when he thought about it. "Let me help you clean up before we go on."

"Memories?" Zeke said. "The dog was nicer to me than my mother. When I think of my childhood, I see a little boy nursing with the litter of puppies. Ever heard of anything so weird?"

Lance was shocked, but all he said was, "I've heard some wild tales from kids in my classroom, so I never question whether things really happened, Zeke. Children often bear the wounds their parents endured. I'm glad you shared that with me."

Zeke didn't answer, but Lance thought he was likely thinking of his childhood dreams, dashed by memories too complex to understand. Lance recalled his own happy, secure childhood. Extracting a wad of Kleenex from his pocket, he wiped the water off Zeke's face and helped him remove his wet tee shirt, noting that Zeke had dropped his sweater in the water as well, so Lance took off his own sweater and gave it to the shivering man.

"Give me your shoes," he said, "so I can empty the water out of them." Without speaking, Zeke sullenly, but with almost childlike obedience, removed his shoes and waited while Lance emptied them and dried them off as well as he could. Zeke put them back on without comment and continued to lead the way. His wet shoes began to squeak. "At least I know where you are with those squeaky shoes," Lance said.

By the time they arrived at the theatre, Zeke's grumbling had diminished somewhat, although he was still annoyed. He walked beside Lance without rushing ahead, not once mentioning how inconsiderate people were leaving their equipment and flowerpots around the yard to trip him while he trespassed on their property. Finally arriving at the theatre, they walked through the parking lot to the backstage entrance, where two young guards stood on duty. "I know George, so he might allow us in," Lance said.

"Hi, Lance," the guard said. "Did you forget something? I shouldn't really let you go back in, but I know you. Check with me when you leave."

"Thanks, George," Lance said. "My friend left his phone on a table. He needs it for work tomorrow."

EIGHT

Lance was relieved that the police presence was evident, but when Zeke didn't move to follow him in, Lance turned around to ask why he'd stopped. He had been so insistent on going back to the theatre in a hurry, but now he was lagging behind.

At the end of the hall stood a man dressed in a tuxedo jacket and jeans, an unlikely mix. He was busily tucking the tails into his pants, then he bent down to pick up a small black suitcase that Lance recognized as a luthier's toolbox. When he stood up, he turned his face toward the two men.

"Well, fancy seeing you here," he said, looking surprised. "I thought you'd be busy playing a concert tonight. What are you doing here?"

"Jeremiah Bastable! I haven't seen you for ages! Where have you been? The concert was cancelled," Lance said. "Freddy was on for the first set and after a quick costume change, he didn't come back. Brutus tried to cover for him, but the crowd got nasty."

"I was hoping to catch up with him at the intermission. Did you say he didn't come back?" Jeremiah looked surprised. "Freddy is always punctual."

"He only sang a couple of songs."

"That's odd," Jeremiah said. "Is that why the theatre is crawling with cops?"

"Lots of damage done to the seats. I had lunch with Freddy at noon but didn't talk to him this evening," Lance said.

"He's a little absent-minded sometimes, but he enjoys performing for an audience. I'll call you if I see him. I got a job to do. Freeway car accident. Damaged instruments.

Have to do some repairs so these people can play a concert next weekend. Gotta go," Jeremiah said.

"I heard about the accident on the news this morning. Two people killed. Were they musicians?"

"No, the casualties were from the car that hit them. The news reporter said alcohol could have been a factor in the accident," Jeremiah said.

"I wondered about that. How did you get past the security? There was a rumble going on."

"We've been friends for years," Jeremiah said. "Went to school together, lived together, worked together."

"I'll see you soon, Jem," Lance said, beginning to move on. "I have to go too. Have a good weekend, eh?"

"Bye. Pop into the shop and see me. We haven't talked for a long time," he said as he walked away.

"Who's that?" Zeke asked when he had recovered.

"Freddy's older brother. Sorry, I thought you knew one another. You must have seen him at the theatre numerous times. I taught them music when they were kids. He plays first violin in several quartets here and in Vancouver," Lance said.

"Is his name Jeremiah or Jem?"

"Jeremiah, but he likes to be called Jem," Lance said. "It's his nickname."

"Why was he tucking the tails of his tux into his jeans?" Zeke said. "He was likely sneaking around the theatre."

"You have him all wrong," Lance said. "He plays lots of concerts with the Mozart Trio, a couple of professional quartets, and he probably just came from some function. You must have seen him before.

"I get bad vibes from him," Zeke commented. "He kept looking over his shoulder, and he's got funny eyes. I don't like him."

"That's silly," Lance said. "The Bastable family are all musical. The kids just happen to have an odd gene. Jem and Freddy both have one blue eye and one brown. That doesn't make them bad people."

"I need to get my phone now," Zeke said impatiently, as he scanned the hallway. "I don't have time to wait around while you talk about some creep with funny eyes. I'd have been smarter to break in than wait around for you to do all that nicey stuff. Come on!"

"Zeke," Lance said, with a shake of his head. "Your phone is probably not here. You'd be better off waiting until tomorrow. There's been a lot of people milling around."

"I want it now," Zeke barked. "Jem doesn't even have the same last name as Freddy. You said they are brothers. Freddy's name is *Gonzaèlas*."

"That's his stage name," Lance told him. "Jem runs the family music store on Cardinal Crescent in Meldrum. He's the instrument repair man."

"Likely story," Zeke said. "If you ask me, he looks like a criminal."

"That's silly. I heard on the news about that car accident. He'd be the one they'd call if they needed quick repairs. Anyway, we're here for your phone. Where were you when you called the cops?" Lance asked.

"I called from the concession," Zeke said, with an exaggerated sigh. "I laid my phone on the table."

"We shouldn't hang around here," Lance said. "Just have a quick look so we can be on our way."

"If he'd hired me as a stand-in I could have kept that crowd under control better than that Brutus person," Zeke said, "I play and sing just as good as him."

"You'll have to discuss that with Freddy," Lance said. "We have to go through the hallway to the concession stand where you think you left it. Come on, let's go." Lance led the way.

"Oh, for crying out loud," Zeke said. "I want my damn phone tonight, not next week. Most people wait 'til they're dead before rigour mortis sets in. You make me sick.!" He pushed Lance aside and grabbed the door handle straight ahead without paying attention to the sign that read, "BOILER ROOM. Out of Bounds. Maintenance staff only." He flung the door open angrily.

"No. You can't go in there. Can't you read the sign?" Lance said, putting a warning hand on Zeke's arm. It was too late. Zeke was already in the room, staring open-mouthed at the scene before him.

"Oh, shoot! This is the last room I want to be in!" he muttered to himself as he tried to back out.

Lance stopped dead in his tracks. He was face to face with a very large police officer and his dog, a heavy-set Shepherd-Labrador cross. He and the officer looked keenly at one another, and a brief moment of recognition passed between them,

The officer said, "Stop. This area is off-limits. Close the door, please."

"Oh, my God! Who? What?" Zeke mumbled, standing nervously by the door, his gaze riveted to the floor.

"My friend here lost his cell phone, and I thought it might be here, but it doesn't matter," Lance blurted. He turned as if to leave, but the scene was so horrific he couldn't move. "Who…? Is that…?" he asked in a weak voice.

"We don't know," said the officer, "but you must remain here for now."

"Why?" asked Zeke.

"Lock the door, please. I don't want anyone else to come barging in. I've called for backup, but until they come, you have to stay here."

"Okay," Lance muttered, the only one with enough presence of mind to do as he was told. He clicked the lock shut.

Sprawled on the floor in the dressing room was the body of a young blonde male, his long hair discoloured by blood, his legs spread grotesquely apart, one hand still clutching his guitar in a death grip.

Across the room, by the open door to the catwalk, stood a dark-haired girl, one foot close to the blonde head lying on the floor. Mesmerized by what she saw and obviously in shock, she looked as though she might faint.

"Oh my God!" she whispered, but loud enough for Lance to catch the words. The officer told Zeke to get a chair for her. He pointed across the room. Lance noticed that Zeke appeared to be moving as if he was made of wood although, he did as he was told, without his eyes ever leaving the officer's face. Lance wondered why.

The dog recovered first. He looked up at his master as if to ask, "What are your orders, Boss?"

"I want my damn phone," blurted Zeke. "And I want it now."

"I'm waiting for two backup officers," the police officer said, giving the dog a pat. "One of them will take you three into another room where you will remain until further notice. After the body is removed, I'll arrange for you to be questioned. I'm sorry," he said, "but I have no choice but to detain you."

"I understand. May I call my wife?" Lance asked. "I don't have my phone with me, so could I use the office phone?"

"Yes, of course, I'll call the number for you now, and before you hang up, give me the phone and I'll explain to her."

"I don't see why we should be treated like criminals,"

Zeke complained. "We ain't done nothin' wrong. I just came to get my cell phone. I left it on a table in the foyer after I reported a riot was about to take place here."

"We'll check for your phone later. Thank you for reporting the riot. When tempers begin flaring, that's always a possibility," the officer said. "You may as well sit down and wait until the backup men get here."

Zeke obviously was not pleased with this arrangement. He openly studied the scene with distaste and glared at Lance as if he were at fault. When he turned an evil eye on the police officer, Lance stared at him in disbelief. If looks alone could kill… It was hard to believe this was the same person who had come to his rescue a short time ago.

Lance did a double take when he heard Zeke snap, "Who is he?" his voice harsh and accusatory.

"We'll know that when the body is identified," the cop said. The cop had to know the victim was Freddy, so why would he say such a thing? It must be a matter of protocol not to name the victim.

Lance had never been a man who had hidden from the harsh realities of life, but he selected a chair by the door as far from Zeke and the body as he could. He wasn't sure whether he wanted the ugly scene behind him so he couldn't see it or in front where he could keep an eye on it. He felt sick to his stomach. He did know that he wanted to be as far from Zeke as he could get. He was horrified by the man's behaviour. It was as if all he cared about was his phone, appearing to minimize the fact there was a dead body on the floor. The police officer handed Lance the phone. He dialled his home number with shaking hands, spoke briefly to his wife, and handed the phone to the policeman.

"Hello, Mrs. Bishop," he said, "My name is Brad Thomas."

Lance studied the officer. So this really is Brad

Thomas? He obviously recognized me. Called my wife by name.

When Lance heard the word *sequestered* he looked up quickly, making eye contact with the officer. He thought about Igor again. For some reason, he couldn't get the cat out of his mind. And Charlie. What would happen to him?

Poor Freddy! What did he do to deserve this? Lance was sure he could identify the body, but he couldn't say a word until asked. Protocol had to be followed whether he liked it or not.

A few minutes later, when the medical officer arrived to examine the scene and pronounce the victim dead, Brad told Joanne, Lance, and Zeke to come with him. Joanne moved as if in a trance, her eyes never leaving the horrific scene until they were in the hallway. Zeke was still protesting loudly.

Lance tried to block out Zeke's tirade. The light tech's anger made him uneasy. He wondered what Zeke would say next and possibly incriminate himself.

"We'll use this office for the time being," Brad said, pointing to a door with *Administration* written in large black letters. "I know this is not what you guys want, but as far as I know you are the only ones who witnessed the scene. We don't know why he died, but we have no proof he was murdered. The detention is as much for your protection as it is to record what you obviously witnessed."

"I understand," said Lance.

"Me, too," Joanne said.

"I didn't see nuthin'," Zeke spoke up. "I need to get out of here."

Brad sighed. "We all feel the same way," he said. "Oh, here are my backup officers, so that makes it easier."

Turning to address the three men, he said, "Got to get these people away from this scene."

"Yes, for sure," the shortest of the three agreed, taking up a position by the door in front of Lance.

"Lance, and Zeke, stay in the hallway with the two men," the dog handler ordered, "and I will take the girl to the small room at the end of the hall for a brief questioning. Then we can decide which room to stay in."

"Why are we being guarded like criminals?" asked Zeke, his face contorted in anger. "I don't get it."

"It's just routine, but you are required to stay until I give you permission to leave," Brad said.

"I have to go," Zeke snarled.

"In that case, I may have to take measures to detain you. I'd advise you to wait until I am finished questioning everyone and then we'll consider it." Brad stood up to his full six-foot-six height, and Heathcliffe glanced at him, questions in his dark brown intelligent eyes. Zeke angrily sat down on a chair and stared at the floor.

He looked up when Brad told Joanne Riker to come with him.

"Don't hurt her," he ordered when he saw Brad beckon her to follow him.

"I don't intend to," Brad said, turning back. "That's not how I operate."

"I know you guys," Zeke said. "You use intimidation whenever you think it would work."

"You're entitled to your opinion," Brad said, "as long as you obey orders. I should be back here in under fifteen minutes."

NINE

Lance waited patiently in the Administration Office while Brad talked to Joanne. He hoped Brad would talk to Zeke next because his fidgeting was driving Lance crazy. Zeke continued to curse and complain. Lance began to feel uneasy as he waited his turn to be questioned.

He got a glimpse of his reflection in a long mirror by the door. His dark blonde hair was a little windblown from walking back to the theatre with Zeke, but otherwise, he looked normal. He felt relieved that he was able to separate himself from Zeke. He had been kind enough to help him with his equipment, but Zeke's mood swings were worrisome.

The round clock above the door read half past nine. Obviously, the concert was cancelled. The smell of death was in the air, and it made Lance feel ill to even think of the heinous act it took to take the life of the man lying on the floor.

Zeke's behaviour was annoying because Lance felt just as miserable as he did. There were times when one had to simply go with the flow, and this was one of those times.

The officers moved Lance and Zeke to another room as soon as the coroner arrived. However, it did nothing to relieve the tension. Lance flinched when the coroner referred to Freddy as 'the body.' How could his old friend be reduced to being called anything but Freddy? It may have been the truth, but it seemed almost sacrilegious.

He thought of his amp and guitar in the back of the van and hoped Zeke remembered where he'd parked. As he waited, Lance had another disturbing thought. Not only did he not know where Zeke lived but he didn't even know his last name. He appeared to be well known in the entertainment circuit so perhaps Lance could ask someone.

The next twenty minutes went by slowly until Joanne emerged from the interrogation room followed by Lt. Thomas. The girl looked upset, but at least she wasn't in tears or shaking like she had done when they were all in the room with the body.

"Is your name Zeke?" Brad asked the man slumped in a chair. "Your full name please."

"Ezekiel George Giesbrecht," he said, glaring at the officer. "Why d'ya want to know?"

Lance thought to himself, at least now I know Zeke's last name.

The officer continued speaking. "Come back with me and as soon as we have talked, if you cooperate, I'll let you go. First, I need some information."

"Waddaya want? I already told ya who I am. What more do ya want? You're playing this cop thing up, ain't ya?" Zeke snarled.

Lance started to say something in Lt. Thomas' defence but closed his mouth before he got himself into hot water too. Why was Zeke so abrasive?

Officer Thomas looked at Lance and gave him a half smile. He turned his attention to Zeke once more. "I don't have time to play games. Follow me to the office so we can get on with the interrogation. When you've answered my questions satisfactorily, you can go. We have to leave this room right away so the coroner can do his work."

"I didn't kill him!" Zeke snarled.

"We don't have a suspect yet," the elderly cop said. He studied Zeke's face. "Come with me, please."

Zeke shoved his chair noisily against the wall and went toward the left, but Brad said, "To the right, please, toward the exit." The door slowly closed behind him.

Lance leaned back in his seat. Across the short expanse of the hallway, he could see cameras flashing while the coroner took photos of the crime scene. Held in the adjoining room, he tried not to look, but it was almost impossible to avoid it. There was not a full wall between where he was seated and the sordid scene.

Lance struggled to stay calm while he witnessed them placing the body of his old pupil in a white body bag and on a stretcher. It wasn't supposed to end this way.

"What are they doing?" Joanne asked. Lance looked around.

"I don't know," he said. He studied her face They were both staring in disbelief at the action straight out of a horror movie in full colour and real time.

His stomach rebelled, and Lance swallowed repeatedly as he struggled to keep his supper down. When the stretcher was barely out of the room, the investigators began dusting and spraying and photographing the scene.

"What does that do?" asked Joanne, craning her neck to see.

"I think they're looking for fingerprints and DNA."

"DNA? You mean that stuff will show up in the photos? I don't understand."

"I think they spray a chemical that's called Alumanescent or something," Lance said. "I don't know much about it."

Lt. Thomas and Zeke returned to the room. The officer grinned when he heard Lance trying to explain it to Joanne. "I think you mean *luminal*. It's used to find traces of blood so we can get a clear picture of what really happened. Lance, I'll be talking to you next. Mr. Giesbrecht, you may go. Don't leave town. You may need to answer more questions. One of my men will accompany the girl home."

"I don't give a damn," Zeke snarled. He turned to Lance

and said, "I'll come back for you. Just give me a holler on your cellphone."

"I would but neither of us has a phone with us. I depend upon pay phones on concert nights."

"My home phone number is 555-000-0000. Give me about an hour, will ya? I forgot that," Zeke said.

Lance pulled a crumpled piece of paper from his pocket, dusted the crumbs off it, and scribbled down the number. He noticed that Brad was watching Zeke the whole time, and wondered what he was thinking as he, too, made note of the number. What district did 555 represent? As far as he knew it was a fictional number.

After he left, Lance said, "Zeke has all my equipment in his van. I hope he comes back for me."

"Well," Brad said, "if he doesn't return, I'll get you home. Your wife sounded miffed when I spoke to her." He closed the door. "She asked if she should come and get you, but I didn't want her coming to the theatre with so many people milling around."

"Oh, thanks. It really is you, isn't it?" Lance smiled one of those smiles a person gives when they've just had a revelation.

"Yep, I was sure I recognized you when you came onstage tonight. Long time no see, eh? Surprised you're playing this stuff, though."

"Not my favourite but we all gotta butter our bread somehow. Your dog seems to dig heavy metal! I can see by the grin on his doggie face that he likes it." He reached out and shook hands with Brad.

They both looked up when they heard scratching from the direction of the ceiling." What the heck is that?" Brad asked, staring up at the corner of the room.

"Unless this place feeds a helluva big mouse, I'd say someone is out there listening."

"Oh, it's just Igor on the catwalk. That cat gets around." Lance waved his arm in a wide arc. "He has the run of the theatre after hours, but I'm surprised he's not hiding tonight, because of the dog. He can get all the way down to here by walking through his secret tunnels between the walls."

"A cat on the catwalk? Sounds like a movie name. Come to think of it," Brad said, "I have seen him here. The hunting must be good."

"Ask Igor. He's an excellent tracker. He's probably near the door right now, so you can discuss it with him in person. I wonder if he just doesn't smell the dog—he'd be gone if he did. He really doesn't go for dogs."

Lance got up and opened the door, and Igor nonchalantly sauntered into the room. He stopped abruptly when he saw that a dog had invaded his domain. He glared at Heathcliffe suspiciously and performed the famous cat hissing ceremony, complete with an arched back, the stiff-legged walk, and the dangerous show of sharp teeth.

Heathcliffe nervously sidled up to Brad and scrunched himself under his knee.

"Well, the cat sure isn't happy about it," Brad said with a hearty *Ha Ha*! "Heathcliffe isn't keen on cats, either. In fact, I'd say after Tiki got through with him when he was a pup, he has great respect for cats. Actually, to put it bluntly, he's terrified of them."

"Who's Tiki?" asked Lance.

"A Siamese we had when I first got Heathcliffe. He'd been napping downstairs, and she wouldn't let him come up."

"I can't say I blame him for being nervous," Lance said. "That was a mighty good show Igor just put on."

"It was, and he's not finished yet."

Igor had remained frozen in that position for a few seconds before he appeared to realize Heathcliffe was probably not a threat. He began washing his face to cover up his embarrassment, as cats do.

"Igor's a Russian Blue mix," Lance explained. "That breed is usually a bit standoffish, but he's used to people and music. He makes himself scarce when dogs are around, as a rule," Lance explained.

Without so much as another glance at the dog, Igor leisurely strolled over to investigate something he spied on the floor by the wall. After he had sniffed it thoroughly and finally concluded it might make a good toy, he gave it a whack and watched it slide across the floor. He obviously decided it was harmless, so he gave it a shove and watched it slip under a chair. He went after it full-bore and played hockey with it for a few minutes.

"Well," said Brad. He got down on his knees to get a better look, "I think we shouldn't stick around waiting for your friend to come back. Let's go."

"Hey, wait! What's this?" asked Lance. "What's Igor playing with?" He got up and dropped to his knees to take a better look at it.

Brad kept right on talking, "Zeke isn't coming back for you, or he'd be here by now. I want to get out of here."

"He has something … Wait!" Lance said as he put a cautionary hand on Brad's shoulder.

Brad clamped his mouth shut abruptly and watched the cat with interest. "If only we could think like a cat!" he whispered.

Igor paid no attention to either Lance or the dog. He dropped what he was carrying in his teeth and looked at it intensely. When it didn't move, he batted it with his paw and watched it slide across the floor. He ran after it and gave it another whack. It rolled away.

Finally, he tried another feline tactic. He walked away and pretended he was no longer interested in it, probably thinking it just might try to get away and then he could pounce on it.

Heathcliffe slowly moved closer to the cat and sniffed his ear.

The two men watched in amazement as Igor deliberately allowed the dog to come right up to him. The two animals stared at one another until the dog sat up and nervously gave his tail a dignified wag, stretched out his neck to sniff the object again.

"He's trying to tell me something," whispered Brad, standing up. "What is it? It looks like a tool of some kind."

"I know what it is," Lance said, "It's a hole reamer. Where did he get it?"

"I wish that cat could talk," Brad said.

"Uh, I think he is talking," said Lance, "but I wish we humans could understand what he's trying to say. I've never known a cat as smart as Igor." Lance picked him up and looked into the blue-green eyes typical of the Russian Blue.

"Maybe we should take a closer look at that thing. Is that blood on the point? It looks funny to me, and Heathcliffe is sniffing it," Brad said.

"Right."

"Don't touch anything, Lance." Brad bent down to examine the tool.

"I know it's a hole reamer," Lance said.

"What's it for?" Brad asked.

"A versatile tool used by violin makers and carpenters," Lance explained.

"I'm puzzled," Brad said. He flicked a plastic bag from his pocket and skillfully picked up the object without touching it.

"Uh," muttered Lance, "I wonder if it was in this room all the time and Igor just found it? I guess he thought it was a good toy."

"Do you use a hole reamer in the shop when you repair instruments?" Brad asked, his forehead wrinkling in a frown as he spoke.

"I have a smaller one in my tool kit for emergencies, but Freddy's brother is the instrument repair man in the shop," Lance replied. "Violins have a wooden scroll, which is actually a fancy peg-box. The holes are made to insert the pegs in order to turn the strings tighter or looser. Master carpenters like my friend Joe often use a hole reamer in the shop."

"Can you give me an example?" Brad asked.

"Yes. He would use one to make holes in a chair seat when bolting it to the frame of the chair. A hole reamer is used because the screw or bolt needs to be counter-sunk."

"I see. It's a lethal-looking tool when you look closely at it," Brad observed. "Don't touch anything else, Lance, because now your fingerprints will be on that guitar."

"Oh, Charlie used to play this guitar when he was alone and my fingerprints were probably already on it as well as his because I've carried it up for him," Lance admitted.

Lt. Thomas nodded. "Charlie?" he asked. "So, he doesn't play this one now?"

"No, I had an extra guitar at home, and I gave it to him just before the concert that night."

"So, you gave him a guitar that belonged to you then?" Brad asked.

"Yes, I felt sorry for the guy because he really loves music."

"Hmmm, I understand but with your fingerprints on so many surfaces, it does complicate things. Let's have lunch tomorrow, and we can catch up over a cup of coffee," Brad said. "Must be twenty years since I last saw you. You were just a know-it-all teenager then, learning to play the violin."

"I'd enjoy that," Lance said with a grin. "You were just

learning to conduct an orchestra in those days. You waved the baton with one hand and the other arm at the same time, so it looked like you were rowing a boat."

"Yeah, somebody else told me that. Did you know Freddy Gonzaèlas very well?" he asked.

"I taught him music when he was a kid, but I haven't seen him for ages. He left Meldrum to go on tour and promised to hire me to play in his band if he came back to play a concert. I thought it was just an idle promise," Lance said.

"I was going to ask why he hired you. You're so much older than the other players. I noticed that you don't pretend to be their age though."

"I believed in him when he didn't believe in himself. He thought he couldn't do anything with his life because he looked different; one blue eye and one brown. He was a brilliant musician from childhood," Lance said.

"Did you talk with him at all before the concert?" Brad asked, his forehead wrinkled in a frown. He bent down to smooth Heathcliffe's fur.

"We rehearsed last night at his parent's house, and we had breakfast together this morning," Lance explained. "At tonight's concert, he sang two songs and went off for a costume change and didn't return to the stage."

"That's what I thought. I came in after that. I mean, I was at the theatre but not watching the concert at that time. Could you identify him?" Brad asked.

"Yes, but I think they will ask a member of his family to do that."

"Right," Brad replied. "I meant if there was no one else. I'll take you home; Zeke's not coming back for you. I didn't expect he would."

"He's got a few thousand dollars' worth of my equipment in his van, so I hope we can find him. It's my livelihood," Lance said with a worried look on his face.

"He can't leave town and I know his address. We'll get your stuff back. What was wrong with him tonight? He changed a lot in just a few minutes. Uncanny."

"Who knows?" Lance said. "Come on, Igor, chowtime."

Lance dug in his pocket and extracted a piece of waxed paper wrapped around a curious-looking object.

"What on earth is that?" asked Brad, leaning over to get a better look.

"Oh, it's a chunk of the fish and chips I had for lunch today," Lance said.

"Probably not really good for him, but it's all I have today. Sometimes I bring him real cat food, but today I just saved him a piece of fish. He likes it—I already took the bones out of it."

"Will the fish still be good to eat after being in your pocket for a while? It smells kind of strong," Brad said, as he held his nose between his thumb and index finger.

"To Igor, it just enhances the flavour," Lance explained.

"I was wondering what that strange smell was. You like that cat, don't you?"

"Yes, he's lived in the theatre since he was a kitten. Sometimes I take him out so he can smell the air, but for the most part, he stays here and keeps Charlie company. The things he has seen!"

"Who's Charlie?" Brad asked again. "You've mentioned him before."

"I thought you knew about his case. He is staying in the theatre until his hearing comes up. He wants to make Canada his home."

"In trouble at home or here?"

"The whole thing is silly," Lance explained. "He told

me that he was in his second year of university in his country and doing some research for his thesis. He was trying to update too, to get the number of credits he needed to take the medical training courses. Someone suggested that he was spying and before he knew it, he was being investigated."

"Was it just a coincidence that he chose that time to come to Canada? Sounds fishy to me."

"No," Lance said. "He already had his visa for coming to Canada, so he wasn't running away. Despite that, his country wanted him deported to face charges, insisting they had proof he was a spy. Canada has also done some investigations and concluded they have no basis for the accusation."

"I see what you mean," Brad answered. "I'll look into it."

"He is being protected here right now, but it probably has the potential to get worse before it gets better because this thing with Freddy means we're all suspects, I bet," Lance said.

"That's true. I didn't want to bring that up, but it does complicate things. I've never met him, so you will have to introduce me to him soon," Brad agreed. "In the meantime, he will probably need food, and someone will have to see he is fed while the theatre is under the cloud of this murder— or we think it could be one. He might even need someone to sponsor him for the time being."

"What a mess!" Lance said. "Everything's happening at once."

"Yes, it is," Brad said. "Anyway, I want to meet you for lunch tomorrow. How about the Keg?"

"That place still there?" Lance asked.

"Same location and name, but not the same place. See you there at noon, eh? I'll drive you home now, and we can meet tomorrow," he said.

TEN

When Lance rolled out of bed the morning after the concert, he had buckets of energy. He wandered around the bedroom in his birthday suit before he pulled on his pants.

Andrea smiled as she let her eyes linger over his wide shoulders and masculine frame. She reached for her purple housecoat. "Would you like to have the shower first, dear?" she asked. "I'll wash your back for you if you want." She felt her cheeks redden while she followed him with her eyes.

"Sure," he said. He grinned and winked at her, obviously aware that he was being observed. "It's warm this morning. I have to meet Brad at the Keg at noon."

"Where's your trailer and equipment?" she asked, privately thinking that her husband of twenty years was rather well-equipped. "What actually happened at the theatre last night?"

"While we eat, I'll try to tell you as much as I know," he said. "I'd better get dressed first." He gave her a wicked grin. "It's warm this morning."

"I think so," Andrea agreed. "Good idea."

She smiled affectionately, surprised by the blush she knew had reddened her cheeks.

"I'll get breakfast going while you shower," she said. She walked down the stairs wearing a smile.

Thirty minutes later, seated at the small square table in the breakfast nook just off the kitchen, Lance fidgeted with his napkin, folding and unfolding it several times. After he'd accidentally spilt his orange juice down his shirt as he tried to describe the concert to Andrea, he said, "I have things to do."

"What's the rush?" she asked. "It's Sunday morning.

You don't have to go anywhere, and the jobs can wait."

"Sorry," he said. "I hope you'll forgive me for being so hyper. The theatre is in a mess from the ruckus last night. The audience was getting unruly because the concert was cancelled when Freddy didn't come back. Some ticket holders wanted a refund from us right away. I knew you'd heard the news and probably were worried."

"It wasn't your fault the concert was cancelled. The announcer only mentioned the possibility of a riot developing. Is that true?

"The beginning of a riot, for sure," Lance said. "It didn't get worse because the police were quick to clear the theatre."

"Why didn't he come back? It was his band. Was he just playing games? It doesn't make sense."

"I don't know all the details, honey, but – oh, it was awful. We all had to get off the stage because the patrons were angry and..." He stopped talking and choked as he tried to hide his emotions.

"What happened?" Andrea asked. She patted his back until he got his breath and brought him a drink of water. She pulled her chair closer to him and put her hand on his shoulder.

"He got beaten up real bad. He didn't come back to finish the concert because he couldn't." Lance set the glass down, missed the table, and spilled water all over his pants.

Andrea took the glass from him and set it on the counter so he wouldn't knock it over a second time. After mopping up the water, she asked, "Where is he now? In the hospital?"

"Ah, no," Lance stammered. "He—well, he had head injuries, I guess. He—he died."

"Died? What do you mean? Dead?" Andrea asked, her eyes wide. "They said on the news there had been an accident, but I didn't think it was that bad."

"I can't even talk about it." He put his hand over his face and sat still for a minute before speaking again. "It was no accident. He was murdered."

"Oh, Lance, That's awful. I can't even imagine what you've been through. Will there be a police investigation?"

"Yes," he said. "Do you mind if I go for a bike ride? I need to clear my head."

"Are you sure that's a good idea, Lance? You are barely coherent." Andrea frowned as she spoke.

"I have to. I'll call you. If I don't keep busy, I'm going to burst. I have to meet Brad at the theatre anyway," he said.

"It doesn't seem like a very good plan. I'm willing to drive you there and pick you up afterwards."

"Ah, babe, I'll be fine," Lance said, as he leaped from the table. "I've been riding my bike for years. It just comes automatically. The trail is all downhill, and it'll do me good." He grabbed his leathers off a hanger in the hallway. Struggling into the chaps, he yanked up the zippers holding them firmly but not tightly over his legs. He walked resolutely out the door. He swung his leg over the Harley parked next to the truck, strapped on his helmet, and, with a flick of his wrist, revved up the motor.

Andrea watched from the front window overlooking the driveway. "Headstrong male!" she said. "Why are men like that? He's a good guy, but sometimes I could choke him." After he had driven away, she felt guilty for her thoughts. How could she think that about him? Lance would go to the ends of the earth for his family.

Before he was to meet Brad at the Keg, Lance stopped at the theatre to check on his trailer and van. He saw Igor wandering around the parking lot. The theatre entrance was behind police tape and guarded at both doors. He phoned

Brad to tell him he could be delayed.

"Hi, Brad," he said, "I just found the theatre cat in the parking lot. He must have been out there all night. They won't let me take him back in."

"Hmm," Brad said. "Did you tell the guard he lives there?"

"Yes. He wouldn't even open the door so the cat could go in by himself. Igor's never been outside without me since he was a stray kitten. I've got the bike so I can't take him home."

Brad was silent for a few seconds, deep in thought. "I guess the best solution is for me to take him home until things can be sorted out," he said.

"I was hoping you'd say that. I suppose I could hold him in my lap. What would I do with my bike?"

"When I get there, I'll put the cat in my car while you park the bike in a safe place, and then I'll drive you back later to pick it up. Would that work for you?" Brad said.

"Yes, a good idea." Lance realized he would have the dubious pleasure of holding a nervous animal on his lap.

"First, I have to drop the cruiser at the station and get my own car. Luckily, I'll be off duty," Brad said. "I'll drive you back to get your Harley. I have Heathcliffe behind the barrier, but the cat won't understand that, and I don't relish a cat and dog fight in my car."

"That should be fun for us. What about our lunch at the Keg?" Lance asked. "I don't feel very good right now anyway, and I was short with Andrea before I left."

"We'll have to postpone it until tomorrow, but we don't have any other choice," Brad said. "Why don't you give her a ring right now? I don't mind waiting."

"Okay," he said meekly. "I know you're right. I forgot we'd made plans to have lunch at the Keg today. When I left home, I promised to call her, but I haven't done it yet."

Heathcliffe was accustomed to changes and well-trained around other animals, but Igor had spent most of his life in the theatre. To him, Heathcliffe was just a dog, so he had become skittish and wanted nothing to do with it.

While the dog was behind the front seat with a barrier separating him from passengers, Lance held Igor on his lap. Heathcliffe was trying to get a better look at the intruder, and Lance was struggling to keep Igor from getting too nosy. He finally removed his shirt and wrapped it around the cat to control him.

"It should be a cinch getting him into the carrier," Brad said, with a confident smile. A few minutes later, the smile changed to a frown. Igor had a different opinion when it came to getting into the carrier. He burrowed under Lance's arm and pushed his head into the sleeve of the shirt. Brad tried to separate the cat from the shirt and got a bloody hand for his trouble. The cat appeared to have acquired eight legs and three sets of sharp teeth. He was obviously bent on using them all at once.

He glared at the carrier and wouldn't budge. It was then agreed that Lance would continue up to Brad's home with him instead of riding his bike.

"This is ridiculous!" Brad said. "I've had less problem with convicted killers than this little demon. I'll bring you back after we've taken him to my house."

"Providing we can get him in it," Lance remarked. "He doesn't seem very cooperative."

Trying a different strategy, Lance picked Igor up and pushed the open door of the carrier toward him. Igor let his feelings be known. The string of feline swear words suggested that the cat wasn't having any part of the carrier.

Finally, Lance grabbed him by the scruff of his neck and shoved him into the carrier, still wrapped in the shirt, which was showing signs of wear and tear. He slammed the carrier gate shut and locked it. Igor stopped arguing and buried his head in the crumpled garment with his bum up in the air.

Brad quickly got behind the wheel, smug in the knowledge that he and Lance had won the battle. Igor stayed frozen in the same position until the car hit a bump in the road. He sat bolt upright and stared at a herd of cows grazing in a field. With a screech, he clawed between the bars of his cage and snapped at Lance.

On arriving at Brad's home, Lance picked up the carrier and followed Brad into the house. After the front door was closed to prevent Igor from leaving for parts unknown, he set it down on the floor and opened the gate. Igor went to the very back of the carrier and clung to the bars.

"You've been paroled," Lance said. "You're free." He reached into the carrier and tried to pull the cat out. Igor clung to the cushioned floor with his claws extended.

While Brad looked on, Lance shook the cage and finally managed to dislodge one set of claws, but Igor magically deployed his spare set on the other foot. With great finesse, he unsheathed them all at once to not only hook into the soft fabric roof of the carrier but to get Lance's hand as well.

"Shoot! The front door is open!" exclaimed Lance. "Close it, Brad, because Igor will go out."

"What? Where did he go?"

"Igor's outside climbing the maple tree by the gate." They both stared at the cat through the open door as he shinnied up the trunk.

"What do we do now?" Brad asked as he watched Igor go up to a high branch.

"Go up after him, I guess. Ask Heathcliffe."

"I haven't climbed a tree since I was sixteen. Heathcliffe has never climbed one."

"Never mind, I'll do it. My chickens have me trained," Lance said.

"Your chickens?" Brad muttered. "They climb trees?"

"If I don't keep their wings clipped, they fly up."

"Oh," Brad said. He stood by the door and watched Lance tighten his shoelaces and walk quietly to the maple. "I hope that works."

Igor watched Lance approach the tree to begin the climb. As he got closer to the branch where Igor was clinging, the cat leaped to the top in one easy jump. Lance said nothing, but he kept his eye on the cat and the cat appeared to keep his eye on Lance.

Brad kept his eyes on them both from the ground. He sat down on a garden bench and stared at the two climbers.

Sensing that Igor was showing signs of nervousness, Lance checked his pockets for remnants of the cat treats he often carried. Yes! he still had some left over from the night before. He held his hand toward the nervous feline and waited.

Slowly Igor came closer. He kept looking down at the ground. When Lance nabbed him, the cat uttered a soft little "mew" and hid his head under Lance's arm.

Lance now had to hang onto him with one hand and make his way to the ground below while Igor purred and chewed in the comfort of Lance's chest.

Brad helped Lance down the last two branches without touching Igor or speaking. Slowly they walked to the house, closed the door, and watched as Igor went back into the carrier to finish the treats. No one, including Heathcliffe, said a word until Igor fell asleep.

The two guys smiled at one another and silently proclaimed victory.

"I'm glad my chickens have trained me so well," Lance said when he heard Igor snore. They both laughed and

Heathcliffe gave a subdued "wuff!" and wagged his tail in a dignified manner.

"Are you ready to go home yet?" Brad asked.

"Yep," Lance said.

"I guess we'll meet tomorrow for lunch, eh? It certainly was an education for me to watch you and Igor. You sure understand animals."

"I'll tell Glenda you said so. She taught me, you know."

"That's nice," Brad said, as he rolled his eyes.

ELEVEN

The next day when they met at the Keg, Brad slid into the booth opposite Lance and asked, "How are your aches and pains?"

"I have a bump on my head where I hit the door frame, but otherwise I'm fine. I have a few scratches too. What about you?" Lance inquired. He rubbed the top of his head and squinted. "Igor gave us a good workout. He should settle in pretty soon now that he's actually got a home. He likes people."

"My wife likes him. When she came in from volunteering at the food bank yesterday, she borrowed a can of cat food from next door and offered him some. He kept his eye on her while he ate to make sure she was friendly, but he became more relaxed in a short time. We'll shop for his food this afternoon. A house isn't really a home until you have a cat," Brad said. "Do you have one?"

"We have two—one is a beautiful ragdoll named Francie. When she was a kitten, she always looked as though she was having a bad hair day. She grew up to be gorgeous with two little ear tufts. The big male cat is a Norwegian forest cat with a thick shaggy coat," Lance said. "I like cats."

"So do I, but my wife is more of a dog person," remarked Brad. "Igor is her first cat--other than Tiki, who was a blind seal point Siamese. What's a forest cat look like?"

"He's a big fellow, weighs nearly twenty-five pounds, with huge feet, but short legs. He's black with a big white V on a black face and ears. Nice boy. Eats us out of house and home." Lance laughed as he spoke.

"How did he get the name Smoker? Don't try to tell me he smokes cigars."

"I wouldn't put it past him to try," Lance said with a chuckle "He lived in a logging camp and would follow the guys out on the deck to have a smoke and a beer, so they nicknamed him Smoker," Lance said. "He's a big boy. He never got into drinking beer, thank goodness, but he likes pretzels."

"Oh, good. The waiter is coming our way so we'd better order," Brad said.

"My treat today," Lance promised. "I want fish and chips.

"In that case, I'll have caviar and… "

"Oh, no you won't. Luckily for me, they don't have that on the menu at noon. Now, order something or I'll withdraw my offer, and you'll have to pay for it yourself," Lance said as he unfolded his napkin and laid it across his knees.

"How long have you been married?" Brad asked when he'd stopped laughing. "Your wife sounded like a nice person when we talked on the phone."

"Yes. She's a local girl from Rocky Creek. We began going together shortly after we both graduated, but we didn't get married for another five years. Our twentieth anniversary is coming up soon."

"So, the same age?"

"Yes. She's two weeks younger than me. We both graduated in 1972. I went to university and got my degree in education, and she worked at the hospital in Kamloops and later went into nursing. Took her training in Vancouver. When we finished our education, we found each other again and got married."

"So, you didn't go to school with Freddy, then?"

"Heavens, no," Lance said. "He's only twenty-five now. He was in elementary school when I graduated. I was his band teacher for two years, and I also gave him private music lessons."

"You must have taught music before you got your degree," Brad observed.

"I helped with the junior band in my last year of school. Freddy quit school in the early eighties, and he's been away from here for a few years. He didn't even write to me after he left Meldrum to make his fortune," Lance said. He picked up a glass of cold water and drained it.

"When did he contact you about playing the concert? Did you rehearse for it?"

"Yes, one rehearsal. He turned up at the Rusty Hinges concert last week and surprised me backstage. He called me at home the following day to make sure I was coming" Lance said. "I was worried I might not fit in with them, but they didn't appear to care that I have kids almost their age."

"Oh," Brad said. "It's beginning to make sense to me now. I seem to remember that musicians don't really care much about age. It's more whether you can play the music than your age."

"Right. My age was never even mentioned. How long have you and Julie lived in Meldrum City? I like the house you live in now—as much of it as I saw from my vantage point of running into things. I remember your old house in Rocky Creek where we rehearsed in your basement family room with the orchestra," Lance said with a chuckle.

"After the kids left home, we moved to this house. It's smaller than the one we had at Rocky Creek, but the grounds are larger. We needed space for the dog," Brad explained.

"What will happen to him when you retire?" Lance asked, wrinkling his nose.

"He's almost eight and time for him to get his Old Age Security too. We'll both retire at the same time. He's been a great asset," Brad answered.

"I've always liked this area," Lance said as he surveyed the mountains from the window. "We own some farmland above the creek. It's a quiet area. Nothing much ever happens there."

"Was your wife in the Rocky Creek Community Orchestra too? You had a crush on Alisha Watkins. Was that her name?"

"Close. It was Felicia Warren. She was a very pretty girl who dressed like a movie star. I was never really serious about her. My wife came later. She's musical but didn't join the orchestra until the following year. Puts up with me hammering away on my guitar but stays away from the band concerts," Lance explained.

"What type of music does she prefer?"

"She comes to the symphony concerts, but heavy metal is too loud for her. I prefer music that's a little more gentle myself, but I like the kids who play it. I guess it's because they're about the same age as the teens I teach in school. They're a great bunch when they aren't trying to be typical heavy metal band players."

"I do security at the symphony concerts, and I think I've seen you playing the oboe. When did you switch to that instrument?" Brad asked.

"I've always fooled around with the oboe, but a few years ago I became serious about it, realizing I wasn't going anywhere with the violin. Eventually, I auditioned as First Oboe and got the job," Lance explained.

"Wow! A professional!" exclaimed Brad. "I'm impressed. You're the guy who gives the whole orchestra the accurate four-forty vibes for tuning. You get big bucks for that."

"I wish," Lance said with a smile. "How about you? You played a mean jazz piano in those days, and you could play classical music as well."

"Yeah, I can hammer on the piano and wave the baton a little," Brad said. "Learned on the Rocky Creek Community Orchestra years ago. To think the Meldrum Symphony developed because RCCO started in my basement is a good memory.."

"Great memories!' Lance agreed.

"Remember Tony, the guy who took over directing that group? I took conducting lessons from him. It wasn't well known that he was actually a musician. I gave it over to him when my workload got a lot bigger."

"I remember hearing something about that," Lance said. "Where is Tony now?"

"He passed away a few years ago. His wife doesn't play the bass now as its too heavy for her. She was younger than Tony, but she must be almost ninety now. Tony taught me all I know about music. Do you still play the violin?" Brad asked.

"Yes, but not in the orchestra. I liked Tony, but at sixteen I was more interested in girls than I was in the violin. I've added bass guitar and oboe to the list of instruments in my music room. My daughter Jeannie tells people I can play any instrument I want to play. Not quite that good, but I've always loved music."

"Kids!" Brad said. "Mine have distorted ideas about my talents too, but that's probably a good sign," Brad said. "I wasn't sure when I was young whether to go into music or the police force. My mother said that a policeman could be an excellent musician, but a professional musician wouldn't necessarily make a good police officer."

"She was right," Lance said. "Now you can have both music and police work. Do you want to jam with me soon? I have an acoustic guitar I can use, and the fiddle, of course."

"Sure, let's have a jam session. Like old times. So, what have you been doing besides getting married to the best-looking girl in Rocky Creek?" Brad asked.

"Making babies." Lance ran his fingers through his dark blond ponytail. "Three kids. Oldest son graduates next June. He's almost seventeen. Good-looking daughter is fourteen; My youngest son is handsome like me. Just turned ten."

"Oh, yeah. What's his name?"

"Lance, of course. We call him Lanny. He's a smaller version of me. Gonna be a big man if he ever grows up."

A youthful waiter approached their table. "Are you ready to order yet?" he asked.

"Yes, please," Lance said. He picked up the menu and pointed to the fish and chips. "It smells good in here," he said.

"Are your kids all musical?" Brad asked after he'd ordered the same thing. "Decided against caviar today."

"Good thing. I refuse to pay for that anyway," Lance said, oblivious to the curious smile of the waiter.

"Yes, the kids all play something. They can choose their instrument so it's fun for them. Occasionally we play all together and that's a hoot."

"I can imagine, "Brad said. "Sometimes these kids do better than the adults with music. Hey, I like these chips the waiter left at our table." He picked up two more and chomped away on them.

"Me too. Lanny has talent," Lance said. "Right now, he's using it to get on everyone's nerves, but in time he may take it seriously. He can't walk past the piano without playing a few chords, even in the middle of the night."

"That's kids for you. Fairly normal, because they don't take it seriously until they graduate from high school and begin to think of a career." Brad said. "He must really like it to do that though."

"Wow! Look at all that food! Smells good," Lance said

as the waiter walked to their table, his arms loaded with what looked like a lot of food for only two men. He grinned amiably as he put the platters on the table and asked what they wanted to drink. He had started to move away when he spied Heathcliffe snoozing at Brad's feet.

"Is that a service dog under your table?" he asked, looking down.

"Yes," Brad said. "He'll sleep until we leave. His name is Heathcliffe."

"I've seen him here before. Better behaved than a lot of the kids we get in here."

"Thanks," Brad said. "He's very well trained and has a large vocabulary."

"Vocabulary? You mean he can talk?" the waiter asked, his eyes wide with curiosity.

"Not quite!" Brad replied with a laugh. "He understands signals and commands and can carry out complicated directions. All our service dogs are well-trained. He holds the rank of a sergeant."

"Wow!" exclaimed the waiter. "Sergeant Heathcliffe. I've heard of service dogs, but I never met one before."

Brad smiled as the waiter walked away and looked back several times before he disappeared into the kitchen.

After a few minutes, Brad asked, "How do you feel about identifying the body?"

"Rotten," Lance answered. "However, he has family here, so I won't be needed unless there's an emergency."

"Right, but just in case."

"I hoped to fulfill my promise to Freddy last night and play bass guitar for him. It's something I've always wanted to do for the kid. This is the first time I've seen him since he left school. You have no idea how awful it was to see him like that."

"I do know," answered Brad. "After more than thirty

years on the force, I still feel upset every time I see another fatality. Did you say that Freddy was only twenty-five?"

"Yes. He was eighteen when he left B.C. He's travelled quite extensively since that time. Have you got plenty of food for Sir Igor," Lance said. "We could pick up some for him."

"We have plenty of cat food. My wife bought a whole case this morning.."

"Know something? I forgot that Charlie can't get out to buy himself any food, and nobody can go in to take him food. If the theatre is behind police lines, the poor fellow won't have much of a diet."

"Charlie?" queried Brad. "Why is he in the theatre? Don't they usually choose a church for that? I meant to ask you before."

"I don't know why they chose the theatre, but maybe it's because it's not in a heavily populated area, and his problem isn't as urgent as many people who seek asylum in Canada."

"I can get in to bring him some food," Brad said. "I'd like to meet him actually. What is his problem with the government in the first place? Why are they talking deportation?"

"I don't know everything about it, but he says he was going to university in the capitol city and doing some research when someone suggested that he wanted the information because he was a spy. It's not Canada that wants him deported. It's been checked out here. It's his own country," Lance explained.

"That's interesting," Brad said. "I'll look into taking your friend some food. He must be lonely too. In fact, I'll do some cautious investigation into his situation. I can do that without creating any suspicion. Do you think he's just nervous?"

"The language barrier may have some influence although he knew some English before he came here. However, he certainly is not fluent," Lance explained.

"English is a difficult language to learn," Brad agreed. "I'm full to the brim. Thanks, I enjoyed the meal. Next time it'll be my treat, but I'm not buying caviar either." He looked at Lance and chuckled.

"I don't care for caviar anyway," Lance said with a shrug. "So there!"

"We may have to ask for a doggie bag although my wife would probably get stuck with it because Heathcliffe is not interested in people food. Even if I drop something, he won't eat it," Brad said.

"Actually," Lance said, "Igor has had too much people food in his time, so he'd probably eat it. On weekends he ate everything from potato chips to chili. I'm glad he has a home now."

"He's a nice, mellow cat, so I think he'll settle down soon," Brad said, standing up.

"Except when he's in a carrier or being chased." Lance picked up the slip the waiter had left on the table.

They walked out the door together after Lance had paid the cashier. Brad said goodbye, climbed into the patrol car, and drove away.

When Lance was pulling out after lunch, he spied Zeke close by. He killed the engine and removed his helmet and hung it over the handlebars. He strolled over to where Zeke parked. He wondered if his equipment was still in the van or if Zeke had already unloaded it.

"Hey, man, how's it goin'?" Zeke said when he saw Lance looking at his van.

"Oh, could be better. How about meeting me at the theatre so we can put your equipment inside."

"I guess I could, but I'm not sure they would let us in

because it's still behind police tape," Lance said. "I haven't got much time though. I should get home."

"It won't take long," Zeke said, ignoring Lance's statement. "I have other things to do too. If they won't let me in, I'll just take it up to your place. I know where you live, but you better give me your address."

"No, it's okay," Lance said hurriedly. "I'll find some other way to get it home. Brad might be able to help. Thanks, though."

Lance observed that Joanne just happened to be Zeke's lunch partner today, but he didn't say a word. *Interesting*, he thought.

After Zeke left, Lance phoned Brad. Luckily, he hadn't driven too far away.

"I really don't want to come back," Brad said.

"I know, but things have changed. Zeke wanted my address so he could take my stuff there, but I don't want him to go to my house, especially when I'm not home. He's meeting me at the stage door in a few minutes "

"Good," Brad said. "Don't tell him you called me."

"No, I won't," Lance said to an empty phone. Brad had already hung up.

Ten minutes later when Lance pulled into the theatre, he was pleased to see Brad was already there. He stomped on the brakes and shut off the engine.

"How did you get here so fast?" he asked Brad.

"I was here already. Got another call. Fight at the stage door. Don't see anything yet, so maybe they cleared it up themselves. "

At first, neither Lance nor Brad saw Zeke arguing with a guard who appeared to be trying to bar him from putting Lance's equipment inside the door.

"I don't think so. Zeke got here first. What's he doing?" Lance pointed a finger toward the door.

"That must be the fight I was called to settle," Brad said,

"Zeke has that big guy down and is punching him in the face," Lance said.

Brad started running toward the scrap, with Lance on his heels. They roughly pulled Zeke off him.

"What the hell?" Lance asked. "What's this all about? Haven't you got anything better to do?"

"That damned cop," Zeke snarled. "He tried to tell me I was going to be busted if I put your equipment in there. Let's get with it. I want to get out of here. The place is crawling with cops. Makes me nervous."

"I think we should find a better place to store it," Lance said. He began methodically taking items from Zeke's van and piling them up in an orderly way to make it easier to move them into Brad's vehicle, not noticing that Zeke was glaring at him.

"Rigor mortis already setting in?" Zeke asked, looking around uneasily. "Most people at least wait until they're dead to quit moving. Can't you move faster than that?"

Before Lance could answer, Brad said, "Get after it, Lance. We have to get out of here. All this stuff won't fit in my car, so we'll have to think of something else."

"Where do I put it in the meantime?" Lance asked.

"I know a good place to shove it," Zeke archly suggested.

"Keep it to yourself," Brad advised him. "I'll put the guitar and smaller stuff in my car, and then give my brother Jack a call. He can put the amp in his truck. It's enclosed so it'll be safe overnight, and I'll pick it up tomorrow and get it to your place." Brad made a quick call and was smiling when he finished the conversation.

"I didn't know you had a brother," Lance said.

"He's just moved here from Ontario. He's on his way to load the stuff right now."

Lance breathed a sigh of relief, although he was still uneasy when he saw Zeke watching him. He flinched when Zeke threw his wallet at him, and said, "If I were you, I wouldn't be leaving your money around. Lots of cards in there just for the taking."

"Did I. . . . "

"Stupid of you, eh?"

Under Zeke's watchful eyes, he and Brad dragged the amp, guitar, and various other things from the van, including his jacket and footrest. He and Brad stood the amp up beside the car before getting into it to wait for Jack.

Zeke strolled over to the cruiser. "How come you ain't arresting me, Copper?" he asked. "I just kayoed one of yer lawmakers. Your big tough guard," he taunted. He stuck his face in the window and guffawed loudly, droplets of spittle from his mouth sparkling in the sunshine. Lance shuddered in horror.

"You aren't being ignored, Zeke," Brad said as he took a Kleenex from his pocket and wiped his face with it. He got out of the police car again and unclipped the strap on his holster with a snap. "You're under arrest," he said.

Two officers approached from the left. Zeke began to struggle as he was placed in handcuffs.

Lance watched in amazement when he observed how quick and efficient they were. He hadn't even seen Brad calling for backup. How did he do it so quickly?

"You idiots think you got me this time?" Zeke snarled. "You'll never get me on anything, Mr. Smartass!" Zeke hollered at Brad while he fought to get away.

"Tell that to the guys at the Station," Brad said.

"Bad scene," Zeke yelled as he was being manhandled. "Hope you find out who killed poor Freddy."

"Amazing man," Brad said. "Never gives up. "

"I wish your brother would get here," Lance said

uneasily.

"Relax, Lance. He's here now." Jack got out of his truck and walked over with a grin on his face.

Lance looked from one man to another in disbelief. Jack was the image of Brad except not in uniform.

"Meet my twin brother Jack," Brad said with a grin. Turning to Jack, he asked if he'd take the amp to his place for him.

"Of course. I'll be glad to drop it off at your place. Are you taking up the guitar now or something? This is a mighty big amp," Jack said, obviously enjoying the look on Lance's face.

"No, it belongs to my friend Lance. Anyway, let's get out of here. I got work to do at the office now." After Jack left, Brad turned to Lance and said, "My brother is a doctor, just moved from Montreal. He's not retired yet and he plans on setting up an office here."

"You sure look alike," Lance said. "I couldn't even tell you apart but for the uniform."

"He's thirty minutes older than I am, but I'm an eighth of an inch taller."

"Interesting," Lance said. "Hey, are you leaving the girl in Zeke's van?"

"No, she's already gone with the guys in the other cruiser. I guess you didn't notice them while we were talking to Jack. They'll question her and take her back home. She'll be okay."

"I don't understand what's going on."

"There are some things that need straightening out before I talk to you about it," Brad said. "I hope you aren't hanging around with Zeke too much. He is not just a talented sound man. He's heavily involved in drugs and their kind of life is harsh and many times it is final."

"Is Zeke...?"

"Just let the law take care of it, Lance."

After a pause, Lance said, "I was short with Andrea this morning. She didn't want me to ride the bike down the trail, and I just went off and hardly paid any attention to her."

"If I were you, I'd count my blessings to have a beautiful and obviously intelligent wife like Andrea," Brad said.

"You're right, Brad. I shouldn't treat her like that. I'll call her right now." He took his phone from his pocket and called home while Brad waited.

"The Coral Reef Theatre was once the site of a lighthouse, and this area has a history of violence. Of course, much of this area was under water many years ago. In recent years, the music industry has given it a whole new meaning, of course," Brad said when Lance got off the phone.

"Yes, I was reading about its history not long ago. Rum runners frequented this area when it was an old lighthouse. Pirates took possession of a ship's passengers and sailors were often forced to walk the plank," Lance said.

"Right! I know some of its history too. It's an ideal place for a theatre, but now it's hard to think of pirates on our shores." Brad said.

"We'd all be surprised at the things that went on in good old Canada years ago," Lance remarked. "What was normal behaviour then would not be tolerated now."

"I'd better go," Brad said, looking at his watch. "See you tomorrow night for music. I might be a little rusty. I don't play enough unless I have someone to play those pieces with."

"I'll give you a run for your money then!" Lance promised.

TWELVE

Before he headed out to Brad's place for the jam session, Lance asked, "Andrea, would you like to come along? I'm sure the kids will be fine to stay alone for a couple of hours. They don't need a babysitter anymore."

"Some night I will," she said, "but not now. I want to get an early night. I know you guys when you start jamming. You're going to take my car, I hope." She gave him a big hug and kiss.

"Hmm! Not bad! Wouldn't take much for me to stay home, "he said. "I should get my van back soon. I'll try not to be too late. I can't ride the bike tonight with my guitar and violin, so I hope you don't mind, dear," he said. "We hope to see Charlie too."

"Charlie? Is he at Brad's place too?"

"No, He's still on the catwalk but we have permission to take him some food. He must be starving unless someone has given him something to eat," Lance said. "The theatre has been behind police tape for two days."

"He must be lonely, too," she said. "He's accustomed to seeing people around and now there's nobody, not even the cat for company."

"By the way, I'm taking the acoustic guitar and my old violin with me tonight. It'll be a different kind of jamming. Probably Brad will play the piano."

"Okay—take care, Lance. I won't wait up for you," Andrea said, suddenly looking concerned. "You look tired, dear. You've had a hard few days."

"True—but I better go so I can get back here quicker. If that makes any sense."

"Not really," Andrea said, "but I know what you mean.

Anyway, be off! See you when you get home. Love you! Don't wake the kids up if you come in late."

"Love you, too, honey," he said, as he picked up both instruments under his arm and headed out the door. "I'll try not to knock anything over like I did one night."

"Good," said Andrea with a giggle as Lance went out the door.

He slammed the car door after he'd put both instruments in the back seat. He climbed into the driver's seat and adjusted it to accommodate his long legs. He called out, "I won't be drinking at Brad's place," he said. For two cents he'd be willing to change his plans and stay home--- but she'd already closed the door and was waving to him through the window. Damn it! That woman was sure attractive! He grinned as he turned on the ignition and checked the foot pedals.

He pulled into Brad's driveway fifteen minutes later and hopped out of the car. No burning rubber tonight. Not sure he would be good at jamming either, but he would try. What he wanted more than anything in the world was a good night's sleep and time to process Freddy's death.

Brad met Lance at the door, accompanied by Heathcliffe, who couldn't rid himself of the urge to check all visitors. The only difference was that Heathcliffe never jumped all over people like Steve's dog usually did. While Boomer's enthusiasm was unbridled, Heathcliffe just wagged his tail gently and gave everyone a big doggy smile, showing all his teeth.

Sharply at seven o'clock, they drove to the theatre in Brad's Bronco to deliver food and toiletries to Charlie. Lance had given him an old cell phone two weeks before when he got his own phone updated to a better model, so they were able to give him a call before they left.

Charlie was quiet for a change. He seemed uncertain

112

about Brad's presence, but he didn't ask what he wanted. He did, however, ask about Freddy.

"Why anyone want to hurt him? I think he take my song. Maybe he didn't really know it was my song," he said, his voice breaking. "I'm sad for him." Charlie's poor command of the English language and the resulting discrepancies in tonal quality and voice inflection somehow made the words seem more meaningful.

"How did Freddy get his hands on your song in the first place?" Lance asked.

"It was my fault," Charlie said. "I left it on a chair by the door. I am sad for him. He didn't deserve to die."

"We are sad, too," Lance said.

"Yes, it is a tragedy," Brad agreed.

"We'll come back again in a couple of days," Lance promised.

"Where you going?" Charlie inquired.

"To my house to play some music," Brad said.

"I wish I could come," Charlie said, his eyes downcast.

"Things will get better for you soon," Brad assured him. Charlie nodded and smiled, but he appeared lonely.

The two men were quiet on the way back to Brad's house. Lance guessed that Brad's reason for delivering food to Charlie was partly curiosity and partly a desire to help him. Although he'd known about Charlie for some time, tonight was the first time Brad had met him.

He was also aware that both he and Charlie were suspects in Freddy's murder just because they were in the theatre that night. Lance was certain he'd be cleared right away but Charlie may have a problem. He hoped it would happen quickly so nothing would hang over his head to prevent him from having a fair hearing with the Immigration Board.

"Do you want to play from music, or by ear?" Brad

asked when they got back to his home. They set up the chairs and filled their cups with coffee.

"Let's start out playing by ear," Lance suggested. "I haven't played the violin by music for a while, but I can remember some of the pieces we played when we were all in the Rocky Creek Community Orchestra years ago. Kind of odd to realize that our little old community orchestra grew up to be the Meldrum Symphony."

"I can remember them, too," Brad said. "I conducted it in its infant years, but I couldn't do it now that it has grown up."

"Funny how that happens," Lance said. "What shall we play?

"Let's play some old-time fiddle music. It's so much fun just to relax and jam. I can chord on the piano and then we can go on to something else," Brad suggested.

After getting a real workout with *The Raindrop Polka* and *The Devil's Dream* by ear, Brad laughed for the first time in days. Lance also enjoyed a good belly laugh. He realized how much he'd missed the wonderful state of relaxation that jamming could give. "

I guess," he said, "everything that's happened recently has gotten to me more than I thought. I liked Freddy, and I wanted to see him succeed. He showed a great deal of talent even as a young boy."

Brad looked up from the piano. "I didn't know him, but when I saw him lying there, I was surprised he looked so young," Brad said. "It said in the paper that he was twenty-five, but he certainly didn't look that old. Do you know the song that Charlie wrote? I'd like to hear it."

"Only a few phrases of it, because I heard Freddy sing it at the rehearsal and it was the first piece that he sang that night. I don't have a copy of it," Lance said.

"Was that Charlie's song? I wasn't aware of that," Brad

said. "Did he say Charlie wrote it?"

"The composer's name, *Stanislav Gladyzuiski,* was on the sheet music, but I didn't hear Freddy credit him with it at the concert," Lance said.

"Do you think Charlie, or Stanislav, could be imagining things because of the language barrier?" Brad asked.

"Charlie could speak some English before he left home, but he didn't know the music was printed until I told him. Of course, our slang terms baffle him too. Charlie knows that more often a song is remembered by the person who sings it first, not the composer."

"Is that true?" asked Brad.

"Yes, it is," Lance said. "It's the vocalist who makes a song famous."

"That seems unfair."

"Charlie wanted people to know he wrote it for his girl back home. I don't really blame him."

It became obvious to Lance that Brad was hanging on every word he said. He guessed it was probably just a cop thing to listen. It was also not typical behaviour for the police to discuss the details of a case outside the office, so he wasn't surprised when Brad cut the shop talk.

"Let's play before the whole evening is wasted," Brad said as he leafed through some books. "I'm glad you came over tonight."

"Sure," agreed Lance. "I love to jam."

They played rollicking bar music, with Lance improvising on the violin. They hammered out dance music with a swing, some almost heavy metal, but not quite, and, of course, jazz with Brad doing all sorts of things with the piano keys. Lance got his singing voice all geared up for what constituted Gospel Rock revival music at one point. *Count your Blessings* had never been rocked so hard.

At nine-thirty, they called it quits. Lance packed up his

instruments and carried them out to the car before coming back in for another cup of coffee.

Heathcliffe accompanied Lance to the door, his tail wagging energetically, and his long pink tongue lolling out of the side of his mouth.

"He prefers heavy metal, but he likes music in general," Brad said.

"I noticed that he didn't even howl when I played the violin."

"He's too well-behaved to howl," Brad said with a smirk," but he looked at you as if he should make a rescue attempt when you played *The Hot Canary* with all those high notes and harmonics."

"Probably hurt his ears," Lance said, giving Heathcliffe an ear scratch.

The two men shook hands and Lance walked to his car, feeling more relaxed than he had for several days.

THIRTEEN

After the jam session with Brad, Lance enjoyed the leisurely drive through the tree-lined road on his way home. He relaxed and allowed his mind to dwell on the memories of the musical get-togethers they had enjoyed years ago.

He powered down both front windows so he could enjoy the scents of an August evening and hear snatches of bird song, accompanied by the rapidly flowing river. Shadows were long and thin as the blue twilight held the sun in the palm of its hand, ready to push the golden globe below the horizon. The symphony of sound lulled him into the restful realm between the hectic day and the gentle night.

Lance was alone on the highway only a mile before it became the long turnoff lane leading into his driveway. He was startled from his reverie when he saw a blue pickup truck coming full speed ahead straight for him. "Damn fool is in my lane!" he blurted as he fought with the steering wheel.

He swerved into the oncoming lane just in time to avoid a head-on collision. Losing control, the back end spun around in a semi-circle, coming to rest precariously perched on the shoulder facing the wrong direction.

He could only see straight ahead with the headlights, so he took his flashlight from the glove compartment, inched himself to the passenger door, and directed the beam over the bank. The passenger wheel was resting on the bank above the raging river.

He sat quietly for a few minutes trying to get his bearings. He could see that the guard rail had been broken, but he was certain it was intact when he came down the hill earlier tonight. Had someone gone over the bank there earlier this evening and crashed through it? Maybe he'd hit it when trying to dodge that truck?

He watched the lights of the pickup reflected in his rear-view mirror as the vehicle spun out of control and drifted sideways before the lights disappeared in the darkness. Whoever was driving it sped away without acknowledging that he'd almost hit another vehicle.

"Who was that? Blue truck? He tried to run me off the road!" Lance asked himself. "Oh my God! Zeke has a blue truck. Was he at my house!" Terror for his family turned his blood to ice.

Should he go after him? He didn't dare move ahead for fear the vibrations would tip the vehicle over the bank. Call 911? No, then his phone would be frozen. For a moment, his mind was blank. Who should he call? He couldn't remember, so he dialled Brad's number.

Shaking with worry, he tried to control his timorous voice as he said, "Hello, Brad? Can you help me, please? I just met someone driving dangerously down my road. He tried to run me over the bank. It's a dead-end road that only goes to my place, so I know he was on that road. Also, the guard rail has been broken and has tumbled down the bank. I don't know if I hit it. I'm hanging over the shoulder in the oncoming lane facing the wrong way."

"I'll report it," Brad said. "Did you get his licence number?"

"It happened too quickly, and I was fighting the wheel. Yeah, I know it was a blue Ford F10. Probably ten years old. I'm sitting here right now in Andrea's car. Every time I move, I can feel the car shift."

"Turn off your engine We'll talk later. I'll be there as quickly as I can. Did you recognize the truck?"

"Yes, it's off. I think it could have been Zeke," he said.

"You really think so?" Brad asked.

"He asked for my address yesterday so he could deliver my amp. I had a strange feeling that's not all he wanted it for. Things had changed, though, because you and I took everything out of his van. He has no reason to go to my house."

"I'm on my way," Brad said. "I'll contact the office myself. Search and Rescue will send a tow truck."

"Search and Rescue? I'm worried about my family, not me."

"They have the tools to get you out safely. I'll have someone check on your wife and kids," Brad said. "Sit tight and don't move around."

"Damn!" Lance said when Brad hung up. "How the hell do I get myself in these messes? I'm stupid. I let that monster into our lives." He sat as still as possible and watched for the tow truck and police cars or whatever would be coming to his aid. He didn't dare look over the bank again or even move back to the driver's side of the car. It was getting darker by the moment and any little movement could dislodge the car and send it careening down into the river below, over rocks, trees, and gravel. Probably to his death.

"I'll never see my kids again!" he lamented. "My wife needs me. Oh God, help me get out of this mess! I'll be good, I'll be good!" He knew that bargaining with God was wrong, but he was just a dumb child who didn't know any better. He was even too frightened to think clearly. Was God even listening? Of course, He does. God always listens. He couldn't remember the words. Deliver us from evil? Zeke was evil. *Why didn't I see that before I got into this mess? I'm stupid.*

Even in his moment of terror, he remembered hearing someone say it was odd how in a moment of fear, even an unbeliever would call upon God to save him.

"Our Father, Who art in Heaven," he said, improvising.

"I'll be a better husband, a better dad, I promise."

He phoned home but there was a busy signal. He hit redial on his phone and got it again. Lance started to panic.

He had to get out and go home! He began to move slowly toward the door to get out, but he felt the car shift. Terror gripped him with the icy fingers of death, driving him into a panic again.

It took several moments for him to stop shaking. He sat motionless for so long his legs ached from the tension.

The seconds ticked by, each one more painful and longer than the one before it. His head ached and when he put his hand up to his ear, he felt a lump above it. His hand came away wet. He didn't know he'd hit his head until now. He shone the flashlight on his hand. Blood. He cautiously picked up a Kleenex from a box on the floor and wiped his face, thankful the blood was already coagulating.

He breathed a sigh of relief when he saw the flashing lights of the tow truck in the distance. The glorious sound of a siren screamed through his brain-haze. The tow truck is here! He let his body relax. He saw someone get out and peer over the bank before walking toward the car. His mind blanked as the scene faded, and Lance succumbed to the painless state of unconsciousness.

His mind wandered in and out of the haze for several minutes, until he finally broke through the low barrier between being here and not being here. When he opened his eyes, he saw that he was free of the car, free of the danger of death. He had been lifted from the car and placed on a stretcher.

My wife and kids!" he said, trying to sit up. "Are they alright? They need me!"

"Relax," a detached voice cautioned. He couldn't see who had spoken but he tried to obey.

"They're in danger," Lance said.

"No, the police are with them now. They are being cared for, so relax. You are going to the hospital and the police are already at your house."

"No! I have to go home!" He tried to get up. "I have to take care of them."

The syringe hit its mark. Lance drifted away again.

***

When Brad arrived at Lance's back door he leaped out of his car, slammed the door, and went up the three stairs in one leap. The door was locked.

"Open the door! It's the police."

"Where's my dad?" Lance's eldest son, Roy, asked as he opened the door for the police officer. "My name is Brad Thomas and I'm a friend of your dad's. He had a little car accident, and the ambulance has taken him to the hospital. He'll be fine; he is not—"

He was interrupted by Jeannie and Lanny peeking around the corner. The younger boy was rubbing his eyes as if awakened from a sound sleep.

"My name is Brad Thomas," Brad repeated, "and I'm a friend of your dad's. He had a little car accident, and the ambulance has taken him to the hospital. He'll be fine; he is not injured. It's just routine. Are you in charge when your dad is away? Can you tell me what happened here?"

"Yes. Some guy came here and tried to strong-arm my mom. You should've seen her fight him off!" Roy said, pointing to Andrea. "He grabbed her, and she elbowed him in the ribs and punched him in the windpipe with her fist so fast he didn't have time to do anything. Hard. Man, she's good," he said proudly.

"I get the message," Brad said. "Was that a self-defence move?"

"I don't know. My dad said you gotta do whatever you can." He demonstrated on Lanny, who stuck his tongue out and gagged as he walked stiff-leggedly across the room.

Andrea nodded. The two boys, anxious to get their two bits in both began talking at once. "Our dad showed us how. Specially Jeannie," Lanny said.

"Yeah," Roy said. "And mom too. Girls need self-defence."

"Okay, I get the message. I need to talk to your mother." The police officer turned to Andrea and said, "I know you've had a traumatic experience tonight, but can you describe what the intruder looked like, Mrs. Bishop?"

"He was probably in his mid-forties, and had a scar on one cheek," she said. "He had black hair slicked down flat. He was very well dressed."

"My brother hit him with a stick of stove wood, "Lanny said, pointing to a big box on the back porch filled with chopped wood.

"Yeah," Jeannie said. "He crawled out on his knees."

"That would do it," Brad said, "So between you two, you chased him away?"

"Yes," said Lanny.

"Okay. What was your little brother doing when he first came?" he asked. "He looks like he's still half asleep."

"He woke up when Mom walloped the guy," Jeannie said.

"I'll call for a guard to stay with you until I get your dad from the hospital," he said. "He's alright. They just needed to check for injuries. Do you know what the intruder wanted?"

"No, but he left in a hurry when we fought back."

"Your dad will be home soon," Brad said.

The sirens stopped wailing when the ambulance arrived at the top of the driveway. The peaceful night disintegrated even as the screaming stopped. Two ambulance attendants stepped onto the gravel driveway and headed into the house with no hesitation.

"No one got hurt, but the guy who broke in might need some First Aid," Brad told them, "but he's gone. Apparently, this little lady fought back. We won't need the ambulance here." A faint smile passed quickly over his face. "I think we passed him on the highway driving erratically. I called it in, so he's probably been picked up by now."

"Thank-you," Andrea said.

***

Brad met Lance at the hospital an hour later. Somehow the fact they'd counted their blessing at the end of the jam session made sense now.

Lance walked slowly in the doorway of his house followed by Brad, who spoke briefly with the two guards and asked them to remain until morning. "I doubt if anyone will bother them tonight, but just in case," he said. "Better to be safe than sorry."

Lance hugged his wife tight, before letting her go. In seconds he and Andrea were surrounded by the three kids.

It was one thirty a.m. when the last surface was dusted for fingerprints and the last question answered. Lance followed Brad to the car and requested a few minutes to say something.

"Could it wait until tomorrow, Lance? We should all get to bed. It's been a long day."

"No," Lance insisted. "This is important."

"Well, okay," Brad said rather grudgingly.

"I think I know what he was after," he said.

"What?" Brad asked, looking keenly at Lance. "Who?"

"The person who attacked Freddy. After the rehearsal at his parent's place, Freddy asked me if he could stash a brick of cocaine in the back of my amp," he said. "When I told him I wanted nothing to do with it, he became angry. I asked if he intended on selling the drugs at the concert, and he said I was hiding my head in the sand if I didn't know that's what he meant."

"He told you that?" asked Brad in surprise. "Why didn't you back out?

"I tried to, but I'd signed a contract and he said he was holding me to it. There are consequences to breaking a contract," Lance explained. "I knew he could get me on that."

"I see. How come you didn't tell me?" Brad asked.

"I didn't believe he'd actually do it. He'd told me earlier he would bring my practice amp to the theatre when we did the concert. Now I wonder if I was wrong to trust him. I truly didn't think he intended on taking that crap to the concert," Lance said. "It never crossed my mind again."

"Where is the practice amp now?" Brad asked. "Why would that have anything to do with what happened here tonight? I don't follow you."

"I forgot it at his house after we rehearsed. I think it was because we didn't use it that night, so I put it aside and forgot to take it home with me. I hope it's still at his parent's place," Lance said.

"Right," Brad agreed.

"He was angry that he couldn't use my concert amp but maybe he thought he could use my practice amp instead."

"Oh, I see what you're saying," Brad said. "You think it could have been planned? And when the drugs weren't there Freddy was killed?"

Lance nodded. "It seemed to be a coincidence at the time, but the more I think about it, the more unsure I am."

"That might be an important piece of information. It certainly puts a different slant on things," Brad said with a frown. "Do you know if it was for someone specific to retrieve it from the amp at the concert?"

"No," Lance said after a hesitation. "Do you think he

was setting me up?"

"I can't say right now. Perhaps not you specifically, but it does seem as though he was setting up a situation. Someone was supposed to find the drugs. You don't use drugs, I hope?" Brad said.

"No, but Freddy knew I smoked a little pot when I was in high school," Lance admitted.

"During the '60s a lot of kids and even older people smoked dope," Brad said. "Lance, we'll meet again in a couple of days to get some more food for Charlie, and we'll talk more about it then. In the meantime, don't talk about it to anyone else. I will follow this up. Do you think it was Zeke?"

"I don't know. It had to be Zeke who called Andrea yesterday. I'm too nervous for my family so I won't talk about it to anyone else," Lance said. "It was definitely Zeke who tried to run me over the bank that night too. I recognized his truck."

"I wonder why?"

"Maybe the drugs Freddy wanted to put in my amp had something to do with it," Lance said.

"You could be right," Brad agreed. "Not a nice thought, but it could be that way. I'll talk to you tomorrow."

Lance slowly opened the door and went inside the house. Andrea was waiting for him at the table, but the three children had gone back to bed. The only sound was the crackling of the fireplace as the log sputtered and the flame died. He shot the bolt into the latch and turned out the lights.

FOURTEEN

When Lance opened the bedroom blinds that Sunday morning, he hoped to see a glorious sunrise. However, the day had begun with a torrential rainstorm instead. He frowned as he saw in the distance the white-capped waves rolling in, the frothing green and blue waters buffeted by gale-force winds. The river-side city of Meldrum was under grey skies. The dismal monotony of the darkened panorama surely fit the city's sordid past perfectly.

Lance sighed as he closed the blind again and opened it quickly to take another look.

"What on earth are you doing? You're kind of old to be playing with the blinds, aren't you?" Andrea sat up in bed and rubbed her eyes. "I hoped to get an extra half hour in this morning, but you killed that."

He laughed guiltily. "Sorry. I thought I was seeing things and there would be sunshine. I'm tired of rain. I feel better after a few good night's sleep though. How about you?"

"I think that guy scared me the other night," she said. "I'm waking up at the slightest little sound, Then I can't get back to sleep."

"You were so brave," Lance said, thinking of the upsetting events of a few nights earlier, and the home invasion. He sat down on the edge of the bed 'You smacked him good. I doubt if he will forget that for a while. The boys were impressed."

"They fought him too. He got what he deserved," she said, rubbing her eyes. "I may as well get up now as I'm wide awake now anyway." She swung her legs over the side of the bed and slid onto the floor.

"I'll get the coffee pot going," Lance said with a grin. "Nice legs."

"Thanks," Andrea said as she pulled her housecoat off a small bedside table beside the bed and wrapped it around herself. She giggled when he bent down and kissed her cheek. She watched him leave the room laughing.

"Such a handsome man," she thought. She felt better already, as his good humour spread across her mind. No wonder Lance's classes at school were pleased to work hard for him. She understood how his happy frame of mind could be catching.

After Andrea had her morning shower and got dressed, she ran down the stairs to the kitchen where Lance was already getting breakfast organised,

"Wow!' she said. "You mean business this morning. Sorry I'm so lazy."

"You're not lazy at all," he said. "Just tired. "We're taking Charlie some food today, but not for a while. I think my cop friend just wants to meet him. The theatre has been taped off for two or three days, so Charlie hasn't had much to eat."

"Is Officer Thomas a good friend of yours?" Andrea asked. "He spoke very highly of you the other night." She smoothed her wet hair with her fingers and smiled.

"I've known Brad for ages. We had a great jam session that night and I was just relaxing and watching the scenery as I drove home. I guess I fainted when they finally came to get me out so they could move the car. When I saw how close to the edge the car was, I was afraid to move. But I'm okay now," Lance said.

"You haven't really told me much about it. What really happened?" she asked, "It was good of him to send someone to stay here until he picked you up from the hospital. It's so isolated out here."

"Oh, a truck almost ran me over the bank," he said, trying to make light of it. "It happened so fast I couldn't think. I called Brad because it was the only number I could remember. He contacted Search and Rescue."

"I wasn't really sure what happened," she said. "Do you know who it was?"

"Nobody from this area," he said, minimizing it. "I'll tell you more over breakfast."

"I see," she said.

"I was okay until I saw how much danger I was in," Lance admitted, not ready yet to tell her that a wrong move might have sent the car tumbling over the bank. "Anyway, here I am safe and sound," he said, making light of it.

"Well, go feed that Charlie person, so you can start being my husband again. I miss you." Andrea looked wistful as she spoke, looking up at him.

"Sorry," Lance said. "I didn't mean to be so remote. I'm really proud of the way you fought that guy off," he said. "Roy told me all about it and said you were so good. I will never underestimate the power of my wife." He put his arms around her and held her close. In moments it became a group hug as the three kids crowded in to be included.

"Are you taking my car?" Andrea asked when she had recovered from the group hug. "When will you get your truck and trailer back? I don't like to be left out here in the sticks with no transportation."

"Is that okay for today? I hope I'll get it back soon. I won't leave you without transportation again. I just didn't think," he said.

"No, I don't feel safe."

"Why don't you and the kids come into town with me and do some shopping and we can arrange to meet afterwards and have lunch?" Lance suggested, after a pause. "I don't think you should be alone here either."

He smiled when she nodded but noted that Andrea was still somewhat hesitant.

"Okay. We won't be more than thirty minutes. Is that okay?" she said.

"Sure, I'll give Thomas a ring and tell him there's a change of plans. He'll be fine with it. Take your raincoat with you. It's still raining hard."

When everyone was changed and ready to go. they all paraded out to the car in a row, as if they were playing a game of *Follow the Leader* much to Lance's amusement. He climbed into the driver's seat and turned on the ignition.

"Would you like to drive?" he asked Andrea.

"Oh, no," she said. "I'm fine as a passenger."

"It is your car," he said with a smile.

"Right now, it's *our* car so I'm not about to quibble about who drives it."

"Okay—I just wanted to make sure." He turned to her and nodded affectionately.

After he'd dropped Andrea and the kids off at the shopping centre, he drove slowly and parked as close to the theatre as possible. The rain was pelting down harder than ever and ran down the windshield as soon as he turned off the wipers. At first, he didn't see Brad standing just inside the back door talking on his phone, so when he flung the door open wide and stepped in, he almost tripped over his foot. Brad moved out of the way and pointed to his toe. "It's okay," he said. "This isn't the foot you destroyed yesterday anyway."

"Sorry," he blurted. "I didn't see you standing there. I gave Charlie my old cell phone so we could call him to say we're here. How did Igor settle in after we'd chased him all over the place yesterday?"

"He's doing okay," Brad said. "We gave him a good dinner last night and after he'd explored the house, and ate some treats, he settled down and went to sleep. Early this morning he came into our bedroom and told my wife in cat language that he'd like to eat, please. For a new resident, he certainly learned quickly who would be feeding him." They both laughed.

"I knew you'd like him," Lance said. "He's a smart cat and loves people."

"I think he loves food too. Igor obviously knows a good thing when he sees it," Brad said.

Lance took his cell phone from his soggy pocket. "I hope this thing still works," he said. He called Charlie to announce their arrival.

"Hi, Charlie. Hope you've got the coffee pot on," he joked. "We have enough food for an army here. Coming up. Are you decent?"

"Huh?" said Charlie, not understanding the joke.

They met Charlie in the office he used as his bedroom. It was sparsely furnished with a fold-away cot, a card table, and two wooden apple boxes that doubled as chairs. A backpack, just large enough to hold a change of clothes hung on a nail to the left of the card table.

"Sorry, I don't have any chairs. You can sit on my apple boxes," he said.

"I'll sit on the floor," Lance said. "Brad's the oldest so he can have the other apple box."

"No, you sit on the box, Lance," Brad said. "I weigh two fifty so an apple box might not hold me. I'm fine to stand up. I'll speak to the theatre management and ask if they will loan you a couple of chairs. If not, I'll bring you a couple from home that we aren't using."

"Thanks, that would be nice," Charlie said with a shy smile. His eyes sparkled as he said the word 'thanks' with the proper accent. Lance nodded.

"The theatre has been taped off for a couple of days, so

we know you haven't had any visitors," Lance said, "and you probably haven't had any snacks either."

"Two days," Charlie admitted. He held up two fingers and looked hungrily at the cans and packages of food, but he patiently waited for them to offer it. He grinned as he patted his stomach.

"Empty, eh?" Lance asked. Charlie nodded.

When Brad handed Charlie the groceries, he graciously accepted them.

"You better eat something now."

"Go ahead and eat," Lance said. "We know you need to eat—you are still a growing boy." He picked up the half-open bag of potato chips and dumped some in Charlie's hand. "This is already open. I dropped it in a puddle, so the bag got wet. You may as well eat them."

"I thank you for the food," Charlie said very quietly. He chewed happily on the chips and wiped his salty hand on his pants.

"I like potato chips. We don't have them at home, but I heard they might start importing them soon."

"Do you have hamburgers there?" asked Brad.

"No, soon come. You like ham-burrgerrs?" he asked, grinning at Lance as he rolled his R's. "See, I learn speak English?"

"Very good," said Lance, chuckling as he handed Charlie two grocery bags.

He unpacked them all into a cardboard box that served as his cupboard, "I have a little stove and an icebox now. What you call it? A keep-colder?" He pointed to the electric cord plugged into the wall. "No ice. My sister's friend, she send them." He showed Brad the new fridge with pride.

"They call it a refrigerator. Where does your sister's friend live?" Brad asked, allowing himself a chuckle, relieved that Charlie could laugh at his own mistakes.

"Keep-colder does describe it, though."

"Long way from here. Van-coo-ver," he said, carefully pronouncing the word right.

"Oh, I wondered how she could send a fridge all the way from overseas," Lance said. He thought he could see sympathy and understanding on Brad's face as he watched the young man gratefully accept the groceries. Brad's a good guy, he reasoned.

"I was wrong to call Freddy a thief," Charlie said, so quietly Lance and Brad had to lean forward to hear. "I feel very solley for him; he was too young to die." Charlie hesitated for a minute and looked down at his feet before he added, "I mean sorry. I want to play with a band too. I guess I was jealous. It was hard to hear guys have fun. good time. I want fun too."

"We understand," Brad said quietly.

"I taught Freddy to play when he was in high school," Lance reminisced. "I knew he was destined for the stage when he was just a little kid. He was so smart that he recorded each track himself on the CD I have. He was amazing."

Lance noticed Brad said very little. At first, he appeared extremely tense but as the meeting progressed, he gradually began to relax.

He was sure that Brad knew Charlie had nothing to do with Freddy's death and was just following protocol, but he almost felt the huge weight physically lift from his shoulders.

As the visit came to a close, Brad shook hands with Charlie. "Good to meet you, Charlie," he said. "Take care. We'll be back to see you again soon. Do you like sardines?" he asked. "What about cheese? You might need a bigger fridge." Charlie nodded and said goodbye to his friends.

"Fridge?" he repeated.

"Yes. It's just a short word for refrigerator," he said.

"Oh," Charlie said. "Good-bye. I see you soon, eh?"

"Soon," Lance said, with a smile.

A few minutes later he and Brad stood talking outside the theatre door. "Thank God the blasted rain has nearly stopped," Lance said. "It's just a drizzle now." "

"Yeah," said Brad, "but I don't like the look of those black clouds. They're so low it seems much too dark for the mid-afternoon. Kind of foreboding. I better be on my way. I have to work tonight."

"Another concert or somewhere else?" Lance asked.

"I'm at the city lockup tonight. Heathcliffe has the evening off. Where do you work when you aren't playing the guitar or farming?" Brad asked.

"Oh, I thought we talked about that at the cafe," Lance answered. "I teach music at Meldrum High School twice a week, and English grammar on Tuesday mornings. I am also first oboe player with the Meldrum Symphony. I get some freelance jobs with other orchestras and bands during the summer holidays. I am playing a concert in Salmon Arm next week, so I have a few nights off. "

"Wow, you are a busy boy," Brad said. "I wonder where the symphony will play their next concert if the theatre is closed down?"

"It will probably be in the paper," Lance said. "I didn't think of that."

"It's almost dinner time so I better head for home. Thanks for introducing me to your friend. He seems shy. I am toying with the idea of sponsoring him. I have to look into his background first," Brad suggested.

"That would be wonderful," Lance said. "Does he know that?"

"No, I don't want to get his hopes up in case it doesn't work. He appears to be very open, and I liked the way he spoke about his feelings toward Freddy. He didn't hide the fact that he was jealous, even to me. The uniform didn't make him tense. However, I have to follow the rules and go through all the steps before I can do anything."

"I am sure he is telling the truth," Lance said with a big smile. "It would be wonderful to give him a chance." He waved at Brad as he drove away.

Lance was still smiling as he got back into Andrea's car and drove to the shopping centre where he had promised to meet her and the kids.

***

After the visit with Charlie came to an end, Lance picked up Andrea and the kids at the mall. They'd had a great time shopping and were anxious to tell him of their adventures, and their purchases. "Do you want to drive?" he asked.

"You're doing fine," Andrea said with a wink. "You are the one who taught me to drive, you know."

"You were a good student," he said. "That was before we got married, so it was an excuse for me to sit close to you. I had an ulterior motive."

"Oh, Dad!" Lanny said.

"Wait until you get old enough to date," Roy muttered, "then you'll understand."

Lance listened with one ear as the other one concentrated on the sounds of the motor, his wife's conversation, and most of all, their safety.

When they arrived at the turnoff to his own road and the spot where he had almost tumbled over the bank, his mind flashed back to the moment when he thought he was going to die.

With his promise to God that he would be a better husband and father, Lance realized that although God knew he had made those promises under duress, they were still very serious promises. He could easily have come to the end of his life, so he had to try to live up to them.

FIFTEEN

Sunday morning dawned with a splendid sunrise. The peach-coloured sky promised a brand new bright and sunny day. The rain had slowed to a drizzle during the night and by early morning, the clouds had gradually floated away over the mountains.

Lance leaped out of bed filled with energy. Chanticleer, the rooster had finally stopped crowing, so Lance knew he'd stationed himself at the gate of the coop ready to bolt into the chicken pen for breakfast. After five years of farming, Lance still enjoyed hearing the old boy's morning greeting. "Cock-a-doodle doo!'

Before anyone else was up, he'd picked a basket of fresh raspberries, gathered the eggs, fed the chickens, and discovered that two hens were missing. Nothing to do but look for them.

"Come on, ladies," he said when he saw them in the tall maple beside the chicken coop. He carried them home one at a time under his arm, vowing to clip their wings before they went exploring again. Just like kids, they took every opportunity to escape the coop. When he said, "Bad girls!" they only looked at him curiously without an ounce of remorse in their small red eyes.

Lance laughed at his own expense, realizing that his idea of farming was not quite the same as most people's notion. It wasn't his livelihood, so his chickens died of old age. He ate their eggs and named each of his 'girls,' as he called the hens. He reasoned that there was no way one could chop off the head of a chicken called Jenny, Hope, or Glenda. He gagged at the very thought of having one of his girls for dinner.

He entered the house through the back porch and hung his sweater on a peg and took his boots off. Andrea was putting the meal on the small table in the breakfast nook. After giving her a peck on the cheek, he washed his face and hands and sat on his special dining chair that had belonged to his grandfather. It wasn't fancy and it didn't match the other chairs, but he liked it. Andrea had upholstered it for him as a gift and he was partial to anything she did just for him.

"What do you have planned for today?" she asked as she sat down opposite him, wearing a blue shirt the same colour as her eyes.

"You look pretty," he said with a smile. "I thought about going for a bike ride after all the chores are done."

"Looks to me like you've already been working. You have a leaf in your hair." She reached up and removed it.

"I had to climb the maple tree to retrieve two hens," he said. "They had flown up to enjoy the view, I guess. They didn't look a bit sorry."

"When will you clip their wings?" she asked. "I had to bring them home a couple of days ago when I saw them enjoying a stroll down the hill."

"Those naughty chickies!" he said, with a snicker. "I'd better do it now." He started to get up from the table.

"Eat breakfast first," Andrea said.

"No, I'd better do it now. My memory is like a sieve," he said with a laugh.

"Not normally," Andrea answered, "but the last few days have been hard for you to handle. Go ahead. I'll wait for you."

When Lance came back in the house, he announced that his naughty girls were looking at the maple tree again, probably hoping to go flying the moment he turned his back. "Mmm! Breakfast smells good!"

"They can't go exploring now but it must be fun to fly up into the branches like the birds they really are," she said.

"Probably a real sense of freedom, "he said. They sat together and enjoyed a leisurely breakfast. "You're a good cook. I lucked out when I chose you to be my wife!"

"Jeannie has the makings of a good cook. If that is all it takes to get a good husband, she already has it made!" They both chuckled.

"It takes more than that, I assure you, but it does help. Time to go now. I really enjoy a good bike ride," Lance said as he cleared his plate, got up, and headed for the porch again. He pulled his chaps down from a top shelf where they were neatly folded and put them on, pulled up the zippers, and put on his black leather jacket. He threw Andrea a kiss as he closed the door.

He felt her watching him as he kick-started the engine. The 1600 cubic centimetre engine of his Harley roared to life. The straight pipes made sure that nothing else could be heard for miles around. Lance began to relax, as he settled into the padded seat, careful of spitting rocks as the big bike kicked up a patch of gravel from his long driveway with the spinning rear wheel.

He could easily have taken the road, but he preferred to take the back road. The bike was meant for the road, but Lance loved the danger. His heart rate pulsed at a dangerous high as he squeezed the accelerator and turned off the driveway onto the path.

At the bottom of the hill, he decided to take a different route than usual. After making sure he had enough fuel he went out onto the open road and cruised along at a leisurely pace, drinking in the country air. Taking a left turn, he decided to explore another trail he'd often thought of taking. The rolling hills and bushy areas were a challenge, but Lance liked to push himself.

I wonder if Brutus has ever ridden a Harley? I hear he used to be a real tough little devil in his time, hockey and all. Maybe I ought to pick him up one of these days. Bet he'd enjoy that.

To put his own mind at ease, he decided to give Brutus a ring on his cell and perhaps go for a drive up a mountain trail he had noticed alongside the highway. It looked inviting.

Brutus lived in Rocky Creek; Lance had only met him once before at a rehearsal but had liked him. He casually wondered if he'd ever ridden a Harley. It would be a treat for him to go for a drive. The kid had probably never seen a Harley close-up. He also wanted to talk to him about doing a farewell concert in honour of Freddy too. Lance felt more than a little annoyed over Freddy's insistence on drugs being good for him, and his wish to hide them in Lance's amp, but he had decided to put the feelings aside for now. Freddy had obviously paid a price for his habit. To hate the singer served no purpose other than to make himself feel angry. Nothing would bring the musician back.

Lance had been speeding along the new trail, but he turned around and came down to the highway again, thinking that the young man might enjoy exploring it with him. It would be fun for them both.

He had already gone past several large estates and landscaped properties, but he thought Brutus probably lived further on, in a little bungalow at the corner of a dead-end street. He wished he had Brutus' phone number because he was just guessing. After Lance went past a pay phone, he decided his best move would be to turn around and take a look at the phone book that would be hanging on a nail in the booth. Not everyone had a cell phone in Rocky Creek's rural districts, and for those who could afford it, there was often no service until they got closer to the city. Lance dug in his pocket and found a quarter just in case the number was out of range for his cell; he could use the phone booth instead. He found an address that could be Brutus, but when he looked at the name, he was unsure. Doctor and Mrs. Bruce Falgaar? Unlikely but he decided to call it anyway. Perhaps someone there could direct him to Brutus' home if they had the same surname.

"Good afternoon," said a familiar voice. "Doctor Falgaar's residence. Brutus speaking."

"Ah," stammered Lance. "This is Lance Bishop speaking. You are just the person I wanted to speak to. I'm out your way and wondered if you'd like to go for a bike ride. We can both fit on my Harley. Are you interested?"

"Sure thing!" Brutus said, his voice cheerful. "Where are you?"

"At the corner of Meadow Road and Fraser," Lance said.

"Good," Brutus said. "You are right across from our house. I'll walk down the driveway and meet you."

When Lance turned around to retrace his route, he looked up at the huge estate where several workers were busily trimming the long evergreen hedge. The home had looked large as he'd passed it the first time, but now he was closer, he could really see that it was one of the most attractive homes in Rocky Creek. Lance stared at it in disbelief. Well, so much for thinking that Brutus was the product of a middle-class family. Lance smoothed his hair behind his ears when he took off the helmet. It probably didn't help much but it made him feel as if he'd tried to tidy his appearance a little bit as he approached the huge estate. He saw Brutus walking toward him.

"Well, hi there!" Brutus said. "I guess we look different off stage, eh?" he said. "Last time we saw each other we were in concert dress, trying to escape the mess that was going on in the theatre. Did you ever find out what really happened there?"

"Yeah, it was terrible. Freddy was found dead in another room. Nobody knows how he died, but we do know it was in the theatre during a costume change break."

"Did you say Freddy died? Why? He wasn't sick, as far as I know. What happened?" Brutus asked in surprise.

"No, but something happened to him. He got beat up real good. I had help getting my stuff out, but we had to come back because the guy who helped me left some stuff behind. He opened the wrong door and walked right into a bad scene. The police were there, and Freddy was dead," Lance said, without going into details.

"Are you sure?"

"Yes, but what happened to you? You disappeared. Where did you get to?"

"I packed up and went home," Brutus said. "After so many people ordered me off the stage, I thought I wasn't wanted, so I took off. That silly little guy kept trying to pick a fight with me, and I finally realized nobody was winning, so I dragged my stuff out and got to hell out of there."

He came after me, too," Lance said. "After he kicked my shins, I put my hand on top of his head and spun him around and got out of his way too." They both laughed.

"Did you really say Freddy died? What happened?" Brutus asked again. "I thought I was hearing things."

"He really died. Nobody knows what happened, but when Freddy didn't come back to finish the concert, the audience got nasty. I left the theatre before I knew he'd passed away, I had to come back and that's when I discovered he had died," Lance explained. "I was stuck dragging that big bass amp around. The casters kept getting stuck on something sticky on the floor."

"Yes, they were beginning to fight before I left. How

did you get out with that huge bass amp of yours?" Brutus asked. "I'd have helped you if I'd known you might have trouble with it."

"Oh, a guy named Zeke helped me get the amp out. My trailer was set on fire, so I couldn't put my stuff in it. Zeke put it in his van, and I didn't actually get it home until a few days ago."

"Zeke?" asked Brutus, in surprise. "Did I hear you say Zeke helped you?"

"Yes, why do you ask?"

"Stay clear of Zeke," Brutus said sternly. "He may be a good light man, but he's bad business. I hope you'll listen to me, Lance, because I'm telling it like it is. He's heavily involved in the drug world and he's unpredictable, except for one thing. You play it his way or no way. There are no second chances with him and no survivors if they don't choose to do it his way. Anyway, let's not waste the afternoon talking about Zeke. Let's go for that drive. I'm dying to get out on the trail."

"Okay," Lance said. "Someone else warned me about him too, but he seemed nice to me. I agree, we need to get out there and go for that ride."

"Sure," Brutus said. "Come to the garage and help me decide which bike to use today," Brutus suggested. He led the way, not noticing that Lance stood goggle-eyed behind him as he opened the big double doors.

Lance looked around at the row of motorcycles parked diagonally along the rear wall. He counted five high-end bikes. He felt rather foolish that he'd assumed that the kid would find it a treat to have a ride on his Harley.

"Which one do you think I should ride?" Brutus asked matter-of-factly, as if everyone had five motorcycles in their garage. Lance pointed to the bike in the centre.

"I've seen that model before," Lance said, "but I don't

know anyone familiar with it, except Steve McQueen. How long have you been collecting bikes?" He grinned broadly, hoping his remark would at least make Brutus smile.

"Oh, you saw that movie too?" Brutus said. "I'm not a collector. I just like to rotate them once in a while. They're all different, you know. Not one the same, except the superb workmanship that went into making them."

"What's that one?" Lance asked. "I've ridden one like that. Fat Boy, or something. I forget its name."

"My father's favourite!" Brutus said. "Built six years ago. Very durable."

"Your father?" Lance questioned. "Isn't he a doctor?"

"He's a Doctor of Philosophy. Don't you think a doctor could ride?"

"Of course," Lance said. "It's just that these are big bikes. You don't expect doctors to ride them." He grunted as he went through the motions of lifting a heavy bike and mounting it.

"That's where you're mistaken," Brutus said with a snicker, obviously enjoying Lance's dilemma. "Doctors and lawyers and even the pastor of the Evangelical Church ride in the Christmas parade to collect food and Christmas gifts."

"Oh, now I suppose you're going to tell me your mother rides, too," he said, trying to be amusing to cover his embarrassment.

"She's not a motorcycle mama, of course, but riding is something that Mom and Dad can do together. Her bike is the one beside Dad's. They belong to a motorcycle club. Anyway," he said, "what did you have in mind? Off road or a specific trip? I'm game for anything you have in mind. It'll be fun to ride with someone who loves his bike."

"Let's just go for a spin now," Lance suggested. "It's getting late, but we could go up the trail to the east of here. I guess I just need to go for a ride and a chat. It's been really rough knowing Freddy died at the concert. He was my pupil, you know."

"Sure," Brutus said, as he wheeled the bike out and locked the garage doors. "Let's go."

"Does your father work at the medical clinic downtown? Or does he have his own building?"

"No," said Brutus with a smile. "He's Dean of the University of Lonsdale County. He was knighted by the Queen in nineteen eighty-two, but he's modest so he only uses his Doctorate in Education. He teaches both psychology and Law at Lonsdale. He could be called *Sir,* but he doesn't bother with that. Actually, he knows I play in bands, and he thought our friends would give me a bad time."

"Oh, no!" Lance said. "It's a great honour."

"Where do you want to ride?" Brutus asked, changing the subject. "Got anything in mind?"

"Yes," Lance said. "Before I arrived here, I noticed a trail off to the right. I think it's called *Ridgeback Mountain.* I rode about a mile up the hill and then I thought maybe you might enjoy it too. Didn't know it was this close to your house. Have you ever been up there?"

"Not yet," Brutus answered. "My father has been on that road a few times. He said it's a great ride, but wild country further up the trail. Lots of hills and wildlife."

"Sure, let's go."

"Okay," Brutus said, "but we need something to drink. Hang on and I'll go raid the wine cellar. All sorts of things in there—some with a buzz and some without. But it's all good stuff."

"Go easy on the wine, please. I don't want to get arrested for dangerous riding."

"Chicken!" Brutus said. He parked his bike up against the garage, and without taking off his helmet, unlocked the door and went in. When he came out, he said, "Have you seen yesterday's paper?"

"Yes, why do you ask?"

"Oh," Brutus said, "just something in the Letters to the Editor page. A girl is missing. Her father wrote the letter. A girl named Joanne Riker was in my math class in grade eight. I always helped her with her homework. Her father said in the letter that he had not reported her missing yet, but if no one answers today, he will report it and offer a reward.

"Riker?" asked Lance. "I didn't see it, but a girl by that name was at the concert. She was trying to get out of the theatre."

"Interesting. I haven't seen her since we left school." The subject was dropped, but Lance couldn't get it out of his mind.

While he waited, Lance looked around the grounds curiously, noting that the home must be sitting on at least one hundred and forty acres of beautifully landscaped property.

Ten minutes later Brutus came out carrying a knapsack, "Not much in here but a couple of buns, some meat and two bottles of something that looked clear but probably isn't water." Lance tried to guess what it contained but Brutus packed it up quickly and just laughed as he put the whole works in his saddlebag.

"I'm not great at making lunches or snacks," he said, "but I do know how to pack for the ride. You'll enjoy it."

You lead," Lance suggested.

"Sure," said Brutus as he forged ahead and flung his leg over the saddle. "This is the bike that Dennis Hopper rode in Easy Rider, you know," He grabbed the throttle and revved up the engine, while Lance watched with interest and a considerable amount of fascination and admiration. This kid knew what he was doing! Brutus was no novice when it came to bikes.

The trail left the clearing and zigzagged through a heavily treed area. The dense foliage shut out the sunshine and felt almost cold as it neared the summit of Ridgeback Mountain. Lance could see patches of colour through the trees every so often where the sunshine penetrated.

Brutus pulled to a stop at the top of a ledge and looked down over the valley. Lance parked behind him taking in the panoramic view of the slope as it followed the roaring river. The sound brought memories of another roaring river he recalled only a few days ago and he shuddered, hoping Brutus didn't notice.

"You nervous?" Brutus asked.

"No. Beautiful view."

"Let's eat," Brutus said as he opened his saddle bag and took out the hastily packed lunch bag.

Lance stood his bike up against a huge boulder and took off his leather jacket. "What on earth have you got in there?" he asked. He leaned over to get a better look.

"Just a few things to munch on," Brutus said. He handed Lance a bottle and a bun dripping with sauce. "I like these and hope you do too," he said. "Hope you don't want a plate. I never bother with one."

"Looks good to me," Lance assured him, wiping the sauce off his tee shirt with the back of his hand. "Smells great too. I didn't think I was hungry until I smelled it."

"Pull up a stump and make yourself at home," Brutus said. He sat down on the end of a rotten log and took a big bite. "Sorry I haven't got any napkins, but those red leaves should work."

"I'll skip them if you don't mind. Never did go for poison ivy."

"Yeek!" exclaimed Brutus. "Poison ivy? It's all around us."

"Well, just don't touch any of it." Lance happily chewed until he had worked his way through another bun, and three cookies, each large enough for a whole meal, and looked up to the forest above. "Look!" he said. "We are being watched." High above them a brown bear stood on duty.

"The bears won't bother us," Brutus assured him. "They're nervous of people."

"That one doesn't know the rules. Time to leave," said Lance. "That's a mother bear with a cub. She just told the cub to climb a tree. Can you see her? Let's go."

The two men looked up and studied the animals for a minute. Brutus hastily put his leather jacket back on and threw his remaining bun in the saddle bag. Lance shoved the bottle in his bag after ramming the cork down as far as it would go. He lifted his bike and swung his leg over it faster than usual.

When they arrived at the turnoff and found Brutus' gate and the long driveway to his house, they both got off the bikes and looked at one another, but didn't mention the bear until Lance remarked, "Nice afternoon. We must do it again. Minus the bear, of course."

"Of course," Brutus agreed. "I've always liked exploring new places. Never been on that road before."

SIXTEEN

On Monday Lance picked up a bag of chicken feed at the Co-op and stopped at the Liquor store for a bottle of wine to celebrate their twentieth anniversary. On his way home, he planned to buy chocolates for Andrea. He flung open the door without paying attention to a familiar voice that pierced the air in the generally orderly shop.

"You?" shouted a man, "Get out of here before I shoot you full of bullets too, you lily livered creep!"

Zeke? What's he doing here?

"What?" Lance blurted. He looked around in stunned disbelief when he heard an angry exchange of words between Zeke and Alphonse, the manager.

"You said I'd get my payoff today and I want it now," Zeke shouted.

"Not here, for heaven's sake. I'll call you later. Keep it down, eh?" Alphonse said. He looked embarrassed when he glanced at the customers seated at tables near the window.

"Now!" Zeke yelled. He drew his revolver from behind his back, aimed above the man's head, and fired. The bullet whined as it flew through the air and hit the long mirror behind the counter. "Let this be a warning to you! Next time you won't be so lucky!"

As glass shards scattered over the customers, they ran for cover. Some ducked under the tables and tried to hide. Others headed for the door.

"As for you...you creep, I got a bone to pick with you," he said as he swung around and faced Morley.

"Huh?" Morley asked. He slunk down under the table, drawing his long legs as close to his body as possible, but Zeke had his scent and closed in.

148

"I'll get you, you dirty-mouthed rat!" Zeke screamed. He pointed the revolver at Morley's head and pulled the trigger. "I hate rats like you."

The bullet went wild; first it hit the ceiling and ricocheted off the light fixture. Faster yet, another bullet whined. Zeke clutched his elbow as blood spurted over the carpeted floor.

"You're under arrest!" said a voice. With a snap, the handcuffs were clamped.

"You half-wit! How dare you call the bloody pigs! I ought to kill you right now!" Zeke screamed as he fought to get his hands free.

Lance was pushed out the door by someone, minus the bottle of wine he'd come to get. Morley was right behind him.

"What's this all about?" muttered Lance.

"I have no idea," Morley said. "I wasn't even in here when the rumble started. That guy was having words outside with someone and I got yanked in here for safety. Then he came in here and scrapped with Alphonse, saw me, and tried to blow my head off. I recognised him because he's the light tech from the theatre?"

"Yes, it's him. I wanted a bottle of wine for our anniversary," Lance said. "Where are you parked? I'm right over here." He pointed to his car parked under a shade tree.

"Right behind you," Morley said.

"What did he mean when he called you a rat?"

"I was working at the hospital when Freddy's body was brought in for the autopsy," Morley said. "I think he was referring to his death. Odd, because I didn't think they have a suspect yet or even know how Freddy died."

"Oh, is that why he was so nasty toward you earlier? Do you mean he thinks you fingered him?" asked Lance. "You must have been in two places at once to do that."

"Not quite," Morley said. "While we were waiting to go onstage the night of the concert, I told Zeke I was on the eleven p.m. to six a.m. shift at the hospital that night after the concert. He accused me of working there to have easy access to drugs."

"He's a strange man," Lance said. "I didn't think he'd pull a gun on anyone though." He shook his head.

"Yeah, I feel all shook up. My job puts me in contact with a lot of people, but I've never met one like Zeke." Morley ran his fingers through his hair, which now puffed up into a large ball over his left eye.

"Oh," Lance said, trying to focus on Morley's green sweater rather than his hair. "I saw Brutus yesterday and we talked about a farewell concert in Freddy's memory. Are you interested?"

"Yeah," he said. "As long as Zeke is not the light tech that night."

"Not likely," Lance said. "I think he'll be out of circulation for a while. Too bad because he was good at his job. Anyway, I gotta go."

"Me too." Morley looked at his watch and remarked that he just had enough time to heat some fish and chips for his dinner before he had to go to work again.

The two men parted company and headed for their cars.

Lance still wanted to take home a box of chocolates for Andrea. He went into Safeway on his way home.

The knowledge that Freddy was no doubt murdered the night of the concert, hung heavily over his head. In his heart he knew he was not to blame, but he still wished he had been more aware that the young man was living in the harsh world of drug culture, an environment where only the shrewd survive. Had Freddy really depended upon drugs? Even after his illegal request, Lance hadn't wanted to believe Freddy was so deeply involved in the drug community.

Lance knew his death was possibly premeditated by the killer, but he couldn't help wondering if he could have somehow stopped it. On one hand he felt guilty because the drugs were not where Freddy had wanted to hide them. On the other hand, he also knew that he was not responsible for the poor choices made by others.

Lance opened the mall door and entered the store, startled to hear live music being played on a keyboard. Lance recognized Steve's crew-cut hair before he actually saw him. Steve? Busking? Was he that broke?

He stood by the door and listened to the music before he went over and spoke to him. Steve had stationed himself close to the little take-out restaurant selling hamburgers and soft drinks inside the mall. Lance sat down on one of the stools and ordered a root beer while they chatted. He looked around at the various salads and sandwiches displayed inside a glassed-in locked cupboard.

"What are you doing here, Steve?" he asked. "Just getting a bit of practice in on we unwary customers or what? Would you like a burger or a drink? I'm buying."

"Lance! Just a drink, thanks. Root Beer's good," Steve said. "To be truthful, none of us got paid for the concert, but we still had to pay the bills. I needed the money."

"I heard that," Lance said, taking a five-dollar bill from his pocket. "Would you be insulted if I tipped you this?" Steve grinned.

"I'm too broke to be insulted," he said. He took the money and smiled. "Did you see the commotion over there on the corner? There was a police takedown.."

"Yes, I just came from there," Lance said.

"I think he works as a light tech at the Coral Reef. I heard someone yelling. Sounded like the light tech at the theatre." Steve babbled. "I heard that some guy pulled a gun in the liquor store."

"Yes, he did. I witnessed it," Lance said.

"I was told that Zeke pointed the gun at the policeman, so the cop returned fire," "Got his arm instead." Steve babbled on, ignoring what Lance told him.

"He refused to drop the gun. Some people came in from the street and told us what they saw."

"Really? You play well, Steve," Lance said, trying to change the subject. "Funny how Heavy Metal music still sounds good even when played on a keyboard."

"I was outside busking when it happened, "Steve repeated, telling Lance what he already knew.

"Steve, let's stop talking about it now," Lance said. "I'm sure we'll read about it in the paper. These things get twisted out of shape when we keep repeating ourselves. I came in to get Andrea some chocolates for our anniversary. I was in town buying chicken feed."

"Is it her birthday?" Steve asked.

"No, it's our anniversary today," he repeated. "Actually, I do get her chocolates once in a while anyway." He laughed, thinking the young man probably wouldn't understand that, so he added, "You know, buy wheat for the chickens and chocolate for my own chick."

"Get her two boxes," Steve advised. "One for her, and one for the kids. That's what my dad does. Otherwise, by the time everyone has had a couple, pushed their fingers into them to see if they are soft or hard, she hardly gets any. Works fine."

"Good idea," Lance said.

"Look! They're loading someone in the police car instead," Steve observed. "Is that Zeke? I thought he was arrested for pulling a gun in the liquor store." He frowned as he spoke.

Lance strained his eyes to see what was going on. "I

don't know," he said. "Oh, Brad Thomas is coming toward us. Wonder what he wants?"

"I'm leaving," Steve said. "He wouldn't be talking to me anyway. He's a friend of yours. My old jalopy is right here so I got no reason to hang around. Anyway, my keyboard and stand are too heavy to be carrying around." He waved and proceeded to load everything in the car, much to Brad's amusement when he stopped.

"Hi," he said. "Your friend seems nervous to talk to me. What's up?"

"I was going to ask you the same thing. Was that Zeke Geisbrecht who took off running up the road? I thought they were trying to get him in the ambulance."

"He escaped, but he's still under arrest and I am trying to catch up with him. Want to come along?" Brad asked. "His arm is still bleeding. He needs medical care."

"What can I do?" Lance asked. "Follow the blood spots?"

"Try to keep Heathcliffe in sight, and when I catch up to you, we might have a better idea what he's up to. He's a tricky beggar. I doubt if he will get too far," Brad said. "If you see him, duck around a corner and phone me. I don't want you to get hurt."

"Where's Heathcliffe?" asked Lance. "I wasn't watching."

"I gave him the order to go after Zeke, but I don't want to lose sight of him. He's headed toward the main highway. He's injured and may pass out. Don't get too close. Keep your eyes open and your mouth shut. Got it?"

"Yeah," Lance said. "Against my better judgement."

Lance had little trouble following the dog's movements. He was obviously following the blood spots on the pavement and apparently enjoying his job of sniffing each and every one carefully. Lance stayed back just far enough to still see the dog in action. When Heathcliffe leaped over a picket fence, Lance had time to note on an envelope in his pocket that the dog spent considerable time checking out the spots.

After hopping two fences, and going down a lane, Lance looked around. He normally stayed on the sidewalk, but Heathcliffe had other ideas. Lance stayed close enough to note the dog's movements until he reached a dead-end street. The only one in Meldrum City was at the site of the Full Gospel Church. Did the blood lead to the church? The precious church of his youth.

The years had slipped by since he and his parents and siblings had been the church orchestra here. Then his wedding. Why was he drawn to this place?

He slowed down when he saw the steeple and walked past several parked cars. The majestic double doors were open a few inches and he could hear the rise and fall of a male voice. He walked up the two steps to the vestibule. Heathcliffe stood by the door as if he was waiting for a command.

What day was it? Lance recalled that his grandmother always attended a senior's prayer meeting on Wednesday mornings.

He peeked in the door and saw a woman offer Zeke her chair and a wad of Kleenex for his arm.

The dog looked up at Lance and followed him as he slowly backed out and called Brad.

"I'm right behind you," Brad said, startling Lance as he pushed past him. "Good dog. Thanks, Lance."

Lance slowly made his way to the last pew and sat down, uncertain what he should do next, but hoping there would be no violence. The dog followed Brad and stood at his feet. Brad spoke quietly to Heathcliffe, and the dog suddenly made a rush for Zeke and grabbed him by the

154

wrist.

The words, "You are under arrest!" startled Lance. He was not certain if he should exit or stay. He saw Zeke grab the first thing he could reach with his one free hand. A silver pitcher flew through the air. Brad dodged just in time to avoid getting it in his face,

Then in a surprise move, Zeke pulled a revolver from his pocket, put it to his temple and pulled the trigger. Lance saw him shudder before he fell, blood oozing onto the carpet.

Brad nodded in agreement when Lance called the ambulance. Maybe it was too late? Then he saw Brad kneel beside Zeke and take his pulse. Was the fugitive still alive? No? Yes! His eyelids fluttered. Lance wanted to run away. *Oh My God! What next?*

He sat still and heard the pastor talking quietly to his parishioners. "Move slowly and quietly out of your seats and walk to the prayer room. There is nothing to fear. The police are here, and everything is under control." Lance marvelled at the older man's calm.

He looked up to the choir loft where a few people were praying. And then he spied the organ. He looked away, as if denying he had seen the instrument at all, bowed his head for a moment, then looked again. It was still there just waiting for him. Slowly he made his way towards it and sat down on the bench. Then as if guided by unknown hands, he touched the ivory keys. No sound.

He touched the switch and felt the power come on. The music swelled ever so slightly. Softly at first, then a mighty swell. "Jesus loves me," he whispered. "Does Jesus love Zeke?" He forgot where he was going with the thought, buried in the sheer magic of the moment. Moving his fingers experimentally over the keys, he played several children's hymns, and the beloved chorus *Hallelujah*. Without looking up he allowed his fingers to wander over the keys, playing whatever came to mind; scales, school songs, jazz tunes, waltzes, always coming back to that magic chorus he had sung in Sunday School as a kid. Lance had come home.

He was startled when the gentle voice of the pastor sounded close to his ear. "Is your name Lance?" he asked. Lance nodded. "I hate to ask you, but the janitor needs to clean the church so he can go home for dinner."

"I'm sorry," Lance blurted. "I guess I lost count of the time. I'll leave now."

"No problem," the pastor said, as Lance turned off the power and closed the lid. "Would you like a ride home?" He walked with Lance to the front door.

"My car is somewhere," he said, looking around helplessly. "I think I left it at the grocery store parking lot." He put his hands over his eyes and began to shake.

"I'll drive you to pick it up and accompany you until you arrive home. You look worn out. I won't leave you until you're home. Is your name Lance?"

"Yes. is your name Michael McKenzie?"

"It is. I've seen you somewhere before."

"At our marriage ceremony, twenty years ago today," Lance said with a smile.

"I remember now. Next year I hope you'll celebrate it with less fanfare!"

"I plan to!" Lance replied with a smile.

When he arrived home, Lance got out of his car, walked back to Pastor McKenzie's car and thanked him for his kindness. He waved as the good man drove away and stumbled unsteadily into the house.

"What in the world happened to you?" Andrea asked as she took the packages from him. "Happy Anniversary!"

"Thanks, honey," he said. "I'll tell you later. I love you!"

SEVENTEEN

Lance was surprised when Brad phoned him Thursday morning. "Will you come with me to Zeke's place to get his insulin? I need an impartial witness," he said.

"Is he still alive?" Lance asked. "I thought he. . ."

"He is conscious but gravely ill," said Brad. "He had surgery this morning, and he's in a lot of pain. He's a type one diabetic, so his doctor said he needs to have his prescribed dose before he can eat anything."

"How come?"

"So his blood sugar level stays normal."

"Oh, but why me?" asked Lance. "I'm a bit smelly. Been working in the top pasture."

"We're short- handed in the office this morning and you do know Zeke. I'll pick you up in ten minutes and drive you back home afterwards."

"Okay, I'll be ready," Lance said. He quickly opened the shed door and hung the rake on a special rack before he locked the door. He looked at his tatty old denim overalls with a hole over one knee and grinned. If his band students at school could see him in this getup they would never believe he was a serious musician. He brushed the dirt off his bare knee and walked briskly down the hill to the house.

"How come he called you?" Andrea asked when he came into the kitchen.

"Brad said I know Zeke so it's not like total strangers going into his house," he told her.

"He must trust you," she said. "You'd better have some lunch before you go. You can eat it while you change. I'll whip up some food in no time." Lance grinned when she handed him a sandwich and a coffee five minutes later. *You have to love a woman who can do that*, he thought.

"Thanks," he said. He took a bite out of the sandwich and just had time to change into some clean clothes before Brad arrived in full uniform. "What do I have to do," he asked as they walked out to the cruiser.

"Just accompany me in. Not too complicated," Brad explained. "Sorry to rush you, but Zeke could have a reaction if he doesn't have his insulin. We don't want him to lapse into a coma."

"Coma?" inquired Lance. They climbed into the cruiser.

"What's in that sandwich? Smells good." Brad remarked.

"Andrea can put a whole meal between a bun," he said. He laughed as Brad sniffed the tantalizing aroma of ham, fried eggs, and cheddar cheese. "Hi Heathcliffe," he called to the dog behind the barrier separating him from the passengers." I see you're ready for work." The working dog gave a dignified wag of his tail and a doggy smile to acknowledge Lance before he quietly sat down again behind the barrier,

Zeke's home was on the edge of town. Brad drove up the long driveway to the front door of the three-story stuccoed home, surrounded by rose gardens. Before he got out of the car, he opened the latch and released Heathcliffe from his spot behind the front and back seats.

The cop unlocked the front door. He was greeted by a big brute of a dog who leaped out of the shadows barking loudly and snapping at Brad's heels. Heathcliffe remained dignified and ignored the other dog entirely. as he glared at the intruders.

"Cool it, Pooch!" Brad commanded. "I wish I knew his name. Normally I'd want to isolate the two dogs, but this is his home and he's only doing his job. Situations do arise. Heathcliffe never overreacts to other animals."

Lance grinned. "Heathcliffe is better behaved than most children. This is Hagar. He and I have met before when Zeke brought him to the theatre once a long time ago. We had a conversation in the parking lot the night of the concert. Come on Hagar. Stay with me. We're just here to get Zeke's insulin." Hagar whined at hearing Zeke's name and looked up at Lance. "Zeke told me he's very well trained. He'll cooperate."

"Hello, Hagar," Brad said, using his name. Hagar stopped growling and stared at him. Brad guarded his face as he slowly bent down so he was the same size as the dog. "Will you co-operate? My name is Brad. I just have to get Zeke's insulin. Good boy Hagar."

He turned to Lance. "Being a dog handler is good experience. He probably smells Heathcliffe, but he seems to understand. You are good, so watch Hagar. Let's just do the job and get out."

"How do you know? You didn't use any of the words familiar to him."

"His master's name and probably the word *insulin* are words he might know. Most people talk to their animals. I have a feeling he's not as ferocious as he appears," Brad said.

"He's part pet and part security. I remember when Zeke brought him to the theatre." Lance said.

"Good. I hope you're right. Easy there, big guy," Brad said. He patted his hip. "Hagar, Heel!" Hagar stayed close to Brad and looked up at him trustingly.

"He said the insulin was in the bathroom. Maybe in the medicine cabinet."

"No," Lance said. "Insulin has to be kept cold. There must be more than one bathroom in this big house. He probably has a small refrigerator either in the bathroom for that purpose of in the hallway by the bathroom door."

He looked around curiously. The house was beautifully styled and furnished. The hardwood floors were highly polished, and everything proclaimed wealth.

"Zeke told me he has a cat too. I think his name is Bigamy. He also has a young man on staff who acts as his butler and feeds the animals. I didn't really listen that closely to what he said the night of the concert, because I was worrying about my own equipment, but it did impress me how he cared about his pets."

"I'll get the girl at the desk to find out if someone is looking after them because Zeke won't be coming home for a while," Brad said.

Brad headed up to the third floor, followed by Lance "It must be up here," he said. "I wish he'd told me what floor he keeps the insulin."

"I seem to recall he said that his bedroom is on the third floor, Brad. His private bathroom is no doubt up here too."

They were startled when they heard a few notes played on the piano. Brad chuckled. "I think we found the cat," he said. He retraced his steps. Lance peeked into a large room at the top of the stairs and found the musician. A big fluffy orange cat was making himself comfortable on top of the piano. He merely raised his head and observed the men invading his home. Both animals appeared well-fed and obviously socialized, Lance thought.

"Hello, Bigamy," Lance said. The cat stretched his long ginger legs and murmured a soft, "Meow!" Lance reached out slowly and ran his fingers over the soft fur. Bigamy purred loudly and nuzzled his hand as he walked back and forth over the lid of the highly polished Lesage piano. He stepped down onto the keys and played his three-note song once more. He turned around three times in a circle and stretched before he went back to sleep.

Even Brad had to smile. "Nice cat," he said. "However, we have to locate Zeke's insulin. There must be a bathroom on the third floor so I'm going up there to look."

Lance followed Brad as he sprinted up the stairs to the third floor.

"Yes, it's up here," Brad called. "Stand where you can see what I'm doing, please."

Brad came down the stairs carrying a small bag. "Okay," he said. "That's all I'm supposed to do. See?" he said as he held the bag open so Lance could see it. "Thanks for coming with me. Now I guess we'd better get on the road. I'm glad you told me it would be in a refrigerator because I didn't even think of looking there."

In the silence that followed Brad noticed that Heathcliffe appeared restless. As they neared the bottom of the stairs his ears swivelled around to focus on a closed door.

"Stay!" Brad said. "He seems restless. I wonder why?"

"Dogs and cats hear things like a moth landing on the window. If our hearing was that keen, we'd go crazy. I guess in the wild they live and die by their ability to hear and see. We don't need to, so we've lost that ability."

"You're probably right," Brad agreed. "Early man likely was more animal-like than we are now."

"My father used to say his goat was better looking and more intelligent than his first date as a teenager." Lance chuckled as he spoke, and Brad grinned.

As he and Brad reached the main floor, Lance heard a sound that caused him to freeze. He stopped to listen. It seemed like someone was crying for help; trying to scream. It appeared to be coming from the basement, although the door was closed.

"Let's go!" Brad said. "We have to get Zeke's insulin

to him. What's that noise?"

"Maybe the wind."

"The dog hears something though," Brad said. "I hate to delay any longer. The door may be locked anyway."

"I hear something. Odd Hagar doesn't seem bothered by it. He could be accustomed to hearing it, I guess. I'll break the door down, if necessary," Lance said.

Brad stood still for a moment and finally said, "I can't hear anything unusual, but I'll take a look. If I need you, I'll holler."

The cop walked down the stairs, turned to the left and continued to the end of the hallway. When he stood still to listen, he could clearly hear a woman's voice in the distance. Lance was right –a woman was crying. He suspected it may be a recording or even a trap, so Brad pulled his revolver from the holster before he opened the door.

It wasn't locked, so he walked in. Barely a minute later he came back to the door and said, "Oh, my God Lance, I need you. Come down, and don't touch anything." His voice held fear and a sense of urgency.

Lance crossed the hall and stepped into the open doorway. This couldn't be real! He stared at the manmade horror before him.

In the centre of the room was a wheelchair inside a metal cage-like structure, secured by heavy cables. Exposed electrical wiring connected it to something behind a panel. A power outlet?

"Oh my God! What is this? She's imprisoned in that contraption! Who?"

Lance stared around the room for a few seconds, tongue-tied as he struggled to think clearly. He had been sure someone was there but when he saw it with his own eyes, disbelief and horror held his mind captive. "Oh, no. This can't be. This is the same girl who was at the theatre. I saw her in Zeke's van the first time he was arrested. I remember her. Joanne?"

Brad knelt beside the cage and looked into the girl's terrified eyes. The tears she must have shed for the hours she was imprisoned here, were drying on her face, leaving smudges of dried mucous on her fair skin. "Is your name Joanne?" he asked.

"Mmmmm!" the girl whispered through a dirty gag covering her mouth. She tried to move but was held tight by the many restraints. Terror was etched into every line of her youthful face, her eyes darting back and forth toward the door, as if she expected someone to open it and come in any minute. Every little sound caused her to shake as she looked fearfully into Lance's eyes.

"Oh, my dear God!" Lance uttered, He stood for a minute and looked at the scene in utter horror. He felt anger welling up in his chest. Was Zeke a killer? How could anyone do this? He wanted to take her hand and promise he could help her, but the fear that he couldn't fulfil that promise haunted him.

If he touched her, he could be electrocuted and need help himself. He felt helpless and angry. He should be able to do something, but knowing he could be a victim, too, calmed him somewhat. He breathed deeply and focused on what he knew he was capable of doing.

Brad studied the breaker box. "I'll check the wires before we touch it. No electricity is going through it now, so what if I just turn off the main breaker? I'm not an electrician and I don't know for sure."

"I bet it's still alive. Zeke is a journeyman electrician, so he's probably installed some traps too. I'm sure this contraption is hooked up to its own breaker and is not part of the main one. Okay if I check the fuse box? I think the power is still on," Lance said.

Brad watched as Lance stood up and walked over to the window A loose wire hung down below the sill. "It's not grounded," he said. He hit the switch and there was the unmistakable sound and smell of a power surge before it fizzled and died. The girl passed out.

"The best thing to do is to call Search and Rescue because they'll know what to do," Brad said.

Brutus' warnings came to mind. How long had the girl been there? Two days? It was at least that long since Lance had seen her in Zeke's van. Maybe longer. He'd lost track of the time. He overheard Brad talking on the phone. "We have a rescue here," he said. It's touchy and dangerous. The homeowner has been in custody for two days. It involves electricity. The girl is injured. Kill the sirens, she's had enough trauma already. My partner is with her. Yes, come as quickly as you can get here. This is an emergency." He gave the address and came back.

There was enough light from the window to illuminate the horror-filled scene. Lance knelt beside the girl again and spoke gently to her. "We will have you out of here in no time as soon as Search and Rescue gets here. Can you hold on for another few minutes? It's just about over."

She opened her eyes and tried to speak, but no sound came out of her mouth. He thought of his wife and daughter as he tried to comfort her. He didn't dare remove the gag because he was almost certain the chair was still connected to power.

While waiting for the medics, Brad took several photos of the terrible scene.

In moments, the ambulance arrived, followed by Search and Rescue. Brad opened the door for them.

Dr. Lee Scotton, whose name tag stated that he had earned his PhD, and his assistant Betty Armstrong scrutinized the situation.

"Oh, my God! That's my friend Joanne," blurted the girl, her voice near to hysteria. "How…?" She put her hands to her face and shuddered. "We went to the concert together. We went to school together!" They all looked up when she spoke, shock written over their faces.

Lance was sure the power was still active in the cage. He leaned forward to take another look. Brad urged him to leave it alone, but Lance knew in his heart that Zeke was devious and smart enough to have done an expert job of deception. "Please let me check it before anyone touches it."

"Stubborn," Brad said. "There is barely time for that but have a look."

A minute later Lance located the switch and turned it off, electrocuting himself in the process. He passed out as he was zapped hard enough to blacken his face.

Twenty minutes later Joanne was removed from the cage and placed in the ambulance. First Aid was administered, and oxygen started.

Lance came to, not certain where he was, in time to see the ambulance leaving. Brad still had to get Zeke's insulin to him at MGH and meet the ambulance at the hospital.

"Are you okay, Lance?" he asked. "You are one of a kind."

"A bit giddy," Lance answered, shaking his head, "What happened? Did I get zapped?"

"Yes, you did. I should have listened to you in the first place," Brad admitted.

Heathcliffe sat at attention and waited for Brad to put him in the cruiser, close the barrier and settle Lance in the front where he could keep an eye on him.

"I've called for someone to pick up the insulin and deliver it to the hospital immediately. Enough time has been wasted already. He should have had it thirty minutes ago. Then you must go to Emergency." he said.

"Why? I feel fine. Lance said. "Sorry I scared the hell out of you, but I knew that trap was still hot. Where's Hagar?"

"We'll deal with that later. You need to go to the ER. An electrical shock is not a little thing. Get it checked. We'll get Hagar and Bigamy from the shelter as soon as we can get in touch with Lief and find out what he wants to do. Don't forget to tighten your seat belt. I don't want to give myself a ticket." He reached over and connected the buckle for Lance before he started the car.

EIGHTEEN

Lance sat by the window in the hall after grudgingly going to the ER to determine if he had incurred any injuries from the electrical shock. Luckily, he appeared healthy so as soon as he was released by the doctor, he waited at the end of the hall for Brad to return from delivering Zeke's medications to the Head Nurse on the third floor,

A tall red-headed orderly walked down the hall. It was Morley, the drummer with *The Sinkholes.* When he saw Lance, he inquired if he had an appointment.

"No, just waiting for a police escort home," he said. "What's going on with Zeke Giesbrecht?"

"Hmm—I won't ask any more questions. Zeke isn't feeling good today, I guess," Morley said, keeping to strict patient protocol. He smiled as he walked away. He turned back to add, "Nice to see you, Lance. I'll give you a holler on my phone tonight."

Brad finally emerged from Zeke's room a short time later, his jaw set in a determined square. When his phone rang, Brad moved around the corner for privacy, but Lance was close enough to hear the one-sided conversation. "Yeah, what does CSIS want with Zeke Geisbrect? He's too sick to come to the phone anyway, but I'll leave him a message," Brad said, as he walked back to speak Lance.

"I have to remain here for a while, so can you find your way home?" he asked.

"Sure. My wife will pick me up," Lance said. "It's not far from here. She won't mind. I'm feeling okay now."

"Good," Brad said. "You better call her before you leave the building. I don't want you passing out."

"Oh, Brad," Lance said. He took a step ahead, "Wait!

What's happening?"

"I don't know yet, "Brad said. "I'll phone you in a bit. There are some changes,"

"Changes?" asked Lance.

"We'll talk later, Lance," he said.

Lance watched Brad walk away before he called Andrea and requested that she come and get him. "Brad had to go back to the office, so I'm stuck and I don't feel like hitch-hiking," he said.

"I'll be there in a few minutes or so. Can you walk down to the post office, and I'll pick you up there?" she asked. "Your voice sounds weary."

"I am weary, but the fresh air will probably do me good. I'll wait on the corner at the bottom of the stairs. I saw Morley and Brad, but they didn't tell me what's going on. I'm leaving the hospital now," he said.

He looked up at the tall hospital building as he turned the corner onto the sidewalk and sat down on the bench, He was surprised he felt so tired. Maybe that electrical shock was bigger than he thought? He wondered how many shocks Joanne may have endured at Zeke's hands. Would she ever recover completely? Then he thought of his wife and daughter and began to shake. If anyone treated his family like Zeke had treated that girl, he knew he would have a hard time keeping his temper in check. He was glad that he had not tried to walk any further. How much worse it would be for her! Tears came to his eyes. He wanted to go back and shake the guts out of Zeke. And yet, he had the strange feeling that Zeke was dying. Perhaps as he stood there Zeke was leaving this world. Second sight perhaps? He shuddered to think of it. Why did the thought of death do that to people? Zeke didn't deserve to live, but still, death was final.

***

Andrea had picked the kids up at the recreation centre

on her way to meet Lance. "You look tired," she repeated. "Hard day?"

He nodded. "Yes," he said.

She moved Jeannie to the front seat and gave the boys bus fare to get home "Be quiet and let your dad have the back so he can stretch out," she said.

He got in, leaned back, and closed his eyes. If they only knew what he'd been through! He opened his eyes briefly and glanced at Andrea, filled with admiration for her. He relaxed again and fell into a deep sleep.

***

At the hospital, Nurse Bradford knocked briskly on the door and called out in a cheery voice, "Mr. Geisbrecht, I have some good news. Sgt. Thomas delivered your insulin." Leaning over the bed, she looked closely at the sleeping patient and frowned. Something wasn't right. Her eyes widened as she tightened the blood pressure cuff around his upper left arm. She felt her cheeks flush when she saw the reading. She took it again, and once more to make sure. No reading?

She then took his pulse once more. No pulse?

She pressed the emergency button. "Doctor? I can't get a reading," she said. She listened for his footsteps as he quickly entered the room. After one glance, the doctor took his pulse again and said, "The patient has passed away." He put his hand to his forehead. "He has gone through a lot in the past twenty-four hours. The poor, lost soul. I wish we could have helped him. No matter how many times we face death, it hurts to fail."

NINETEEN

When Leif came home after work at five-thirty Friday afternoon, he was surprised to see the house surrounded by yellow police crime-scene tape Two uniformed RCMP officers stood at attention by the wide double gate at the main entrance leading onto the long driveway. A sign on the gate announced that the property was off-limits.

"Everything was fine when I left for work this morning," he said. "I don't understand. I live here." He showed his ID but no dice.

"You'll have to phone the police station to find out. No–one has permission to enter the property without a pass," the guard said.

Leif sighed and called the station on his cell phone to get the goods directly.

"Good afternoon. Leif Fergusson speaking. May I speak to Lieutenant Brad Thomas, please? I came home from work this afternoon and found the property guarded behind police crime tape. "

"Oh, yes," said the man. "Lt. Thomas was expecting you to call. I'll connect you to his office right away," the Desk Sergeant explained.

"What's happening?" Leif asked when Lt. Thomas answered the phone. "What is this about a crime?"

"I'll explain when I get there," Brad said. "Stay in your car. I'll be there in about fifteen minutes." He cut the call.

"Okay," Leif said as he automatically locked the car doors, although he was certainly not nervous about being beaten up under ordinary circumstances. He ran his hand over his muscled arm and smiled as he visualized how shocked the big man would be if he picked him up and tossed him across the room. Not that he intended to do it, of course, but it was entertaining to imagine it.

When Brad arrived, Leif asked, "Was there a robbery here? Everything was normal when I left for work this morning."

"No," Brad said. "Your landlord was taken to the hospital yesterday, but earlier today I came in to get his medication and my partner and I discovered a girl was being held prisoner in a room. Do you know anything about that?"

"Girl? Zeke hated women," he said. "There were never any girls here. What are you talking about? Where is Zeke now?" He frowned as he tried to picture the scene.

"Mr. Fergusson," Brad said. "There is no gentle way to tell you. Zeke fired a shot at a police officer yesterday and he fired back as a warning. Mr. Geisbrecht had a superficial wound. He escaped from an ambulance and went into a church to hide from police, but when we did catch up to him, he attempted to commit suicide. He survived that, but he only regained consciousness briefly and died in MGH this afternoon."

"Suicide? Church? He never went to church. What are you talking about?" Leif asked. "He must be out of town. He just forgot to leave me a message." Leif shook his head in disbelief.

"No, Mr. Fergusson, Zeke passed away in the hospital. Did no one notify you of his death?"

"Death? Where is he now?"

"Uh—Leif, do you mind if I call you by your first name? Zeke passed away in the hospital this afternoon. We found your name and address in his pocket as next of kin. Are you related to Zeke Geisbrect?" he asked.

"No, I was just the hired man."

"Okay. The house is out of bounds until the tape has been removed, and we get things sorted out. Would you like to get some clothes from the house? I could accompany you past the tape. Perhaps you could stay at a hotel for a couple of days until we know what happened?" Brad said, attempting to make Leif understand.

"Can I stay in my apartment? I live there."

"No," Brad said. "Against my better judgement, I'll accompany you in the house to get some of your belongings and food, and get you settled for a few days. My friend Lance will help you. I'll give him a call and get him to come. Okay? I know this is difficult, but Zeke did pass away. "

"I want to go home. Where are the dog and cat?" Leif asked.

"At the animal shelter waiting for you to pick them up when you know where you will stay. When Lance gets here, we'll take you inside to show you the crime scene. A restoration company will be in tomorrow to clean up the room," Brad explained. "I wouldn't ordinarily do this, but you need to see it."

"What room?" Leif asked. "How do you know? What were you doing here? The doors were locked."

"We came in earlier to get his insulin. I needed a witness, so Lance came with me. My dog seemed upset, and we heard whimpering coming from a room by the stairs and thought it was a cry for help. The door was not locked so we looked in and discovered a girl held prisoner here. The medics said she would have died if we had not called them today. You would not want to stay here. She was rescued in time and taken to MGH where she is being treated. We may never know what happened unless she recovers."

"No, I don't believe you," Leif insisted. "No girls ever came here. If the door wasn't locked, what prevented her from leaving?"

"That's why we need to take you in and show you the scene. She was held captive in a locked cage. I am telling you the truth," Brad said.

***

Lance was surprised when Brad called him to request he come to Zeke's home right away. "How come?" he said. "I thought the restoration crew was coming to clean it up."

"They'll be here tomorrow, but Zeke's renter, Leif Fergusson was not informed of the circumstances, and no one let him know that Zeke had passed away. We found Ferguson's name in Zeke's pocket, but we don't know if he is the next of kin or not. The house is taped off so he can't enter without permission," Brad explained.

"I see, I think," Lance said. "Where are you now, and when do you need me? I am not working tomorrow. I've just come in from school We're out for the weekend.

"I know," Brad said. He explained the circumstances very briefly. After thinking it over, he said. "As soon as possible. This is an emergency. "

"Okay, I'll talk to my wife about it. Glad it wasn't yesterday—our anniversary, you know. I've just about had enough emergencies already," Lance said. He went into the kitchen and found Andrea getting dinner.

"Leif?" she asked. "Is he the same guy who teaches Lanny martial arts?"

"Yes, the same fellow. He's really messed up right now. Brad thinks because I work with kids, I can talk to him." Lance said.

"You probably can," Andrea agreed. "Go, but don't forget you are MY husband and father to OUR kids."

"I won't," Lance promised. "I'll be home as soon as I can." He got back into her car and drove up to see Brad, who was waiting by the gate with Leif.

He pulled over, parked beside the police cruiser, and got out. "What's going on?" he asked as the two men approached him. A second plain-clothes policeman parked next to Lance.

The tall, good-looking man got out and introduced himself as Lt. Josh Peters. "I work with the Federal Dangerous Crime Unit," he said. He offered his hand to Brad with a smile. He presented his ID cards. Lance stepped back and listened.

After Brad had looked at the papers, he said to Lance, "Lt. Peters will be accompanying us through the crime scene. It seems our federal Bureau is very interested in your boss, Leif," he said.

"Please act as though I'm not even here," Peters instructed, "Mr. Giesbrect had worked with my agency for several years. It seems he might have operated above the law on occasion."

"Means nothing to me," Leif said. "The boss had his finger into a lot of pies. I stayed out of his affairs." He fidgeted with his keys."

"I'm sure he did," Peters said. "Go on with your business as usual."

Brad cleared his throat and turned to Lance, "Well, like I said on the phone, Lance, Leif wasn't informed that Zeke was in MGH or what had happened, so he just thought he was out of town on a business trip when he didn't come home for two nights. Can you help him?"

"I'll try. Have we met before?" he asked, turning to Leif.

"I think so," Leif said uncertainly.

"Were you with Zeke at the Sinkhole's concert?" Lance asked.

"Yes, now I remember you," Leif said. "I'd had a drink or two that night and was in a fighting mood. Was I speaking Japanese?"

"Yes, an Oriental Language," Lance said, with a smile. "I didn't have the faintest idea what you were saying."

"Probably a good thing," Leif said. "I'm embarrassed to admit I don't remember what I said either."

"I thought that could be the case," Lance said with a grin. "Everything was mixed up that night, so I'm not surprised. You did surprise me when you tried to pick a fight with me though, but now I understand you knew you could take me. You are my son's martial arts instructor."

"Oh, no," he said. "I'd have remembered that the rule is to never use my skills for anything but self-defence. What's the deal on the cop tape around the house?"

"Lt. Thomas has probably explained to you about finding a female victim in the room by the stairs and we called the ambulance to take her to hospital. She is gravely ill and badly injured. It is not known who victimized her, Leif, because she was unable to speak. The two dogs were acting funny, and I heard a noise as I walked past the door and told Thomas. It wasn't locked so we went in." he said.

"That's odd. He had no female friends at all." Leif said.

"Lt. Thomas will take us in so you can see for yourself. I'll come with you," Lance said. He glanced at Brad. "Where will you stay?"

"I want to go home."

"When the room has been cleaned up and the police are finished examining it, I'm sure you'll be able to," Lance said. "In the meantime maybe, you could stay at one of the cabins above. We'll come in with you, while you get some stuff. Then we'll get the dog and cat, so you'll have company. Unless you would prefer to stay at my place. We could put a bed in the music room."

"No," Leif insisted. "I want to stay here. If I can't go home, I guess I could stay in one of the cabins. I look after this place, you know."

"They said you are probably his next of kin. Do you think Zeke left any instructions for you?" Brad asked.

"I don't know."

"Leif, are you related to Zeke? Your name and address were in his pocket."

"He said he was related to my father, but I don't remember him being around at all," Leif said. "Zeke always left instructions for me when he had to go out of town. I was a hired hand. He said he didn't know if he even had a father."

"Would you allow me to have a look at Zeke's instructions? Then we'll have a clear picture of what he wants you to do," Brad said. "Lance is my witness should I need to verify any of this. You don't mind, do you?"

"No, but this time he didn't say he was going out of town, so I don't have any instructions," Leif said.

"Let's go take a look, Leif, and then we can make a decision. Where would he leave them if there were any?" Brad smiled at Leif and exchanged glances with Lance.

"Upstairs in his office," Leif said. "I'm the only person who had permission to enter that room."

"He may have left some instructions for you this time, Leif. He could have forgotten to tell you. May we go up and take a look?" Brad asked again.

A large oak desk stood against the north-facing wall of the big room that Zeke had furnished as an office. It's carved roll-front was bordered in gold-leaf and was locked. Leif walked to the safe and standing with his back to Lance and Brad, put in the security code, found the key, and unlocked the desk under Brad's watchful eyes.

"Wow!" Lance mouthed. Brad nodded.

Leif found the brown manila envelope with his name on it but hesitated before he opened it. Brad nodded his head and gave him a half smile. Leif opened it and read a few paragraphs, frowned, and nervously handed it to Brad.

"Okay, your immediate instructions are to take care of

Bigamy and Hagar as usual until you receive the papers giving you full rights to this house and property and further orders will be there. It should take a month," Brad said. "He writes that there's four thousand dollars in cash inside a gold box in the safe. Did you know about that?"

"Me?" Leif asked, in surprise. He sat down on the arm of the big easy chair in Zeke's room. "He didn't tell me anything about it. When I put the key back in the safe, I'll look for the box. I never touch anything of his, so I have no idea what is in there."

"Mr. Fergusson, you've obviously been a good employee. You and I don't know one another," Brad said, "but it appears as though you will legally own this house along with Hagar and Bigamy. You will be required to care for them. I'm guessing, but I think this could be Zeke's only selfless act. He's a difficult character to understand. He seems to truly have loved his dog and cat though. He said it had to be clear before he died. He doesn't want them to perish in the meantime. Did you know about this?"

"No, it's all news to me. This is a large estate," Leif said. He shook his head as he waved his arm in a large circle. "It goes right up to the tree line. I couldn't afford to maintain it, without him."

"His letter reads that all their needs and yours for now are covered, but as soon as the will is probated you will have all rights to it."

"He said that?" Leif asked. He was shaking and Lance thought he might pass out from shock. He remembered Leif kicking Brutus after the concert, but this young man hardly resembled that bad-tempered fellow.

"Yes, that's what is written here. Mind you, we have to find a legal will before we can follow up on anything, so the only thing we know right now is that Zeke did pass away. We know nothing else other than we rescued a girl from here yesterday. Zeke will never go to court, and we'll never know until the girl recovers and tells all. In the meantime, a restoration company will dismantle that room tomorrow."

"Where does that leave me?" Leif asked.

"Right now, you have your hands full taking care of the animals. Did you know about the girl?"

"No. He hated women. What is her name?" asked Fergusson.

"Her first name is Joanne. Did you never meet her? Was she a girlfriend of Zeke's? Lance and I saw her in his van last Saturday at the Keg."

"He didn't have a girlfriend and vowed never to marry. He did have one odd request when I was hired. He said not to bring girlfriends here. I thought it was odd, but I obeyed. I've never found one shorter than me anyway, so that wasn't a problem." He gestured from his feet to the top of his head, referring to his diminutive stature.

Lance had been quiet up to now, but he grinned in response to Leif's remark. "He was helpful to me the night of the concert. If not for Zeke, my equipment might have been damaged in the riot. He helped me get it out of the theatre. I feel bad that that he ended his life so tragically," Lance said.

"I'd only seen the man once or twice when I did security at the theatre. I heard he did some good things in his life," Peters said. "It's always sad to know a man with his talents really wanted to die. He was well known for his precise sound and light co-ordination for various theatre groups. Why did he think life wasn't worth living?"

"When he and I walked back to the theatre the night of the concert to get his cell phone," Lance spoke up, "he told me his mother wasn't good to him, and he thinks the mama dog they had cared for him much more than she did."

"I guess that explains why he loved Bigamy and

Hagar," said Brad. "How old was he when his mother died?"

"He told me," Lance said, "that one day she just disappeared. He lived with her until he was sixteen, but there was little love lost between them. I think she may have been a sex trade worker."

"Disappeared, eh? Interesting," Brad said. "Many sex trade workers get a bad rap from society. Without any skills, they think it's an easy way out. it's not their choice of a career, but it's hard to find a job that pays enough. They do the best they can but often lose their children. We are more tolerant nowadays, but years ago women even put up with domestic abuse to care for their children."

Peters nodded, as he followed Brad and Lance down to the horrible room in the basement. "Prostitution is a harder life than many people think," he said. They stood in the doorway of the basement room and looked at the metal cage still in the center of the room.

"From what I have read, the girls are literally owned by their pimp, so they are forced to do things that they hate. I wouldn't wish it on anyone." Lance said.

"Oh!" uttered Leif as he stood in the doorway shaking, He grabbed the doorknob to steady himself. He slid slowly down to the floor, without another word.

Lance knelt beside the fallen man and put his hand on his shoulder.

"This is a bit much for him. From what he has said, Leif didn't expect this. Poor kid," Lance said. "He's not much older than my son."

A few minutes later Leif opened his eyes and looked around the room Lt Peters supported Leif's shoulders as he held a glass of water to his lips.

"Where am I?" Leif asked as he looked around the room for something familiar.

"You fainted," Lance said. "You are at the bottom of

the stairs.”

“It was to be expected,” Lt. Brad Thomas said. “I’m sure you didn’t expect it to be this bad, but you had to see it. This is why the police taped the property off and the reason you cannot stay here until the investigation is over.”

“I understand.” Leif tried to get to his feet but fell back onto the floor again. Lance gently lifted him and supported him as he stood up.

“Poor kid,” Lance said after Leif finally was able to walk away on his own steam. “Zeke mentioned a martial arts expert he knew when he and I walked back to the theatre the night of the concert. He must have been referring to Leif Fergusson. I think this is a bit too much for him. He’s just a teenager.”

“He’s older than you think. Because of his size and youthful appearance, one would never know he is almost thirty years old. I checked him out after you identified that picture, Lance. I had so much on my mind that it didn’t seem that important at the time. Leif may have just realized some truths about his landlord,” Brad said.

“Zeke mentioned a martial arts expert he knew when he and I walked back to the theatre the night of the concert. He must have been referring to you,” Lance said when Leif came down with a suitcase filled with clothes,

“Probably. I think there are others in Meldrum, but I may be the only one in Rocky Creek. I’m anxious to get the dog and cat back as soon as possible. I’ve been feeding Bigamy and Hagar for the past two years, so that won’t be a

change,” Leif said. “They are my kids now. I promise to be a good dad.” He walked away to get some canned food from the kitchen.

“I know you will,” Brad called after him.

TWENTY

Leif had not wanted to leave his apartment at first when he talked it over with Lance and Lt. Brad Thomas. "I live here," he said, "It's been my home for a long time."

"I understand," Brad said. "However, I think I'd find it very hard to live here with the knowledge that someone almost died not far from where I was sleeping."

Leif frowned as he looked down toward the stairs leading to the first floor, as the three men stood in the hall outside his rooms talking. "I'm not thinking very clearly, I guess. I wish it didn't happen, but I know it did, and I…" He stopped and put his hands over his eyes for a minute. "I don't know where to go if I can't stay here. I have no friends. I have to get out of here. I can't handle it." He shook his head as he looked down.

"I can't even imagine how you feel," Lance admitted. "It would be terrible even thinking of that room. I think you're making the right decision. Getting away for a while so you can think clearly is a good decision. You do have friends, Leif. I'm your friend and my son Lanny is your friend too."

The officer nodded his head. "I agree. If you would like, Lance and I will help you gather up some essential items and then we can review your options."

"Are there any other choices?" Leif asked. He looked up at the large police officer and tried to smile. "Or is leaving the property the only possible option I have?"

Brad Thomas nodded. "Yes, there are. Often when a house has been the scene of some terrible deed it is destroyed. I don't know how you feel about that."

"Better for you not to be here until a decision is made,"

Brad said. "If you own the property, it will be your decision so you will have to wait until the will is read. It will be a new beginning. Do you mind if I call you Leif?"

"Not at all," answered Leif with a faint smile. "After all it is my name."

He rather unwillingly packed several suitcases and boxes from his apartment with enough food, clothing, and other essentials to last for a week. He took a last walk around the rooms and packed enough cat and dog food to last for a while.

He looked towards the stairs leading to the lower floor with a sad smile, Brad and Lance exchanged glances. "Have we met before?" Brad asked, trying to change the subject.

"Yes," Leif said. "I think we met once at the theatre."

"That's what I thought. You were with Zeke."

"Yes," Leif said. "I went to the concert with him, but I didn't stay. I wasn't quite myself that night." He hesitated and looked at the officer and smiled.

"I noticed that," Brad said. "Although a lot of people were the same that night. It was difficult to know the difference."

Leif smiled guiltily.

"I understand how you feel about being in a place where you know bad things happened," Lance said. "You will eventually have to come back and deal with it but right now the best thing to do is get away somewhere quiet so you can think. However, we must do what Lt. Thomas thinks is best as he is in charge,"

"I would leave if I were you. No matter how you look at it, this house will carry the stains for a long time, and you may not want to move back into it," Brad advised.

"If it will be for a long time, how will I get all my things out? I don't want to leave them here, and I may never be comfortable living in this house again," Leif said. "What if

I find out I really do own it?"

"It will depend upon what memories you have of your time here as a child. If. However, it is accepted that a house of bad memories such as a murder or other happenings could be torn down. Such as a room in a house where a murder was committed or in this case a torture chamber, often the house is destroyed."

"I don't think I would want to live here knowing that room existed," Leif said. "But I …." He hesitated. "Actually, it was added a long time after the original house was built. What if it was not cleaned up by the Restoration Company, but torn down?" He walked over to the window and studied the scenery.

"Hmmm," muttered Brad. "You are right. Mind you, there are some legal issues we would have to clear but it would certainly be a solution. I'll look into it. We have taken a number of photos of the room as well as fingerprints. I believe that would be the best solution, Leif. As soon as we know if it belongs to you, the work could be done.

"Anything you want to take with you can be moved by our crew. Just let me know and I'll arrange for it," Brad promised. "Have you ever thought of having Hagar trained as a sniffer dog?"

"What's that?" Leif asked.

"Narcotics. He's not a puppy but he is well-behaved and has obviously had some training. He could become a therapy dog too," Brad said.

"I will think about it," Leif said "I like the idea of having him trained as a therapy dog. He sure comforted me on a few occasions. And Bigamy could be a therapy cat. Do they have therapy cats?"

"Why not?" Lance said with a smile as he and Leif exchanged glances

Leif Fergusson decided it was high time the Lab, as

Zeke had jokingly called it, was dismantled entirely now that he was gone. He was excited to realize he would no longer have to operate the illegal business for him. Because of his university training, he'd learned quickly but now the lab was no longer needed. He certainly was not planning to mix up any more concoctions if he didn't have to do it. His ambition was to mix medications for the good of humanity, and to save lives, not for the wealth of someone willing to prey on vulnerable addicts. It made him angry to think of his role in that business. He knew that Zeke would never have to answer for any of his crimes. Maybe the rightful owner would, though. He shuddered when he realized that could be himself.

He'd slept fitfully the night before because there was so much on his mind. The central cabin's room was comfortable enough, although it was sparsely furnished and rather unattractive. For a man who loved the artistry of mixing up a prescription to save a life, the plain cabin hardly fit the bill.

The temperature had climbed into the high thirties Celsius, so he revved up the dirt bike and roared up the hill. At the top, the building was hidden by the lush evergreen trees. He parked the bike and unlatched the door and let himself inside.

As long as Leif had obeyed his wishes, Zeke had been a reasonable boss. There were days that Leif felt as if Zeke owned him, and that was not a good feeling. He was tired of the slavery, as he secretly called his association with him. He knew he'd paid off the debt long ago, yet Zeke always found something else to pin onto him to keep him under his rigid control.

Leif wasn't sorry he'd borrowed the money to give his mother a few more years, but somehow Zeke had found a way to make him indebted to him for what appeared to be the rest of his life.

He asked himself, *How can I put this behind me?* He struggled to think up a way. The lab had to go. With that in mind, he loaded the Jeep with everything associated with the lab. There were boxes of empty bottles, cases of dried leaves, liquids, and powders. He drove up the hill until he reached an old, abandoned gravel pit. The only way to get rid of them permanently was to destroy them. Without thinking of it as covering up the evidence, he started up the Bobcat he used during the spring run-off season to keep the roadway from flooding. He actually smiled as he destroyed the drug paraphernalia with a sledgehammer. What a good feeling it was to see that hateful crap smashed to smithereens!

After scattering the remaining powders and dried leaves over the gravel, he covered it with lime and used the machine to smooth it over tidily. It was getting dark when he was finished destroying it all. The final job was to pour the many bottles of liquids into small excavations he had dug just above the tree line. After he'd covered them with soil and more lime, he smoothed them over, he admired his handiwork. He loved using the powerful little Bobcat The only thing that still bothered him was the fear that the contents of the bottles would affect the wildlife in the area.

The bottles and beakers were another problem, so he broke some of them up, put them in the garbage bin, and hauled them to the dump. He smoothed that area with the Bobcat too. Its small size made it the perfect machine.

The sweat dripped off his body as he looked distastefully at his dirty clothes. "Ugh! Why didn't I go for a swim while I was near the creek?"

He parked the jeep at the work site at the top of the hill after he'd cleaned up all the dirt. Just as he was climbing onto the bike to go to the cabin that was now his home, a car pulled up and two uniformed officers approached.

"Mr. Fergusson, I'm glad we found you at home. You look as though you've been working. Do you mind if we look around?" said the tallest of the two men. He introduced himself as Sgt. Tom Higgins and his partner as Jon Erickson.

"Go ahead," Leif said. "Anything in mind you'd like to see?"

"Yes, I'm interested in the laboratory you run up here." He pointed to the small building, a sarcastic smile on his face. "May we go in?"

"Sure," Leif said, purposely overlooking that he'd called it a lab. "I'll unlock the door for you. Nothing much to see. It's just an empty building. I come up here every so often to keep it clean and free of rodents" he said, glad that it was the truth. "The creek attracts them, you know." He opened the door and gestured for them to go in first. "I'm thinking of building some more cabins. Golden Harp Creek runs through the property up above. There's a small lake too. I plan to look into it and probably have it rezoned as a business." He pointed toward a grove of evergreens.

"How far does this property go?" Sgt. Jon Erickson asked, looking up the hill.

"Another half mile above the tree line. Zeke Geisbrecht left the property to me in his will, which still has to be probated, but he once told me he thought about building cabins," Leif said, amazed at his calm state of mind. Before they'd arrived and put him on the spot, all he'd wanted to do was destroy a part of his life he hated and no longer needed to survive. Now he'd done that, he felt as if a huge burden had been lifted from his shoulders.

Ten minutes later, the two officers climbed back into their car looking rather sheepish.

As the last rays of sunshine disappeared over the

186

horizon, Leif walked to the cabin carefully pushing the bike ahead of him. He said a silent prayer as he opened the door and ushered Hagar inside for the night. Bigamy had already made himself comfortable on Leif's bed.

***

Officers Higgins and Erickson reported to Brad the following day. "I thought you said there was a drug operation going on up the hill at Zeke Geisbrecht's place," Higgins said. "We went up to see it yesterday and nothing there. We saw the little guy who will own the property and he took us into it and let us look around."

"Nothing?" Brad uttered. "Interesting. We knew Zeke didn't use drugs himself, but we were told he had a meth lab among other things, going on up there. He was a ruthless SOB. However, the electricity bill never exceeded the usual charges so we thought he might be tapped into someone's meter."

"Nope," Erickson told him. "Fergusson said the Golden Harp Creek runs through the summit and Geisbrecht had wanted to turn it into a fishing lodge eventually. It would be a big job and require clearing some of the trees and bushes away, so he said he'd have to give it some thought.

"Good idea," Brad said, still looking skeptical. "I'll believe it when I see it. I think Fergusson is straight enough, but Zeke was a strange character. He may have used Ferguson. Zeke probably took advantage of his gullibility and worked him hard."

"Possible," said Higgins.

"Right," said Erickson.

"By the way," Higgins announced, "We may as well get rid of the police tape. It's not serving any purpose now, anyway."

"Yeah?" Brad asked. "It may be too soon. I'll look into it, but I think it should stay up until the case is closed."

TWENTY-ONE

Lance had just finished gathering the eggs and having an in-depth conversation with his three favourite hens, Hope, Jenny, and Glenda when his cell phone rang. "Brutus! It's great to hear from you. I was just thinking of calling you. What's up?"

"Are we still planning to do the Freddy Gonzales Memorial Concert? Haven't heard from you for a while."

"Yeah. Things have been kind of busy recently, but I still want to do it." He tossed a handful of wheat on the ground from a shiny tin bucket and filled their water trough. They stared at his cell phone when he turned it to speaker phone. He brushed the stray kernels of wheat off his sweater and sat down on a bench outside the coop to chat on the phone. "I haven't forgotten it, Brutus. I did talk to Morley and Steve about it, and they're interested. Do you want to talk to Glenda? She seems really fascinated by your voice."

"Only if she is more attractive than you are. Her voice is a little cracked, like a chicken. Are you in the chicken coop by any chance?" He laughed at his own joke.

"Yeah, I was feeding the girls."

"That's nice," Brutus said. "Don't forget to call me when you do plan the concert. We can't have it in the Coral Reef though. Any idea where we can have it?"

"Not yet but we're working on it," Lance assured him. He hung the bucket on a nail just inside the chicken coop.

"Oh, by the way, Joanne Riker is the same girl Zeke had locked up in that horrible cage in his house. I knew her in school and used to help her with her homework. I went in to see her at the hospital and she remembered me too, so she gave me permission to call her father. He was pleased when

I told him I'd been to see her."

"That's great, Brutus. Is she improving? That was a cruel experience she went through. I'm glad you visited her and talked to her family."

"Yes, she is recovering, and her dad is glad I called. I had to laugh when he said he was honoured to know a big strong guy like me would look after his little girl. I didn't tell him that I'm only five feet eight, so my bigness is not very impressive."

Lance joined in the laughter but became serious, reminding Brutus that a man does not have to be huge to have a big heart. "He's right…you have the inner strength to take care of her."

"Morley works on her floor, so he also called her family and confirmed she was there. He said her father came in to see her. She is not able to speak yet and she can't walk, but she is alive."

"I hope she will have a full recovery. Poor soul! It made me sick to imagine how terrible it must have been. I kept thinking of my own daughter when I saw her. Her dad must be beside himself with worry and anger. We want the best for our kids, and feel protective toward them," Lance leaned against the door.

"I'd like to get my hands on that idiot and teach him a lesson he'd never forget. I'd beat him to a pulp and after he'd dirtied his britches, I'd rub his damn nose in it," Brutus snarled. "I hope he gets the book thrown at him."

"I don't blame you," Lance agreed. He visualized doing it himself. "It would serve him right. How did she communicate?"

"She only moved her lips, but I could read what she was trying to say. She appeared happy to see me. We had lost touch after graduation." Brutus said, his voice becoming very quiet.

"Funny how that happens. Same for me and Andrea. Getting in touch again must have been in the stars." Lance said, certain that Brutus would know by the sound of his voice that he was smiling.

"The doctor said she has a good chance of a complete recovery because she is young and in good health. I was surprised that he spoke to me at all, but he seemed to welcome my interest. After speaking with Morley and the doctor, I felt that Joanne was in good hands."

"That's good news, Brutus. She must have gone through hell before she was taken to the hospital," Lance said.

"I think you're right," Brutus answered.

"Oh, Brad and I are getting together to play some music tomorrow night. My kids and Andrea are joining us so why don't you come along, too? Perhaps the music would be good for you. Mind you, we will not be playing concertos or Beethoven and Brahms, because the youngsters are just learning."

"Sure, as long as Glenda and her girlfriends aren't coming too. I guess we could play the Chicken Reel for them, though." Brutus suggested and chortled.

"No, seven o'clock is past their bedtime." He could hear Brutus still chuckling on as he hung up.

***

When Brad came over that evening armed with a music book, and a list of tunes they might be able to play together, he was somewhat negative, "I'm surprised you want to put on a concert in Freddy's honour after the rude way he treated you," he said as he dumped the books on the coffee table in the music room and pulled up a chair. "Is this where you want me to sit? I've had a rough day at work, so I hope you don't mind if I sit down."

"Fine with me," Lance said. "When Brutus gets here,

ask him where he wants you. He plays lead guitar. We aren't very formal, but the kids like to join us once in a while." He sat down at the piano and played a series of arpeggios.

"Hey I like that!" Brad said. He looked up in time to see Brutus park his red convertible next to Steve's Monarch and, with his guitar under one arm, quickly march to the door.

"Here's the boss-man and Steve," Lance said, getting up. "Now we can organize ourselves properly!" He opened the door to the music room for Brutus with a big grin. Heathcliffe wagged his tail and gave Lance a doggy smile.

After the usual greetings, Brutus took his place in the coveted lead guitar spot and grinned at the members of the new group. "What's the name of your group?"

"The Deadbeats!" Jeannie said as she played a few somewhat disjointed chords on her mandolin.

"Great name for the maverick group," Brutus said. He took his guitar from the brown leather case, dusted it off with a white cloth and tuned it.

"Maybe we should call ourselves the Mavericks," chirped Jeannie.

"Nope, let's stay with the Deadbeats," Brutus said. "I like that name." He played a G major chord across the six strings and sat down.

Lanny picked up his clarinet and tuned it to the piano without speaking.

"Clarinet?" his dad asked "You haven't been playing the clarinet for very long. Do you think you can handle it tonight?"

"Yes. Since Mr. Thomas and Mom are taking turns on the piano, I'm playing the clarinet. I'm not good enough to play in the school band yet." He grinned at his dad.

"I know. I'm the director," Lance said with a chuckle. "Come on, Jeannie, get your mandolin tuned to the piano.

Deadbeats are on stage!"

"What should we play first? A rousing chorus of Twinkle-twinkle little star?" Roy asked. "I think I'll play rhythm guitar tonight. "

"Sure," Andrea said, "Even I can play Twinkle. Learned it when I was six." She giggled.

"Good. We won't talk about my clarinet playing then!" Lanny said.

"About the same as my level on the guitar," Roy said. He looked at Brutus and grinned self-consciously.

"And mine on the mandolin," Jeannie piped up, as she played her unique version of a couple of bars from The Entertainer

"Hey that's good! I recognise it. Let's play easy stuff tonight, eh?" Steve pushed Lance off the piano stool. "Go play the drums or something. I can't stand here with these crazy drumsticks in my hand while you murder everything on the piano."

With a peal of laughter Lance picked himself up, grabbed the drumsticks and did an impressive drum roll on the top of the coffee table, the side of a jug of lemonade and the corner of the door.

A few minutes later Brad asked, "Jeannie, how come you're playing 'Mary had a little lamb, while we're playing Round and round the Mulberry bush? It's not even in the same key."

"I can't play any more pieces," she said with a shy smile. "I'm only on page six of my book."

Brad leaned over and looked at her music. "Okay, but it won't work if we aren't playing in the same key. Try it in G Start on B and it should work. It's in the same count so that's a good thing. "

"Really?" Jeanie piped up "You want me to play it by ear?"

"Yes, if you can."

"I'll try." After a good natured laugh, she managed to play it in G without too many mistakes.

"That doesn't sound bad, really," Roy said. "A few strange harmonies but surprisingly, it's not as bad as I thought. "

"Right," agreed Brad. "It's possible to play two tunes together; they call it counterpoint."

"Hey, that worked!" Andrea got the giggles, again, and nearly choked from laughing.

"I like The Deadbeats, and I'm proud to be a member of this very talented group," Brutus announced. He bowed to an invisible audience.

***

And so the evening commenced. While the tomfoolery was part of the fun, the mood was set to play an hour of real music too. With much laugher, the session ended with ginger ale, chips, and cookies.

"Thanks, Lance, for a great evening. I'll keep your comments in mind. Bye now! It was fun. I'd be honoured to call myself a member of The Deadbeats any time!" Brad said with a chuckle as he walked toward the door. "I haven't had so much fun for ages."

"We should do it again. The Deadbeats are a talented bunch. The cookies are good too," Steve announced, as he dumped the last five off the plate into his duffel bag, much to Andrea's amusement.

"Oh, Brutus, "How is Joanne Riker doing? Is she the girl you knew in school?" Andrea asked.

"Yes, I called her family and told them," Brutus said. "Morley saw her as well."

"Good, I asked about her, too and the doctor said she was suffering from anxiety and hadn't been able to sleep."

"I'm not surprised," Lance said quietly.

TWENTY-TWO

On Sunday morning Lance decided to visit Brutus to talk about the concert in person. He knew he should get it together, but his mind had been so filled with negative thoughts he found difficult to concentrate. Perhaps Brutus' straight forward manner was what he needed. After telling Andrea where he was going, he hopped into his truck and made an impromptu visit.

"Hi, Lance. What brings you up here this morning?" Brutus asked as he looked up from the book he was reading while seated on an ornate garden bench in the park-like area at the front of the Falgaar home. "Have a chair."

"Hi Brutus. After you phoned, I realised we do have to talk about the concert. Should we really do it?" he said as he got out of his car and slammed the door. "This is a magnificent piece property. Every time I see it from the road when I drive by, I am in awe. Your dad's gardeners are true professionals when it comes to landscaping." He looked around at the big trees and the magnificent rose gardens above the home.

"Yeah," Brutus said proudly. "He hires the best." He studied Lance for a minute. "You don't seem very positive about the concert. I thought you still wanted to do it." He laid his book on the bench and stood up.

"I do" Lance said. "I guess I'm worried about paying for it. Renting the venue and all the other things. Well, you know…"

"I thought I told you that my dad has already put a down payment for it. Quit worrying about it."

"But it costs big money for the Convention Centre. How can we pay it back?" Lance looked worried.

"By putting on a terrific concert with all the best music from Freddy's repertoire and making him proud that Meldrum City produced such a well-known performer as Freddy Gonzales. You really are a goose." Brutus said with a laugh.

"Down payment?

"That's what I said. He has already put money down on it and there is more in the bank set aside for any surprise debts. Your job is to begin getting the group together to rehearse. Now get with it," Brutus said, as if spending thousands of dollars to put on a concert was an every- day occurrence.

'Okay, I gotcha!" Lance said. He sat down on the end of the bench without looking what he was doing and exclaimed, "Ouch, that hurt!" as the other end flew up and dumped him on the ground.

"What happened?" Brutus asked as he ran over to assist Lance to get up. "Are you okay?"

"Yeah. My own fault. I guess I sat on the end of the bench where the ground was uneven. Bet I have a nice bruise on my you-know-what!" Lance said as he pulled himself up

Brutus put his hand over his mouth to stifle a laugh. "I saw you land hard enough to rattle the whole house. I hope you didn't break anything." He threw back his head and laughed.

"No, I'll live. It wasn't *that* funny! I probably have a nice bruise." He joined in the laughter.

"I'll take your word for it and put the coffee pot on. There's nothing like a nice hot cup of coffee to make it all better," Brutus said. "Let's go around the back." He led the way and pointed to another sturdy bench. "Sit on this one. It won't dump you. We dump-proofed it this year." He pointed at another bench at the end of the lawn below the steps leading to the back entrance. and headed toward the house.

"What have you got in there?" Lance asked when Brutus came back with a tray and a saddlebag filled with something edible, he hoped. "Booze?"

"No, not this time," he said. "Bandages to mend your hiney! And a couple of soft drinks to get you in a better mood. Come on, let's talk about the concert. You're the guy who lectured us about only remembering Freddy for his music."

"Okay." Lance looked down at his shoes.

"Let's forget all the other things. Not worth it. This will be the best concert we have ever given." Brutus parked himself into a white garden chair near to a picnic table and opened the saddle bag."

Lance leaned over to get a better look. "Cookies, drinks, glasses, fruit, chocolate. ---Good heavens! You packed a banquet. If I eat all that…!"

"There will be no room for bad thoughts," Brutus finished the sentence as he handed Lance a bag of goodies and proceeded to help himself to a dark chocolate bar. "Do we have a date yet?"

"No, but…"

"No buts. How about October first week?"

"Yeah, but …"

"Okay, that'll work. Who's in charge of decorations?

"Uh."

"Great! I think that would be a job for Charlie."

"What about a budget?"

"We won't need one. Dad said the rest of the money is in the bank for it," Brutus stood up and said, "It's all arranged. Now you just use your energy to keep thinking positively. Work out the programme and leave the cash thing to us. And in the meantime, here's some salve for your butt! Take it home and spread it on the area. I don't know what's in it, but it works. Drink your coffee before it gets cold."

"Yes dear," Lance said with a chuckle as if he was talking to his wife.

Brutus snickered and said, "You're welcome!" in his best falsetto voice.

After a good laugh Lance sat thinking about the concert while he ate the doughnuts and listened to Brutus chatting. *The best one we've ever given? Now that would be good.*

When at last the goodies were all consumed and the plans appeared to be making themselves, Lance had to smile at the way Brutus handled things.

TWENTY-TWO

As Lance drove past Zeke's big house on his way home from visiting Brutus he smiled as he compared the two men. They were so different from one another and yet Brutus' family was equally as wealthy as Zeke.

Did Zeke have other investments, such as stocks and bonds? His home was one of the most beautiful places in Meldrum City and Zeke had given the impression as being a very clever money manager. It took cash to keep up such a prestigious estate.

Since his death there had been so many changes. Leif was now considered to be the legal heir to Zeke's wealth; the cat and dog had to get used to not seeing Zeke for special treats, and a young girl was in hospital because of her association with him. How many others had suffered a similar fate at his hands? In Meldrum City alone there were a number of missing persons. Were any of them associated with Zeke? Lance felt sick to his stomach when he thought about it.

He decided to take a detour on his way home and stop at the Convention Centre. He didn't expect to find it open but when he saw Charlie's sports car parked there, he decided to go in.

"What brings you here?" Charlie asked when Lance met him coming down the stairs.

"I wanted to see the building because I'm in charge of all the plans for Freddy's Farewell concert, and I don't know where to start." Lance looked around at the massive building.

"*The* beginning—that's where you told me to start when I was learning to speak English," Charlie said, with a smirk. "I'm cleaning it after last night's concert, but I didn't expect to see you here."

"No, I was thinking the same thing. I guess you are working hard," Lance said.

"Brad and his wife are very good to me, and I get lots of work. He told me last night to keep an eye who comes into the building tonight."

"How come?" Lance asked.

"Maybe I'm not supposed to say anything," Charlie said. "Last week his dog digged up a bone. Ugh I mean–dug up a bone near Coral Reef. You see in paper?"

"No, I missed that," Lance answered. "Did Brad seem worried? He's not really involved with that case now, you know."

"He just say it was odd that new bone found. And something else too. Dog bring it to Brad."

"What was it?" Lance asked.

"Don't know," Charlie said. "He left it in the room. Probably a cat toy. I clean room and leave it there for Igor."

"Does Igor go to the Coral Reef theatre when Brad goes there?"

"Sometimes Brad takes him there because he knows the place better than Brad does" Charlie tried to contain his mirth, but a snicker escaped his lips.

"A kitty detective, eh?" Lance said with a chuckle. "I'm really glad you are getting more work. You speak English much better now you are working with others. Do you get to play the guitar and sing now, too?"

"I play lots now, in the evenings when I'm not working. I miss the theatre though," Charlie said wistfully. "It was my home for almost a year."

"So do I," Lance said. He looked thoughtfully into the distance. "I miss seeing you too. This concert is more complicated than school concerts, though. The band members expect me to choose the music and decide how to decorate the stage, as well as hire someone to do the lighting and the sound. I will need some help. As odd as it seems, we will miss Zeke."

"You think he killed Freddy?" asked Charlie. Lance looked at him curiously.

"I don't know, Charlie. I don't have any answers. I'm not sure there are any other suspects. However, we can leave that for the law to handle. Zeke died in the hospital three weeks ago, so let him rest in peace now," Lance assured him.

"Okay, Boss," Charlie agreed "Lots of people in theatre. Big fellow threaten you, try to burn your trailer. I scared I be trapped in the theatre, so I wented out. I see some bad things."

"Charlie, did you tell the police what you saw? "Lance asked.

"No, I was scared," Charlie said.

"I understand because we were all being questioned that night," Lance said. "Zeke acted strange, and it did make everyone wonder if he was involved. I understand he told the cops he would kill himself if he had to go to jail, so I think it was accepted that he killed Freddy."

"I not see him for long time," Charlie said

"No, he died in hospital," Lance repeated. "Three weeks ago. I'll find an old newspaper so you can read it for yourself."

"Good," Charlie said. "I help with concert. I know stage stuff too. No concerts in theatre now. Come in so I can go home."

"Okay. You must talk to Brad about what you saw, eh?"

"Okay," he promised. "Brad works real hard. He likes the cat, and the dog likes him too. I'll say you told me to tell him."

"Please come with me while I see the stage, Charlie. I don't have a key yet," Lance said.

"Okay. I like stage but I like Coral Reef better. I at home there, and Igor visit me when everyone leave," he said.

"Well," Lance said with a chuckle, "You get to visit with Igor every day still, because you both live there. He is still your best buddy."

Lance smiled as he allowed Charlie to guide him through the massive Convention Centre. He was amazed at how much Charlie had learned in his short time away from the theatre. Where once he had been uncertain about his future, Charlie appeared more confident.

"Where is Igor today?" he asked.

"He is Brad's cat, but he sleep in my closet sometimes," Charlie said. "When Brad goes out he puts Igor in my apartment. We need to go now."

"That's good for you both. Bye, Charlie," Lance said. The two men walked to their cars, He watched as Charlie jumped into the front seat of his green sports car and drove away. It was good to see him working and not hiding out in the theatre. It was a better life for him. No doubt he still missed his family and girlfriend back home, but he was young, and would adjust.

He puzzled over what Charlie had seen that night, besides the fellow who set fire to his trailer, and hoped he'd recall it soon. Did he see something more important? Why did Zeke want to die if he hadn't killed Freddy? Why did he just accept that he was more than a suspect? Who was in that room at Zeke's house besides Zeke and Joanne? He hoped Joanne would remember. She still was not very lucid and was unable to speak above a whisper. She had worn a gag but perhaps she was blindfolded as well. He vowed to speak to Brad about it. Charlie was right. If Zeke had not killed Freddy, even in death, he should not be blamed for a crime he had not committed. Where was the real killer? Walking around free to kill again? He drove home feeling satisfied with good visit with Charlie, at the same time wishing he had all the answers.

***

No," Lance said. "I was here chatting with Charlie. He looks happy now he's working. He was just leaving."

"Great guy. Good trustworthy worker," Brad said. "I'm glad you introduced me to him."

"I liked hm. He's still shy but his English has improved immensely. He reads a lot and studies a great deal. He is lonely for his family though. I think he wants to talk to me about something, but he seems too shy to bring it up. He's started a couple of times and then walked away," Brad said.

"He told me something today that you ought to know. I wasn't going to bring it up, but since you have, I'll tell you what he said. Please be diplomatic if you talk to him because he was very nervous," Lance said.

"It's good if he told you what's bothering him. Spill the beans, eh? I will go easy. He's a good person and I am glad I gave him a chance to have a suite of his own and a job and get out of the theatre."

"He said on the night of the concert he was afraid of being trapped in the theatre and he let Igor out, and he was up on the fire escape observing how some people were acting. He saw the guy who set fire to my trailer, and he doesn't think Zeke killed Freddy," Lance said. "I did find Igor out there the next day, if you remember."

"Interesting," Brad said. "I have some doubts also. There are other suspects so it will go to court. Yes that was the day we bought the carrier. However, Zeke is dead. If it wasn't him, then the killer is still at large. Who tortured

Joanne? When she is able to testify, we'll know the truth. There are a lot of questions. Zeke acted so odd that night he made himself a suspect."

"Yes," Lance agreed. "Maybe he was protecting someone. Anyway, talk to Charlie. He's afraid to tell the police what he saw."

"I will." He looked around the Convention Centre and pronounced it perfect for the Concert. "You had better reserve it right away, Lance. Dr. Faulgaar is a generous man. So kind of him to pay for all of it."

While Lance and Brutus were actively planning a Farewell Concert for Freddy, Brad puzzled over the identity of the person who had murdered him. If it wasn't Zeke, who could it have been?

The day after the concert Heathcliffe dug up what appeared to be a human bone in the shrubbery of the parking lot at the Coral Reef Theatre, but there was already an active investigation of the surrounding area. The bone proved to be part of a human remains discovered a month ago and may have been several years old. Obviously there had been suspicious activity at the Reef for some time. The area surrounding the theatre was already known for its gory history, but this bone was of a more recent death, the pathologist said.

After Lance told him Charlie wanted to speak to him but was nervous, Brad had to raise the subject himself. When he and Charlie sat at the table enjoying a last cup of coffee and chatting casually about his observations that night, he mentioned it. He knew Charlie was telling the truth. There had a been a good deal of suspicious activity the night of the concert, which had never been fully investigated.

"I got scared me and the cat would be trapped in the burning building, so I found him, and we went out the fire escape.," Charlie said, his broken English sometimes making it difficult to understand him. "I saw some guys breaking into cars and fighting. I didn't know the fire they set was in Lance's trailer, but I saw them setting fires in lotsa other parked cars too." Charlie had repeated what Brad already knew, but his impromptu eyewitness account gave some new insight as to what the vandals were looking for. "Did you hear anything else?" Brad asked.

"Yeah," Charlie said. "I hear them say cocaine. One guy, he say cocaine all gone. Not where Freddy said it would be. They were bragging about choking him because he wouldn't tell the truth. They were real mad. I saw them breaking into cars and trucks "

"Did you tell anyone about it?' Brad asked.

"No. I on fire escape. Nobody saw me hearing what they said," Charlie said, forgetting the English lessons he'd been taught.

"What were they talking about?" Brad asked.

"Drugs," Charlie explained. "I was scared. Igor scratch me so I let him go because they would have heard me there. They went away but I couldn't find Igor. I got scared so I wented –how you say it? I wented back in and left from the other side. I was scared. They had clubs and guns."

***

The heavy-set Detective Morris sat across the table from Brad in his office. "I think the first person we need to investigate is Jeremiah Bastable," he said. "You already have the murder weapon—that hole reamer came from Bastable's tool case."

His brother?" Brad asked in surprise.. "What would his motive be?"

"That's for us to find out," Morris said. "We got the information from a reliable source."

"Who?" Brad asked.

"The light tech that night, as well as Aldo Cody, one of the roadies from the Shot-glass Five," he said. "They were the opening band that played before the concert. We heard about that before you came and gave us your info. We're way ahead of you," Morris said smugly.

"Are you talking about Zeke Geisbrecht? Did he tell you that?" Brad asked, his eyes wide with surprise.

"The same. Maybe you weren't aware that Geisbrecht has been a reliable informant for years. He's helped us solve a number of bothersome cases."

"Are you sure he wasn't the killer?" Brad asked.

"We suspected him, but couldn't to prove it," Morris said. "We always found him to be very reliable, and very well educated. Just a guy who wanted justice to be done."

"Was his DNA ever tested?" Brad asked. "What about Al Cody?"

"Nothing," Morris said. "The cases are closed."

"I see," Brad said. "Zeke's dead now, so he's no longer a source of information. I think his DNA should be tested. What about the opera singer who was missing two years ago and the band leader who disappeared without a trace? There are countless mysterious cases in this theatre alone. It's about time Zeke Geisbrecht was tested too. Don't just test Jeremiah Bastable, and think you've covered everything." He got up, slammed his fist on the table and stomped out of the office.

"Well, you don't need to get sore," Morris called after him.

Gnashing his teeth, Brad got into his squad car and drove away. "Reliable source of information, my ass!" he snarled. "More like he's the killer. I'll be so glad to get out of this business next month."

***

Jem was shocked when he was arrested early Saturday

morning. As soon as he came out of his house ready to walk the ten blocks to work, three police officers came out of the shadows and surrounded him while a fourth man clamped the handcuffs on his wrists. "You're under arrest!" he said.

He didn't resist the arrest, although he was startled. He looked the arresting officer in the eye, and asked, "What am I charged with?"

"Aggravated assault among other charges. We will discuss it on the way to the station," he said.

"In that case you may have the wrong man," Jeremiah said. "I have not been in any altercations. I have no idea what you are talking about."

"They all say that. Tell it to the boys at the station," the uniformed officer said. He read the charges, told him of his rights and led him to the waiting paddy wagon. It all happened so quickly that Jeremiah had no chance to ask questions.

"May I call my father at the shop so I can tell him I will not be coming into work?" he asked, as he quietly did as he was told.

"You can request one phone call when we get to the police station." Officer Forbes said.

"I'm supposed to open up the shop this morning," Jeremiah explained.

"Well, your plans have been changed, haven't they?" Forbes said rather rudely. Jeremiah settled quietly in the back seat and looked around him as the shock of what was happening began to sink in. The bars between him and the two men in uniform were something he'd only seen in the movies, and for some reason, he found them claustrophobic.

When they arrived at the station, Jeremiah was dragged none too gently from the van and escorted into the station where he made his phone call. His father was eating breakfast at home when he received his son's call.

"What are you talking about?" he asked. "You're supposed to open the shop this morning, damn it!"

"I know, Dad, but I've been arrested, and I can't leave."

"Hogwash!" his dad said. "Why? What did you do?"

"Nothing, honestly. I was just leaving the house to come to work when they arrested me. I don't know why."

"Yeah, right. I'll cover for you, but you get down there as soon as you can. It's my day off." Jeremiah could hear his father complaining in the background as he was roughly taken away from the phone and informed that his call had ended. "Your time is up."

He was shoved into a cell until *further notice* and processed. It all happened so fast he had no time to think.

"What are the charges?" he asked.

"Quit pretending you don't know. You can tell it to the judge," the guard said as he turned the key.

It was three o'clock in the afternoon before Jeremiah was formally charged with the murder of Freddy Bastable Gonzaèlas and released in the custody of his astonished father, Frank Bastable.

The ankle bracelet irritated his skin, his orders were strict, and he was only allowed to leave the house to work at the store. His parents had the additional stress of answering all calls themselves. He tried to discuss the charges with them, but they didn't really understand the seriousness of it.

Emergency calls went to another luthier in Meldrum City, taking business away from the shop. His professional quartet was off limits to him as he prepared to spend a considerable amount of time behind bars for the murder of his brother. He may not be able to appear at the Farewell Concert and as he sunk into bed that night, he felt his life was over.

Brad was furious when he discovered that Jeremiah was charged with the murder of Freddy, without even considering that Zeke could have been lying when he gave his so-called reliable information, never had his DNA tested or charged when any of the infractions that Brad knew about, besides the one that sent him to jail two weeks ago What about the torture of Joanne Riker, and the missing opera singer whose shoes were found in his car, or the recent discovery of human bones just above his estate? What about the child who had died as a result of a candy apple given to her Halloween night by one Zeke Geisbrecht, and the woman who was tortured to death in his van five years ago? Brad wondered why he'd been so blind not to have connected the death of the boy who'd overdosed on a drug laced with a lethal dose of an opiate drug traced to Zeke?

What was Leif Fergusson doing associating with a man like Zeke? Reliable informant? Killer?

TWENTY-THREE

Joanne Riker was beginning to recover from her ordeal. With daily therapy, her legs were gaining some strength, and the speech therapist was pleased with her progress.

Brad was pleased, too, because her recovery meant she could testify in court about her experiences and the horror she had endured at Zeke's hands, and probably recall some things he may have told her. She was not a girlfriend of Zeke's, but he likely thought she knew too much about him already. "Women are like that, you know," he had told Lance. the night they had walked back to the theatre after the ill-fated concert, "The less they know, the better."

Joanne was someone he used and if Zeke had lived, she may have died at his hands. Out of all the females Zeke had romanced, Joanne was likely the only one who had survived him, as far as Brad was aware. He had checked his notes several times for information. The facts always stopped short of giving him the information he needed.

Brutus was pleased for a different reason, and his parents agreed with him. Dr. Falgaar enjoyed giving his money away for a good cause, and his only son's happiness fit the bill. Brutus' three sisters had enjoyed lavish weddings, and he deserved to be noticed as well.

Brad intended on visiting Leif at his apartment in Zeke's big estate. The young man had not yet moved from the small rooms he rented from Zeke, preferring to wait until the will legally granted him more privileges.

A few days later, Brad phoned Leif. "Good morning Mr. Fergusson," Brad said, "I'd like to come over and chat with you about your plans, if I may. They sound interesting—but I really want to see how you are managing and make an offer to train Hagar as a police dog. I'll be retiring shortly, but I will still be active with the force training dogs."

"Sure, come on over," Leif said. "Hagar is too old to train. He's not a puppy like your other beginners."

"Yes, for some things he would be too old, but he could be trained as a therapy dog," Brad said.

"He's had some obedience training, but I don't want to lose him. I like him and Zeke wanted me to look after him and the cat. Anyway, come to see me and we'll talk about it," Leif said. "Only if I'm involved. I'm not giving up my dog."

"Oh, you wouldn't be required to give him up," Brad said. "Perhaps you could join him and work as a team. I recognise that Hagar is a smart dog, or I wouldn't have suggested it."

"When did you see Hagar?" Ferguson asked.

"The day Lance and I came up to get Zeke's medication when he was in the hospital. Hagar could have chewed us up, but he responded well to me talking to him," Brad said.

"Well, okay," Fergusson said. "I guess so. Two cops were up to see me the other day and wanted a tour of the property for some reason. How come you guys are hassling me?"

"I hope you don't think we're just giving you a bad time," Brad protested. "I'm merely interested in your plans." He nodded wisely to his reflection in the hall mirror at his home. Leif may not be as easily manipulated as he thought. Perhaps he should call Lance to come with him? Lance had a way with young people that Brad didn't possess. He gave him a call.

"Hi, Lance," he said. "I should have called you earlier, but I just thought of it now. I'm going over to visit with Leif Fergusson in about thirty minutes, and I realized I don't

210

have as good a relationship with the younger generation as you do. Would you come with me? I wouldn't ask you, but I know you are still on summer holidays from school."

"Okay," Lance said. "You've just blown my last excuse. Any reason you're going to see him that I should know?"

"Well, yes, but no reason for you to panic," Brad explained. "I was told awhile back that Geisbrecht ran a drug operation on that property. We sent two men up to see Fergusson and they came back with a story that it was an empty building. Fergusson told them he intended on building a fishing lodge."

"I've never heard any stories, Brad," Lance said. "I'll go with you, but don't expect me to contribute anything. I've only seen Fergusson a couple of times."

"I know but your presence would help him relax.'

Brad piled into the car with Heathcliffe in his own space behind the barrier, and headed over to pick Lance up before he went to see Fergusson. Heathcliffe was always pleased to go to work. His tongue lolled out of the side of his mouth as he looked around at the scenery, probably wondering what he had to do this time.

Leif Fergusson met them at the gate when they arrived and directed Brad to a parking area not far from a tumbling creek rushing somewhere in a hurry.

"I didn't notice that creek the last time I was here," Brad said.

"It's swollen a bit since you were here," Leif said. "The last snowpack has melted up above and will be finished about the time more snow falls next month. Anyway, welcome to Zeke's estate."

Hagar came running out to greet Leif and was very curious when he noticed Heathcliffe was in the car. He stood up on his hind legs to get a better look at Heathcliffe through the window.

"Not yet, Heathcliffe," Brad said. "Be quiet." Heathcliffe settled down and sat watching Hagar without making any more noise. At Leif's direction, Hagar stopped barking and watched him without another doggy comment.

"I suppose you want a tour of the property, too?" Leif said, pointing up the hill to the long building up above. We'll drive up in the Jeep. It's too hot to walk up today."

He jumped in the front seat and indicated for Lance and Brad to get in.

"No, Brad said. "I'll drive up. Heathcliffe is all ready to go, so Leif in the front to give me directions and Lance in the back."

It only took a few minutes to get up to the tree line where Leif opened the cabin door and directed them to go in.

"Take your time," he said. "It may take a while to see everything that isn't in here, but it's worth it." He laughed at his own joke.

"What's above here?" asked Brad, ignoring his humour.

"Golden Harp Creek, an old gravel pit and evergreen trees. A whole forest of them. Which tree would you like to see?" Leif asked. "The one on the left is about one hundred and twenty years old. It's an old growth forest so no clearing will be allowed here. There's a waterfall up a couple of miles. About the only thing I might do is build a few more cabins and open a fishing lodge where the creek runs into Winfry Lake. What do you think?"

"Good idea," Brad said rather weakly. "What will you do with this cabin?"

"If I subdivide, it could become another house. I haven't thought much about it. I'm too shocked yet at the idea of owning all this property so I haven't had time to digest it yet," Leif admitted.

"Let's walk up to the creek and old gravel pit," Brad said.

"Sure," Leif agreed, feeling confident. "It's not far. Not much to see up there." He pointed to a well-used trail and lead the way.

Hagar ran ahead exploring all the scents and sights of the old gravel pit. Heathcliffe walked sedately beside Brad, looking up at him every so often for new orders even though he was not wearing his working cape. "I'm glad that the two dogs are friends," he said. "It makes it so much easier. Hagar has just had enough training to follow orders well." He looked over his shoulder and tripped on an exposed rock.

"Oops!" Brad exclaimed, flailing his arms and doing some fancy steps as he regained his balance. "What's that?" He bent do to see what he had tripped over.

Leif turned white. A piece of glass shining in the midday sun was in plain sight.

"You never know what you'll run into in a wild place like this," he said, trying to look confident. He tried to catch Lance's eye. That didn't help as Lance was looking at the object too.

Brad bent down and picked it up. "Looks like it's from a glass bottle," he said. He stumbled again and dropped it.

"Oh, kids come up here to drink now and again," Lance said, with a chuckle. "Not always soft drinks, either. Even when I was a teen, this is where we came. One time I stubbed my toe on the top of a coke bottle, maybe twenty years old. Come on, let's go. It's getting late."

Brad smiled knowingly. "I remember those days, too," he said. "Kids will be kids."

"When do you legally take possession?" Lance asked Leif.

"There's no time frame," Leif said, glad to change the

subject. "These things are always painfully slow. All I know at this point is that I must look after the two animals, and Zeke doesn't want a funeral or memorial service."

"It could take a while to be probated," Brad commented.

"In the meantime, what will be done?" Lance asked, filling in an awkward pause.

"He'll be cremated and his ashes destroyed. My orders are to care for his two animals, and Zeke's estate forever. I like them both so no problem. I intend on fulfilling my obligations to Zeke," Leif said.

Brad drove down the hill deep in thought. Leif climbed out at the bottom of the hill and walked toward the house.

"He's a cool dude," commented Lance.

"I'd say so," said Brad as he drove out onto the main highway. "He may be young, but he's been around the block a few times. I think he's sincere about taking care of the cat and dog, but I am certain that Zeke used him to run some sort of a drug operation above." He made a mental note to go back up the hill and investigate the gravel pit. "I heard that he was an unwilling partner, but for some reason he did the work."

"I hadn't heard a thing about him other than he taught martial arts downtown. Could be that now Zeke is not his boss he no longer needs to do that work. If he did, it has vanished into thin air," Lance said. He leaned back against the seat and studied the scenery.

"Hmm!" said Brad as he entered downtown Meldrum. "You could be right. At one time he owed Zeke a large sum of money, but we have reason to believe he paid it off. I think Zeke was holding something over his head, It's an awful thought, but it happens. The police have been monitoring it for a while because we were told that Leif was not paid for his work there. Strangely the only thing we could find out of order was that Leif didn't keep any of the money he made working for Zeke."

"That doesn't seem right," Lance said. He shook his head and frowned.

"He got a paycheck, but he couldn't keep the money. When we looked into it, we found that Leif's salary was a farce for income tax purposes. He had to return it all to Zeke," Brad said.

"That's awful!" Lance said. "How was Leif able to run the operation with the limited knowledge he would have had?"

"That's where Zeke took advantage of him big time," Brad explained. He tapped a drum rhythm on his knee, "We'd been watching Zeke for a while. Leif didn't have a pharmaceutical degree, but he had taken one year of university before he dropped out for no apparent reason. He was an honor student. When we looked into that, we knew there was something very sinister going on."

"How could Zeke get away with that?" Lance asked. "That's almost like blackmail. Enforced labour isn't lawful."

"It happens more often than you know," Brad said. "Leif may not have done anything, but Zeke seems to have known him for ages and accused him of something unlawful. It may have been a scam."

"Gives me the shivers." Lance was on the verge of getting steamed up. "Do you mean he could have been tricked? Someone may have been blackmailing him."

"It certainly appears so. We haven't finished investigating it, but we know Leif did borrow a sum of money from Zeke when his mother was ill. We believe there was more to it than a cash debt. The only person who knows the truth is Leif himself.," Brad said. "This may be the reason Zeke left him everything."

"Do you know what Zeke was holding over Leif's head?" Lance asked. "Perhaps we should try to find out. If this has been going on for some time and Leif gave up his education to work for Zeke without pay, it seems to me we shouldn't turn a blind eye to it."

"No, but you're putting a different slant on it. Zeke won't pay the penalty now, and Leif is free anyway," Brad said. "However, maybe there were others caught up in the web."

"Exactly what I'm saying," Lance said. "Maybe an extortion ring working under Zeke, to take money and labor from others in return for silence. Zeke's death doesn't mean that someone else in the extortion ring will not take it up and continue harassing him. Zeke won't pay the penalty, but neither will the others unless the ring is broken."

"That's a sober thought," Brad agreed. "I'll look into it. It definitely is not over."

Both Lance and Brad were thoughtful as they headed toward Lance's long driveway. "What puzzles me more than anything are the things that Charlie observed the night of the concert. We talked about it last night after dinner, but I'm not certain where it fits in."

"Did he mention any names?" Lance asked.

"No. He did refer to some guy who worked with the opening band but didn't know his name."

"Maybe he meant the guy who manages the Shot-glass Five. He's that big mouthy guy who orders everyone around. He also works as a roadie. They're a good band but I don't like him. He and Zeke never got along." Lance said.

"Aldo Cody?" Brad asked.

"Yes, I saw him at the theatre often and he was nearly always arguing with someone," Lance recalled.

"Charlie said that cocaine was involved but the brick of cocaine the recipient got was laced with something else and everyone involved was mad," Brad said. "Do you know anything about that?"

"No, but I wonder if that was the one Freddy wanted me to hide, or a different one?" Lance asked.

"Could be the motive for killing Freddy. Do you know that roadie's name," Brad wanted to know.

"Not sure. Funny name. Same guy. Surprised he didn't change it," Lance said.

"Parents call their kids some odd names. I went to school with a girl named Nita Bath," Brad agreed. "I'll look into it."

"Wow!" Lance said. "She must have hated that. I knew one called Urini Potts. That's even worse."

"That's awful," Brad said. They both chuckled.

"Did Charlie know his name?" Lance wanted to know.

"No, but he heard him tell his friends he choked Freddy in his dressing room. That wouldn't do the damage we know Freddy had," Brad told him. "Charlie said he overheard them talking while he was hiding on the fire escape and wanted to get away before he was discovered."

"Probably talking about a drug deal. Would it smell different if it was laced with something else?" Lance said. "I'm not very knowledgeable about it."

"It smells the same and looks the same," Brad said. "Only the effect is different, and I understand it's hard to tell without using it. It's easier to overdose on it."

"I guess the chemical they lace it with is the one that kills."

"Probably. It is in most overdose cases," Brad said as he pulled the car to a halt and thanked Lance for coming along, "The name Aldo Cody does ring a bell in my head, and I'll look into it. Charlie didn't know the names of anyone in the opening band. See you in the next few days. Keep all of this to yourself, Lance. Bye."

"I will," Lance said. He got out of the car and hopped nimbly over the gate and walked up to his back door.

****

Late that night Brad drove his old jeep to the gravel pit by the upper road. With Heathcliffe by his side, he retraced his footsteps of the day before when he had tripped over the bottle. He found the spot finally, after digging around in the wrong place twice. Eventually he got down on his knees and felt around with his gloved fingers. Heathcliffe got down on his haunches beside him and carefully examined the pile of gravel.

"Found it," he whispered. The dog leaned over and sniffed.

Brad scraped up a pile of dirt and put it in a brown glass container. "Shhhh!" he whispered to the dog. "It's not just gravel. I don't want to get Leif in trouble, but at the same time…" He got up from his knees and climbed back into his car, intending to go to the Forensic Laboratory with the jar. However, Mother Nature had other ideas.

Brad had just tightened his seatbelt when he heard a roar. He had barely started the engine when his vehicle was carried in a huge volume of water over rocks and debris across what used to be a field of potatoes.

What had caused a flash flood this time of year? The skies had been clear all day. He looked up at the ski hill ten miles above as the lights turned off. "Oh-oh—melting snow?" It was very hot.

It seemed to last forever as he struggled to keep control of his car. The moving water flung him every direction, until his jeep came to a full stop leaning sideways up against a huge poplar tree. "Damn!" he exclaimed.

What had started a flash flood tonight? Had he tampered with something he should not have done? His fault??

When the water finally stopped flowing, he realized it was probably an act of nature. He gingerly got out after calling for help. "Come on Heathcliffe," he said.

Heathcliffe crawled out and tip-toed through the mud. He looked up at Brad.

He could barely see the mess of uprooted spuds, garbage and something that smelled strong and made his nose run. He was right. It had been a meth lab. Did Leif run it? What?

An investigation? Leif? What was his role? Would he come clean now he was about to be caught red handed. Brad shuddered at the thought.

Just as help arrived on the scene, the irate owner of the potato crop also arrived, dressed in a peculiar getup of jeans over his pyjama pants. The blue flannel legs hung in a muddy mess longer than his jeans, dripping water in his already muddy shoes.

"What the hell is going on here?" he snarled. "Look what you did to my spuds!" He focussed his flashlight at a murky mess of muddy roots and broken leaves.

"This is the police," Brad said, forgetting he had not checked into the office first. "I was caught in a flash flood. I didn't mean to destroy your crop."

"What's that funny smell?" asked the farmer after he had introduced himself as Andy Cummings. He took a length of toilet tissue out of his pocket and wiped his eyes. "Smells like some toxic chemical. Was there a lab of some kind above here?"

"I have no idea. There's an old gravel pit and some cabins," Brad said lamely. "Look, Mr. Cummings, I'll take your information and name and get back to you in the morning. Sorry about the mess but I think Mother Nature was to blame for the flash flood. Here is my help." He breathed a sigh of relief as he pointed to two police cruisers covered with mud parking to the left of the potato field.

Brad was surprised when Leif came out of the shadows. He hung his head. "My fault," he said. He held out his arms. "Cuff me! Let's get this whole mess over!"

"I'll pick you up tomorrow at ten a.m. No need for cuffs. I'll see you then," Brad said. "Go home and look after your dog and cat. We know what happened, Leif, but hearing it from you is what we want." He drove away, leaving the property owner and Leif staring after him.

"Is your name Leif Fergusson?" Mr. Cummings asked.

"I think so," said Leif.

"I getcha!" Cummings replied. "I wouldn't own up to a name like that either. *Gotta* go home. Have a beer and go back to bed. Wanta join me?"

"No thanks. I better go home like he said." He waved as he headed toward the big house.

The following morning when Leif appeared at his office promptly at ten o'clock, Brad was sitting at his desk ready for him "Leif," he said, "I have reviewed the circumstances thoroughly. As you probably know, we have been watching Zeke Geisbrecht for over a year and we know exactly what happened here. "

"Yes, Sir, I understand," Leif said. He wiped his forehead with a red handkerchief.

"I am not entirely excusing you, because you did know what you were doing was wrong. However, if Zeke was alive today, he would be charged with blackmail. Considering the circumstances, we would advise you to compensate Mr. Cummings for his losses." Brad said.

"How much?" Leif asked, his voice shaking.

"He lost about five thousand dollars worth of produce. It would have just been the crop but for the chemicals being used in the laboratory you were obliged to run." Brad said. "However, the work he will have to do to recover the property will be enormous. You are looking at twice that much.”

“I’m sorry,” whispered Leif.

“I think, considering the circumstances, if you offer Mr. Cummings ten thousand bucks from your settlement, he would accept it, and we can close the case.” Brad stood up and offered his hand to Leif.

“You mean I can go?” asked Leif. He wiped his hand across his forehead. “I don’t have to go to jail?”

“No,” Brad said. “The case is closed. I’d like to see you go back to university and achieve your pharmaceutical degree the way you intended. You are still young. Goodbye.”

Heathcliffe wagged his tail in agreement as Leif walked out the door. His master greeted Officer Higgins who *just happened* to come through the door as soon as Leif was out of sight.

“Good job, well done,” Higgins said with a big smile.

***

After arriving home Leif cleaned the mud off his shoes and put his jeans in the laundry basket.

“I’m a lucky man,” he told Hagar, as he climbed back into bed. The dog looked knowingly into his eyes and laid down at the foot of the bed. “Brad Thomas knew all along I was guilty of running that laboratory.” He switched off the light and pulled the sheet over his head and tried to hide from himself. When that didn’t work, he got up and sat beside Hagar on the floor and was soon joined by Bigamy. Bitter tears of remorse ran down his cheeks as he whispered the words he hadn’t wanted to say for the past three years.

“Now I have to think of all those young people whose lives were changed because I was too much of a coward to stand up to Zeke and say ‘no’ All the good I have ever done was cancelled out because I was too scared to do the right thing," He collapsed with his head on the bare tiled floor.

Bigamy purred loudly in his ear and kneaded his shoulder and Hagar cuddled up beside him on the floor until they all fell asleep from pure exhaustion.

The next morning, he called Brad Thomas at home before he'd even had breakfast and tried to turn himself in again.

"Leif, I appreciate what you are saying. You cannot change the past, but you can change the path you will take for the future. It takes courage to face the truth and you have done that. I'll drop in to see you tonight at seven o'clock. There will be no charges, but there are things you can do to reverse the path you were taking. We'll talk about it tonight."

Leif made himself a cup of coffee and ate a doughnut. He looked at himself in the mirror and thanked his lucky stars he had the affection of his two furry pals.

What did the police officer mean? He looked forward to Brad's visit although he also dreaded it at the same time. He admired the beautiful home that would soon be his to keep as many complex thoughts invaded his mind.

Reverse the path into the future? Yes, he wanted to turn his back on what he had done, and the beginning would be paying off the damage done to Andy Cummings' potato field. Next?

His back hurt from sleeping on the bare floor. He whispered to Bigamy, "This is how homeless folks feel every morning!"

He thought about how they must feel after a night on the sidewalk or bare ground. He shuddered as he visualized himself in that predicament.

"There must be something I can do. Money to build homes they can afford?" he told Hagar while he filled up his dog food dish. "Maybe a job so those who have fallen through the cracks can earn some money and feel good about themselves?" The dog wagged his tail while he wolfed down his breakfast.

***

Lt. Thomas arrived punctually at seven o'clock in his trusty old jeep, now free of mud. Leif met him at the door with a smile although the pangs of guilt nagged at his mind. "Come in," he said. "I have already put the coffee pot on. I hope you drink coffee."

"I do," said the officer, "but I'm surprised an athlete like you drinks it."

"Actually, I try to stay away from caffeine, but I serve it to my guests. I do have less lethal beverages on hand. Perhaps we should both be good tonight." He laughed for the first time since the flash flood.

"Good idea," Brad said with a smile. "I've had enough for today anyway. I came to talk to you about some things you could do that would help others and help you as well. Do you have orange juice?"

"Sure do!" Leif said. They both chuckled and Leif felt the negative vibes begin to fade.

"Okay," the officer said. "Orange juice it is." He became serious.

"You mentioned this morning that it is possible to reverse the dangerous path I've been travelling on. Got any suggestions? I had a hard time sleeping last night and I ended up on the floor with Hagar and Bigamy. I actually bawled all over them" Leif admitted, hanging his head.

"I'm not surprised," Brad said. "I've done that too. You are not the only guy who found himself in that predicament. Dogs and cats as natural therapy animals and they know when a human or another animal is hurting."

"I can't imagine you ever blubbered like a baby."

"You'd be surprised to know most of us have done the

same thing." Brad ran his hand over Heathcliffe's back, and smiled sheepishly, recalling an episode he had tried to forget by putting it far into the back of his mind.

"I guess you're right," Leif said with a sniffle. He gave a watery smile.

"Yes," said Brad. "Hagar could learn to be a professional therapy dog. When I retire in a week or two, Heathcliffe will begin training too, and the two dogs could work together. They are already friends. We would benefit also. What do you think?"

"You mean I would have to work with him?" asked Leif.,

Brad smiled as he thought about it. "We both would. I have some experience in that field already. You wouldn't have to give up your dog or quit the Martial arts job. In addition, you would be reversing your own future path."

"Yes," Leif said. "You knew all along I was on a dangerous route, didn't you?"

Leif fidgeted with his pocket watch, turning it around several times before he put it back in his pocket.

Brad smiled at the somewhat fallen soldier before him. "That's behind you, Leif. Life is complex enough already. Rather than looking backward, let's see what tomorrow will bring. You did the right thing in wanting to get rid of the lab It takes a big man to admit he is wrong. Those of us who have had to do it know it takes more strength to come to terms with a mistake than anything else we have ever done. You are that strong man." He paused for a minute before he asked, "Where's that glass of OJ? I'm thirsty!"

TWENTY-FOUR

Brutus called all his friends to announce his engagement. His mother was happy, his sisters were overjoyed and Dr. Faulgaar had another reason to share his wealth.

"I thought the bride's parents paid for the wedding," Brutus said.

"Sometimes they do," Donna Faulgaar said, "but you know if your father gets it into his head to take out his wallet, he can't be stopped." She opened the sliding glass door on the china cabinet and selected a cream coloured teapot, hand painted with gold swirls.

"They might let him contribute, but they may be insulted if he gets too pushy," Brutus said. "I guess I'll have to deal with that discussion when it comes. Joanne wants a three-month engagement so there might be time to head him off at the pass. I'll help you set the table, Mom." He got out the matching cream pitcher and sugar bowl.

"Thanks," his mother said. "He might just get all wound up by that time. He admires that girl. What she went through was terrible, but she has done so well with your help. I'm very proud of you. Your dad knows her ongoing therapy will cost money. He will do something special for her. Your father is such a good man." She smiled indulgently as she looked at his photo hanging on the dining room wall.

"My mother is a good woman too," Brutus said with a wink. He got two matching cups out of the cupboard and put them on the table.

"I'm not really," she said, with a broad smile. "I'm just trying to make up for my only son's badness!" She giggled and Brutus burst into laughter, as she poured the tea and offered him a piece of chocolate cake.

"Mmmm! This is good cake!" Brutus said. "Hey, Mom, do you remember the Mother's Day when I was about fourteen? I decided to be a good son all day, and I brought you breakfast in bed, and cleared the dishes from the dishwasher."

"I sure do," she said. "What was really memorable about that day was that you brought me a cup of tea in the afternoon and a chair to put my feet up on and…"

"Yes," Brutus butted in enthusiastically. "Then you begged me to quit being so damn nice! Those were your actual words. You said you couldn't stand it any longer and told me to be my old rotten self!"

"I remember that. I guess you being normal was easier to take. *Nice* for the first ten minutes was okay but all day niceness was a bit much," she said. "Besides, now we have something to laugh about." They both chuckled.

"So glad you and I can laugh over almost anything," he said, taking a gulp of hot tea. "I was a little devil when I was a teenager, but I've changed my ways since planning to get married. I sometimes stretched the truth, and I thought rules were to be broken. Now I actually wash my hands before eating and I cough or sneeze into my sleeve. "

"I'm impressed, but don't change too much, Brute," his mother warned, using her pet name for him. "Joanne is probably fascinated with your sense of humour and the fact that you always have things to do, and to laugh about. Being unable to laugh is a terrible curse. Laughter will help her heal."

"Well, then you and I ought to stay healthy for the rest of our lives," he said. "I can't recall a day in my life that we have not laughed. Joanne hasn't had much to laugh about recently. While she was in the hospital, she learned that the extent of her injuries could mean she would never walk again, and she is afraid.”

“How long did she go with Zeke Geisbrecht,” Donna asked. “He was twice her age.”

“He only asked her out that one time, so it was not a regular date. He was handsome and threw money around and offered her the moon. Before that one date was over, she was afraid of him,” Brutus explained.

“You are handsome, too,” said his mother.

“You are biased,” Brutus said with a chuckle. “My nose is too large, and my eyes are too small. My generous mouth makes up for any other faults I have.”

“Your eyes are not small!” she said, with a twinkle in her own eyes “We will not discuss the size of your mouth!”

“Thanks,” Brutus said. “Mouths are made for laughing. I hope Joanne will learn to laugh again.”

“I hope so too. I recall she was a happy schoolgirl when you helped her with her homework.”

“Yes, when Joanne was young, she was a happy girl except in her math class.”

“She will heal, but it will take time. As for the math, she won’t ever have to worry about being numerically challenged again after you are married,” his mother observed. “Both your father and I like her. She has the potential to be a wonderful wife. She will learn to do things, and she will laugh again.” “That’s true, but she can practice her budgeting skills on me,” Brutus said with a snicker. “Between learning to cook and money management, she will have no time to remember Zeke.”

“You mean she can’t cook?” She shook her head as if everyone knew how to cook.

“I think she can boil potatoes and make tea, but she’s never cooked a whole meal. She said her grandmother lives with the family and she will teach Joanne to cook. I think Gran is Joanne’s dad’s mother. I haven’t met all her family yet," he said. "That will be good."

"When we were kids you let us cook and I remember those meals now as a fun time with you or Dad. We had to be able to eat whatever we cooked, so we had some interesting food to eat up before you got home!" he recalled. They both chuckled, remembering the various interesting and not-so-interesting meals produced by the amateur cooks, shuddering at the memory of undercooked meals, over cooked ones, and those in between horrible and barely edible.

"Do you remember that horrible roast I did for a Sunday dinner?" he asked, covering his nose.

"How could I forget it?" she asked

"I can't remember what you seasoned it with, but it smelled so strong of garlic it brought tears to my eyes," Donna said with a snicker as she held her nose.

"That was to cover the smell of catnip I put in it by mistake," Brutus reminded her. "Then we had to eat it."

"Right, I allowed you to cook, and you all knew the rules. You had to clean up after yourselves too." Donna said. "Food is not something to play with. It's what keeps us alive and keeps us happy. Catnip can be eaten by humans though we usually save it for the cat."

"Dad can cook pretty good, too," Brutus remarked. He looked toward the kitchen and grinned.

"He certainly can, but he doesn't want to cook. You have a lot to look forward to. Has Joanne chosen her bridesmaid yet?" she said, changing the subject.

"Her friend Betty Armstrong will stand with her. She wants two flower girls, daughters of another school friend." Brutus said. "I might ask Lance to be my best man. He's older but he is a fun person. I thought of Steve or Morley. We have a few months yet."

"I think it's usual to have a single man as your best

man," his mother said," but these days people seem to make their own rules."

"Yes, I know, but with her white wedding dress and red roses, we have gone traditional. Steve would be the obvious choice but he's a bit of a slap-stick person. I don't know how serious he would take it."

"He'll be okay, once he knows what he has to do, I'm sure Steve will be just fine. Morley and Lance could supply the music, and then you would have all your friends around you to share in your special day," she said. "When will the rings be ready to pick up?"

"They'll be resized by tomorrow. The engagement ring was too large for her. I was just guessing because I wanted her to be surprised," Brutus said.

"Did you hear what I said about the music?"

"Yeah, I never thought much about the music but you're right. Lance is a good piano and organ player, and Morley has a nice baritone voice. He's a tall man and with his fire-engine-red Afro hair style, he gets an additional foot at least. We can go easy on the decorations," Brutus said.

"That's an interesting thought. However, we don't usually think of the attendants as part of the decor," Donna Faulgaar said. They both laughed. "It would be a good idea to talk to Joanne about that, anyway. The music is usually the bride's decision, but make the suggestion. I'm sure she will be happy to have your input. She strikes me as a girl who is easy to discuss things with."

***

Lance was surprised but overjoyed when Brutus called him to ask if he and Morley would provide the music for the wedding on November 15, 1997, to be held at the Full Gospel Church in Meldrum City.

"I wondered if you two would be tying the knot, Brutus," he said. "Somehow I couldn't see you walking away from that gal."

"Nope. I'm smitten!" Brutus agreed. "She came into my life at the right time. Actually, she has been part of it for a long time. She dated others in High School, and so did I, but nothing became serious. We've been friends since grade eight when I helped her with her math homework."

"That's the way it happens," Lance said.

"I have a favour to ask of you, Lance. Will you play the organ for the wedding? I'll ask Morley to sing, if that's okay with you?' Brutus said.

"Me?" asked Lance. "It would be an honour, Brutus. I'll make a note of it right away—not that I would be likely to forget such an event. Morley has a very strong baritone voice. He's a good choice. I heard him sing years ago at a Christmas concert. What about Steve?"

"Thanks, Lance. I haven't talked to Steve yet, but we thought he would be a good best man. What do you think?" Brutus asked. "You fellows have been so supportive, and Steve isn't taller than me. He's a little bit flighty but I think he'd be a good choice."

"I guess that's important. I know Steve will step up to the plate. We'll all be with you, man! I'd better start working on the organ again, or you'll throw me out. There's a pipe organ in the Full Gospel church but the electric organ might be better for a wedding."

"Have you ever played a pipe organ, Lance?" Brutus asked.

"Funny you should ask," Lance said. "Not long ago I was feeling down, and I walked into the church. The door was unlocked, and the janitor was cleaning it up for the evening service. He said I could try the pipe organ, and I got carried away. The pastor finally asked me to go home so the janitor could have his dinner before the church filled with worshippers again."

"What did you play," asked Brutus with a chuckle.

"Everything from hymns to rock and roll, and foxtrots. Rather comical," Lance said. "Will you have traditional music or something more modern?"

"My bride will be wearing a white gown, and she will carry red roses," Brutus said proudly. "That's what we both want. I guess we better have traditional music, eh?"

"Sounds good to me, Brutus. Does Joanne have any special requests? "

"She wants our moms to help with choosing the music," he said.

"Good idea. No motorcycles or anything?"

Brutus laughed and said, "No, Joanne isn't ready to try that yet. Maybe someday she might come for a ride with me, but right now, no bikes. She's adventurous but she has never been on a bike. I took her out to see them, but she is still on crutches and sometimes she still uses the wheelchair, so I haven't really brought it up."

"Andrea doesn't ride either. She doesn't mind me riding, although she does often point out to me the dangers of the trails I like to ride on. She's not really interested in bikes. My boys might take an interest in it eventually, but my daughter Jeanie wants no part of it. I doubt if that will change unless she marries a biker. Anyway, man, I'm glad you asked me to play. It's an honour."

"Thanks, Lance. I'll give Steve a holler. Do you think he'll be surprised when I ask him to be my best man?" Brutus asked.

"He might be, but I know Steve well enough to be sure he'll be pleased. The groom chooses his best friend, and he will like that."

"I'll call him now. Bye. Talk to you tomorrow."

"Bye!" Lance hung up the phone and went to tell Andrea the news.

***

Brutus met Morley, Lance and Steve downtown later that day and told them the good news again, not just once, but three times in the half-hour they sat at a table in the *Tavern In The Town* to have a hamburger and fries. The tavern was busy, but not too busy to give Brutus a free lunch as the good news spread among the regular patrons of the popular cafe.

"I knew you intended to pop the question," Steve said, as he moved another table closer to where the other guys were. "I hope they won't object to us moving tables around."

"They won't mind as long as we put them all back when we're finished," Lance said. "I thought you might ask her to marry you."

"So did I," said Morley. "I was going to warn you to close in before it was too late. I had a girl like that once and she ran off with my best friend."

"Oh, she won't do that," Brutus said. "She already said 'yes.'"

"Great!" Morley said. "Zeke really hurt her badly. It will be a long haul, but we're all behind you. You'll need a lot of moral support. We'll be there for you anytime, man!"

"Count me in," Lance said. He adjusted his chair and wiped the crumbs off his pants.

Steve had been quiet up to that point. Finally, he said, "It must have been a terrible thing he put her through. I hate pain, and she must have endured a lot of pain in the short time he had her in his life. I never liked Zeke."

"I didn't either," Brutus said. "He was rude to me when he came in late for that concert."

"He was a good light and sound tech, but I didn't trust him. His eyes were cruel. Once I saw him pick Igor up by the tail, and I told him off. He threatened me. He said, 'he's just a cat' and I said that was cruelty and he hated me after that," Steve said.

"Good thing I didn't see that," Lance said. "He seemed to like his own cat and dog. A very odd man."

"I didn't like Zeke, but they say he was wonderful to his own pets. He hated women. Odd guy. Funny that he would treat Igor like that. Saying he was only a cat is awful," Steve said.

"Igor is not *just a cat*. He belonged to us all at The Reef. Before the concert, I delivered some food to Charlie on the catwalk, and Igor startled me by meowing in my ear when I was coming down. When I recovered, I had quite a conversation with him. I thought it was the theatre ghost."

"I remember you came down late," Brutus said. "Dodging the ghost, I bet."

"Yep! I thought he was coming to get me. There's a poem called 'Just a Dog' that expresses how we depend upon our pets to be there for us when we feel bad, and when no one else can fill the bill. There should be one about cats, too," Lance said.

"We'll have to write one," Steve said. "Igor spent a long time as a theatre cat. If he could only speak our language! When the holidays are over and you get back to teaching, maybe you could have your students write one as a project."

"Good idea!" Lance said with a grin. "Has anyone heard how Hagar is doing with his therapy dog training?"

"Last I heard he was doing great," Steve said. "I ran into Leif, and he said he and Heathcliffe were really having a ball working together. Do they have therapy cats too?"

"I think they do," Lance said. "When Igor was in the theatre, we all loved him, so I think he was a great therapy cat."

"He has a permanent home now, but we will never forget the old boy. Will you get a cat when you are married?" Morley asked Brutus.

"Sure thing and we'll call him Igor the Second. Igor the First deserves to be knighted, don't you think?" Brutus said.

"Sir Igor sounds important. Will Joanne want a cat?" Steve asked.

"Of course," Brutus said. "Joanne loves cats and dogs too. She doesn't like snakes, but she doesn't mind frogs. "

"Girls are scared of snakes," Steve said with a snicker.

"She is leery of turtles, too," Brutus said. "She told me one time when she was about six, her mother sent her to pick some rhubarb from the garden and she came back in the house complaining that the rhubarb plant growled at her. Finally, her mother went out to see for herself and there was a big snapping turtle hiding under a rhubarb leaf."

"Wow! That wasn't in town though, was it?" asked Morley.

"No, when she was a child, they lived in the country. Did you see last night's paper?" Brutus asked, changing the subject.

"No," Morley said. "Anything interesting besides your wedding announcement?"

"Yes, Aldo Cody is missing. He's that big-mouthed roadie with the *Shot-glass Five*. His father reported it two days ago. He went out to meet some friends and never came back, his father told the police. There is a reward for his return.," Steve said.

"Did they talk to his friends?" Brutus asked.

"Apparently he never met up with them," Steve told them.

"He wasn't a very nice guy," Morley said. "However, I still don't like the thought of something terrible happening to him."

"I don't wish him ill. Well, I better go," Brutus said. "Thanks for all your support. It's nice to know you will be there for both Joanne and me."

TWENTY-FIVE

Lance sat at his pump organ in the music room, deep in thought. It was a serious thing to be asked to play for a wedding. He would be playing an electric organ in the church for Brutus' wedding, but at home, he just had the pump organ his mother had played in church many years ago. He smiled at his reflection in the wall mirror, thinking of long ago before every church had big expensive organs that didn't do the job any better. Besides the player got some exercise pumping with his feet to keep the bellows filled with air. With practice, the organ produced a full-bodied tone. He felt secure playing the old songs his mother had played and revisiting his childhood.

Lance tried to get his mind off Leif's problems, but even the peaceful old instrument with its many memories was not enough to discourage the ugly thought from invading his mind. Leif must have been living in fear for years.

What could Leif have done to give Zeke the power to order him to work for years without pay? Now that Zeke was gone, would he be released? What was the secret Leif was hiding? Why was he scared of Zeke? He could probably easily have overcome the older man. According to Brad, Leif had even given up his studies to serve him, although the money he'd borrowed from Zeke was not the issue.

He got up from the organ deep in thought and walked out to the garden. What a peaceful place it was to sit and think!

A month had passed since Zeke's death. Although his DNA proved he was not Freddy's killer, the case was no closer to being solved than it had been in the days following his murder. The only thing they knew for sure was that an extortion ring had existed under Zeke's leadership. It was by no means disbanded with his death. The members were probably just lying low under new leadership. Leif was undoubtedly still in danger.

"He finally broke his silence," Brad said when he and Lance met for coffee at MacDonald's on Third Avenue. "He told me that there was a bounty on his head. Zeke was holding that over him."

"Did Leif actually tell you himself what Zeke was using against him?" Lance asked.

"Not willingly," Brad said. He added two sugar sachets to his coffee and vigorously stirred it. "He said he knew he was being scammed. You were right, Lance. It was blackmail. It is something that Zeke said happened nearly twenty-five years ago when Leif was only five. The family was planning to travel to Japan where his dad worked with the Canadian Embassy," Brad explained. He drained his coffee cup and sat quietly for a few minutes before he spoke again. "The trip was delayed because of a house fire. Zeke said that Leif was playing with matches, and no one was watching him. His little sister was asleep in her crib when a blanket caught fire. Leif ran crying to his mother, but it was too late."

"You mean the child burned to death?" Lance asked, in horror.

"To put it bluntly, she did not survive. She could have died of smoke inhalation. I investigated the incident but cannot find any information on it. Leif was not named as the person who started a fire although he recalls playing with matches, once when he was little. Zeke may have made up a story to use against him.

"So," Lance said, "it may not have happened. Why was Zeke there in the first place? You've lost me? How long was

Zeke involved with Leif? And why? What was the connection?"

"Yes," Brad said with a sigh. "I wish there was no previous connection, but it appears Zeke was a third cousin to Leif's father. Leif said he can't recall him being in his life at all as a child, but Zeke made the incident sound so real that Leif doesn't know if it happened. He is confused and can find nothing in his research to connect him to a fire.

"Oh, for Heaven's sake!" Lance exclaimed. He swiped his napkin over his lips and put his cup down with a bang. "Then why are you making something out of it?'

"We have to look into it, Lance. I doubt if there's a case, but it appears that Zeke convinced Leif that there was a fire and that the death of his sister was his fault. He was only a child, and the person who should have been watching him is more to blame if it even happened. She died so cannot be charged," Brad said.

"So they went to Japan anyway?" Lance inquired.

"They lived in Tokyo while his dad served two four-year terms with two years between each term, making Leif seventeen when they returned to Canada. During that time, the boy learned martial arts and would have forgotten the incident but when they returned to Canada, Zeke kept bringing it up and using it against him, until he began to feel guilty," Brad explained.

"Balderdash!" Lance said. "It sounds like a made -up story to me. I don't believe a word of it. Zeke was just trying to make him think he was responsible for his sister's death. As for the familial connection, the only thing that explains is why Leif was mentioned in Zeke's will. Perhaps it was Leif's money all along."

"What do you mean by that remark?" asked Brad. He frowned.

"Maybe Zeke was assigned Leif's custody, including

the money in trust until he came of age. It appears obvious to me that Zeke was making out he was a rich man because of smart money deals he made but in all likelihood the money he claimed belonged to Leif," Lance said.

"Hold on there, Lance. "Those are serious charges," Brad said.

"Perhaps he used the family connection to *take care* of the child's needs after his father died. Do you know when Leif borrowed the money from him?" Lance asked. "No one has been able to establish that Zeke really did anything to earn the riches he has been flaunting. Do we even know who owned that estate before Zeke got it?"

"This could have been when Leif was younger. I don't know."

"Then I suggest you find out from Leif," Lance snapped. "This whole thing stinks to me! Find out where Zeke got the money he is so generously leaving to Leif. It doesn't sound that complicated to me. The man was a good light technician, but he was a ruthless bastard." Lance was so steamed up by this time, he was shaking with anger.

"Wonderful!" exclaimed Brad. "Now we have to investigate Zeke for more than just his torture room. I must say you've probably opened up a can of worms. So what you are saying is that Zeke bought that estate with cash that legally belonged to the Fergusons."

"Yes, Leif mentioned to me a couple of days ago that he remembers living in a house like the one Zeke said was his own home. All you really have to do is find out where the Fergusson's lived in Canada, either before or after his father's service in Japan. Zeke may have assumed ownership of the property and at the same time assumed guardianship of the child. I think it's worth looking into, even if it's only to ease Leif's guilt over the death of his sister in the fire."

TWENTY-SIX

Lance was directing the Meldrum High School Senior Band during an early evening concert when he noticed Brad in the audience of parents and siblings of the players. He had half turned toward a soloist at his far left and caught a glimpse of Brad before he turned back to the band. The march came to the final notes with a flourish, and he faced the audience to acknowledge the applause.

The days were getting shorter as September quickly changed from bright summer days to the colours of Harvest time. Before the long holiday weekend, Lance enjoyed directing the school concerts. He had the knack of encouraging each student to do his best.

The big music room at Meldrum High School was decorated with bronze, yellow, red, and amber leaves. The stage was set with the podium facing the rows of chairs and music stands. Lance had wisely chosen to direct the dress rehearsal in the school auditorium because he knew the acoustics would be different to the classroom they were accustomed to use. From his own orchestral experience Lance remembered as a young player the excitement when at last they could graduate to the real concert hall.

He bowed as he proudly coached his students through the formal acknowledgements for soloists and the niceties of concert performances.

As the applause died away, and the audience made their way out onto the street, Brad walked to the front of the stage with a broad smile. Heathcliffe wagged his tail politely but didn't utter a sound.

"Wow!" You know your stuff!" Brad said, as he looked up to Lance. "Your students are very good. I wish I had been here for the whole concert."

"I did see you once," Lance answered. "Did you enjoy what you heard? "

"Yes, it took me back to my own conducting days long ago. However, I dropped in to tell you I had just come from the Agricultural Land office."

"What did they have to say?"

"I'll call you later tonight, Lance. You will be interested. What time?"

"About eight-thirty, eh? These kids are good, but sometimes I wish I had just one with the drive that Freddy had. It breaks my heart to think that he allowed drugs to interfere with his career." Lance said rather wistfully. He looked down at his shoes.

"I understand," Brad said. "No matter how many years have gone by, that excitement and pride never go away. It always gives me a thrill to meet one of my old orchestral buddies on the street. For you it was Freddy, but I had my favourites too."

"Yes, I can relate. I knew I wasn't one of them," Lance said ruefully under his breath as he watched Brad hurrying to the exit and disappear into the crowd of students, friends, and families of the players.

Later that night Lance was at home drinking a hot cup of tea and eating a cinnamon bun when Brad phoned him "Okay," he said. "What's the verdict?"

"I enjoyed the concert immensely and I'm glad I came to it," Brad said. "What I really came to tell you was that I got a shock when I called the Agricultural Land Office today to find out if they had traced the past property owners of Zeke's estate. Your intuition was right. The Fergussons had owned that property for over thirty-five years. Zeke was the caretaker while they were in Japan and had a position of trust with the family. When Leif came of age, he was supposed to take possession of it.”

“Then why was it not turned over to him?” Lance asked with a frown,

“That’s the catch,” Brad explained. “His mother passed away from cancer before Leif came of age. His father has Alzheimer’s Disease and doesn’t even know Leif, or Zeke. Before Leif can take possession, there has to be an investigation and then a court order. Two doctors and a psychiatrist must assess his father before the property will go to Leif. The handwritten will must be assessed, but in the meantime, Leif can go on living there. The lawyers see no reason that he could not take possession of it now. It appears legal and it was witnessed by a Notary Public. However, they have to go by the rules.”

“What about the fire?” Lance asked.

“There was no fire associated with his sister’s death, or the house other than the one Zeke accidently started when he was doing a spring burn,” Brad said. “Leif had nothing to do with his sister’s death. She was born with a heart condition and passed away in Japan. She was four at the time of her death in a hospital. Zeke was fabricating stories. He used it to force Leif to do all the illegal grunt work.”

“Any idea why? What did he have to gain?” Lance’s frown deepened.

“He got out of the hard work, and he got the money while Leif was always in danger of being caught. Hey, go finish your tea and go to bed. Hellava good concert tonight. You should be proud of your students. I enjoyed it. Goodnight! See you tomorrow.” Brad said goodbye before Lance could respond.

Lance had another cinnamon bun before he got washed up for bed. He knew it had been a good concert, but it was nice to hear someone with Brad’s experience say so. He was proud of his students.

Andrea barely stirred as he crawled into bed beside her. Lance wanted to talk, but he didn't want to disturb her sleep, so he sighed and closed his eyes tightly and drifted off to sleep. It could wait until tomorrow.

Lance's four kids always looked forward to the long Thanksgiving weekend, with two extra days off school. The fourteenth of October marked that special day.

After the holiday weekend even, Lance was weary after a day of teaching teenagers the finer points of playing the guitar. He looked forward to a quiet half hour in the local pub so he could watch the final period of the Canucks game before he called it quits for the day.

Lance enjoyed all his pupils, no matter what their talent. "I'll play along with you," he told his grade ten band class. He demonstrated how to seamlessly change between chord shapes.

"D major, A 7," he chanted. "Back to the tonic chord, that's right! Jim, you are playing a C chord, not a D major. Relax your hand, Marlene. Hum along with the music! See how much better it sounds. Now it's music, not just notes."

Some students caught on quickly, but many stumbled all over the notes, trying to copy the moves Lance made so easily. He used rhythm to inspire those students who found it difficult. It usually paid off.

"One, two, three, four! Don't whack the edge of the drum. That's for special effects. You don't need to hammer with the drumsticks because the drum-skins are pulled tight to reverberate with the slightest touch. Keep a loose wrist. Enjoy it. Let your heart sing along with it. George, I like that! Fantastic! You got it! Tom, you're a great bass player. A little more sound on the lower strings. Give it all you've got!"

Rap was the choice of many students. Lance enjoyed his kids, even those who would never make it. Those who did really take an interest in the music made up for those who couldn't.

***

It was Hockey month, a time when the big game took over television sets and often husbands, who could talk of nothing else. Andrea enjoyed the game too, but hockey fever was not quite as exciting to her and Jeannie as it was to Lance, Lanny and Roy.

After school that Friday, Lance looked at his watch and realized he had forty minutes to spare before he was due to meet with Brad to talk over Brutus' wedding music. Time enough to catch the last period of the game before Brad arrived.

As he walked into the *Roaring Tiger Pub* and sat down in a booth, he saw Leif sitting at a table alone drinking, not just one beer, but three at a time. He hadn't thought Leif was a drinker.

Lance looked around at bright yellow and bronze menus posted on the cream walls, with photos of plates filled with fish and chips, different hamburgers and frothy glasses of the favourite drinks lined up in rows of three. The bartenders were efficiently serving drinks and plates of delectable looking food as the pub filled up with patrons hoping to see the game while enjoying the company of friends.

He loaded up his tray at the counter and headed for a booth. He was so engrossed in the game when it started with his favourite team scoring a goal in the first twenty minutes that he even forgot Leif was there until he slid into the seat opposite him.

"Hi Leif," he said. "It's nice to see you, but your head is blocking the screen completely. How about moving it so

I can see the game." He tried to be polite, but it was an effort. He guessed Leif had been in the pub for a while by his very first words.

"Hi, Lanshh. How'sh it going? S-s-s screen?" he slurred. "I don't see no screen."

"Neither do I," Lance said. "Your head's in front of it. Quit blocking it, will ya? You seem to be celebrating. What's the big deal? You win the lottery or something?"

"Want to hear something funny?" Leif asked.

"Later, I want to watch the game."

"This g-g-guy comes into a bar," Leif said, bobbing his head and smiling to himself.

"Okay," Lance said, as he waited for the punchline.

"Uh?" Leif said. "I forget. I think I been drinking. I don't drink, y'know. Never 'ave. I'm sort of celebratin' somethin'. I forget what it is. I think its money."

"Money? You got paid?" Lance asked with one eye on the game, and the other on Leif's beer which he was waving as he spoke. As it came dangerously close to landing in his lap, Lance suggested Leif eat some food instead of drinking. He handed him some chips from a small cardboard container and called the bartender over to bring Leif some food.

"Yeah. Zeke just gave me my own house," Leif finally said, his mouth full of chips. "My father left it to me. Zeke was just the trustee until I reached twenty-six. I'm twenty-nine."

"That's nice," Lance said. "Hey! Canucks just scored another goal! That forward is sure good. Goalie let another one in. Wow! Fantastic defence!"

"Yeah," Leif murmured holding himself up with his elbows. "Zeke made out that he owned the house and was leaving it to me, when it was mine all along," Leif said..

"Yes, that's what you said," Lance said, handing Leif a handful of napkins. "Wipe the beer off your chin."

The second period ended with a score of three to one for the Canucks. In the Meldrum Memorial Arena, the audience probably crowded to the Concession stand chatting about their favourite team with excitement. Leif, wanted to order another beer, but Lance stopped him.

"You've had enough," he said sternly. "How are you getting home?"

"Home?" repeated Leif. "Oh, yeah, somebody's coming for me. I need to go home."

"Who is coming for you, Leif?" Lance asked once more.

"James," Leif said. "All chauffeurs are named James, ain't they?" He giggled like a schoolgirl and Lance was about to chastise him when Brad came in the door followed by a man wearing a chauffeur's cap.

"I think this is who you are looking for," Brad said, pointing to Leif.

"Thanks," Leif said. "Your name James?"

"No," the chauffeur said. "My name is Harry, and I came for Leif Fergusson."

"I haven't seen him," Leif said, as Brad and Lance both shoved him toward the man.

"He needs to go home," Lance assured Harry. "And when you get there, make certain the dog and cat are fed, and –"

"Get him into bed so he can sleep it off," Brad said. "I don't want to arrest him."

As Leif was led out the door, he dropped a ten-dollar bill on the table. "'ave a beer on me to keep yer nappers clear," he said. He rubbed his head.

"My napper, as you call it, is already clear. I came to see the last period of the game," Brad said, after Leif's dramatic exit. "Who's winning?"

"Canucks, I think. Sit down but don't block the screen.

Leif talked all through the game and his head was in the way," Lance said sharply.

"You *are* bitchy," Brad complained. He sat on the same side as Lance and was just getting comfortable with a beer when the last period began. "This good enough for you?" he asked.

"Sure," Lance said, biting into a ham sandwich. "I've had enough beer already. Leif damn near spilt his last one all over me. That kid sure can't drink."

Brad said into his phone. "I'm off duty and I've got a beer. I don't have the squad car. Can't you send someone else? I've just taken a sip, but it probably smells on my breath."

"He likely won't co-operate unless you are there. We're short-handed. We know he's difficult from his behavior at the concerts. He does know you. I'd appreciate it if you would come," said the officer in the office.

"Damn!" said Brad when he got off the phone. "Want to come for the ride? I have to pick up Heathcliffe first."

"No," said Lance, "I don't want to, but I will come with you. I want to see the Canucks win. I haven't seen much of it anyway. I was going to take a taxi home."

"I'll drive you home," Brad said. "I know I'm pushing you, but I don't relish tackling those guys alone."

***

"Why are we driving into Leif's driveway? What's going on?" Lance asked. "Is Aldo Cody at Leif's place? I heard his voice in the background."

"I should have explained, He and three other guys are holed up in that vacant cabin we thought Zeke was using for a drug lab," Brad explained. "Leif Ferguson's chauffeur saw them when he took Leif home tonight. He saw Cody get out of a truck that came by the upper road. That was him on the phone. He said he'll stay with Leif until we get there, and maybe the night, if necessary.”

“Do you plan on taking on the whole gang, Brad?” Lance asked, in alarm.

“No, they will send two cops as backup. Sounds like there could be four guys. Cody and three others.”

“I thought Cody was missing,” Lance said, with a frown.

“His father reported his son was missing, but apparently he’s been holed up in that cabin the entire time. Nobody knows why.”

“Is that all you know about it, Brad?” asked Lance.

“They headed up the hill and parked behind a grove of trees. “That’s all I know right now. Stay in the car, Lance. You don’t need to get involved.” Brad got out and walked toward the cabin, keeping as far out of sight as he could.

“This is stupid,” murmured Lance. “Brad could get killed.” He craned his neck to see through the trees, but it was too dark to see much. He couldn’t relax. He wanted to get into the action, but Brad had told him to stay in the car. He closed his eyes and tried to think of something else.

A few minutes later, Lance was startled by a tap on the window, and looked up to see the diminutive figure of Leif standing there.

“I couldn’t sleep after Harry left,” Leif explained. “Can I wait with you? I’m sobered up now. The thought of action does that to me. I may have to help Sgt. Brad Thomas out.”

“You?” Lance asked in alarm. “What the hell can you do?”

“Yeah, me. Did you forget what I do for a living?”

“You mean you will use some of your martial arts moves on them?”

“Who else?” Leif asked. Lance was sure he detected a chuckle in his voice.

Lance heard two popping sounds coming from the

248

general direction of the cabin.

"Gunfire?" he asked. He opened the door as quietly as possible. "Get in, no use us both getting killed."

"No," Leif said. "We're safer outside the car."

"You kidding?"

Leif shook his head. "No," he said. "Those gunshots are from a couple of low calibre guns, but they can still kill or wound." He crept closer to the cabin, staying out of sight. Lance got out cautiously and followed him. They heard shouting and several oaths being sworn. The voices got louder. Lance walked back and slid behind the car. More gunfire. He heard Brad's voice as a bullet exploded when he came in obvious contact with one of the men.

"You're under arrest!" Brad threatened. He snapped his holster as he pulled out his pistol.

"Yeah? You and who else?" It was Cody's voice. From the sounds he heard, Lance concluded that Cody had tackled Brad. When he ventured a look, he saw that Cody had knocked Brad to the ground, where two other guys took advantage of the fallen cop to jump him. Three to one was not good. Brad was ready to retire, and Lance shuddered to think what could happen if the fugitives got the upper hand.

Lance watched as the area was suddenly flooded with light. In the spotlight he saw Leif ready for action.

A car door slammed. Two more followed. Then a scream. The amazing sight of Leif in action flabbergasted not only Lance but four other men. He could see them standing around in shocked disbelief as Leif flung Aldo Cody over his shoulder, to land on his back on the ground, where he continued to fight him. As Cody tried to recover, Leif grabbed the second man and did a thumb lock, taking control of his balance. As he also sunk to the ground, the backup cops arrived.

Instead of withdrawing, another man broke from the

cabin and came at Brad from the back. They had been kicking Brad and all four of the men were on the elderly cop at once. One punched him hard in the face and blood spurted from his nose, filling his mouth and eyes. Lance knew that Brad was going to get creamed, so he came out of hiding and was about to advance on the thugs when he heard Leif's voice. Obviously, the little man was ready for them, standing in a Modified Front Stance, as his son Lanny would call it. Lance knew from watching Lanny training with Leif a few times.

Aldo attacked Brad from behind, ignoring Leif. As they continued fighting, they rolled behind a thicket of blackberry brambles. Lance stepped forward and knocked Aldo backwards off Brad, so the elderly cop could get his second wind. Wiping the blood off his face, Brad got to his feet, but Aldo did too, being younger and heavier.

Aldo pulled a collapsible nightstick from his pocket, snapped it open and swung the weapon at Brad, but missed his target as Lance moved out of the way.

Brad tried to step back when Aldo swiped at him with the weapon but was unable to avoid taking a blow to his right shoulder. Heathcliffe grabbed Aldo by the arm and held him firmly until Brad recovered. The driveway and cabin were simultaneously bathed in bright lights as two more police cars arrived with spotlights playing on the three thugs just outside the cabin doorway.

As Lance watched, Leif delivered a drop-kick to one of the two men, while blocking the other one who began throwing punches to Brad's face and neck. Leif did a fancy sidestep and with a guttural 'Hi you" he whacked the second thug on the temple, knocking him out.

The two officers moved in on the two thugs, quickly cuffing them before they could do any more harm.

Lance, Brad, and Aldo were out of view on the other

side of the bush. Leif hurried to them in time to see Lance narrowly avoid another blow from the night-stick.

One of the two cops followed Leif around the bush while the other one stayed with the two prisoners. "Hold it!" he ordered Leif. "Police! Stay where you are."

Leif froze, following orders. The officer trained his weapon on Leif until he saw Brad and Lance fighting Aldo, and then let him go.

He watched as Aldo swung the weapon at Brad again, but Leif advanced and did a terrific move. Grabbing the club, he spun around backwards, connecting with Aldo's mid-section with his foot. With a "Yyyecht!" Leif took possession of the weapon and brought it down on the back of Aldo's head, knocking him out cold.

Lance, Brad, and the young cop watched Leif as he bent down to inspect Aldo.

Staring in disbelief at the small Martial Arts expert, they were flabbergasted at the intricate moves he made with almost no effort. Lance was the only one who had no Martial Arts training, but even he could see this man was an expert. Lance was pleased that the times he had watched Lanny work out at classes had given him some knowledge of the craft. He may not have been able to execute the intricate moves himself, but he knew what they were.

Later that night Brad called Lance. "This will hit the newspapers tomorrow," he said. "But you and Leif deserve to hear it first. Remember that unknown DNA on the hole reamer? Well, when a certain person was reported missing, we got a sample of his DNA from a hairbrush, and guess who it matched?"

"I'm not good at guessing games," Lance said. "Besides, my nose won't quit bleeding. You better tell me."

"Not over the phone but if you and Leif hadn't been there, I'd be in the hospital."

"Are you saying that you know who killed Freddy?" Lance asked after a pause.

"I'd like to think I do, but I'm only guessing," Brad said.

TWENTY-SEVEN

Charlie took Lance by surprise when he called with a complaint. "How come you ignore me?" he asked.

"Gee, I hadn't intended on neglecting you. My mind has been occupied by a whole lot of worries," he explained.

"Where you been?" inquired Charlie. "I not see you for long time. You left town or something?"

"No, I'm still here," Lance said. "I've been training my students for the fall concerts, of course. The Senior Band will play a concert next weekend and the Junior band the following week. I've just been working hard. What about you, Charlie? Anything exciting?"

"Yah, I got news. I getting married, you know."

"Married?" Lance asked. "You find a new girl or what? Hurry up and tell me. How come?"

Charlie chuckled. "You better sit on chair," he said. "No new girl. I keep old one. New one scare me. Still speak funny English, Canada girls say. "

"You leaving Canada?" asked Lance in alarm.

"No leave," Charlie said. "She coming to get me. Church man, he bring her here. We have long wait, then we get married. It getting all fixed. How you say it? I ask her again on phone."

"That's wonderful news Charlie," Lance said. "Your English has improved lot." He smiled to himself. "Those Canada girls are wrong."

"Thanks, they should have heard me before, eh? That really bad English. Even I laughed." Charlie snickered.

"You're a good sport, Charlie. Love must be in the air." Lance selected an apple from a bowl on the table and took a big bite out of it. "Brutus and Joanne are getting married too.

I'll play the organ for his wedding and Morley' going to sing."

"Already I know. Birdie say it. You play for my wedding, too, eh? Not guitar. Organ, eh? I come to Brutus wedding to hear you then ask for mine too. Suzanna will want it same. Canadian wedding. Her daddy he die, but momma she come to Canada. Live with us in big house like at home."

"That's very exciting, Charlie," Lance said, secretly thinking it could be not so exciting after all. "Will you want to share your home with your mother-in-law?"

"Ya! We will have big house. Not little apartment no more," he said. "What you doing so you not have time for me?"

"We should meet soon for coffee and talk about it, Charlie. How is Igor?" Lance said, not wanting to address Charlie's question.

"Ha ha!" snickered Charlie. "Igor have girlfriend too. Her name is Tootsie. Not bother to get married. Kittens coming in three weeks. Igor fast worker."

"I'm sure Igor will do the right thing," Lance assured him.

"Yah! He be good daddy. Bring mouse for babies."

"I hope it won't be as smelly as the mouse that Kitt brought us for a welcome home gift when we came back from a camping trip last summer," Lance said.

"I tell Igor what you say," Charlie said. "We good friends just like when live on catwalk. Igor's gift be nice."

"I didn't intend to ignore you, Charlie, so could we meet on Friday at The Crossroads?" Lance suggested.

"Where it be?" Charlie asked.

"It's a new restaurant is two blocks from your basement suite at Brad's place. How about four o'clock on Friday afternoon? It's close to the high school so I can get there soon after school is out. Would that be okay with you?" Lance suggested.

"Good idea! I like to see you again. I working every day now. Brad find job for me doing building . . . main. . . how you say it?" Charlie said.

"Building maintenance?" Lance asked. "That's a good job, but you must work hard."

"Ya, I like hard work. Muscles get soft hiding on catwalk," Charlie explained. "I like to show you how hard my muscles are, but you canna see on phone."

"Charlie, I'll see you on Friday afternoon, and you can show me your muscles then. I'm glad you can stay in Canada, and Suzanna is coming soon. Will you sing the song you wrote for her at the wedding?"

"Maybe," Charlie said, after thinking it over for a minute. "If you play organ with me."

"We'll practice it together," Lance promised.

***

The Crossroads Restaurant was within walking distance of the Meldrum High School. Lance left his car there and walked the four blocks to the cafe. So much had happened in the past month that he enjoyed the freedom of walking through a shortcut used by students on their way to school. It reminded him of his own school days when it was exciting to take shortcuts through the woods.

Lance walked in a few minutes late and sat down across from Charlie at a small table at the back of the restaurant. "Sorry I'm late,' he said. "Those teens sure hold me up sometimes. They forget I have a life too. They don't pack up and get out as soon as the bell rings. They want to talk. Today it was all about how Leif Ferguson beat up four guys last week, all by himself."

"Well, that was really something to talk about," Charlie said. "I not have time for lunch today so I was hungry. Have some cherry pie. It is good."

"Just some coffee. Your pie does look good. Next time I will have some. Nice to see you, Charlie and hear your news," Lance said. He made himself comfortable and moved the ash tray onto another table. "Ugh, that smells awful. You don't smoke, do you, Charlie?"

"I did for a while, but Brad's wife doesn't like it, and I'd have to quit when Suzanna comes anyhow. The girls there don't smoke," Charlie explained. "I at Courthouse all morning."

"Courthouse?" asked Lance.

"Ya, I tell you about it when you get your coffee. The girl is coming now."

Lance ordered his coffee, and said, "On second thought, that cherry pie smells good. I'd like a piece too." The waitress took his order and smiled as she walked away.

"Why were you at the courthouse, Charlie. Were you a bad boy?" he said, turning his attention back to Charlie.

"No, not me, but Brad wanted to know who I see night of concert. He say important for me to remember."

"It is, Charlie, but you mustn't tell anyone about it, but Brad and me. I think it was important. What you saw that night may have been the guys the police were looking for," Lance said.

"Ya, I be quiet like mouse," Charlie promised.

"What were you doing at the courthouse?" The waitress brought Lance his pie, and more coffee. "I better not eat too much because I won't want dinner," he said.

"I talk to lawyer lady what I saw. She said it crew-shall evvy-dance. What that mean?" Charlie said.

"It means that you have important evidence. You must be a witness to help find the bad guys," Lance explained, allowing himself a smile.

"I tell Lawyer lady what I see. That Cody guy and his

friends all bad guys. They mean to Freddy," he said.

"Did you see what they did to Freddy?" Lance asked.

"No, no. I no see them kill Freddy, but I see them push Freddy into boiler room. Cody threatened him with big knife. I afraid to tell Brad until I see picture in paper. Then I tell him. He come to Courthouse too." Charlie said. "We tell Lawyer lady everything."

"Oh, Morley and Steve, and Brutus. Come in door. You tell them to come?" Charlie asked.

"No, but it's nice to see them. I wonder why they are here?" Lance said.

"Hi, you guys. Mind if we join you? We could move this table closer so we can talk," Brutus said.

"Sure," Charlie said as the three members of The Sinkholes noisily moved the furniture much to the consternation of the waitress.

"We'll move it all back before we leave," Morley promised.

"Coffee?" she asked. "Refills for you fellows?"

When they nodded, she filled up all the cups and walked away smiling.

"She knows we tip well!" Brutus said with a grin. "These guys are planning my stag party. Just don't make it too noisy, eh? And no strippers,"

"No strippers?" Steve asked. "You spoiled our fun."

"Well, it is his party after all," Morley said.

"Actually, Charlie will soon be getting married too," Lance said. "And Igor's girlfriend is having kittens soon, so love is in the air."

"Too bad we couldn't give Igor and Charlie a party at the same time," Steve suggested.

"My dad said he will pay for it all. I didn't tell him about Igor," Brutus said.

"Suzanna and me wait for our party," Charlie said. "We

be good Canadians first, eh? Have flag and eat hamburgers, and we tell everyone we no live in igloo and our dogs no mush us to work with dog team. We not leave Igor and Tootsie out. We all have party together."

TWENTY-EIGHT

When Lance heard that Cody and his friends were reported missing, he had wondered if they were just in hiding. In that case they must have had a reason. Was Cody even a suspect up to that point? What was the motive? Drugs? Jealousy over the music? It didn't make sense that the manager of the opening band would be jealous. The two bands were not even in completion. Out of respect, Lance didn't want to draw any conclusions. He did know that Cody and even Zeke had tried to make everyone think Jem had killed his brother, but Lance always knew there was no motive.

He waited anxiously for his paper the next morning, curious as to what the reporter had written. He thought of Leif taking on four big guys at once and marvelled at the little man's tremendous stamina and the many hours of expert training he had gone through to be so well able to tackle that many people at once.

"I'll race you up the hill to the mailbox," Lanny said. When the paper came, Lance eagerly put on the speed, but Lanny got there first. There it was right on the front page in big letters. MELDRUM MARTIAL ARTS INSTRUCTOR TACKLES FOUR FUGITIVES.

Lance cleared the dishes from the table and spread out the paper The headline was followed by a photo of Leif in action.,

"I'm glad they didn't print a picture of me hiding in the bush," Lance told Lanny ruefully, as he slid into a chair at the table beside him.

"Oh, Dad! You aren't that bad. You've never been a coward. Leif is a good teacher, but I didn't know he was that tough either. If you had the training he had from the age of four, you'd have been right in there too," Lanny said. "I'd have hidden behind a bush too. Those guys are tough characters. All drug addicts. I've seen their mug shots in the newspaper before."

"Does anyone know why they were hiding?"

"No," Lance said. "Probably something to do with drugs, but apart from that, they aren't nice guys. They've all been in trouble before. We think there must be an extortion ring working, and perhaps they were involved. It's too soon to know."

"That's right, Lance," said Andrea, as she looked over her son's shoulder. "I've seen them too. Look at that huge guy being tossed by our little hero."

She handed Lance his cup of coffee and offered him the plate of cookies. "Aren't you proud to know him?" she asked.

"I am," said Lance as he bit into a cookie. "Some time in the future our Lanny will be that good."

"Not me," Lanny said with a chuckle. "I'm just interested in learning self-defence from him. I don't have any ideas of becoming a champion. Here comes Roy and Jeannie." Lanny stood up in the horse stance with his feet apart and knees bent. His hands moved independently of one another

"I've seen that one before," Roy said. "Horse something?" he said as he tried to mimic his brother. "Hey, our teacher. Mr. Ferguson is in the paper, some of the kids at school got to him. He teaches Kung Fu and everything." He put himself in the front stance, made a mock punch at Lanny.

Lanny blocked it with his left and landed a right blow on Roy's solar plexus. Andrea stepped in between the two boys, and everyone laughed,

"Let me see!" Jeannie said, pushing her way in between them. "Yep, that's him. He's sure brave. He's a hero!"

"I know!" Lanny said with a superior air. "He's *my teacher*."

"Will you be able to do that, too?"

"If I stayed with it for about thirty years, maybe I could, but I'm not that serious. Leif has made it his life work. He is much better than I would ever hope to be," said Lanny.

"You looked pretty good to me!" Jeannie said. "You should call him *Mister* Fergusson, you know."

***

Brutus and Joanne were deeply involved in their wedding plans. The wedding originally was to be the following spring, but neither one could bear the thought of waiting that long to tie the knot. They finally decided on a day in September.

"Can't we have it now?" Joanne whined.

"What does Brutus say? Why the rush?"

"The quicker the better," she said.

"No," her mother, Louise Riker, said. She was putting the finishing touches to the wedding gown. "Can't you two be patient? Hopefully, it will be a once in a lifetime event."

"Well, maybe a little while, but we want to get married NOW!" Joanne said, pouting like a little girl and stamped her foot. "The reception isn't as important as the wedding."

"I'm sure you do want to get married right this minute, dear," her mother said. "However, you will have to wait. Brutus is not going to run away. Try this dress on again, please. The waistline is too low. You are petite so your waist is shorter than those real big girls." She waved a measuring tape back and forth as she impatiently waited.

"Brutus likes to do things his way," Joanne said, as she took off her jeans and tee shirt for the third time.

"My dear child," her mother said, helping her to put the

dress on, "if he runs away, it means one thing. He is not ready for marriage. Hold still or I'll poke you with a pin."

"Ouch! You just did." Joanne jumped back.

"Sorry. There's no blood. You'll live."

"Thanks," Joanne said rather sourly as she smoothed the dress over her knees.

"There are many disappointments in life. You are still recovering from a traumatic experience at that dreadful man's hands, and we don't want you to have a relapse. You've had to learn to speak and to walk again. Brutus cares enough to wait. Now, go read a book or something. Just get out of my hair," she retorted.

"Mom! Don't you remember your wedding day? Weren't you excited?"

"Oh yes," Louise said with a big smile. "My aunt made my cake, and it was the funniest looking thing you've ever seen. She decorated it with what she called icing roses, but they looked more like red and pink globs all around the cake." She laughed at the memory, her eyes lighting up with delight.

"Weren't you disappointed? I hope mine won't look like that. I don't want my cake to be funny," Joanne reproached, with a nervous smile.

"No, I adored my aunt, but she sure failed at cake decorating Your wedding cake will be something to remember, too," Louise said. "Our friend Chrystal is very artistic. I love her cakes. She made one that looked like a truck for her husband. It even had treads on the tires. She also decorated a cake that represented an owl house. Lovely!"

"Where did you live when you got married," asked Joanne.

"Chase Creek," Louise said. "It was a wonderful farming community. I made my own dress, between milking the cows, mucking the barn, and churning butter. I loved that healthy life, but it sure played hell with my hands. The air was fresh smelling, like newly baled hay, with only a hint of the cow pasture."

"Sounds lovely," Joanne said, holding her nose. "I can do without the cow pasture. Did you have a long engagement?"

"Almost a year. I didn't mind because he was worth waiting for. Now, be patient. Take off your shoes; you'll get the skirt smudged."

The door slammed and Henry Riker walked in. He covered his eyes and snickered. His red plaid shirt hung limply over baggy work pants. When he took off his straw hat, his mousy gray-brown hair hung in damp strands over his forehead, and his once red-brown whiskers framed his square-jawed chin.

"Hi, ladies," he said. "Nice dress. You'll look real fine in that, I tell ya."

Joanne mentally compared her father to the dashing Brutus. She wondered if her mother thought he was as handsome as her man when he was younger. She thought of the wedding cake with blobs of icing all around it, and imagined what Brutus would look like in thirty year's time. With a big smile, she picked up her jeans and shirt, and slipped into the bathroom to change. *I guess it's all depending on your point of view. Brutus will look handsome even when his hair turned white.*

TWENTY-NINE

Jem walked into the classroom late Friday afternoon just as Lance had dismissed his last class of the week. However, his workday was not finished when the students went home. He still had papers to correct as well as plan for Monday's workload.

He smiled when a chorus of, "Goodbye Mr. Bishop!" followed the last students out the door. Lance was champing at the bit to get out of there, but now Jem was here to talk.

"Nice to see you, Jem," he said, turning to face him. "What brings you here?"

"Oh, just the usual," Jem said with a smile. "Don't tell me you have no ailing instruments for me to fix this week." He picked up a guitar from the shelf and wiped the grime of fingers off it with a small sheet of pure silk.

"It's the dirty hand syndrome," Lance said with a knowing smile. "There are a couple of guitars needing new strings, and one with crack in it. Of course, the piano on the third floor needs tuning again."

"Sure," Jem said. "I'll do that on Thursday. "I should have time by then. I'm glad to get back to work."

"I am really glad to have you here," Lance assured him. "I was so happy to know you had been cleared. It has been a difficult couple of months for everyone, but your family still believed in you, and I did too."

Lance was startled to hear a choking sound coming from Jem as he sunk down into a desk and put his head down. "My dad brought up the times I disagreed with Freddy over music. We argued like all kids do, but I never thought about killing him."

"It was just nerves, Jem. We all knew you were

innocent." Lance, put his hand on Jem's shoulder.

"I had to wear that ankle monitor for over two months after they let me out of jail."

"Thankfully they realized they were wrong," Lance said. "The newspaper did report the DNA found on one of your luthier tools matched DNA found on a hairbrush in the theatre but said it didn't match yours."

"That should have been enough, but even Mom mentioned the times I said I didn't like to see Freddy using drugs as if it was normal behaviour," he said

"I told him the same thing, and I expect they did also," Lance said. "That shouldn't have made anyone think ill of you. You were showing concern for Freddy's wellbeing."

"I was always worried about Freddy getting into trouble with drugs." He paused and wiped the perspiration from his brow with a piece of Kleenex from his pocket. "One tool is still missing from my case, but there were two other tools that had DNA, hair fragments and blood on them that didn't match mine."

"Do they know who…" Lance paused and reached out to touch Jem's shoulder.

"They may do but are not saying yet. Of course, the police confiscated my tools, and they all have my DNA on them—but that one tool also had Freddy's DNA as well as DNA belonging to someone else. I think they know who killed Freddy, but they aren't saying yet," Jem said between sniffs and blowing his nose.

Lance sat in the desk behind Jem and managed to talk him down finally. "Did they put all that information in the newspaper?" he asked. He didn't mention the hole reamer that Igor found the night of the concert. "I haven't read it yet."

"Yes, they did, but it's too soon to reveal who they think is the guilty person.

"That always affects the innocent ones," Lance said. "The media sometimes manages to blow things out of proportion. It makes it hard when they publish names. Your parents are merely reacting to the gossip right now."

"I never thought my family would turn against me," Jem said.

"The stress of having you as a suspect has been hard on them. We have all been subject to that, though. Until they narrow it down, we are all suspects. Leif Fergusson beat Aldo Cody up a week ago and Cody has been in the lockup ever since," Lance said.

"I saw the pictures. Rather funny. Those guys were huge in comparison to Leif." Jem lifted his head and flashed a watery grin. "Thanks, Lance. I feel better now," Jem said. "I'm glad they figured it out finally."

"You should have seen Leif in action. He saved Brad and me from a real beating by those guys. The pictures were no comparison to the real thing," Lance said. "He sure got those big guys good."

"Now I can get on with my work. Mom was hit the hardest," Jem said, as he began to recover. "She couldn't even look at me until this morning. She said she didn't believe I was capable of murder but looked at me as if she had some doubts."

"She knew you couldn't do it, Jem."

"Well, life goes on, I guess," Jem said. "I have work to do. So, I'll go to the shop and get started. There's nothing like work to make me feel better. Thanks for everything."

"Sure, I understand."

Lance helped Jem load the instruments onto a school trolley and wheel it down the hallway and out to his van.

"I hear you're planning a Farewell concert for my brother. I think he'd like that. Who's playing?"

"Band members, and maybe Charlie."

"Who's singing Freddy's part?"

"We don't know yet."

"I could."

"Yes, you could. Your voice is a lot like Freddy's," Lance agreed.

"I'm not as explosive as my brother, but I know all his songs by memory. It would be one last thing I could do for him," Jem said, his voice breaking. "He has never heard me sing them, but I can. We used to sing together when we were kids, but all that changed when he earned some fame."

"It often does," Lance remarked. "I'd better run." He checked the time on his watch. "I'm meeting the boys at the pub in twenty minutes. Want to come along? We want to go over the concert together and make plans."

"The Roaring Tiger Pub?" asked Jem.

"I like that place. Only been there once before," Lance said.

***

They both arrived at the pub a few minutes later, and Lance parked just behind Jem's van and the two men walked in together. Charlie, Brutus, and Morley were seated at table chatting when Lance and Jem arrived.

"Where's Steve? He's supposed to come," Brutus asked.

"Probably trying to pick up all the pieces that fell off his car on the way over," suggested Morley with a snicker.

They ordered a beer each and were just beginning to take a drink when Lance heard the familiar pops and growls of Steve's vintage car as he parked close to the window.

"Maybe we should take up a collection for him to get a new car," Brutus suggested.

They watched Steve open the driver's door and pick up his door handle from the concrete and screw it back on the car with a screwdriver from his pocket.

"Does he do that every time?" Lance asked.

"I think so," Morley said. "He'd be insulted if we noticed so don't anyone say a word, eh? He's very independent. That car is probably worth a mint."

"Yes, I think so," Brutus observed. He craned his neck to get a better look. "I know an antique when I see one. Nineteen forty-nine was the year they used the lion hood ornament. It's ninety-six now so it's a vintage car. I'll ask my dad. He knows his cars as well as motorcycles. He might offer Steve something for it."

"Really?" Lance said. "It was a nice car when new. It's a Mercury Monarch. My father had one. High end car in its time. Good heavens! Who is murdering one of Freddy's songs? Is that Pothole Rock?"

"Yes," the waiter said. "They've been trying to kill Freddy's songs all week. I'm getting tired of hearing them."

Steve entered the pub hot and sweaty, and shoved the screwdriver in his pocket. "A little car trouble today," he said. "Who's singing one of our songs?"

"I don't know, but he won't be our singer when we do the farewell concert," Lance said. "I was thinking that perhaps Jem could; His voice is a lot like Freddy's."

"Would you feel comfortable doing it, Jem?" Brutus asked.

"I'll be fine, but I'm not as wild as Freddy. Fanfare is okay in its place, but I would not like to have guitars exploding. I like to fix them, not wreck, them," Jem said.

"Would not be appropriate," Steve argued.

"I think the pub is about to kick us out. I'm sure they overheard what we said about some of their performers ruining Freddy's songs," Morley said, half joking.

"Well, they did sing them badly, Lance agreed. "I think we've got our singer anyway. Jem will do it."

"Can I have an audition?" Jem asked, looking at the

square clock on the wall.

"Sure," Lance said. "When do you want it? We can arrange it any time you say."

"How about now?" Jem asked, turning to the waiter. "Pothole Rock, conventional way. No exploding guitars or other noises." He started to walk up to the stage.

"Hey, don't you have to be on their list for the karaoke?" Lance asked, grabbing his arm. "You can't just walk up there and start singing."

"I am," Jem said. "I've sung here before. Why do you think I wanted to come here today?" He continued walking to the stage, while the drinkers applauded enthusiastically.

"Oh, my gosh," Lance uttered, "I didn't know he sang here, but it looks as though he has been doing it for a while."

"I haven't been here before," Steve said. "What about you, Brutus?"

"This is a new place, and I don't hang around pubs really. Not my thing, but if he says he's done it before so it's okay with me."

The introduction was played again. Jem began to sing, without looking at the words flashing on the teleprompter screen.

Lance listened as if mesmerized as Jem seamlessly began to sing with feeling and a voice so close to being Freddy's voice, it was as if Freddy had returned. The only thing missing was Freddy's bombastic style and the long blonde hair.

"There's our man!" Lance whispered. "What an audition!"

"I like his style," Steve commented. "He doesn't try to copy Freddy. It's his own style."

"Right," Lance said. "So many singers do that instead of being themselves, so this was a treat."

"Bravo!" Brutus cheered, as Jem walked back to the

table, and seated himself. "Good job! You're hired."

"Thanks everyone. I didn't expect you'd be that enthusiastic," he said. "Yeah, I'll do it for Freddy. I'm not as good as him, though."

"Hi, guys," Brad said as he walked toward the table with Charlie beside him. and Heathcliffe trotting along wearing his blue work cape. "We just came for a beer before going home. We were standing just inside the door, listening. Good job Jem!"

"Yeah, we worked today. I learn to be a dog handler. Heathcliffe good teacher." Charlie said, as Heathcliffe crawled beneath the table and laid down. "Of course, that is not what I want to do as a career."

"You are very good, Jem," Lance said, after the excitement had died down. "Charlie, it's great to see you. Living with Heathcliffe is a good way to learn and then the dog will not have to quit work when Brad does What a wonderful idea."

"He'll learn to be a therapy dog, so he won't be confused," Brad said, pulling out a chair to sit down at the next table. "Retired Service dogs make wonderful therapy dogs, and Charlie can continue with his medical studies at the same time. Anyway, let's drink to Jem's success."

"Charlie," Lance said. "You were about to tell me your plans. What do you intend to do with your life in Canada?"

"I marry Susanna," he said. "I want be clinical biologist and a therapist. Heathcliffe will help. I be nurse in my country. I study hard. Then Canada want me. I study all about medicine. Susanna and me be nurses in hospital. She say her name like Canada girl now."

"That's wonderful, Charlie. Well, Jem, before I go home," Lance said, "we should arrange for a few rehearsals so you two fellows can get accustomed to singing and playing with the band. Then we can organize the Farewell

270

Concert." There was a round of applause. "I'll be in touch. Do you want a ride home?"

"No," Charlie said, "Have own car now. Not fancy like Steve's car. It drive real good." There was a round of applause, as he and Brad left.

It was a quarter to five when Lance arrived home. Roy and Lanny were squabbling over who would choose tonight's TV program, as usual. Andrea and Jeannie were discussing the intricacies of making pizza.

"How did your meeting go?" Andrea asked when Lance came home.

"We got a surprise tonight," Lance said. "We talked about who would be the lead singer and Jem asked if he could audition. He's been singing Freddy's songs and planned to sing at the pub today. When he got up and took the microphone, we were amazed."

"I didn't know he could sing," Andrea said. "Is he good?"

"He sure is," said Lance. "Of course he sings straight, but he is our man. We hired him right away. We begin rehearsing this Saturday. Brutus and Steve were in favour, and so were Morley and Charlie."

"What does Charlie have to do with it?"

"He plays the guitar. He will sing the song he wrote for Suzanna."

"Was Brutus there?" asked Andrea.

"Yes, he's excited about his wedding, of course. Steve turned up with his rattletrap of a car. Darn near deafened us with the thing, but Brutus said it's a valuable vintage car," he said with a grin. "Trust our boy Brutus to think of cash. He said his dad might be interested in it."

"I doubt if Steve would sell it to him. He needs the car and the car needs Steve."

THIRTY

One of the last rehearsals for Freddy's Memorial Concert was held in his old sound proofed studio. Jem was all smiles when he greeted the band members at the door. "I think Mom and Dad miss having people fill the house with music," he told the group as they tuned up for the rehearsal. "Dad would open the door upstairs so they could listen to us playing Sometimes they would even join us."

"Was that before Freddy introduced fireworks and explosions?" asked Steve.

"Freddy never rehearsed those," Jem said. "Actually, before he went away on tour he didn't use the props or the fireworks. That was a new thing he said they started doing to excite the audience."

"Like we often did at our house," Lance said. "Freddy used to tell me how he enjoyed it when the family would get together."

"A week or two before he left home he got a little too loud and that's when our parents sound proofed this room," Jem explained.

"Yes, when he came back, I did find him somewhat changed, but I guess that happens to all of us," Lance said. "Anyway, let's get down to business. Charlie has been practicing with Brad at home and he and I have been working on the songs too."

Lance and Morley had made up a list of songs suitable for the concert and their suggestions were enthusiastically accepted by Steve and Brutus.

"I suggest we not play Pothole Rock because that is what we planned to play when Freddy came back after the costume change. It wouldn't be appropriate to play it now,"

Brutus said.

"Won't the audience s expect it?" asked Steve.

"Maybe, but we know it was during that interval that something happened to Freddy," Morley explained.

"We might have to tell the audience something," Lance said.

"Do you guys realize I have to do a costume check before you will be approved to play in the Meldrum Conference Centre?" Lance asked.

"I heard about it," Morley said. "We're just wearing jeans anyway. Is this something new?"

"There were some complaints about another group, so we have to comply," Lance said. "Costumes are easy. Jeans without too many holes are acceptable. It's an unwritten rule that the more personal parts have to be intact. It's my job to inspect the clothing."

As he checked the clothing for hidden hazards, the boys guffawed and made piggish grunts as they melodramatically threw themselves on the floor with their legs in the air.

"Come and take a good look, Boss," yelled Steve, flinging his legs open to display his inseam.

"Don't forget mine!" Morley said with a snort. "Drummers are notorious for breaking the rules."

The shouts of laughter heard through the open door of the music room attracted the attention of Jem's parents. They walked down the stairs to the first floor and peeked in the doorway to see what could possibly be going on down there.

"You are a very accomplished guitarist, Charlie," Brutus said. "You have learned the songs quickly. It's a good thing because there isn't much time to practice all the music we want to work on before the concert."

"It might be a good idea to practice at home, too," Lance said.

"Lance good teacher," Charle told the band members. "He teached me good."

Steve smiled as he said, "Lance can play every instrument here better than even Freddy."

Lance's head swelled a little bit, but he tried to hide it. "Thanks, Steve," he said. "I'd like to think that was true, but Freddy was much more talented than I am. He used everything I taught him in writing these songs. Plus, he used a few chords he picked up on the way. Freddy was a natural musician. I'm just me."

"We should really play Suzanna, too," Morley said. "After all, Charlie wrote it for his girl back home. We should play it Charlie's way, not Freddy's way."

"Good idea," said Brutus.

Charlie picked up his guitar and showed the band members the chord changes, as well as Freddy's changes. "I can use Freddy's ideas to improve what I had written."

"Almost the same," he said. "Freddy, he fix my chorus good. I like."

"Good," said Morley.

"Will we be playing something special for Freddy?" asked Charlie.

"I have a song, but I don't know if I'll be able to sing it," Lance said.

"Why? If you wrote it, you should be able to sing it." Steve said. "That's kinda silly."

"Oh, for heaven's sake, Steve. That's not what he means. Freddy was a good friend, and a student of Lance's. Don't you have any feelings at all for anything other than filling your belly?" Brutus said.

"Forget it, you guys," Morley ordered. "This is not the place to argue." Turning to Lance, he said, "Perhaps we could all sing it together. If we flash the words on a screen behind the band, the audience could sing it as well.

"Good idea," Lance agreed. "Let's go. No more talking. Tune to the piano. Come on, Steve, give us a G chord. Nice piano."

"Yeah, but you should use the keyboard you'll be playing for the concert instead," Morley suggested.

"Is this okay for tonight?"

"Of course."

"Come on, Charlie. Get your tonsils tuned up, man, so we can get with it."

"Tonsils?" Charlie repeated. "That new guitar?" He looked for another instrument.

"No, he's just being funny," Morley said. "He means your voice."

"Oh," said Charlie, rubbing his throat. He quickly opened his case and tuned his guitar to the piano. "Where your keyboard, Steve?"

"I didn't bring it tonight."

"Sure, it' s fine for one rehearsal, but next week you should bring your own keyboard so we can do it exactly as we will in the theatre," Morley said.

"Well," Steve said, looking sheepish, "I don't have it right now. I hocked it last week so I could eat. Sorry about that."

"You *hocked* your keyboard? Really? Oh, no. I'd never do that!" Brutus muttered. "If you don't have your keyboard, how can you earn the money to get it back?"

"Come on, you guys," Lance ordered, realizing that Steve's financial problems were out of bounds for public scrutiny, not to mention the absurdity of Brutus' query. He vowed to have a chat with Steve and get his keyboard back before it was sold. "We can deal with that in private, later. Let's get down to business. Morley count us in."

"A one and a two and a three-four!" Morley chanted, hitting a rhythmic beat on the snare. "And away we go!"

The room filled with music.

In spite of some touchy moments in the beginning of the rehearsal, the music went well. Jem sang even better than he had done at the Roaring Tiger Pub, so much like Freddy that his mother quietly pushed the door open. "Leave the door open, boys," she said. "I want to listen. It's almost like having Freddy back. I miss him so much."

"We all do," Lance said. He thought of the last time he had rehearsed with the gang in this room. It was the night before Freddy died, and yet tonight marked a whole new era.

He and Steve walked out together. "Nice playing," he said,

"Thanks, Lance," Steve said. They watched Brutus jump into his car, slam the door, and swing onto the highway.

"Uh, Steve," said Lance hesitating for a moment. He looked the young man in the eye, and spoke, carefully measuring his words. "Let's get your keyboard right now. Did you leave it at Martin's Pawn Shop? How much did you get for it?"

"Just enough for a few days," Steve said. "I have to pick it up by Saturday or he'll add more onto it, and maybe sell it on me. I haven't got the money to get it tonight."

"That doesn't answer my question, Steve. I want to know how much he gave you for it," Lance asked. He put his hand on Steve's arm.

"One hundred dollars but he wants one hundred and thirty dollars to give it back to me and I don't have it," Steve said. He looked down at his feet.

"Your keyboard must be worth a lot more than that, Steve. I know it's one of the best on the market. What time does he close?" asked Lance.

"Ten tonight. Weeknights it's five o'clock. Why do you want to know?" Steve said.

"That's just three blocks away on Gryphon Street," Lance said. "I'll give you the money to get it out tonight, but you have to promise me you will come to me the next time you are broke. You mustn't do this again, Steve. Come on, lead the way." He put his hand up to stop Steve from protesting. "No time for words. Let's go. Move, boy. We have thirty minutes to get there and redeem it."

He watched Steve get into the old Monarch after he'd tightened the door handle. Lance wondered how much gas the old car burned and vowed to help him have it serviced. Steve was a good keyboard player, but he obviously wasn't good at handling his money.

At the pawnshop when Steve started to get out of his car, Lance said, "Let's do this right. We need to talk it over before you go in." He got into the car and put his hand on Steve's shoulder. "Tell him you have the cash to get your keyboard."

"Come with me," Steve insisted.

"Well, okay, but wouldn't it be better if you went alone?" Lance observed the woebegone expression on the younger man's face.

Steve shook his head. "No, I don't trust him."

"He's there to loan money, not terrorize customers."

Mr. Martin was not in a good frame of mind when Steve and Lance walked through the door. Steve laid the ticket on the counter and counted out the money. The shop owner frowned when Steve said, "I came to get my keyboard."

"What did you do, rob a bank?" the proprietor asked, narrowing his eyes.

"No," Steve said. "I saved for it."

"Oh, really? Not likely. I know how you save money. Next time ask me before you go makin' deals with somebody else, will ya? I don't like nobody playin' my game. I stick my neck out to help you and then you double-cross me," Martin said, as he grudgingly accepted the money.

It was a happy young man who left the shop a half hour later, carrying his keyboard, but a decidedly unhappy pawnshop owner.

"Bad tempered old devil!" Steve complained to the closed door.

"Does he always give you the runaround?" Lance asked.

"Usually," Steve admitted.

"How many times have you pawned your keyboard?" Lance asked.

"Once a month, unless I'm lucky," Steve answered.

"That many times?" Lance asked. "So, you are a regular customer. I guess that was why he resented me coming in with you."

"He wants my keyboard because he knows it's a high-end model. One of these days he hopes I'll be unable to pay him, and he can sell it for what it's worth," Steve admitted.

"We'll talk about it tomorrow, Steve," Lance said. "Do you have enough groceries for the week?"

"I have enough for a day or two;" Steve said. "Thank-you. I was wondering what to do. I'll pay you back as soon as I can."

"Don't do anything until we've talked about it, Steve," Lance said. "I'm sure we can work out something better than Martin would."

"I want to pay my bills," Steve said.

"Of course, you do. I'll see you tomorrow. I have some odd jobs for you to do around my place," Lance said. "Lanny and Roy do some but often there's more than they can do. You'll have money to pay your bills and get groceries. How does that hit you?"

"Nice," Steve said with a grin. Steve walked to his car

with a lilt in his step after the two men had shaken hands.

Lance headed home after seeing Steve pull away from the Pawn shop. He thought of Freddy and the money deal that had cost him his life. He recalled his own youth and knew from experience it wasn't easy being young. Lance remembered it only too well himself. In an age when there were so many more things to investigate, so many more attractive places to explore than in the days before free love was offered generously. It was difficult to say 'no' to all the delights of the twentieth century. An age that had the motto "Make Love, not war."

When Lance arrived home at eleven o'clock, the house was in darkness, except for a light in the bathroom. He opened the back door and brought his equipment in as quietly as possible. He had enjoyed the rehearsal and the camaraderie he had with the young people.

He was still putting his instrument away when Andrea came into the music room wearing her bathrobe. Her blonde hair was damp and sticking up all over her head, but she still appeared attractive to him.

"Awesome hairstyle," he said. "Is it a new one?"

"Goodness no!" Andrea said with a chuckle. "I wouldn't want anyone but you to see me like this. Hang on and I'll drag a comb through it. It's kind of scary like this, but there is an actress who wears this style and seems to get away with it, but I wouldn't recommend it." She came into the bathroom next to the music room and picked up a comb.

"I know the one you mean," Lance said as she walked away.

He watched as she shook the water out of it and combed the tangles away. She pushed the waves into place with her fingers. "Ah, that's better," he said.

"Was your rehearsal good, tonight?" Andrea asked.

"Yes, but Steve had pawned his keyboard so he could

buy groceries, and I talked him into letting me pay the man so he could get it back," he explained. "I feel sorry for the kid."

"I know you care about these kids, Lance, but you can't solve everyone's problems. What about his parents?"

"They live in Vancouver but he's too proud to ask them for help. I offered him some odd jobs around here. I helped him redeem his keyboard tonight. Is that okay with you?" Lance asked.

She thought for a moment. "If it's important to you, Lance," she said. "We aren't made of money, but I know we always have work to do here. We'll talk about it tomorrow."

"Okay," Lance said. "If you are finished with the bathroom, I'd better go clean up. Trying to keep up with those young players certainly gets my adrenalin flowing. I need a shower."

"You certainly do, but I love you just the same." With a cheeky smile, she disappeared down the hall.

THIRTY-ONE

Lance raced the boys to the rural mailbox by the upper gate to his farm for the Friday morning paper. They wanted the horoscope, the funnies, and the weekend TV schedule. Lance wanted the headlines of the week and the Stock Exchange news.

He was shocked when he casually glanced at the headlines and saw a familiar name. On the front page in large print the words jumped out at him. KILLER STILL ON THE LOOSE. Under it in smaller print a one-liner read, *DNA always tells the Truth.*

Lance sat down on a log and stared at the mugshot of Aldo Cody.

"Come on, Dad!" Roy said. "Are you going to read the whole thing here?"

"No, but this is of interest to all of us. I don't like this."

"Who's Aldo Cody? Do we know him?" Roy asked.

"Only too well," he answered.

With Roy looking over his shoulder he went on to read the entire story, unable to digest the information it contained. It ended with. a warning. 'If you see this man, do not approach him. He is armed and dangerous. Call 911 or Crime stoppers at 555-1212 immediately and report the sighting. Anonymous calls are accepted.'

"Dad!" reproached Lanny. "You took the whole paper! I just wanted the horoscope!"

"Sorry," Lance said as he pulled the pages out. "We should buy two papers from now on." He made a quick check to make sure he'd given the boys the appropriate pages.

Lance had last seen Aldo Cody two days ago lying on

the ground with Leif Ferguson standing over him. How could he be on the loose? Lance had witnessed him being handcuffed and thrown into the paddy wagon with two other men. Had he escaped? Lance read the column again.

Killer? Who was the victim? It didn't say. Just that his DNA matched that found at the site of a murder. When? The night of the Sinkholes concert tour featuring a visiting heavy metal band?

Freddy's killer?

He walked back down the hill to the house, planning to phone Brad, but the phone was already ringing. Lanny beat him to it and handed the receiver to his dad.

"For you again," he said. "How come you get all the calls around here? Even more than Roy or Mom."

Lance just smiled and took the phone call. "Hi Lance," a familiar voice said. "Brad here. Have you read the headlines?"

"Yes, I just picked up my paper. I thought he was already in jail."

"The paper said he was charged and released on bail," Brad said. "I'm worried about Leif. He sure made an ass out of Cody that night. Mind you, that little guy can probably take care of himself, unless taken by surprise."

"That's true. But the columnist called Cody a killer. How can they write that before there has even been a court hearing?" Lance asked.

"You're right, Lance. I questioned that too. However, if he's on the loose and armed, there's every reason to believe he is dangerous. I'll pop up to see you after dinner tonight?" Brad said.

"Sure, about seven thirty will be good. Okay?"

"See you then," Brad said, as he signed off.

It was nearly eight o'clock when Brad turned into Lance's driveway where he sat talking on his phone before coming to the door.

"He's still at large," Brad said when Lance opened the door. "Cody's been seen several times, but we haven't caught up with him yet. We have a fairly good idea where he's headed."

"Leif's house?" asked Lance.

"Maybe, but I think he'll go across the border. He has dual citizenship," Brad said.

"Well, come in and sit down., "Lance said. "I didn't know he was from the States. What did they mean about DNA telling the truth?"

"Yeah, he's from Oregon. Before he was arrested," Brad said, "his father reported him missing and we took his hairbrush to collect his DNA in case he was in an accident."

"I'm surprised the newspaper columnist wrote that. Then it was published in a daily newspaper as if it was true."

"I am too. There will be a hearing and a trial unless he admits to it, and even then, it must all be legal," Brad said.

"When the newspaper published his name and called him a killer, they were wrong then?" asked Lance.

"Legally they are. Saying he is a killer before he has been charged is against the law. Cody likely could challenge the newspaper for writing that and delay the process, and that is within his rights," Brad said, "but he's wanted for questioning as well, so he will be arrested and charged with assault."

"Would you like a coffee before you head home? Or are you planning to check Leif's place first?" Lance asked. "How is Hagar making out?"

"Right on all counts. I'll take the coffee, check on Leif and be on my way. Hagar and Bigamy are doing fine. Leif is good to them, and he likes their company. I intended on asking how the plans for the memorial concert for Freddy are going?" Brad said.

"Everything is going fine," Lance assured him. "The dress rehearsal is this afternoon."

"When's the concert?"

"Saturday night. I hope you're coming. You and Heathcliffe are running security. Did you forget?" Lance said in alarm.

"My mind is busy, but I didn't really forget. We'll be there," Brad assured him. "It's been one hell of a week. I'll be glad when it's over."

"Me, too, but I'm looking forward to the concert. It should be one of our best. Charlie and his crew have done a terrific job of decorating the Convention Centre. It's also his first Canadian concert as a performer. "

"I know," Brad said as he finished his coffee. "Cody makes me nervous. I wonder what he'll do next. When he's located this time, there won't be any release. He's burnt his bridges behind him. There were conditions and he has already broken them."

Lance felt somewhat uneasy as he got ready for bed that night, but he brushed it from his mind and thought about the dress rehearsal. "

***

Morley began the dress rehearsal with a drum solo. Music filled the air, while the rafters literally vibrated with the sound. Standing in the centre, Charlie nervously tried to start the program. His English faltered and his face reddened with embarrassment.

"You won't have to start off at the concert," Lance told him. "Brutus will do that. I wonder what's keeping him? He's never late. Tonight, we get to make all the mistakes we like. That's what dress rehearsals are for."

Jem and Charlie fit in with the band very well after only three rehearsals. For the rehearsal, held in the Bastable music room, Charlie had brought his acoustic guitar with him so they could sing the non-electronic version of the song Lance had written for Freddy. *Farewell My Friend.*

"Good idea, Charlie," Lance said. "I hope the audience will take part in this one because I'm not sure I can sing it. Brutus said he can put the words on a screen for the audience like they do in other concert halls."

"They do that in churches now, too," Charlie said. "Even back at home before I came here, a technician would flash the words to our music on the wall so everyone could sing it."

"Yep," Lance said. "We did a Sing-along Messiah concert one time and the words to the choruses and even the solos were on a screen, so the audience could take part. The Halleluiah Chorus was wonderful with seven hundred and twenty-five voices."

"What on earth is a 'singalong Messiah'," Jem asked, looking confused.

"Members of the audience are invited to sing the choruses and even the solos," Lance explained. "Local choir members love to get a chance to perform without any stress. It's fun, although it is serious music that most of us know."

When Brutus arrived, Lance and Charlie were still setting up for the rehearsal.

"Hey, guys," Brutus said as he bustled through the open door, "Who's that blocking the parking lot? He sure don't know how to drive. He's parked halfway out into the street, and I darn near hit him when I came around the corner."

"Could be the *Shot Glass Five*. They want to join us for the Farewell concert too. They were at the theatre the night we lost Freddy," Lance said, as he looked through the window. "I forgot they wanted to come to this rehearsal and open up before we begin to play, just like they did at the concert."

"Well, okay, I guess," Brutus said. "They want to say

goodbye to Freddy too."

"I was the one who suggested to Lance that we reach out to them too," Jem said.

A few minutes later the Shot Glass Five bunch walked in behind Brutus and entered without knocking according to the old custom of entering quietly as to not disrupt a rehearsal. in progress.

"We're here!" Shotglass Five drummer Tommy Bergen announced "Who are those guys parked on the road? Snotty bunch of creeps!" he said. "I thought our roadie, Al Cody, was out of town, but I see him here."

"Shush!" warned Steve. "Look who just came in."

Brutus jerked to attention when he saw Aldo Cody sneaking in behind the band members followed by three other men. Cody led the way, his gun aimed straight ahead at Lance. He pushed aside the other three men and stepped into the light.

"Stay where you are and keep your hands in the air, where I can see them. This is not a social visit. I'm here to get what belongs to me."

"What the hell?" Brutus muttered, putting his hands up.

"The cops already have the coke," Jem said, lowering his hands slightly. "You're too late."

"If you don't want to get shot, Mister, keep those hands in the air. Gimme what's mine now."

"I said you're too late. The cops have it," Jem repeated; "I don't have any coke."

"Oh, I'm not here for that. anymore. I came here to get all the cash. I'm getting to hell out of this dump. I want that cash, all of it, before I jump the ditch into the States where I belong."

"Cash? What cash?" asked Lance. "None of us have much cash on us."

"Jem the Bastard has cash," Cody snarled. "I know you

286

didn't stop at the bank when you left the Music shop. I followed you here."

"Oh $****," Jem mouthed to Lance. "There's an envelope with cash in it upstairs. I'll go up and get it," he said aloud.

"Oh, no, you won't," Cody snarled. He turned to his gang members "Watch these creeps while I take this idiot up and get the dough. I'll come down when I've settled with him." He roughly shoved Jem into the lower hallway, and toward the stairs and followed him up to the kitchen. Through the open door Lance could see the gun shoved into the centre of Jem's back. He flinched every time Cody rammed the barrel into Jem again.

Charlie had been tuning his acoustic guitar just outside the hallway when the gang walked in. No one appeared to notice him because he wasn't a regular member of the band and he had learned a few sneaky moves while hiding on the catwalk.

One of the gang members told Charlie to get over with the other band members but Charlie pretended he didn't understand. He suddenly broke into a stream of foreign words which were gibberish to the musicians.

"Shut your mouth," a gang member roared, as Charlie moved closer to the Shot glass Five group instead.

"Hey, we didn't even know about this," Jackie Gordon, the lead singer for the other band blurted. "What's going on?"

"Get over there with the others," growled another gang member. He brandished his gun in Charlie's face.

Charlie moved again, keeping the phone hidden. Suddenly he slammed his guitar against two of the three gang members,

Guns fell to the floor as one of the Shot Glass members slammed into the third guy, knocking him to the ground.

Lance kicked all three guns across the floor and Brutus, Steve and Morley grabbed them, pointing the weapons at the invaders.

Cody and Jem were at the top of the stairs during the commotion. Lance heard Cody say, "Happy landing, Chump," as he got a quick look at Jem falling down the stairs. Cody must have escaped through the upstairs exit, because a second later he heard the unmistakable sound of Brutus' sports car being driven away. Lance wondered how he did it without the key.

Lance ran outside through the basement door and watched as Brad spoke into his car radio before he took off. He figured he was calling for backup, before he and Heathcliffe raced to the Bastable house, and knew he had witnessed Cody getting into Brutus' sports car. Lance lost sight of Brad as he swung around the corner on two wheels.

***

"I want two cars to join in the pursuit of a red nineteen ninety-one Alpha Romeo Spider sports car and send two more to the Bastable house at three twenty-two Mock Orange Boulevard." Brad gave chase himself, while continuing to talk into the radio. "The suspects are presumed to be armed and dangerous. Proceed with caution."

Heathcliffe barked while sitting in the back seat. The partition was not up so the dog was ready for action.

"Keep calm," Brad commanded as he took the turn onto the freeway at one hundred and twenty miles per hour. Shaking with excitement, the dog jumped into the front seat and watched the sports car careen down the highway.. The top was down making it easy for Aldo to point his gun at the SUV and fire off a couple of rounds of ammo at it. The windshield cracked on the passenger side.

"Heathcliffe, to the back!" Brad instructed the dog. He immediately obeyed. He went to the very back of the car beyond the seats.

Cody aimed at the SUV again and lost control of the sports car he was driving. The Alpha Romeo swerved, and the backend continuing the turn out of control until the car went into a spin, landing in a ditch upside down. Aldo fought his way out. Like a drowned rat, he crawled out and sprinted through the ditch. He kicked bull rushes out of his way, sloshing through the mud and filth and headed toward a thicket of blackberry bushes to hide.

Two police cars travelling in the opposite direction came to a halt. One of them yelled, "Freeze! Police!" before he jumped over the ditch.

Brad got out of his SUV to warn the other cop to be careful. "Cody is armed and dangerous. Heathcliffe…" He gave the order for the dog to go after him. Heathcliffe leaped out of the open door and bolted toward the ditch.

In a clearing, the other officer got close to Cody and again ordered him to freeze. Instead, the fugitive swung around, his gun in his hand and aimed it toward the cop.

With lightning speed Heathcliffe did what his police dog training had taught him to do, the second Brad gave him the order. He came in from the back and grabbed Aldo Cody's wrist. The gun fell to the ground and Heathcliffe let go of his wrist and placed his teeth around Aldo Cody's neck to hold him securely.

Brad crawled up the side of the ditch and ran to the clearing as quickly as he could and spotted the second cop just ahead.

"Hold!" he ordered the dog. Heathcliffe held Cody securely without breaking skin. The two cops got the gun from him and placed it in a plastic bag.

"Release!" ordered Brad. Heathcliffe released his hold on the man, while the other two officers stood with their guns drawn. Cody was handcuffed and taken into custody.

"Take him downtown, boys, "Brad said. "I've got to get to the Bastable house and see if everyone is okay. He stole an envelope of cash belonging to The Bastable Music Store, and he has it on him."

"Gotcha," one of the arresting cops said as he shoved Cody into the back of the car, behind the bars. The lock clicked behind him, the first of many locks, Brad thought, as he got into his SUV and drove away.

***

Back at the centre, the police had taken the rest of Aldo Cody's men into custody. A big paddy wagon was parked in the driveway. Both the Sinkholes and the Shot Glass Five members were talking with the police when Brad arrived.

"If it wasn't for Charlie's quick thinking, that guy would have gotten away," Brutus told Brad when he came back. "He saved the whole works of us single handed."

Brad walked over to meet Lance when he arrived, but Heathcliffe got to him first, trying to tell his version of the takedown of Aldo Cody.

"I know exactly what he is saying, you know!" Lance said. "We're old friends."

"What did happen and how did you know to call me?" asked Brad.

"In a nutshell, Charlie saved the day, plus an envelope containing about eleven grand belonging to the Bastable Music shop. It's marked with their name."

"How's my car?" asked Brutus.

"It's a bit sick, but your insurance will cover it," Brad said.

"I know, but I just got it waxed and serviced for my wedding this weekend. Where is it?" asked Brutus.

"Sitting in a ditch about five miles from here," Brad said. "I'm sure it can be fixed."

"Oh no! How come?"

"He was shooting at me. I didn't shoot back at him, but one of the other officers had a shootout with him."

"The top was down, and I wanted it to be perfect for the wedding." Brutus moaned.

Lance patted him on the shoulder and promised to stay up all night if necessary and wax his own car so Brutus could have it. Steve said he would play the piano for the reception. He patted him on the other shoulder. Charlie said he would do anything Brutus wanted. He slapped Brutus on the first shoulder again.

"If you guys don't mind, just give me a handshake. "Brutus advised, "If I get smacked anymore I'll be getting a ride in an ambulance. Your happiness is going to cripple me."

"I don't know why you are complaining, Brutus," one of the guys from the Shot Glass Five remarked. I'd like it if our group was like that after work time. We hardly speak unless we're on stage."

"Yeah," said their lead singer, "Me too. Even the cop's dog loves you!"

Lance summed it up with a few words. "Life is too short not to care!"

THIRTY-TWO

Lance and his musical buddies didn't have the heart to continue with the rehearsal after being held up by Aldo Cody's gang. They quietly packed up their instruments after the police and took the criminals away in the paddy wagon.

"I just thought of something that will make everything go right!" Steve said a with a grin so large his face literally shone. "I'll drive you home. My car is old, but it still drives. What if I wax it up real good tonight and you can have it tomorrow."

"Your car?" blurted Brutus. "You'd loan me your car?"

"Sure, we could fix the door handle tonight and clean it up. It needs a little work, but it drives well, and I have some wax," Steve said.

"I'll call my dad right away. He likes your car. What is it, a forty-nine Mercury Monarch? That's the last year they used the lion hood ornament, you know," Brutus said, his eyes lighting up.

"Yeah, something like that," Steve said. "I think they got sued because it was so much like the jaguar ornament. I'm sure it's not worth much but I don't want to get rid of it."

"Nope," Lance said, "That's the nineteen sixty-seven Mercury Cougar, I think."

"Really? I've always liked that old lion. He's a handsome beggar," Brutus said. "I'll miss my little Spider! but getting a chance to drive the Mercury Monarch will make it easier.

Morley and Jem listened to the conversation as they packed up and prepared to go home. Jem and Charlie had just returned from the police station where they had each written a statement about the home invasion by Aldo Cody and his gang. Lance was able to tell the police what he had witnessed as he stood in the rehearsal room by the stairs. Brad met them there and assisted Charlie with the English legal terms as much as he was allowed to do.

Brutus called his father right away with the bad news and the good news. "Hi, Dad," he said.

"How did the rehearsal go, son?" inquired Dr Falgaar. "All ready for the wedding this weekend? Bet you're excited. You got a concert to do too. What's up?"

"That's what I phoned to tell you. Aldo Cody and his gang pulled a home invasion tonight, stole money that belonged The Bastable Music Store and got away with my car. He…?"

"Your car?" he asked. "Stole it? Your Alpha Romeo sports car? They won't get far in that without being caught. It can be seen miles away."

"They didn't just use the Spider to get away in. About two hours ago they used it for a shootout with the police. It's upside down in a ditch between Washington and B.C. You know the place they call *The Ditch* on Highway 99."

"Not personally," Bruce Falgaar said, "but I've heard of it. How are you getting home?"

"That's what I phoned for," Brutus said. "You know my friend Steve? He's driving me home and has offered his car for the wedding." There was an ominous silence on the other end of the phone.

"The Mercury Monarch?" Bruce Faulgaar asked. "He would actually loan it to you?"

"The same," Brutus said. "The door handle has to be fixed tonight and it needs a wax job."

"Really Does he know how much that car is worth?" his father asked.

"He knows it's an antique but has no idea what it's

worth. He says I can have it tonight," Brutus said.

"Stay there. I'm coming for you right now. Don't move. I'm on my way," his dad said. Brutus grinned to himself. He knew his father was familiar with that car, and probably would insist on driving it. He forgot to tell him they would have to drive Steve home first, and either loan him another car or give him a ride. He was the best man, so he had to be at the wedding.

Both Lance and Morley were overjoyed. Steve didn't know what the excitement was about. "It's just an old car," he said. "The door handle still falls off."

"Is it the original handle," Brutus asked.

"I think so," Steve said. "I've never thought about it. I just pick it up and tighten the screws every time I drive it. Don't matter to me."

Dr. Faulgaar took no time at all to arrive at Jem's studio, to get his hands on Steve's car. He leaped out after parking hurriedly on the street.

"You must have wings," Brutus said. "It only took you twenty minutes to get here. It takes me thirty minutes at least." He watched in amusement as his father gently ran his fingers over the Monarch.

"May I drive it?" he asked.

"Sure. That's what it's for. As long as I don't have to walk home," Steve said. "Nobody has offered me a ride yet."

"Oh, no," Dr, Falgaar said." I'll give you a loaner for the weekend. Just don't go knocking the door handle off. You and Brutus can follow me up there and you can drive my Lincoln. When we get there, I'll give you one of my cars for the week." He giddily got into the Monarch and tightened the door handle with a radiant smile on his face. "Any other parts that might fall off?"

"Nope!" Steve said cheerfully. "None that I know of.

Don't forget to put on your seat belt. I installed a new one a few days ago." He chuckled good naturedly as Bruce Falgaar started up the Monarch.

Steve climbed into the Lincoln with the expression on his face of an astronaut about to land on the moon. He looked around at the spacious seats, the wide body and flawless upholstery. He started the Lincoln and looked at Brutus sitting beside him.

Are you sure your father really meant I was to drive this car? Maybe he meant you were to drive it," Steve said, with a nervous chuckle.

"Nope, Steve. He really meant you were to drive it. He's like that. Just enjoy it. He has wanted to drive the Monarch for ages, and you gave him a chance to do that. He's doing what he likes the most."

Lance and Jem watched from the front driveway as the two men drove away.

***

Instead of having a traditional stag party on the eve of his wedding, Brutus was treated to a car-waxing party.

The cement pad behind the Faulgaar house had been swept clean. "I'll move these two work trucks," Brutus said, "and get the water hoses and pails. I see you've already got overalls. You guys thought of everything, even sponges! Wow! You mean business!" He beamed with happiness.

"I brought some car wash, too," Steve said, with a big grin.

By the time the car was gleaming in the moonlight, everyone was soaking wet.

When his brother-in-law George arrived with a case of beer, the scrubbers and polishers were happy to take half an hour out to indulge.

"Why didn't Dad just loan you one of his cars instead of all this trouble?" George asked, as he passed out the bottles.

"Because he's my dad," Brutus said, proudly "He's wanted to get close to this beauty for ages. He sees a beautiful antique car."

"Because that's what it is," Bruce said as he picked up a clean rag and polished a door handle. "Let's get back to work, guys!"

They sat down at a small table Brutus brought from the garage.

"Okay. Wow!" You'd never know it's just a beat up old car," Steve said with a chuckle. "Traditionally I get to drive it to the airport when they leave on their honeymoon."

"Well, you do own it," Jem said, who just arrived with more clean rags.

"Grab a sponge and make yourself useful," Brad said, when he, Charlie and Leif came around the corner followed by Heathcliffe and Hagar. The two dogs had a reasonably friendly relationship after a few visits together recently. Heathcliffe was always friendly, but Hagar still had a lot to learn.

"Have a beer," said George. "They're on the house."

"Nope, I don't want to speak gibberish today. Last time I had a drink or two I even disowned myself," Leif said. "Who's gonna do the hood ornament?"

"You," Brutus told him, as he waved the hose in his direction. "You aren't wet yet."

"I'm sure you'll remedy that," Leif said. "Hoist me up there and I'll do it. On second thought, I'll jump up and someone can pass me the bucket." He spun around and with a flip, he landed on his knees close to the lion.

Eventually the Monarch came out looking as handsome and regal as the king of the jungle it represented. Steve stared at it with a smile on his face.

"Would you like to park it in the garage now, Steve?"

asked Bruce Falgaar, examining the beautiful vintage car. "A right–hand drive? Wow!"

Steve nodded, as he picked up the screwdriver he always kept handy and took his place behind the wheel. "I didn't know it could look like this with a little care. What is there about this car that interests you, Sir," he asked. "It's just an old car."

Bruce grinned. "The right hand drive is very unusual. I thought I mentioned it before."

"Oh yeah. The guy who sold it to me was pleased about that because he was from England. They drive on the left there. When it got old and cost him money, he just wanted to get rid of it."

"Funny," Bruce said. "It makes it more valuable. Do you do your own repairs?"

"Oh yeah. It rattles a bit, but it still drives okay. I don't care what side the steering wheel is on," Steve said with a chuckle.

"Why don't you fix the door handle so it won't fall off?"

"Damned if I know." Steve shrugged his shoulders. "No reason, I guess. It will be fixed for the wedding,"

***

When she arrived home from the dinner with her girlfriends the night before the wedding, Joanne thought seriously about her wedding gown and the jewelry she had chosen to go with it. Everything had to be perfect. There was only one way to find out, and that was to try it on. She couldn't ask Brutus because tradition said the groom was not to see his bride until the wedding. She had a shower, being careful not to destroy her hair although she had an appointment with the hairdresser before the wedding.

She slid the closet door open and examined the dress. It was beautiful. She felt like a princess as she touched the white satin skirt. It wouldn't hurt to try it on one more time. No one needed to know. It was her secret. She stealthily slipped it off the hangar and laid it out on her bed while she took off her nightgown in this room for one last time. Tomorrow night it would be a different matter.

Joanne pulled the zipper down and slipped the gown on over her head. When she zipped it up again she realized how tight it was. Very form fitting. Her reflection in the full length mirror told her it looked perfect. She clasped the pearls around her neck and put on the beautiful drop earrings. They were the gift of the groom's parents and the real thing. She pranced up and down the room smiling at herself. Then she remembered the 'something old, something new, something borrowed and something blue.' That was easy. She had a blue garter, and plenty of new things. She picked up the borrowed shoes and the old watch her grandmother had worn years ago. Perfect!

"I'll be a beautiful bride," she told her mirror image. "Mom did a great job of making this dress. She is a wonderful seamstress. Look at the neckline! Gorgeous lace. Mom even made the lace herself." She walked up and down the room, twirled around twice and admired herself in the full-length mirror. Smiling, she curtseyed one more time just to make sure she was really as regal as she felt.

After a half hour or so, she checked the time. It was eleven o'clock and if she wanted to look as beautiful as she felt, she'd better go to bed. She took off the necklace and earrings and put them away and tried to pull down the back zipper.

It stuck halfway down. She yanked and pulled it and shed tears over it. She couldn't pull the dress off without unzipping it. She tried to twist it around so she could unzip it easier. Nothing worked so she sat on the bed and cried.

She knew her mother was asleep. There was no one to

call for help.

"I don't want to get married anyway!" she sobbed. Wiping her tears on the nightgown lying on the bed, she tried one more time. Nothing worked. "I'm trapped in the thing! If I sleep in it, it will look like a rag. What will I do? Why am I so vain? "

Finally, she sat on the bed and cried hard for several minutes. Then she thought of something.

Chocolate! She always felt better after eating chocolate. Why didn't she think of it before? What if she got it on her dress? There was no time to clean it if she dribbled chocolate on it. Just one little square! She had a whole bar right on her dresser.

Joanne gave in to the lure of the lovely, sweet bar and broke off one delicious square. As it melted in her mouth, she swallowed it and forced herself to calm down. Ten minutes later she tried one more time. The zipper slid down easily, and Joanne slipped out of the dress and hung it up in the closet.

She smiled at her image in the full-length mirror. "Tomorrow my husband will be able to help me take it off."

***

In another part of town Brutus wondered if Joanne felt nervous too. He knew he was about to find out. He'd heard stories of weddings that almost got cancelled at the last minute over some small thing that probably didn't matter at all. Like last night.

He had to laugh when Joanne told him about getting stuck in her wedding dress the night before. He knew it was no laughing matter at the time and almost brought everything to a grinding halt. Well, not really. Joanne was more sensible than that. Besides, if she gets stuck in anything after this, he'd be there to save her. He relished the thought.

The song went, "Get me to the church on time." Maybe she'd be late, and he'd have to wait.

Steve picked him up at four-thirty and delivered him to the church for the five o'clock ceremony. The old Monarch shone in the evening sunshine. And the handle didn't fall off. Steve looked quite dashing in his dark suit and tie.

After talking to the pastor, Brutus walked to the alter and stood quietly waiting. The strains of music filtered through the hallways and out onto the courtyard welcoming the many people in the congregation. He stood with his back to them. Who would be there? Old girlfriends? Those who wanted him for his money and those who didn't want him at all but were curious.

Brutus heard the music change as the bride walked up the aisle. He gasped as her father brought her to him. Wow! She did look beautiful. Stunning in fact, Henry Riker was quite handsome in his dark suit, while his wife, looked very nice in a lovely blue gown. Joanne's friend Betty was charming as a bridesmaid.

Lance as organist was superb and Morley sang 'Oh, Promise Me' with feeling. Brutus was impressed. Brad and Charlie sat together in one of the front pews while Leif was the usher. Brutus wondered what Leif would do if Cody and his gang should turn up? The visions of a takedown in the church hallway calmed his bridegroom nerves. He walked to meet his bride with a smile on his face.

Luckily, the only interruption was when Hagar tried to assist Leif at the door and took exception to one of the guests getting too close to him, but as usual, Heathcliffe was the picture of authority in his working dog uniform.

The reception took place in the Moose Hall overlooking the mighty Fraser River in Rocky Creek.

THIRTY-THREE

Early Sunday morning Steve drove the bride and groom to YVR to catch a plane for Los Angeles for a five day honeymoon. Brutus would miss the rescheduled dress rehearsal before the concert, but he felt sure the rest of the gang were capable of carrying on without him. In fact, he was so happy that he barely gave it a thought!

On Thursday afternoon, the Faulgaars, the Rikers and the bridal party waited at the airport to meet Brutus and Joanne. To the amusement of other passengers, the familiar strains of 'Here Comes the Bride' could be heard as Lance played the melody on a large alto recorder just outside the entrance, accompanied by Steve on the ukulele and Morley on a small acoustic guitar. Charlie sang the words, forgetting to sing them in English, but it mattered not because the sentiment was the same in any language.

It was those first sounds of home the newlyweds heard as they trudged along the exit ramp with other travelers entering Canada. The electric doors opened to reveal the Monarch and the newly outfitted Alpha Romeo at the curb.

After going through customs, they were met by the welcoming party and escorted to the waiting vehicles. Steve had the honour of being the chauffeur in his Monarch. "Your Limousine awaits," he said, holding the door open, with a courtly bow.

The door handle didn't fall off, and there were no squawks or groans coming from the newly tuned up engine.

"Wow!" gasped Joanne as her new mother-in-law leaned out the door of the Spider and gave her an affectionate hug. "Hi, Mom!" she whispered, using the unfamiliar words for the first time. They smiled shyly at one another.

Louise and Henry Riker were next but no less enthusiastic as they greeted the happy pair. "Hello, Dad," Brutus said with a grin when Henry approached him. They looked at one another and laughed.

Henry hugged his daughter and clapped Brutus on the shoulder.

"Now we are all one big happy family!" Bruce Faulgar declared. "We'll meet at Hayle for lunch, it's already ten thirty so we'll be out of the heavy traffic by that time. See you in about an hour for lunch. There's a fenced off area on the bank side of the highway, but on the river side there are blackberry bushes. It's a tiny place so you can't miss it. That's where we'll be.

He looked at the Monarch admiringly and said to Steve," Young man, you take care of the car from now on. It's very valuable."

"It's just an old car," Steve said. "Much better to drive after you got it overhauled for me—but it's so old nobody but you and I would want it. Who wants a fifty-year-old crate? The steering wheel isn't even where it's supposed to be."

"That's what makes it valuable, Steve," Bruce said. "A right-hand drive is rare. Drive carefully. This car is a gem. We must think of that. Let's go so we'll all meet for lunch."

Steve smiled at the word 'lunch' as he started the car and led the procession from the airport. Taffy said 'Ruff!" meaning that she agreed. If she was lucky, she might get a piece of ham or a sausage for lunch.

"Good dog!" Steve said. "We'll soon take you for a doggy stop and a drink of water." Taffy smiled as only a dog can smile. She wagged her tail in response and stretched out on the seat beside him.

Steve couldn't help admiring at himself in the rear-view

mirror. There is something magic about a new haircut, and a freshly waxed car. Taffy was beautiful too.

As they rounded the hairpin turn where the railway tracks cross the highway at a three-hundred-and-sixty-degree angle, Steve pointed out the mighty Preston River below. "Don't look down there," he advised as he followed the highway through Hidden Gold Creek, past Martha's Landing and across Roaring Creek Bridge.

"Why don't you stay with Highway one?" Brutus asked, as he looked from the window.

"Because there's a detour," he said. "The bridge is washed out. Didn't you see the sign?"

"What sign?"

Steve snickered. "Good thing you aren't driving then. I'd call you a distracted driver!"

"Guess who's distracting me?"

"I'm not going there!" Steve said with a chuckle. "We can still get to Hayle from here. I've been this way before. We go through Two Mountain Canyon to Pringle Rock

"Good grief!" Brutus said. "The elevation up at Pirate's Hideaway is over three thousand feet above sea level, so hold onto your stomachs."

"We're coming down. Everyone's following us."

"Look at those gorgeous evergreens," Joanne said. "That must be Mount Gregory from the opposite side Such beautiful scenery. There's Mom and Dad."

"Hey," muttered Brutus, looking over Steve's shoulder, "That crazy driver is too close to us. What's he trying to do?"

Steve's foot hovered over the brake pedal. "He's driving too fast, for one thing. Looks like they're drinking. Oh my gosh, he's crowding me on purpose. "

Brutus tightened his seatbelt and checked Joanne's to make certain she was buckled up. "Hey, do you know who those jokers are? They're that crazy Cody's gang."

Steve took as much of the road as he could without going into the oncoming lane. "I know. He's making me nervous," he said."

In another trick, the driver came right up to the Monarch, passed it, and as the driver pulled in front of the Monarch he suddenly came to a full stop, causing Steve to jam on the brakes to avoid a collision.

As the brakes squealed, the car lurched sideways. The other driver slammed his door as he got out and leaned into the Monarch. "You SOB," he hollered. "Why doncha learn to drive? I have a good mind to report you, I got your license number. Oh, the bride! Ain't she pretty? Want a thrill, little lady? We could all break you in for your old man! How about it, guys? She's here for the taking! "

He punched Brutus in the face. As blood spurted from his nose, the intruder shrieked with laughter. "Try to stop us and you'll get a lot more of those." He flung the rear window open and grabbed Joanne's arm. trying to drag her out of the car, but Steve was too fast for him.

He swung around and with one hand on the steering wheel, he grabbed the rear passenger door handle with the other hand and slammed it shut, barely missing the heckler's fingers.

The thug ran alongside the car hollering. His language would have melted the paint off a whole warehouse filled with new cars, but Steve didn't let that bother him.

The driver could be heard yelling threats as he made a U-turn to move behind the bridal car once more. They could be heard jeering as they passed in the wrong lane, nearly going over the bank.

"Keep calm, if you can," warned Steve. "I have no idea what this guy is going to do next. He's not finished yet. They're all drinking. My reflexes are fast, but I had no

304

passengers when I was stock-car racing. Sometimes we even pretended to crash just to give the onlookers a thrill."

"Idiot!" Brutus muttered as the driver in the rogue car suddenly made an attempt to pass the Monarch on a blind corner, pushing Steve onto the soft shoulder. He gripped the steering wheel until his knuckles were white.

Gritting his teeth, Steve avoided another collision by centimeters. Fighting the steering wheel, Steve outran the renegade car twice more. "He wants to force us off the road."

"What's he trying to do now?" Brutus asked.

"Probably not what he *is* doing," Steve observed as the heckler's car careened off the side of a telephone pole and landed in the ditch. "We'll send the cops to help you!" he yelled as they passed him.

"I have his number, so as soon as we are within cell phone range I'm calling the police," Brutus said. "I wish my nose would quit bleeding. Steve, you're doing great. There's a campsite ahead and we can make a call from there." He hesitated for a minute then asked, "By the way, was that fancy door maneuver you did back there really safe?"

"I wouldn't do it for fun with a carload of passengers, but I do know what I'm doing," Steve said. "If you and Joanne weren't behind me it wouldn't work. Luck was on my side. There's the campsite." He swerved the Monarch and parked as a second car whizzed by missing them by a whisper. Brutus hurriedly made the call to the police and was assured that the incident had been reported by another driver and the authorities already had it on their radar.

"Someone else reported them," he told the passengers after making the phone call. "The police are waiting for them at the ESSO Service station about a mile from here."

Ten minutes later the Monarch passed the service station The drunken party had just been terminated and the group of drunks were standing outside the car looking forlorn as they were being handcuffed and questioned. The car that had hit the telephone pole was nowhere in sight, but as the Monarch was driven by, the officers gave Steve a friendly wave.

"I think their party is over," Joanne observed. "That's their car."

"I have my screwdriver," Steve said, as he put his hand in his jacket pocket "I knew I wouldn't need it, of course."

"Why?" asked Brutus.

"You never know when it might come in handy."

"Where are we meeting for lunch," Brutus asked. "I should've written it down, I guess"

"No worries," Steve said with a superior air. "As the chauffeur I had it all written down."

"Good thing," Brutus said with a grin. "I was too excited to get anything straight. Not every day a guy gets to marry the best looking girl in Rocky Creek." Joanne hopped out of the car, as soon as Steve parked, and said "I need a bathroom."

Henry and Louise Riker arrived next followed by Lance and Andrea with the three kids. Behind them was Morley and his current girlfriend, a pretty girl who came barely to his shoulder.

"I was beginning to think we'd never get here," Joanne admitted. She hugged her parents again.

"I think that's the sixth time you've hugged me," Louise said as she tried to straighten her hairdo.

"You two look wonderful!" Andrea said as she got out of their car. "Lance said he'd lost you at one point but as we all agreed to meet here, we weren't worried. I'm hungry after all that."

"Brutus forgot where we were supposed to meet," Joanne said. "Until he saw the sign we were in the dark."

"Typical Brutus style," said his mother. "You'll get used to it."

"Excellent driving, Steve," said Brutus. "You did a terrific job. Thanks a million! You're one tough guy!"

"Steve, you really know your stuff when it comes to driving," Bruce said. "I agree. You had the presence of mind to apply your knowledge for a cause."

"Thanks, Steve. You saved my life," Joanne said. "When he tried to drag me out of the car, I was petrified. "

"So was I," Brutus admitted.

"You saved us all. I'll never forget that. Thank-you."

Steve said nothing but he grinned as he stood on the sidelines stroking his trusty old Monarch. Taffy looked up at him, with a loving doggy smile. Perhaps it was the sweet smell of food as Louise, Donna and Andrea whipped up a lunch. Then again it could have been the combination of romance, food, and satisfaction in a job well done.

As he joined Steve, Lance and the boys discussing stock cars, Bruce asked, "Now do you see why I was so excited over the Monarch having a right hand drive? You could not have done that stock-car trick if you were driving anything but this car."

"It's just an old car," Steve said with a nervous chuckle. "That idiot was out to get us, and someone would have gotten hurt or maybe killed. I have no training whatsoever."

"Perhaps not but you have common sense. I like old cars," Bruce said. "Brutus always helped me in the shop when he lived at home. He won't be able to spend much time doing that now he is a married."

"Let's go eat or the ladies will have our heads," Bruce said. "The food is served."

"Well, we wouldn't want that," Steve agreed. "Taffy feels the same. Look at her tail wagging. She knows the sweet smell of lunch."

THIRTY-FOUR

It was a short drive to Rocky Creek from Hayle, but it was late when at last Brutus and Joanne arrived at the cottage they would call home for many years to come. His parents had arrived earlier and turned on the porch lights for the happy couple.

A gift of the groom's parents, the cottage was on a two-acre lot bordered by seven poplar trees, a lilac hedge, and a swimming pool. "How come they call it a cottage?" Joanne asked. "It's larger than the house I grew up in."

"That's my dad for you," Brutus explained. "Anything less than fourteen rooms he considers a cottage."

Before they went to bed that night Joanne wanted to explore the property, but Brutus said, "I think we should wait until daylight to do that, dear. We have no idea what goes on in the dark at the end of a forest. Wild animals come out at night."

"Wild animals?" she said. "You mean bunnies and deer, don't you?"

"No," Brutus said with a chuckle. "Bears, mountain lions, and foxes. Deer, too but bunnies and little animals stay out of the way of those who might eat them. "

"Really? Mountain lions?"

"Yes, mountain lions. We can go tomorrow in the daylight. Did you forget that we have an important day ahead of us tomorrow?" Brutus asked, as he took her hand and lead her to the big picture window overlooking the panorama below.

"Tomorrow? What are we doing tomorrow?"

"We have wedding gifts to open," Brutus said. "Our parents will meet us for dinner and a family get-together," he said.

"Wedding gifts? For us?" Joanne said, her eyes wide.

"Yes, there's a whole room filled with parcels. We get to open them tomorrow. It's time to go to bed now so we'll be rested up for more parties. It isn't over yet," he said with a chuckle.

The following morning Brutus sat up with a start. "We slept in!" He blurted. He looked at the clock hanging on the wall by the dresser. It's seven o'clock already. What happened? I feel like I've been hit by a truck."

"It's only seven o'clock. This is the first time I've been called a truck," Joanne said with a giggle. "I feel groggy too, but we don't have to go to work this morning. We're on our honeymoon. We have the rest of the week off."

"Oh, yeah! Honeymoon. I'm hungry. Do people eat on honeymoons?" Brutus asked. "What's for breakfast?"

"I don't know," she said. "I don't think we have any groceries. We didn't shop."

He bounced out of bed and pulled the covers off his new wife. "Come on, Lazy bones. I need food or I'll pass out from starvation. Step to it, Mrs. Faulgaar!" He chased her down the stairs and into the kitchen,

"May I get dressed first?" she asked, not sounding a bit pathetic.

"Yes, but make it snappy," he ordered, trying to look fierce.

THIRTY-SIX

Brad's retirement evening was already underway when Lance and Andrea arrived. As he came through the door of the police conference room, he recognized some of the officers he'd seen on the streets of Meldrum city. He remembered seeing two of them at Leif's place the evening the Martial Arts teacher had tackled Aldo Cody's gang while he cowered behind a thicket of blackberry bushes, but understandably Lance preferred not to share that information.

Wearing his uniform for the last time, Brad sat to the right of Captain Tweedsdale at the right of the podium. Heathcliffe wore his working dog cape.

When the wonderful steak dinner was served to the men and women on the force, Heathcliffe sniffed but didn't pay much attention to the food until a smiling waiter pulled up a platform and placed next to Brad's chair. The dog was mildly interested when he put a dark blue dog dish on it containing a luscious looking steak, but Heathcliffe stayed put until Brad, his master beckoned him to jump up on the platform. He looked at the steak with interest without moving until Brad gave him the signal. With shining eyes and a doggie grin Heathcliffe willingly joined the diners and enjoyed his steak dinner. The applause didn't startle him as he looked up at Brad and softly said, "Mmm!"

Lance knew that it was a bitter-sweet experience for both Brad and Heathcliff on their retirement dinner. They both liked their work, but Brad had admitted to Lance that he looked forward to retirement. Now the time had come for them to put away their coveted uniforms and stay home, Lance couldn't help but notice that there was a sadness in

Brad's smile and even in the dog's eyes, as if he understood his longtime partner's mood. Brad was proud of the seven years they had worked as a team.

After dinner, Captain Tweedsdale walked to the podium and smiled benevolently at the crowd of off-duty officers and cleared his throat. Brad was called to the podium where he was presented with his forty-year service pin. The captain had to stand on tiptoes to pin it on the taller officer's uniform until Brad bent his knees to make himself shorter. They both laughed when the captain patted Brad on the head

"I'd forgotten how tall you are. Tell us again."

"Six feet six," Brad answered.

"Six inches taller than me," Tweedsdale said.

Heathcliffe happily accepted an edible dog bone and another badge to add to his cape. He favoured everyone with a doggy smile showing all his teeth as Captain Tweedsdale talked about him.

"Seven years ago, when Sgt. Heathcliffe was a police puppy, and before he was fully trained, he once brought a fugitive in all by himself. Brad had been trying to catch the culprit for ages, with no luck," Tweedsdale said. Brad patted the dog's head, knowing right well the story that would be told. He couldn't help chuckling as it was a good story about Heathcliffe, and how he was already earning his points.

"Brad was doing traffic duty with his faithful police dog in training by his side when Heathcliffe went after someone on the street. Without waiting for orders, the dog took off running. Brad got a glimpse of him chasing a man down the street and recognized him as a person of interest. Thomas finished his shift as soon as he could and went off to find his dog. Heathcliffe had disappeared entirely. An hour later Brad went into Headquarters to report the incident. Heathcliffe was sitting in front of the desk grinning with satisfaction. All by himself the police puppy had brought the criminal to the right place, although his method of arresting the man was not quite in the usual manner. Obviously, by the look of the man's torn trousers Heathcliffe had dragged the criminal around the corner and right to the police station, growling ferociously Onlookers said that every time the man tried to shake the dog off, Heathcliffe would snarl. Luckily, another cop drove up and recognized the criminal and the dog, so he opened the door and let him in. Private Heathcliffe proceeded to drag the man inside, and up to the counter. On the wall the man's mug shot was displayed, so there was no doubt in anyone's mind that the dog knew exactly what he was doing."

Brad stood up and acknowledged Heathcliffe's first "job" as being well done in spite of the circumstances.

"There was no way I could call him on leaving his post because he did a good job," Brad said, getting serious again. "He has always worked hard and deserves his retirement too. He might even get to chase a cat or two now—but I doubt he would bother. He's too well-behaved for that." The dog gave a dignified howl as Lance joined in the laughter at his own expense. Heathcliffe nudged his knee and looked up into his eyes.

Lance thought he heard a wee catch in Brad's voice as he listened to the stories. It must be a bittersweet moment when an officer turns in his badge and completes his last day at work. He stood up and said, "I have a story too. Would it be okay if I tell it?"

"Of course," said Captain Lawrence Tweedsdale. "The more, the better, Go for it." He moved from the podium and beckoned to Lance to take his place.

Lance grinned as he began to speak without notes. "My name is Lance Bishop, Meldrum Secondary School band teacher and guest bass guitarist for the ill-fated Sinkholes concert last summer in the Coral Reef Theatre. I had not seen Brad for a long time, so I was surprised to see him at the theatre doing security with Heathcliffe that night. He is an old friend of mine from the days when the Meldrum Symphony Orchestra was in its infancy as a Community Orchestra. Brad was a super jazz pianist and a temporary conductor for rehearsals played in his basement Rec room for our first concert. He worked hard training us, but he overlooked a few things. One was that the only experience most of us had was in high school bands and for Brad as a stand-in director, difficult to conduct," he said.

Brad put his hand to his mouth as he listened in horror to Lance speaking. His heart sank when he realized Lance was talking about his backstage meltdown at the first concert. The perspiration trickled down his neck and ran down the centre of his back.

Oh, no! He's going to tell everybody, and I won't ever be able to face these officers again. I'll be a fool forever. I just know it.

I was so relieved when Tony Lorenzo couldn't take it any longer and pushed his way backstage from his seat in the audience where he had a good view of Elise, his wife. After arguing with me he finally grabbed the baton out of my hand and did it himself. I didn't know at the time that Tony had run away from music too. I guess my meltdown made him able to face his own problems. Surely Lance won't tell that awful story! I'm sweating all over my shirt. Yuck! I didn't just sweat that night though. I gagged and damn near brought up my dinner. Oh! Please don't tell that story! He put his head down and stared at the floor as Lance continued. He finally managed to look up and smile. The audience would run with it if he stared at the floor much longer. Oh, I just realized that Lance was just a teenager then and probably didn't know what happened anyway! He grinned confidently at the audience and nodded his head.

"Interesting, but not perfect, was our rendition of *The Nutcracker Suite*. The overture was great with all the excitement that it should have, but when the sugarplum fairies danced in next with hobnail boots, it was a shock. Despite stomping fairies and numerous cases of stage fright which we hid from the patrons, Tony and Brad came out together and bowed to the audience. Orchestra members stood up to accept the applause, and thanks to Brad's love of music and ambition, the orchestra is all grown up now. Long live Meldrum Symphony Orchestra. We had a surprise guest conductor that night too. Many of you may remember Tony Lorenzo who directed the earlier version of the Meldrum Symphony. We didn't know he had been asked to direct the New World Symphony that night, so it was a shock when he came out."

Brad lifted his head and grinned as he listened to the catcalls and laughter. Breathing a sigh of relief, he smiled at Lance, who nodded in Brad's direction and acknowledged the audience.

Thank goodness he only told that story, rather than why Tony Lorenzo was the guest conductor. He's a good guy, I appreciate him. It could have been so much worse.

He grinned when he made eye contact with Lance. Heathcliffe gave his master a doggie smile.

"Lieutenant Bradley Thomas has been with the precinct for forty years, "Captain Tweedsdale said. "He has worked with four police dogs, training them, and living with them until they each retired from active service. We are proud of the many years of service that he worked with us. It is with some sadness that we wish him a happy retirement, but with appreciation for his many years of dedication to our cause." He shook hands with Brad.

The evening ended with Brad turning in his badge and

accepting congratulations for a successful career. Sgt. Heathcliffe stood up and leaned against Brad, looked up into his eyes and gave him a doggie smile.

"I like that dog! I'm glad I decided to adopt him. We're the perfect pair!

THIRTY-FIVE

Steve was startled to receive a call from Bruce Faulgaar a few days after arriving back in Meldrum after the drive home from Vancouver airport.

"Steve, are you busy?" Dr. Faulgaar asked.

"No, sir, I'm not busy. What can I do for you? I hope you aren't angry at me. I know I pushed the boundaries a bit when that guy was trying to run us off the road, but, well, you know, I was worried about having an accident."

"No, not angry, but I'm impressed at your presence of mind. I'm convinced you prevented my son and daughter-in-law from having a serious accident. I want to talk to you about something different."

"Sure, tell me!" Steve cleared his throat.

"Brutus has moved out of our home now and will not have time to work on my cars and bikes. Would you be interested in doing it?" he asked. "With training, you will be a top mechanic in no time."

"Me?" Steve said. "I do want to see the vehicles you have, though. I have no training at all, and I can't afford to go to school. I only know how to drive those old stock cars."

"You certainly do," Bruce agreed. "Stock cars have souped-up motors. I'll bet you did that type of work on the ones you drove."

"Well, yes, I did. They were old cars no one wanted. Some had been in accidents and were already dented and rusted. They came from the car graveyards. Nothing could ruin them any more than they were when I got them," Steve said with a chuckle. "I wasn't a star pupil in school. You might be disappointed. What do you have in mind?"

"I want to send you to school and have you trained to

work on my cars. Don't sell yourself short. Two o'clock tomorrow. Don't be late. I have an empty cabin on the property. I am offering you the cabin and a wage to work on my hobby. You're a smart driver and I know you'd learn fast. I need someone to test drive them and keep them in top shape. Are you interested" Bruce asked.

"Yes, of course, I am," Steve admitted. "I have no experience. When the handle fell off my car door I just picked it up and screwed it back on. I like my Monarch, but I have no idea how to keep it in shape. I'm a novice."

"I'll show you my cars and motorcycles. Nothing is in stone. Get your ass in gear! This is important. You're the guy I need!"

Steve wanted to laugh at those words coming from Bruce Faulgaar. Maybe he wasn't so stiff after all? He sure did like his cars. Steve began to relax. "Trained? You mean you want me to be a mechanic? Certified and everything? Me? I can't afford it."

"Don't worry about that. After being trained, you will earn every cent of it. I recognize talent when I see it. I'll show you the house you can have too. "

"Okay, two p.m. I hope you won't be disappointed."

"I won't." Bruce shut off his cell phone.

***

On September 14th, 1996, the ample stage in the Convention Centre was beautifully decorated for the Farewell Concert. Equally as large as the stage in the Coral Reef Theatre, Lance was pleasantly surprised. It was not quite like the familiar theatre, with its catwalk, balconies and all the complicated sound and light equipment. However, the band had a large enough sound system of their own for this concert, which was to be quieter and more controlled than Freddy's bombastic style.

Lance was impressed with the stage setup. On either

side were four pots of blue forget-me-nots and white chrysanthemums. The graduated stage was built to showcase every member of the band.

The raised platform of three stairs covered by a royal blue satin spread could be seen above the band. Freddy's two concert guitars were displayed on either side of the top stair with his first guitar in the centre. Beneath it on the two lower levels was Freddy's favourite costume. The Shot Glass Five's equipment was on the lowest level.

"You'd better be ready to go on stage," Lance said to the opening band. They gave a thumbs-up and focused on the stage.

"Five minutes," the stage manager announced. He held up five fingers. "There must be hundreds of people waiting to get in and at least five hundred already sitting down. Come on, boys, step lively."

A hush fell over the theatre as the house lights came on, and the opening act took their places one by one. They played the same songs they had at that earlier concert, but Lance felt sure they played much better. After their set they left the stage, high-fiving The Sinkholes on the way past.

The three roadies, John, David and Herman, all friends of band members, removed the extra equipment and checked the set up of the microphones on stage. Steve's keyboard was ready for him. This concert would be different from the first one. It was not all about entertainment or making money. There were no exploding guitars as gentle drum rolls welcomed the mourning crowd.

There was an excited burst of applause as Brutus walked on stage, carrying his guitar. followed by Lance and Morley. Steve walked to his keyboard and sat down. He looked at Lance over his horn-rimmed glasses and smiled. Charlie walked confidently to his place and picked up Lance's guitar by mistake. He grinned when Lance gently exchanged guitars with him. When Lance whispered, "We can do this," Charlie nodded his head.

Steve and Morley played their version of "Fanfare" on keyboard and trumpet, which was Morley's first time to play it before an audience. Nobody noticed that he missed a few notes because Steve skillfully covered them up by playing all the notes on the keyboard. Steve's expertise highlighted not only his talent but brought to the concert to those who knew him, a gentle reminder that he was a concert pianist in his own right.

Lance walked to the front to deliver the eulogy, turned to see Freddy's guitars and costume, and became choked with emotion when he attempted to speak. He knew he should have resisted the temptation to see them once more, but he couldn't help himself.

He was relieved when Morley quickly and without being awkward, took his place. Lance moved away and sat down. He had forgotten to give Morley his notebook, but it was too late to worry about it now. His friend would have to improvise on the spot. Could Morley do it? He hoped so. How well did he know Freddy?

"Good evening, everyone," Morley said, as he adjusted the microphone. "Freddy was my friend and Lance's student. He was a fine example of what determination can do for a person who didn't believe in his own talent until a short time ago. We are here tonight to pay tribute to Freddy Gonzaèlas and to celebrate his life. We are aware that no one person could ever take Freddy's place, but we also know that he would have wanted the band to carry on. This concert is dedicated to his memory. May I introduce *The Sinkholes Minus One.*" Morley bowed low and with a wave of his hand, said, "Charlie Gladyzuski, soon to be a Canadian citizen, shares the spotlight with Freddy's brother Jem tonight." He stepped away for a moment to allow Jem and

Charlie to have centre stage.

"Welcome to Canada, eh?" someone in the audience called out. Charlie nodded his head and smiled shyly in the direction of the voice. There was a short burst of applause as Charlie had a few moments in the limelight. It died down quickly as Morley continued speaking.

"The Sinkholes Minus One will open the program with "Suzanna" written by Charlie Gladyzuski," Morley said, coming back to centre stage. "Translated literally, the words mean, 'Goodbye, this may be the last time I will see you, Goodbye.' I think those meaningful words express our sentiment for Freddy, although they were written by Charlie when he left his home country. For Charlie, it was not the final goodbye. Suzanna is in Canada now and she and Charlie will soon wed. For Freddy, the goodbye is real. We say it with sadness, for we will miss Freddy Bastable / Gonzaèlas for his music and his dynamic personality long after this sad day is forgotten,

Lance picked up his guitar and read the bass part that Charlie had just written that afternoon, remembering that when Freddy had sung the song, it was incomplete.

He wondered how Jem managed to look so composed given the fact it was a farewell concert to his younger brother. He guessed it was all about professionalism, but even so, he recognized how difficult it was for him.

Lance felt better as he busied himself playing because it was comforting to think of the music rather than how much he would miss his former student. The band toned down the bangs and crashes Freddy had made his own as part of his stage personality; they were not appropriate for a farewell concert so there were no fake gunshots, but there were coloured lights and drum rolls.

When at last the concert came to an end. Lance stepped up and announced the last song. "Freddy had just returned from a world tour," he said. "His life ended much too soon. This is a tribute to Freddy, my friend, and my student. We worked together for many years. Please join us at the end as we sing the chorus. The words will be on the screen kindly loaned to us by the Roaring Tiger Pub as we pay tribute to our own Freddy Gonzaèlas. Farewell, My Friend."

When the golden sun set once again
And that sad day came to an end
There were no rainclouds in the darkened sky
But all the heavens began to cry.
His friends all knew the reason why
That one dark cloud in the midnight sky
Let the rain fall gently down
Chorus
I'd like to say farewell, my friend
Though I know it's not the end
In another life, we'll meet again
And you'll always be my own best friend...

As soon as Lance had sung the last words, as one, the audience stood up to sing the song in unison. The chorus was repeated three times until it faded away. The words "We'll always be best friends" hung in the air until they, too, blended into a precious memory.

Morley, Steve, and Brutus walked together to centre stage and joined hands with Jem, Lance, and Charlie as they bowed to the audience.

In the brief moment of silence that followed, Heathcliffe bolted to the edge of the stage, with Brad tugging on his leash to keep up. His usually well-behaved dog led the way. He pushed his way between Lance and Brutus at centre stage. Wagging his tail wildly he threw his head back and clearly said "Oh, whooooo."

Lance smiled as he patted the dog affectionately. "I

think I know what he said. He wants to tell you it was a
wonderful evening, and we all thank you for coming. We all
know why Sergeant Heathcliffe had to have the last word.
He has attended every concert for over seven years because
he really is The Dog Who Digs Heavy Metal! Way to Go,
Heathcliffe!! All together now—Oh Whooooo!"

About the Authors

This son and mother writing duo was a noisy but happy alliance between two family writers. Within the music world there are many styles, from the serious opera to the carefree heavy metal. Al Betts is a master of heavy metal and rock, while June Carter Powell plays and listens to old time music as well as the more gentle baroque music. However they recognize that all styles of music are important, so this book takes the reader on a musical ride into the exciting world of heavy metal.